ALSO BY GINNY BAIRD

Right Girl, Wrong Side

the Holiday Mix-Up

GINNY BAIRD

sourcebooks
casablanca

Published by Sourcebooks Casablanca, an imprint of Sourcebooks
P.O. Box 4410, Naperville, Illinois 60567-4410
(630) 961-3900
sourcebooks.com

Printed and bound in Canada.
MBP 10 9 8 7 6 5 4 3 2 1

For John

ONE

One Week before Christmas

KATIE SMITH PAUSED WITH HER coffeepot held midair and stared at gorgeous Juan Martinez. "Wait. You want me to do what?" Her heart skipped a beat. She'd probably misheard him. He wore a starched white button-down shirt under a charcoal suit jacket with no tie. His slacks matched his jacket. Juan was always dressed to a T, and his sturdy build filled out his business clothes expertly.

"Pretend to be my girlfriend"—he shrugged sheepishly—"for Christmas dinner?" His eyebrows rose. "You said you don't have family plans, right?" He sat at the counter on his customary stool, eating a piece of gingerbread cheesecake. Beyond him, a Christmas wreath adorned the door, and swags of fake greenery dripped from the cracked plaster walls. It was slow season in wine country and a dead time of day at the diner. Only one other patron sat in a booth, waiting on his late lunch and reading his tablet. Tiny Castellana, California, did its fair share of tourist trade three fourths of the year. From December through March though, not so much.

Katie's mind whirled as she refilled Juan's coffee cup. She'd crushed on him for the past three months, which was approximately how long he'd been coming in for coffee. When he'd begun asking for her advice, she'd secretly hoped their quasi friendship would lead to something more. Like a real date, not a fake one. Although beggars couldn't be choosers. Not that she was begging, exactly. He was the one who seemed borderline desperate.

He dropped his voice to a whisper. "Remember when I told you about my Titi Mon coming from Puerto Rico for Christmas? Well." He winced. "She's already here, and my great-aunt takes her double role very seriously."

Katie returned the coffeepot to its warmer. "Double role?"

"She's also my godmother. And as my *madrina*, she feels a certain obligation to find me a 'nice Latin girl.'"

Katie didn't exactly fit that profile, what with her extremely Anglo roots, light brown hair, and basic brown eyes. At least she wasn't *that* pasty—when she wasn't wearing makeup. Only medium pale.

Juan leaned toward her and continued. "Last year was such a disaster. She had three poor women lined up. One for Christmas Day. Another for New Year's Eve. And a third for Three Kings' Day."

"Three Kings' Day?"

"The Spanish tradition of the wise men bringing gifts to Jesus. In our house, they brought presents to us kids, Mateo and me, when we were small. Last year, my Titi Mon invited her best friend's second cousin's grandniece to my parents' house for dinner to meet me. I don't think she was much interested in being there though, because she stayed glued to her phone."

Katie laughed when he pulled a face. "Oh no. But why would these women even agree in the first—" She looked at Juan and bit her tongue. Why wouldn't they? Nearly every living, breathing soul in Castellana wanted to go out with him once they'd seen his picture. Katie had to pinch herself to believe she might actually get a chance. She dropped her chin when she blushed. "Never mind."

"I can't figure out why they'd do it either," he confided huskily. "I think mostly as a favor to their moms or grandmothers or great-aunts." His eyes sparkled. "Or maybe their *madrinas*." He shook his head. "Seriously. If not that, then probably on account of my connection to the winery. I mean, come on. The place is beautiful. What's not to love?" He laughed self-effacingly. "I certainly don't think it's because of me."

She appreciated that he didn't have an ego. At least not as big a one as he rightly could own, with his deep brown eyes and his nearly black hair. Juan was very handsome and accomplished. He also had somewhat of a checkered dating history. Katie had read about that online. None of his relationships ever lasted very long, but that was likely because he kept dating flighty jet-setters. Maybe if he settled down with somebody stable and ordinary, things would go differently.

"Well, if you don't want her to fix you up—"

"Katie," he said smoothly, and her mouth went dry, because he looked so helpless, and ooh, how she wanted to rush to his rescue—with open arms. "There's no talking to my Titi Mon. She's trying to set me up this year with Adelita Busó."

"Who's Adelita Busó?"

He sighed. "Only her grandniece's second cousin's cousin—by marriage."

Katie winced. "That sounds complicated."

"It is complicated—by the fact that I don't even know her. She supposedly lived in Castellana years ago and has recently returned to town. So what if she's the CFO of some mega media company that she now works for remotely? Fact is, I'm not interested. But it's hard getting through to Titi Mon, especially with Abuelo on her side. The two of them are always going on *and on* about how I don't value my culture." Juan's family had owned Los Cielos Cellars for generations.

She hesitated and then asked, "Do you?"

"Sure I do." Juan took a sip of coffee. "I also value my independence. So I think I should be able to make up my own mind about who I do—and don't—see. Don't you agree?"

"Well, sure." That sounded reasonable enough.

His expression oozed sincerity. "Look. You're a nice woman. Kind. Genuine. Once my family sees me with someone like you, they'll finally back off."

"Back off how?"

"By letting me lead my own life." Juan squared his shoulders. "I'm thirty-two. A man and not a kid. Old enough to make my own choices."

Over the past few months, he'd told her about some of those. While the rest of his family lived at the vineyard, Juan owned a fancy modern condo in town. He also followed his industry and was keen on modernization. Always up on the latest trends.

Her heart beat harder when she imagined herself with him. Juan was active on social media, and pretty much every single woman in Castellana followed him. Maybe a few of the married ones too. What if fake led to forever and they actually coupled up?

She bit her lip, knowing that was a stretch, but still. A girl could dream.

Katie had never had a serious boyfriend. Well, not since Wes in high school. He'd been smart and ambitious and had gone on to do other things. He was an entertainment lawyer in Los Angeles now. He also had a girlfriend. Katie checked in on him once in a while on social media. Members of their old friend group too. It was hard to believe she'd once been one of them. But that was before her life had taken a different turn.

"I don't know, Juan." She frowned. "I mean, I get what you're saying—"

"Then please, say yes."

He pleaded with his eyes, and Katie found it impossible to resist him. Why would she turn down an opportunity like this? The diner was closed on Christmas Day, and all she had going on was her regular volunteer stint at the soup kitchen. Maybe she'd get to experience a real heartwarming holiday for the first time in forever. Plus, she'd get to meet Juan's family.

The family that wanted Juan to date someone *not like her*.

Her stomach clenched.

Maybe this was a bad idea.

But no, Juan would be there with her, holding her hand. Possibly even literally. *Yes*.

"Just for Christmas dinner?" she asked, acting like her cheeks weren't burning so, so hot.

He grinned, reading her expression, which must have looked goofily giddy.

Gah.

"So, what?" His face lit up. "You'll do it?"

Katie pursed her lips. It was only for a couple of hours, and maybe after doing him this favor, she'd stand a chance with him for real. Assuming she impressed him enough. She'd also have to win over his family. This last thought filled her with dread. She was a simple person, and the Martinezes were, well, the Martinezes, with their beautiful winery and all that land with so much history behind it. She'd never been there, but she'd seen Los Cielos Cellars written up in area wine magazines and online blogs. She'd bookmarked all the pages that had photos of Juan on them. Embarrassing.

"Okay, yes," she agreed. "I'll do it." She peeked at him shyly. "If it will help you out." And *helping* was a good thing. *The right thing*, especially to do at the holidays.

"Great!" His cell dinged and he took it from his pocket, scanning an incoming message. "Ugh, sorry. I've got to respond real quick." He texted back, engaged in a fast exchange, then set his phone down by his plate, grinning at her. "Thanks, Katie," he said. "You're awesome." He winked and her stomach fluttered. "I won't forget this. Just promise me one thing."

"Huh?"

He lowered his voice. "Don't breathe a word about this being fake to my family. This has got to be our secret." He glanced over his shoulder, but there was nothing behind him but the coatrack, holding the lone other customer's jacket. "None of them would understand."

Katie swallowed hard. "Okay. Sure."

Panic gripped her when she realized she had nothing to wear.

But that was fine. She had a whole week to think on it. It was a lot more time than she'd had to prepare for some of her last-minute dating-app meetups, none of which had ended well. Maybe she was being too picky, but she wanted someone she was comfortable with and whom she could talk to. Someone like Juan.

Although, technically, when Juan was here, he did most of the talking and rarely asked her about herself. Okay, not rarely. Never. But hey, that would change now. He'd have to get to know her at least a little better before bringing her home for Christmas dinner. If they wanted to convince his family they were really a couple, they'd need to put their heads together and plan. That could be fun.

Juan finished his gingerbread cheesecake and set down his fork. "This is delicious. Can I take a piece to go?"

Katie nodded and boxed up the slice, setting it beside Juan's coffee cup. This was going to be good. No. *Amazing.* She was going out to Los Cielos with Juan! She wiped her damp palms on her apron, and her cell phone jiggled in its pocket. Too bad she didn't have someone to text with her stellar news. Like Jane. Or Lizzie. But she'd lost touch with those girlfriends so long ago, it would be weird reaching out to them now, all of a sudden and over something like this.

"Order up!" The diner's cook, Mark Wang, spun from the griddle, setting a plate on the high metal shelf beside Katie. His dark eyes gleamed, offsetting his amber skin. "BLT with a side of fries." Mark was in his forties and married with two kids. He was also a secret romantic and forever ribbing Katie about her private crush on Juan, goading her to do something about it.

So there. Now, she was.

Mark sent her a sly look, rolling his eyes toward Juan, like he suspected something was up. Katie smugly set her chin, deciding she could tell him later. She wanted to tell Daisy first.

"Sorry." She glanced at Juan. "Duty calls."

"Sure." He stood and grabbed his overcoat from the stool beside his, sliding it on. He held his cell phone in one hand and lifted the pie box in the other. "Thanks for this." He smiled. "And thanks especially about Christmas."

She picked up the lunch order and delivered it to the other customer, who asked for more coffee. When she turned around, Juan was already at the register, and her boss, Daisy, was ringing him up. Before he left, Juan said to Katie, "We'll work out details tomorrow."

She couldn't wait. "Sounds good!"

As soon as he'd gone, Katie scuttled over to Daisy, dying to share.

"Juan's invited me to Christmas dinner," she said in an excited whisper. She had to stop herself from squealing.

Daisy's forehead rose, the creases in her dark complexion deepening. "Is that right? My, my." Daisha Santos had come to Castellana from Panama and still had a bit of an accent. Everyone knew her as Daisy, as that was the name she'd given her diner.

Katie nodded, beaming.

This was really happening. She was going out with Juan!

Sort of.

"Well, congratulations. I'm glad the boy has finally seen the light." Daisy shared a motherly smile, and Katie wanted to hug her, but she didn't. Daisy and Mark were the closest things to family she had, but they each had families of their own. So Katie kept her relationships with them friendly but distant, because distance was what she knew best.

She sighed, hoping that Daisy was right and that Juan really would come around. She didn't tell Daisy that her Christmas date was just pretend, because that part didn't matter so much. The important thing was that she'd been legit invited to Los Cielos.

By Juan.

Who knew what would happen from there?

Daisy's eyes twinkled. "You know, if Juan hadn't asked you to his parents' house, I would have invited you to Christmas dinner myself. You'll always have a place at our table."

Daisy was so kind. She'd invited Katie home for various holidays before, but Katie had never been able to let herself cross that line. Daisy already had five kids and a husband, plus multiple grandchildren. So Katie typically invented excuses, saying she'd made other plans. She never mentioned those plans involved eating sandwiches alone while working online crossword puzzles, because even to her, that sounded a little sad.

"Thanks, Daisy."

Daisy glanced at a spot in front of the register and frowned. "Oh no."

Katie saw what she was staring at. Juan's wallet.

"He set it down to check his phone," Daisy said. "It kept buzzing."

Who'd been texting him like crazy?

Maybe his mom or his Titi Mon?

Katie's pulse stuttered. What if he'd already told them about bringing her home for Christmas dinner? Maybe he had and they were going ballistic.

Stop being so negative and paranoid.

Or maybe he had, and they were super happy?

Sure, that could be it. Think positive!

It's Christmastime. Good things happen.

It was true they very rarely happened to her, but now she had a date for Christmas. So things were looking up.

Katie grabbed Juan's wallet and dashed for the door. "I'll catch him!"

Luckily, Juan hadn't gone far. He had paused at a crosswalk and stepped into the street, carrying his pie container in one hand. He held his cell phone in the other and was one-handed texting. If he wasn't answering his family, maybe he was caught up in some business deal.

"Juan! Wait!" she called, but he was so absorbed in his messaging, he didn't hear her.

Katie hurried toward the crosswalk, moving faster. "Juan Martinez!"

The lights changed and a large white van screeched around the corner, driving way too fast. Katie's heart lurched.

It was heading right for him.

"Juan!"

He startled and his eyebrows shot up.

Next, he saw the oncoming van.

But it was too late.

The van driver hit his brakes.

Tires squealed and the van slid sideways, a two-ton lightning bolt of metal streaking in Juan's direction. Katie shot into the street and shoved his arm with all her might, pushing him out of the way of the oncoming van, which slammed past them and into a lamppost with a thundering crash.

Juan tumbled backward toward the curb, and she tripped and fell.

People called out and a woman screamed.

Then everything went black.

TWO

"MISS? MISS, ARE YOU ALL right?"

Katie opened her eyes, realizing she was sitting on the very hard—and cold—street in her dirt-smudged uniform. Gooseflesh covered her bare arms and legs. She shivered, and an EMT wrapped a blanket around her shoulders as paramedics loaded a stretcher into the back of an ambulance. *Juan. Oh no.* "Is he—?"

"We're taking him to the hospital."

Hospital? Wait. "But he's going to be okay?"

From the grim looks on their faces, Katie feared the worst.

Another medical worker bent near, checking her vitals. "Boyfriend?"

She spied Juan's smashed wallet on the road beside her, along with his shattered phone. They'd dropped these things when they'd fallen. The pie box was crushed flat, and brown-tinged goo squished out from beneath its edges, staining the road.

Katie's stomach churned. If she hadn't moved so quickly, that van would have run over Juan too—and her. She scanned the huddle of emergency vehicles around her with brightly flashing lights, but the van was nowhere in sight. "There was this white van..." Her head spun and she felt woozy.

A police officer with olive skin and a short black ponytail strode toward her. "Yes, we have eyewitness accounts on that. The driver seems to have fled the scene, but don't worry. We'll find him." She noticed Katie's gaze on Juan's wallet and picked it up. "Do you know this man?"

"Yes. His name is Juan Martinez." Katie tried to get her bearings again, but her surroundings grew fuzzy.

The paramedic who'd been examining her put away his stethoscope. "Do you think you can stand?"

"Yeah." She was a touch light-headed but basically okay. When she'd pushed Juan out of the way, she'd landed on top of him, so he'd cushioned her from the fall. "Think so."

"Easy does it." Two EMTs helped her to her feet, and her knees buckled. "We're taking you in for observation too."

The police officer going through Juan's wallet spoke up. "I'll contact Juan's family."

Four hours later, Katie was discharged from the emergency room. Daisy had called the hospital to check on her, offering to come by, but Katie had declined. She had a few scrapes and bruises but was going to be all right. As she passed through the lobby, Katie stopped at the hospital registration desk to ask about Juan, but the worker there wouldn't say much because she wasn't related to the patient. "Can't you at least tell me if he's still in the ER?"

A commotion erupted near the gift shop, where two police

officers spoke with the huddled-together members of a family. Periodic snippets of Spanish conversation peppered the air. She didn't know tons of Spanish, but after living in Castellana, where there was a sizable Hispanic population, her whole life, she'd picked up words here and there.

Katie recalled the female officer was one of those who'd been present at the accident scene, surmising the family was the Martinezes. The officer nodded toward Katie, and an attractive middle-aged woman turned in her direction, her face brightening. She tugged at her companion's arm and they strode over, accompanied by an older couple and another woman.

"Katie?" the brunette asked gently. "Are you the woman who saved my son?"

"Well, I don't know about saved—"

"I'm Juan's mom, Pia." She embraced Katie firmly, her chestnut-colored hair sweeping over Katie's shoulders. "Thank you." She spoke to the man beside her. "This is Juan's new girlfriend."

Ooof. Katie's pulse raced. So Juan had told them already.

She started to explain but then clammed up. Maybe she should leave any explanations to Juan. He'd sworn her to secrecy after all, and she wasn't entirely sure what he'd said in the first place. Katie licked her suddenly dry lips. "Is he going to be all right?"

The group grew silent, and her heart thumped.

The handsome man beside Pia had extra-dark eyes like Juan's. "I'm Raul, Juan's dad." He shook her hand. "Thank you for your bravery."

Katie didn't feel so brave at the moment. She was petrified. Something was very wrong.

The man's expression seemed strained as he glanced at his wife.

"We were just on our way to see Juan," Pia said. "He's been taken to the ICU."

Raul frowned. "He's in a medically induced coma."

A coma? What? Unconscious? That couldn't be right. Her stomach flip-flopped, and the hospital's lobby lights seemed to gleam brighter. If Juan wasn't awake and couldn't talk, then that would mean... "For how long?" she asked, her voice shaking.

Pia sadly shook her head. "We don't know."

No. She was... Wait. Stuck playing his girlfriend?

She had to tell his family that she wasn't. She had to tell them now.

Juan's voice came back to her, haunting the recesses of her brain.

Just promise me one thing, he'd said. *Don't breathe a word about this to my family.*

Katie swallowed past the burn in her throat and asked weakly, "But he will wake up?"

Pia herded the family toward the reception desk. "Come with us," she said, latching on to Katie's arm. "We're going to talk to his doctor now."

Hang on. Where was Pia taking her? To the ICU?

The hospital desk lady tried to stop them. "I'm afraid she can't go with you," she said, talking about Katie. "Not if she's not family."

Pia raised her chin and dragged Katie along. "Of course she's family, if we say so." As they hurried toward the escalator, she introduced the older couple as Placida and Esteban Martinez, Juan's grandparents, whom she referred to as *Abuela* and *Abuelo*, and the redhead in the palm tree–printed blouse as Monsita Rebelles, Juan's Titi Mon. They all greeted one another, and Katie's heart ached at Juan's family's worried looks.

Well, most of them looked worried.

The redhead's look was...judgy. "You were such a surprise," Titi Mon said when they reached the landing.

Abuela tugged at her colorful fringed shawl. "But a *happy* one." She had a heavy Spanish accent and Titi Mon a very slight one. The others didn't seem to have any.

Katie's thoughts skittered all over the place like a frantic mouse lost in a maze. How had this happened to her? And *why* had this happened to Juan? He had to recover. He just had to. The sooner the better. For his sake, one hundred percent. Okay, maybe a small smidgen of a percent for hers. What was she going to tell the Martinezes? What if they started asking questions?

Don't panic. You don't even know Juan's prognosis.

If it was good, she could heave a big sigh of relief.

If it was bad...then she could panic.

Raul and his parents led the way. Pia, Katie, and Titi Mon trailed behind them at a fast clip. A bank of elevators sat up ahead. Katie had the urge to veer off to the left and go racing down the escalator and out the hospital's front door. But no, she couldn't do that. Besides, Pia had her arm pinched to her side in a death grip. Juan's mom was really strong and athletic. She and Juan's dad both wore running clothes like they'd recently returned from a jog. Jogging sounded good right now. Running even better.

Titi Mon pinned her scary dark gaze on Katie. "So? How did you meet our Juan?"

Her cheeks burned hot. "I...er. I'm a waitress at Daisy's Diner." At least that much was true.

Titi Mon's eyebrows arched. "And you've been seeing him for how long?"

A signal flashed through Katie's brain like a bright neon sign pulsing in blinding colors. *Juan's in a coma...in a coma...in a coma.* One did *not* betray a comatose man. What kind of friend would that make her? It had been his last wish! His last conscious wish, and Juan was going to have tons more wishes. Once he woke up.

Ooh, her stomach ached.

The elevator doors slid open, and Pia handed her a fresh tissue. Katie dabbed at her damp forehead. "Seeing? Um. About three months, but—"

"Three *months*?" Titi Mon gaped at her. "And yet Juan didn't mention you until today?"

Katie's face grew hotter, and perspiration dribbled down her neck. Also inside her cleavage. *Oh no. I'm melting.* "That's, um, probably because..." *Think. Think. Think.* "We were still getting to know each other?"

They crammed into the elevator, and Pia patted her arm. "New relationships take time." She shot a pointed look at Titi Mon, who rolled her eyes.

"New relationships should be properly *announced*," Titi Mon said as the elevator doors clamped shut. "To the family. Not dropped on them like an atom bomb."

Pia leaned toward her. "Titi Mon's just concerned about Juan.

We all are, and your relationship with him seems so"—she lifted a shoulder—"sudden." Then she said to Titi Mon, "Now's not the time for a million questions. Look at her." She nodded toward Katie. "She's a mess."

Titi Mon clucked her tongue. "We're all a mess over Juan." She huffed. "Let's hope we'll get a little more notice before the wedding."

Wedding? Oh no, no, and no.

"Oh *sí*." Abuela clasped her hands together like a hopeful little girl. "A wedding would be *wonderful*." Her eyes danced when she looked at Katie. "You'll make a beautiful bride."

Wait. Katie had to dial this *way* back. "Actually," Katie said, "Juan and I aren't... What I mean is... We're not...*super serious* about each other." Stick to the truth, because that will be easier. "In fact, it's mostly been one-sided." She sucked in a breath. "Up until now."

Pia viewed her sympathetically. "Oh dear. You poor thing." She frowned. "Well, don't you worry one bit. We'll all make sure Juan understands the sacrifice you made." She glanced at her aunt. "Won't we, Titi Mon?"

Titi Mon gave her the side-eye. "Of course."

The group watched the floor numbers lighting up in silence. This situation was pretty terrifying, but it was way worse for Juan. Nobody should be in a coma, least of all someone as incredible as him.

Katie stared down at her uniform, knowing she couldn't dare lift her arms. She'd totally pitted out. Gross. Fortunately, Juan's family didn't notice. Or if they did, they were being polite about it and acting like they didn't.

They reached the ICU floor, and Pia inquired at the nurses' station. She and Raul went to find the doctor while the others gathered in a small waiting room, leaving Katie alone with Juan's grandparents and Titi Mon, who watched her like a hawk. Pia and Raul returned a short time later, their expressions drawn.

Pia held a balled-up tissue as Raul addressed the group.

"Juan has stabilized now."

"And?" Abuelo's heavy mustache matched his thick gray hair. "The prognosis?"

"Dr. Giblin was encouraging," Raul said. "Because Juan is young and healthy, his prognosis for a full recovery is excellent. There's been some swelling in his brain due to the trauma he suffered when his head hit the curb, but all indications are good that things will return to normal once the swelling goes down."

Titi Mon's eyebrows arched. "What about his coma?"

Raul sank his hands into his jogging pants pockets. "They'll bring him out of it once they're satisfied with the reduction in his brain swelling. For the moment, it's helping his brain rest while keeping his condition from getting worse."

"They'll run new tests every twenty-four hours," Pia explained. "And bring him out of it as soon as safely possible. They're hoping it's a matter of days, not weeks."

Abuela whispered, "*Gracias a Dios*." Then she clutched her hands to her chest and gave a small cry. "*Ay*."

Abuelo shared a worried frown. "*Querida*, what is it?"

Her breathing grew ragged. "My inhaler."

Raul rushed forward, and he and Abuelo settled Abuela in a chair.

Raul spoke to Abuela in Spanish, and she opened her small purse. He pulled an inhaler from its hollow and gave it two swift shakes, uncapping it.

Abuela held up her hand, rasping out, "Water?"

Katie was the first to react. "I'll get some." She returned quickly with a paper cup from the kitchenette adjoining the waiting room, handing it to Abuela, who'd just taken a draw from her inhaler. She nodded and released a small puff of air.

"*Gracias*, Katie." Abuelo sat beside Abuela, rubbing her back.

"She'll be all right," Pia assured Katie. "Now that she's had her medicine."

Titi Mon's forehead furrowed. "Are you sure you're okay, Placida?"

"Yes." The older woman nodded. She eyed Katie and smiled. "And now so much better with Juan's fiancée here."

"Girlfriend," Pia corrected gently.

Katie's heart pounded.

What was she going to *do*?

Stay calm. Focus.

Yeah, but on what?

Abuela sent her a happy grin, and Katie's jaw clenched, giving a painful twinge. And then another. Ow.

Pia spoke to Raul. "I'll take her to see her specialist in the morning unless things get worse."

Katie wasn't sure how much worse things could get. How had things snowballed like this? One day, Juan said. A few hours. And now it was seven days until Christmas, and she had no clue when Juan would wake up.

Once it was Katie's turn to see Juan, she entered his room with Pia.

Katie covered her mouth to hide her gasp. Juan was ensnared in tubing and breathing apparatuses. He was apparently on a ventilator and IV with tons of monitoring equipment coiled around him, and his eyes were closed. In spite of his bruises and bandaged head, he looked like he was peacefully sleeping. Still amazingly handsome, even lying in a hospital bed.

"He's beautiful," she murmured, mistakenly out loud.

"He's always been," Pia whispered. "Our firstborn son." She paused, then added, "Although Mateo's very special too."

It was a small town, so Katie recalled hearing that Juan had a younger brother. Juan had also mentioned him, but only in passing. Mateo was definitely the less-public figure of the two of them. His photo wasn't plastered on their winery's website or elsewhere online.

Pia scanned Katie's eyes. "You really care for him, don't you?"

"I…uh." Katie nodded when a lump formed in her throat. "Was hoping for more time."

"You'll get it," Pia said. "We just need to remain positive." Her gaze misted over. "All of us, hmm?" She smiled softly. "Sounds like Abuela already has her heart set on a wedding."

Katie hedged, "Well, I don't know about *that*." The possibility of them actually dating—much less a wedding—would be *zero* if poor Juan didn't get better. "Will you let me know how he's doing?"

Pia nodded toward the family waiting room where they'd left their cell phones. "Why don't you give me your number?"

Katie returned home exhausted. Her run-down house needed loads of work on the outside, none of which she could currently afford. She was saving up for a new slate roof, and the wood siding could stand a fresh coat of white paint. So could her peeling black shutters. The fake Christmas wreath on her front door had a frayed red ribbon and chipped gold-painted pine cones on it, but at least she'd decorated for Christmas. When her dad was alive, he hadn't been big on the holiday, but now the place was hers, such as it was.

She pushed her way inside and locked the door, tension draining from her body. The threadbare furniture had been purchased at secondhand shops by her folks years ago, and the decor was minimal. The artificial tree in the corner added a homey holiday flair when she turned on its multicolored lights though. Several of its branches were permanently bent in the wrong direction, and it had shed some of its plastic needles, but none of that mattered. She'd found some old ornament boxes in the pull-down attic, labeled in her mom's handwriting.

She pressed a palm to her chest when her heart ached. But no. She wouldn't feel sorry for herself tonight. She had so much to be grateful for. A steady job. A roof over her head—when it wasn't leaking—and the good news that Juan was most likely going to be okay. So what if she was stuck pretending to be his girlfriend for a few short days? It wasn't like she'd be spending gobs of time around his family anyway.

Katie dropped her purse on the sofa to remove her coat, admiring her cool wall collage. It was as wide as the back of the sofa and about three feet tall. She'd started working on it her senior year in high school, when she'd still been close with Lizzie and Jane. They'd helped her at first by finding pics of fun travel locales in various magazines. Her gaze swept the iconic emblems of each city. Big Ben in London. The Colosseum in Rome. The Eiffel Tower in Paris, which she'd desperately yearned to see.

She'd kept adding to her collage over the years, even after losing touch with Lizzie and Jane. She'd had to do *something* to keep herself from going stir-crazy while being trapped in tiny Castellana and caring for her disabled dad. She could either fantasize about a future she'd never have or break down in tears. And Katie hadn't wept in years. Not since the sixth birthday she didn't celebrate because she'd been attending her mom's funeral instead. Her dad hadn't wanted to put up a Christmas tree that year. Or any year after really.

Katie hung her coat in the closet by the front door that was now mostly empty. It had taken her a while to get up the energy to go through her parents' things and donate them to charity, but she'd finally done that last summer, during her time off from the diner. It wasn't like she'd had the funds to go anywhere else, so she'd opted to be productive during her staycation. The only clothing she'd kept from her mom was her old collection of Christmas sweaters, which were still in decent condition. They reminded Katie of her and happier times.

She sighed and changed into her pj's, getting ready for bed, taking two headache tablets when she brushed her teeth in the bathroom. Daisy had given her tomorrow off, so she'd stop by the hospital in the morning to check on Juan. Maybe she'd see his cute family again. And maybe she'd get lucky and Titi Mon wouldn't be there, giving her the hairy eyeball.

She pulled back the covers and shimmied underneath her weighty comforter, her body aching from her fall. But her scrapes and bruises would heal, and she had to keep the faith that Juan would fully recover as well.

Her cell phone buzzed on her nightstand, and Katie picked it up.

It was a text from Pia.

Lunch tomorrow at Los Cielos?

We'd love for you to come.

Please say yes.

THREE

Six Days before Christmas

MATEO WAS NOT HAPPY ABOUT having Katie out to Los Cielos for lunch. While of course he was grateful that she'd saved his brother's life, in his opinion, his family was going overboard with their thank-yous. It would have been nice for the group to have had private time to discuss Juan's situation without an outsider in their midst.

He'd just returned from a business trip this morning, so he hadn't been here yesterday when Juan had his accident. He'd caught the first available flight home and was anxious to see his brother. They hadn't parted on the best terms, and he felt terrible about that.

And now this.

"Mateo," his mom said as he headed for the front door. "Your best manners, please."

His mom worked at the stove on the kitchen island, cooking something delicious-smelling in a large cast iron skillet. Copper-bottomed pots and other kitchen gadgets hung from the suspended ceiling rack above her. The large house had vaulted ceilings with exposed wood beams and was decorated in a southwestern motif.

Its open living area spilled out from the kitchen adjoining a dining section.

She was obviously cautioning him about lunch, but he didn't intend to be rude. He could be as gracious as the rest of them, although this didn't seem like the best time for entertaining.

"Of course, Mom," he said, but then he scowled. This whole thing about Katie didn't add up. Juan hadn't even mentioned having a girlfriend until he'd sent that group text about bringing Katie home for Christmas yesterday. Everyone in his family had texted back with a bunch of nosy questions. Especially Titi Mon. Juan hadn't answered any of them. Now they knew why.

"She's special, Mateo." His mom met his eyes. "I can feel it. I saw the way she looked at your brother." She shrugged. "Maybe we didn't know that anything was going on, but in her case, I'd say there's been something developing for a while. And she's a nice girl. Really sweet. You'll see that when you meet her." She tasted a sample from the skillet on a small spoon, then turned off the gas burner.

"Sure." Maybe Mateo should feel sorry for Katie. Coming out here to lunch for the first time without Juan wasn't going to be easy. Then again, she'd had the chance to say no. Savory scents wafted in his direction, but Mateo was anything but hungry. His trip had been unsuccessful, and he was still processing through the painful truths about what that meant.

His mom softened her tone. "I'm really sorry about New York."

His shoulders sank. "Yeah, me too." He'd tried to get their distributor to extend their credit, but they'd already done that—twice.

As much as they wanted to support the Martinezes' wine business, there was only so much they could do. Their organization had its own expenses and obligations as well.

His mom wrung her hands together. "Do you think we'll need to lay off staff?"

"Most likely." His heart twisted. "I've already talked to Abuelo and Dad about it." It had been a brief discussion and a tense one. His dad had gone down to the stables immediately afterward, and Abuelo had decided to join him. They were probably putting their heads together, struggling to find another solution.

His mom's eyes brimmed with sadness. "Not now, Mateo. Not right before Christmas?"

He shook his head. "Everyone's already on vacation anyway. Let's let them enjoy their break."

"Then after?" She swallowed hard.

"Yeah, I'm afraid so."

Her face fell. "How many?"

"I'm still working out that part." Mateo pursed his lips. "Eight, maybe ten."

She gasped, going pale. "No."

He raked a hand through his hair, wishing there was another way. Any other way. But they'd been losing money so badly, hand over fist. Unable to compete in the brisk and evolving marketplace. "The only way for us to hold on is by cutting back, I'm afraid."

She steadied herself against the island, bracing herself with her hands. "That will mean us practically running Los Cielos by ourselves."

His heart sank. "I know."

Her eyebrows knitted together. "Do you think we can do it?"

"I'm afraid we'll have to." He inhaled deeply. "At least until we get things under better control." He didn't want to voice what she clearly feared, that that day might never come. They'd already made cutbacks in capital improvements and equipment, opting to put funds into upgraded packaging to help with better product placement. Laying off personnel was the next unfortunate step. None of the family was salaried. They divided the vineyard's profits—and now its losses—among themselves. Los Cielos was hanging on, but by a very fine thread.

"We'll get through this," she said, putting on a brave face.

"Hope so." He zipped up his jacket, spotting a fancy-looking envelope on the kitchen counter. He picked it up and flipped it over, seeing the return address. Another sucker punch to the gut. "What's this?" he asked, waving the piece of mail.

His mom sighed. "I meant to tell you."

He opened the envelope and withdrew its contents. It was a wedding invitation. Gabriela's wedding invitation. His heart thudded dully, and he stared at his mom.

She wiped her hands on her apron, then untied it, taking it off. "You know how close we are to Paco and Marie," she said, referring to his ex's parents. "Marie asked me about it. They didn't want to exclude us."

Mateo couldn't fault his parents for attending. The two couples had been friends even before Mateo had been born. At one time, they'd thought they'd become linked as families, back when Gabriela and Mateo had been dating. But that hadn't lasted.

Evidently, Gabriela had found her prince. For the groom's

sake, he hoped her roaming days were done. "When did you know?"

His mom hesitated. "Last week."

"Wow, Mom." The hurt showed in his voice in spite of himself. "And you didn't tell me?"

"Your dad and I wanted to tell you. We'd planned to. But you were in New York, and then this came today."

Mateo grumbled. What did it matter anyway? Learning about it sooner wouldn't have changed anything. It wasn't like he was going to go chasing after Gabriela, begging for another chance. Their relationship had ended in a huge dumpster fire after Gabriela had taken a match to it. His emotions still smoldered from her scorching goodbye. Not that he loved her anymore. He didn't. He was just mad at himself for falling for someone so untrustworthy to begin with. Next time, he'd be much more wary.

"Mateo." Her eyes glimmered sadly. "I'm sorry."

"I know. It's not your fault."

He walked outdoors, greeted by the brisk air and glad for the chance to clear his head. Cool winds swept across the vineyard, where row after row of gnarly vines fanned out toward the blue and gray mountains. Cypress trees rimmed the property, and the occasional imposing valley oak studded the landscape. The bare-limbed desert willows would sprout colorful blooms in the spring. After a successful fall harvest, the vines had dropped their leaves and appeared to lay dormant, but those vines still worked their magic underneath, creating more impeccable Los Cielos Cellars wines.

He got into his SUV and snaked down the gravel drive leading to the paved road. One day, if this place survived their current crisis, his parents would cede ownership of the winery to him and Juan, just like his grandparents had turned it over to his parents. And that would be fine if Juan pulled even half his weight around here. But he didn't. Mostly, Juan stayed enamored with one new get-rich-quick scheme after the next that cost the business more than it made it. Some accountant. Juan was only great at doing the books when he didn't hold the purse strings, and right now, they couldn't afford to gamble with their finances.

Mateo passed the large barn that held their production facilities. Its basement area contained their fermentation tanks and multiple kegs of wine being aged to perfection, and the main level housed their tasting room and entertainment venue. His apartment was upstairs.

Their wine operation wasn't about quantity, it was about *quality*. A bit of their heritage went into every bottle. Los Cielos wasn't just about wine making, like Juan seemed to believe. It was about family. Love. Mateo was still stymied by the fact that Juan had a girlfriend. While he had a history of dating around—a lot—Juan had never brought a woman home. So maybe his mom was right and there was something special about Katie.

Mateo would reserve judgment about the woman until he met her himself. In any case, good for Juan. It was horrible he was in a coma, but at least he had love in his life. For his part, Mateo was enjoying his freedom. Far better to be free than saddled with the wrong woman. He'd learned that the hard way.

———

Mateo lumbered through the hospital lobby, holding a leafy fern. He'd stopped at the florist on the way here because he didn't want to show up empty-handed. Even if Juan wouldn't know, he wanted to do something. No matter how meager.

A small Christmas tree stood on the reception desk, wound with twinkling lights. The man there gave Mateo a visitor's pass, which he attached to his jacket.

He couldn't believe that Juan was really here and in a coma. Even though the doctors had induced it for his safety, his brother being completely unconscious was still very scary. They'd run more tests today to see if the induced coma needed to continue for an additional twenty-four hours. If so, they'd undertake additional tests tomorrow.

Mateo's stomach sank.

Even if Juan recovered, would he suffer any permanent damage or lingering effects? No matter how young and healthy Juan was, it couldn't be good for anyone to be in a prolonged state of unconsciousness. Juan had to pull through and get better.

The woman directly ahead of him held a big cluster of shiny helium balloons. They had hearts and flowers and *Get Well Soon* painted all over them. One was just a great big scary smiley face. She strolled along in boots and jeans, wearing a pullover sweater with a reindeer design on it. A brown ponytail bounced behind her, swinging from side to side as she moved at a quick pace. Some of her balloons lagged behind her, dipping down the escalator stairs and nearly bopping him in the chin.

He frowned and pushed the offending things away.

When she reached the landing, one of the balloons broke free.

"Hey!" he called out, but she didn't hear him. He reached up and caught the balloon's string just in time as it floated away. Then another balloon escaped as she beelined toward the elevators. The very scary smiley-face one. "Excuse me!" he called. "Balloon lady!"

She paused and turned around, her small frame blocked by the bobbing balloon bouquet.

He rushed up to her. "I believe these are…"

She lowered the balloons, and heat warmed his neck. She was *very* pretty, with big brown eyes and a blush sweeping her cheeks. A lump formed in his throat.

"…yours."

She smiled in surprise, viewing the balloons in his hand. "Oh! Wow. Thank you."

"No problem." He handed them back to her, and she added them to her collection.

"I didn't even know they got away."

"It happens." He tried to make a joke. "Renegade balloons."

She giggled. "Yeah. Real rebels."

"Hospital rebels." He dropped his voice in a whisper. "Those are the worst kind."

She tilted her cute chin. "That's what I hear."

"Don't let them give you any back talk."

Her eyebrows knitted together, and he grinned.

"I hear they're full of hot air."

She belly laughed, and the musical sound filled his soul. "I will keep these guys reined in." There was a sweetness about her, something warm and enticing. She glanced back over her shoulder at the elevator that had arrived. "You going up?"

He nodded. "Let me grab my plant." But while he was doing that, a big family group crowded into the elevator with her. She held open the elevator door, but there was scarcely any room. "You go on ahead," he said. "I'll get the next one."

Mateo took a different elevator, arriving at the ICU nurses' desk a few minutes later. Weirdly, the balloon bouquet was there, anchored by a paperweight. He didn't see the woman who'd been carrying it though.

"I'm here to see Juan Martinez," he told the male nurse at the station.

"Sorry, sir," the nurse said. "You can't take that plant in there."

"What?"

The nurse glanced at his fern, then at the balloons, and recited, "No flowers, no plants, no balloons."

"Okay, then should I...?"

"You can leave it here and get it when you go."

Mateo nodded. "How's he doing today?"

"About the same, but stable. And around here"—the nurse smiled—"stable is good."

When he reached Juan's room, Mateo stopped short. A woman was already inside it. The same woman in that reindeer sweater and with the ponytail, but without all those balloons. She sat in a chair beside Juan, speaking to him.

Mateo's heart ached at the tender portrait. Then pain seared through his gut. He'd never seen his big brother looking so helpless. At the same time, he didn't seem to be in distress. So that part was good. He pressed open the door and overheard her soft plea.

"So please wake up and get better. Otherwise, how will we have our future? How will I ever tell you how much I—" She turned toward the door and froze, her big brown eyes on Mateo. "Oh, hi!" She blinked. "It's you."

"Yeah, I... Sorry." He cleared his throat. "Didn't mean to interrupt."

She awkwardly stood from her chair. "No, really, it's fine. I was just talking to Juan." Her cheeks colored. "They say that they can hear you," she said. "People in comas." The room was quiet except for the low hum of medical machines and the steady beeping of a monitor.

He studied her a moment, oddly mesmerized. "I've heard that too."

"You must be Mateo." She smiled, and his heart thumped. What was that all about?

"You're Katie." He extended his hand, and she shook it. Her grip was strong. Firmer than he expected for such a petite person. She couldn't be much over five foot four. Taller than Abuela but shorter than his mom. *And* she was Juan's girlfriend. His mom obviously believed that. So did the rest of his family. So why shouldn't he?

Because she'd basically come out of nowhere.

"Nice meeting you." She frowned sadly. "But sorry about the circumstances."

He rolled back his shoulders. "Yeah. Me too."

He scanned his brother's face and his throat swelled up.

He needed a minute.

"I've just gotten back in town," he told Katie, "so this is the first time—"

"Of course," she said, preparing to go. Maybe his mom was right about Katie. She seemed nice enough and honestly concerned for Juan. If she wasn't, then why else would she be here, bringing balloons?

"So I guess I'll see you back at Los Cielos?"

Her forehead rose and she looked innocent somehow, even vulnerable. Mateo regretted his earlier thoughts about not wanting her at lunch. Since Juan cared about her, it was his duty as Juan's brother to help Katie feel welcomed by the family.

"Yeah," she said. "See you there."

Katie slipped out the door, and he turned toward Juan, pulling up a chair.

"Hey there," he said hoarsely. "It's me, Matt. I'm sorry, man. Really sorry that this happened to you. I'm also sorry"—he swallowed hard—"about those other things I said about your mishandling of the family business." Mateo sat beside the bed. "But you know, I get it," he said. "You've always had the best intentions. Only this time... Juan, those intentions are wrong. Los Cielos is our legacy. You don't throw something like that away." He clasped his hands together. "You hang on to it."

He considered his brother a moment, knowing that if Juan had been a more responsible person, then their parents would be passing the winery on to him alone. But he wasn't, and so they weren't going to. Meaning Mateo needed to forget about his dream of running his own business someday. But that was okay. Family came first. And he would be running a business with Los Cielos Cellars. Just not the one he wanted.

His eyes burned hot when he realized his brother's life was

on the line and that he was fighting for it. "But we'll talk about that later. In the meantime...*look at you.* Picking up a girlfriend." Mateo paused and collected himself. "She seems all right too. Very sweet. *And* she's a cutie. Nice work, man." He gave a low chuckle, pretending they were engaged in a real conversation. "For once."

Wait. What was that tiny tug at Juan's lips?

Had he actually been trying to smile?

Mateo's heart caught in his throat.

No. He'd probably imagined it.

"Anyway, brother, rest well." He patted Juan's shoulder. "But not too well, if you get my drift." His eyes warmed again, and he drew in a breath. And then another. Inhaling and exhaling a third time. "The family wants you home for Christmas."

FOUR

KATIE DROVE UP THE LONG driveway, surveying the beautiful estate. While she'd seen the winery's tasting room in photos, she'd never gotten a glimpse of the main house where the family lived, and it was impressive, with white stucco walls and a red tile roof and lots of windows everywhere. She'd stopped by the grocery store to pick up some flowers on the way here. She also had Juan's balloons.

Mateo must not have stayed too much longer at the hospital than she had, because he was already here. He came out of the house as she parked her car. He was a little taller than Juan and leaner. His long strides carried him along in his jeans and sweater as he approached her car. He smiled and motioned her toward the patio, indicating she should enter through there.

A buzz of current coursed through her. She'd had that same sensation at the hospital when she'd first met him. He was really nice-looking, like the rest of the Martinezes, but that wasn't it. It was more like...she didn't know what. But she did know that he was waiting. So. She got out of her car and opened the back door to grab the balloons and the flowers.

He came over to help her. "Need a hand with that?"

His eyes shimmered in the sunlight, and she noticed their color. Not all dark like Juan's but a little coppery gold around the center, and he smelled fresh and outdoorsy, like a lush pine forest after a storm. And—*eep!*—she'd knocked him in the head with her balloons. "Oops! Sorry!"

He chuckled and took the collection of strings from her, holding the balloons aside. "It looks like you came armed and dangerous." He raked a hand through his curly hair, which was chestnut-colored like his mom's, but that dimple in his chin came from his dad as well as Abuelo.

"Armed?" she asked. His gaze darted to the balloons, and she laughed. "Yeah. I thought if I left them here, Juan would get them eventually."

"Good thought." He observed her as she grabbed the flower bouquet off the back seat. "Or you could give them to him yourself, later."

Her face heated under his stare. Juan's family had been so kind to her. She didn't really fault Abuelo for being reserved or Titi Mon for her inquisitiveness. It was actually kind of nice being around a family again, even though the circumstances were terrible.

"Come this way," he said. "The others are inside."

Mateo held back the door, and Katie stepped into the enormous foyer. Its tile floor connected it with the kitchen, which still had a way of looking homey despite its size. The great room straight ahead of her had a large hearth and huge windows framing the vineyard and faraway mountains. She was surprised that the house wasn't decorated for Christmas, since Juan had bragged about always being the one to pick out the family Christmas tree. Maybe the Martinezes were the late-decorating kind.

Pia rushed to hug her. "Hello!"

"Hi, Mrs. Martinez."

"Please, call me Pia."

Katie smiled when Pia released her. "All right." She handed Pia the flowers.

"Oh, gorgeous," Pia said. "Sunflowers. I love these. Thank you. They'll make a great centerpiece for our table."

"Thanks, Katie." Raul took the flowers from his wife. "I'll put these in water."

Abuela stood at the counter rolling out dough and cutting it into triangle shapes. "Ooh!" she said delightedly, staring at Mateo. "Balloons?"

"I took them to the hospital for Juan." Katie grimaced. "Unfortunately, they wouldn't let me bring them into his room."

Pia shot her an admiring look. "That was thoughtful of you. We'll hold on to them for him. We're bringing him here to recuperate once he gets out of the hospital." She glanced at Mateo. "Can you put those in Juan's old room with your nice plant?"

Titi Mon was busy setting the table. Katie waved shyly. "Hi, Mrs. Rebelles."

The woman's eyebrows twitched. "It's *Miss* Rebelles these days, but Titi Mon is okay."

"Oh no, I—"

"Why not?" She sounded vexed. "I'm not good enough for you?"

"*Titi Mon*," Pia said.

Abuelo chuckled, seeming to get a kick out of this.

"Oh no!" Katie said. "Really good. Excellent. Super. I didn't want to"—her shoulders drooped—"offend."

Titi Mon straightened a napkin. "All this political correctness."

Katie gritted her teeth. "Ah. Is there something I can do to help?"

She removed her jacket and Raul took it. "Not today," he said.

"It's true," Abuela chimed in. "You're our guest of honor."

Pia addressed Katie. "I made us a simple *tinga*. I hope chicken is okay."

Katie detected the scent of braised poultry with hints of spices in the air. A covered skillet sat on the stove, and a plate of tortillas was beside it. A cutting board held sliced avocadoes, and bowls of other condiments stood nearby.

"It smells wonderful."

"I made the *pico*," Abuelo volunteered gruffly. He dipped his chin. "Welcome, Katie."

"Thank you all for inviting me," she said. "And that *pico* looks fantastic," she said to Abuelo. He groused and cleared his throat, but she could tell he was pleased by the compliment.

Abuela's eyes twinkled. "We're so happy you're here. I've been thinking about you, Katie. *Dreaming* too."

Pia widened her eyes at Abuela, and Abuela shrugged. What was that all about?

"Are you feeling better today?" Katie asked Abuela.

"Oh yes, so much better."

"I took her to her doctor this morning," Pia said. "And everything checked out."

Mateo returned and Pia said, "Mateo, why don't you and

Katie go select some wine for our lunch?" She reached in a kitchen cabinet and pulled out two wineglasses, examining them in the light. "Oh, and can you please grab some fresh wineglasses when you're down there? The old ones are looking a little scored."

Mateo gave Katie a cautious perusal, and her pulse raced. Even though he was cordial enough on the outside, she had the very strong sense that he was watching her and trying to figure her out. Or maybe he was trying to figure out her relationship with Juan.

"Mateo?" Pia nudged again.

"Great idea."

Katie was struck again by Mateo's stunning caramel-colored eyes and guessed he had a way with women. Then he smiled and that dimple settled in his chin, and she was sure he did.

"Follow me." Mateo sauntered through the kitchen, and she tried to ignore how in command he seemed of his body and himself. He had a quiet self-assurance that was understated and not shouty, and that only made her want to learn more about him. If she started for-real dating Juan, she'd be spending a lot more time around his brother in a potential sister-in-law kind of way. They approached a narrow spiral staircase made of wrought iron. He glanced over his shoulder. "Ever seen a wine cellar?"

Katie shook her head, her face warming. She had to stop this. Mateo wasn't *that* handsome. Juan was the one who was movie-star gorgeous and totally the guy for her. They had a friendship. A connection! A soon-to-be deeper connection, once Juan recovered.

"Then you're in for a treat." He grinned and his dimple etched into his chin.

Katie grabbed on to the railing, trying to remember if Juan

had any dimples. No, he didn't. But that was okay. Juan was one hundred percent perfect the way he was.

They descended the narrow stairs, and the temperature grew noticeably cooler. Mateo swept his hand over the room and its sturdy racks loaded with wine bottles. "Red?" he asked cutely. "Or white?"

"I'm partial to dryer reds myself."

"Yeah?" He smiled at her like he'd made a friend, and she was glad. "Me too."

She trailed a finger down a label on a bottle that looked very old. "May I?"

"Sure. Pick it up and take a look."

She was aware of him standing very close, peering over her shoulder. Nerves shot through her, because—obviously—she wanted to impress Juan's family, starting with his brother, whose body heat was almost palpable in the chilly space. She removed the bottle from the rack, drilling Juan's image into her mind.

It was easy to imagine her and Juan, snuggling close on the sofa by the fire and enjoying a glass of this yummy wine. It was a tempranillo from thirty-five years ago. The fancy label was the same one the winery still used today. It portrayed the embossed-gold seal saying *Los Cielos Cellars*, overlaid on an image of an oak cask. The design was set against a cream-colored background in the shape of a family crest.

"My parents served that at their wedding." His words tumbled toward her like a symphony, smooth and sophisticated. "The batch was a very limited edition. We started experimenting with that grape that year."

Her heart thumped at the idea of weddings and Juan. She stole a peek at Mateo, who'd make a super handsome groomsman. He probably had a girlfriend or two—or three—like Juan. But that was the old Juan. The new Juan had assured her he'd turned over a new leaf and had given up casual dating. Which left the perfect opening for her.

She admired the bottle, spinning it around in her hands. The back had a brief description of the wine. *Full-bodied, single varietal with a hearty structure. Contains fruit-forward flavors: dark cherry, plum, and fig, with notes of tobacco, cedar, and spice. Pairs well with grilled meats and tomato-based dishes.* "It's fascinating that the vineyard has been in your family that long."

He set his jaw, appearing distant. "Even longer than that."

"So your parents run it now, and you—?"

Mateo leaned a shoulder against one of the square posts supporting the exposed-beam ceiling. "I'm the general manager."

She could breathe a little easier with him over there and her over here. For whatever reason. "Will you own the business one day?"

"I'm supposed to eventually take it over, yeah. With Juan." Mateo's forehead rose. "But I'm sure he told you that."

Katie flushed, feeling tongue-tied. Juan hadn't said much about the future of Los Cielos Cellars, appearing more focused on the present and how to improve it. "Um, not in so many words." She returned the bottle she'd been holding to the rack.

"Juan tends to keep a lot of things to himself." He grinned at her like she was a case in point. "Obviously." His eyes met hers for a lingering moment, and she felt warm all over, even in the chill of the wine cellar. That was twisted. Were it Juan here with her instead, she'd be experiencing a great big overwhelming…heat wave, for sure.

"Well." She forced a laugh. "That's Juan!" She stared down at Mateo's loafers, desperate for something else to say. Anything. *Think. Think. Think.*

She looked up and blurted out, "It must have been fun—" at the same time as he said, "So how long—"

He chuckled, then gestured. "You first."

He'd somehow moved away from the post and closer to her. Which was fine, totally fine. They were merely conversing, getting along, even better than she'd expected.

She fiddled with the hem of her sweater before speaking. "I was about to say it must have been really fun growing up at Los Cielos." She recalled the grand approach to the main house. "It's probably hard to imagine yourself anywhere else."

"Oh, I've imagined it," he said lightly.

Her eyebrows rose. "What do you mean?"

He paused before answering. "I briefly considered going to business school. I've got a hobby I wanted to explore." His frank admission surprised her. Mateo seemed really laid-back and not like the business-school type. Het read her questioning look. "Okay, I thought about it more than briefly." He laughed like it was no big deal. "It was truthfully an obsession I had." He sadly shook his head. "But you know how it is. People grow up." He shrugged. "You let things go."

She was about to ask him about his hobby when he turned the conversation toward her.

"How about you?" he asked, strolling toward another section of the wine cellar containing a vast selection of red wines.
He motioned for her to follow him, and she did, keeping at a
safe—*no, polite*—distance. "Have you always worked at the
diner?" He smiled. "That's what I was about to ask you before."

Oddly, Juan had never asked her this. "Oh no. I only went
to work there out of...necessity. Don't get me wrong. Daisy's is
great, and the people I work with are the best. It's just not what I
envisioned for myself earlier."

Her heart ached at the distant memories. Looking back, it
was like viewing a different person's past. She felt so disconnected
from it now. Jane and Lizzie had kept up some during their first
two years of college, but then they'd drifted away. Lizzie moved
to the East Coast to start a career, and Jane was married with
babies, so she had a real homelife in addition to her job. The sort
of homelife Katie aspired to having someday.

Mateo scanned a wine label, then returned the bottle to its
rack. He seemed to be hunting for the perfect pick. "Life can be
funny sometimes," he said, examining another label. "It doesn't
always go how we think it will."

She frowned. "No."

"So before the diner?" he asked, continuing his wine search.

She liked it better when his attention was divided between that
task and talking to her. It kept things more casual between them.
Less intimidating. Not that she was intimidated by Mateo. She'd
met plenty of intimidating types at the diner, and Mateo wasn't
that sort of guy. It was more like he put her weirdly on edge.

"Before the diner?" She exhaled sharply. "Things were pretty different." She frowned when her emotions went haywire. Her high school dreams of an advertising career had gone up in smoke during her dad's fiery car crash her senior year. There hadn't been money for college after that, they'd been so swamped with medical bills.

"Life happens?" he intuited softly.

"People grow up." She sighed, echoing his words. "You let things go."

Fine lines creased around his eyes, giving them a warm cast, and her stomach swooped. "I'm sorry, Katie."

Mateo was so kind. So easy to talk to. Maybe too easy. If only she'd been able to chat like this with Juan. But she'd get that opportunity soon. She hoped.

"So you and Juan? Huh. Where's he been hiding you all this time?"

"Hiding?" She blushed. "Oh no. It's not like that."

"My mom seems to think you and he are pretty tight."

"Yeah, well, your mom's so sweet."

"And trusting." He arched an eyebrow and she blanched. If he suspected bad motives of her, he was wrong. She was only trying to do the right thing for Juan's sake, because of what she'd promised him. She wished she could explain all this to Mateo, but she couldn't.

"I'm not sure what you're getting at, Mateo, but please believe me. You've got nothing to worry about with me and Juan."

He stepped closer. "Don't I?"

"No. You don't." She licked her lips. "Listen. I care for him, I really do, and I totally want him to get better so he and I—can have our chance."

Mateo stared down at her. "And that's what you want? A chance with Juan?"

"More than anything." A small sliver of doubt crept into her soul like a beam of light streaming from beneath a closed doorway, and her palms went clammy. But that was silly. She was freaking herself out. She wanted Juan. Of course she did. It wasn't even a question.

"Then I'm sure you'll get it." His voice went husky, and he turned away.

She fought the noise in her head caused by Mateo running his interference. He was only looking out for his brother. She knew that. But his inquiries made her uneasy. She wiped her damp hands on her jeans. Ick. Really? Okay. She wiped them twice. Super fast.

"Aha!" Mateo snatched two bottles of red wine off the rack behind him. "Here's the year I was looking for." He smiled, then said briskly, "Our best cabernet sauvignon. Want to try it?"

She pasted on a grin, mimicking Mateo's breezy tone. "The cab sounds great!"

"If you'll please hold these—" He passed her the bottles, and their fingers brushed. Current buzzed through her, and butterflies flitted about in her belly. *What* was happening here?

Mateo swallowed hard, and she tightened her grasp on the bottles, pressing them against her sweater and forming a barricade between the two of them. She was *not* attracted to Mateo. *Juan* was the brother she was head over heels for. *Juan.*

"I need to…uh…" He appeared lost in her eyes as the seconds ticked by.

She heard laughter upstairs and Titi Mon saying something to Abuelo in the kitchen.

Mateo blinked. "G-go grab those wineglasses from the back room."

"Of course!" Confusing emotions washed over her, and her gaze darted to the staircase. "Should I run these up to your mom?"

"Good. Yes. Great idea." He backed away and into a wine rack. It clattered and some of its bottles collided. Not too hard though. Nothing broke. "Oh, sorry." He apologized to the wine, backing farther away and toward an open door behind him.

She backed up too, inching toward the stairs while firmly clutching both bottles of wine with her—ugh—still-slick hands. The last thing she needed to do was drop them. "All right." Her breath came in fits and starts. "See you upstairs!"

"Yep. Um-hmm." He raised his hand and waved. "See ya!"

FIVE

TWO HOURS LATER, THE MEAL wound down with chuckles and Abuelo and Raul swapping tales about how the boys had misbehaved as children. This seemed to really embarrass Mateo, especially when a story centered around him. Katie was glad for all that wine. Mateo had gone to retrieve two more bottles during the meal, and everyone was definitely in lighter spirits. Her awkward exchange with Mateo in the wine cellar was now a thing of the past, forgotten in all the stories and laughter. Katie didn't know why she'd been so nervous around him anyway. She'd worked herself into a fit over nothing.

"And then there was the time…" Abuelo held his sides and cackled. "Juan called you Mate-oreo." It was fun to see Abuelo loosening up. He was in a much better mood than he'd been in at the hospital.

Mateo frowned, but he didn't look seriously mad. "That wasn't funny."

"Oh yes, it was," Raul said. "Because of all the Oreo cookies you ate."

Pia leaned toward Katie and giggled. "Mateo was our original Cookie Monster."

Mateo dragged a hand down his cheek. "Mom."

Titi Mon nodded. "Mateo has always had a sweet tooth."

"That is so not true." Mateo shook his head, but she could tell he was used to his family's good-natured ribbing.

"How about you, Katie?" Raul asked. "Do you enjoy sweets?"

"Let's hope so," Abuela said. "Because I made sopaipillas for dessert."

Katie's mouth watered even though she was already stuffed. She'd tried the tasty Mexican fritters dusted with powdered sugar and cinnamon and drizzled with honey before. "That sounds delicious."

"Do you have brothers and sisters?" Titi Mon asked as they continued eating.

"No. My mom..." Katie frowned. "She passed away when I was young."

Abuelo's brow creased. "How sad."

"What about your father?" Pia asked gently. "Is he in Castellana?"

"He was, but he died two years ago." Katie got that painful twist in her gut that she always did when thinking about it. "He was in a car accident—not his fault—but he was injured pretty badly. He wasn't able to work after that."

"We're so sorry, Katie," Raul said.

The others concurred, offering their condolences.

Mateo lightly touched her arm. "We didn't know." He was the low-profile Martinez brother. The one who stayed out of the limelight. But the goodness in his spirit shone through brightly.

"It's all right." She sipped from her wine and glanced at everyone. "Thank you." It was hard to imagine having a family like this and getting to be a part of them every day. It would be like living in a fairy tale.

Titi Mon addressed Katie. "What did your father do, *mija*? Prior to his accident?" This time, her tone sounded far less judgy and a lot more caring. The fact that she'd called Katie *mija* made her feel accepted already.

"He ran the pawn shop in town," she said. "I used to help out there sometimes."

"Oh yes," Pia commented. "I remember seeing it."

"Closed now, isn't it?" Raul asked.

Katie nodded. "Yeah. They put a laundry in there now."

"Well, I think it's very fine you helped your father," Abuela said.

Abuelo nodded. "We have a family business too." He picked up his wine. "With Los Cielos Cellars." He frowned and stared into his glass, and Abuela rubbed his arm.

"It's been in the family for four generations," Raul said to Katie. "When Mateo and Juan take it over..." His voice trailed off when Abuelo sank lower in his chair. The other faces around the table fell too. Raul addressed Katie directly, finishing his statement. "That will make the fifth."

Mateo drank some wine, and Katie detected an off vibe from him as well. They were probably all worried about Juan and his recovery. Or maybe Mateo was remembering what he'd told Katie earlier about his former business school ambitions.

"Wait a minute," Mateo said after a pause. "Smith Collectibles? I remember that place." He turned to Katie. "I got my first guitar there in high school."

Katie smiled in surprise. "I didn't know you played the guitar."

His neck colored under his collar. "Yeah, I play a bit."

"He plays more than 'a bit,'" Titi Mon informed her. "My nephew's very talented."

"Mateo doesn't just play guitars; he makes them," Pia said proudly. "He studied as an apprentice in Seville for a whole year."

"Seville, Spain?" Katie surveyed Mateo with new eyes. The notion of him building and playing guitars seemed intriguing and romantic. Yet another layer to this multifaceted guy. Maybe this was the hobby he'd mentioned during their talk.

Mateo nodded. "Yeah."

"What a cool experience," she told Mateo. "I've never travelled like that." She'd made so many plans though—in her imagination, especially about going to France. Strolling down the Champs-Élysées. Touring the Louvre.

"No?" Raul asked. "Well, that's a shame."

Abuela's eyes danced. "Maybe there will be more chances for that in the future?"

Katie's spirits gave a hopeful lift. Then Mateo glanced her way. It was easy to envision him crossing a bridge over the Seine, his guitar strap slung over one shoulder, then pausing in the historic square fronting Notre-Dame.

When she tried to picture Juan there, all she saw was pigeons fluttering up to the sky.

Pia smiled around the table. "Okay! Who's ready for Abuela's delicious dessert?"

After the meal, Mateo loaded the dishwasher while his dad rinsed the dirty dishes in the sink, passing them to him. Katie tried to help clear the table, but Abuelo shooed her out of the way. He removed the two plates she carried from her hands. "The women cooked," he said in a mock-stern fashion. "The men will clean."

Mateo's mom relaxed on the sofa, propping her feet on the coffee table. She'd kicked off her shoes and rested them on a throw pillow. "You made the *pico*," she said brightly to Abuelo.

He grinned and passed the dirty plates to Mateo's dad before returning to the dining table for the rest. "That was my pleasure."

"*Gracias, mi amor.*" Abuela swished her long skirt as Titi Mon retreated to the great room with her wineglass. Abuela motioned Katie aside, her eyes twinkling. "Come with me. I have something to show you."

Katie glanced at Mateo, but he shrugged. Abuela obviously liked Katie and wanted to spend more time with her. Maybe show her some of those treasures she kept in her hope chest, like old photos of her family in Mexico. Titi Mon settled in next to his mom on the sofa, also propping her feet up to enjoy the fire, as Katie disappeared down the hall with Abuela.

Juan's new girlfriend was certainly compelling to be around, maybe too compelling. He didn't know why she'd left him feeling as skittish as a colt in the wine cellar. Thankfully, things had gone smoothly at lunch, so she probably hadn't noticed the unexpected buzz between them when their fingers touched. Meaning it had been all in his head. He had no business thinking about her in those terms anyway. She was with Juan, and Juan was lucky to have her. Katie was a strong person to get through losing both her parents on her own. Mateo admired her for that.

His dad rasped hoarsely while Abuelo gathered the remaining silverware from the table. "Abuelo and I were talking"—he leaned closer to Mateo—"about this predicament we're in financially."

Predicament was a light way to put it. Los Cielos was in dire straits. Mateo hated that they had to face that now on top of Juan's accident. "There's really nothing we can do until after the holidays." He pulled out the top rack of the dishwasher, filling it with water glasses.

Deep lines furrowed his dad's forehead. "I don't want to lay people off, Mateo. Our workers have obligations. Families." He had his shirtsleeves rolled up and hand-washed the pretty crystal serving dish Abuela had used to hold the sopaipillas. It was a special piece that Abuela and Abuelo had received as a wedding gift. His dad rinsed it carefully, and Mateo grabbed a dish towel. "We do have another option." His dad shut off the water as Abuelo walked over, picking up on their hushed discussion. The pain showed in his dad's eyes. "We can sell the horses."

Mateo's heart raced. "What? Dad, no." The crystal dish slipped in his grasp.

"Whoa!" Abuelo reached out and caught it before it crashed to the floor.

Titi Mon and his mom looked over at them. "Everything all right?" his mom asked.

"Yes, fine!" Abuelo grinned, lightly buffing the crystal dish with the towel he'd yanked from Mateo's hands. He held it up for the women. "Isn't this beautiful?"

"Such an heirloom." His mom smiled. "Yes."

So did Titi Mon, who said, "It's lovely, Esteban."

Abuelo turned his back on the great room, shielding their conversation.

His dad spoke quietly to Mateo. "We don't farm the land beyond the stables. We could subdivide Los Cielos."

Mateo's stomach flip-flopped. The horses weren't merely livestock to them. They were bonded with the people here, part of their family. They'd had them for years, plus his and Juan's stallions were elderly. He couldn't stomach putting them out to pasture somewhere else. "We are *not* selling the horses," Mateo whispered. "Not any land either. This acreage has belonged to our family since Papi Monchi and Mamacita—"

Abuelo met his gaze with red-rimmed eyes. "Even *they* would have put people first, and you know it."

Mateo rubbed the side of his neck, unable to believe it had come to this. "Let me look at the numbers again. Maybe there's a way to work things by reducing some hours rather than letting staff go completely."

Abuelo motioned with his thumb and forefinger. "We're *this close* to the edge." He glanced toward the great room. "Even Abuela and Pia don't know how bad things are. We could lose this farm, everything."

His dad frowned. "Abuelo's right. Our distributor's decision was a blow. We can't take one more hit like that. It will break us."

"Then we'll just have to get through the holidays in one piece," Mateo said. "Once Juan recovers, he can help us with our next steps." Mateo placed one arm around his dad's shoulder and then another around Abuelo. He met their eyes, one at a time. "Let's not give up yet, okay? It's Christmas. Maybe we'll find a way."

Abuela led Katie to a beautifully decorated bedroom with sweeping views through the windows. She took Katie's hand, and her crinkly skin was soft and smooth as she pulled Katie along. "You sit here," she said, positioning Katie on the four-poster bed. A large mahogany hope chest sat at the foot of it. Abuela went to it and heaved it open. She peeked over the lid at Katie. "I've been saving this for so long, and now someone else in the family will have a chance to wear it." She pulled out a gorgeous wedding gown made from antique lace.

Katie gasped as Abuela held it by its shoulders, and delicate fabric tumbled toward the floor. "Oh, Mrs. Martinez—"

"No, no." She smiled warmly. "It's Abuela to you."

Heat burned in Katie's eyes. She'd never had a grandmother that she remembered, or a grandfather either. "Abuela," she whispered. "It's gorgeous. Is that—"

"My wedding gown, yes." She smiled proudly and held it up against the front of her. "It may need a few adjustments, but I think it will fit you."

Katie flushed. This was all going too far. "Oh no. I couldn't."

Abuela lowered her voice and said, "I'm not supposed to tell you this, but I had a vision."

"Vision?"

"*Una visión, sí.*" She grinned happily. "And you were wearing this dress."

Katie's skin burned hot from her head to her toes. What was Abuela thinking? No one had made any promises here. Then again, Juan was *her* dream. Was it too much to hope that her dreams could come true? Maybe once Juan recovered and with the support of his family, they finally would.

"Oh, Abuela, that would be lovely, but I don't believe now's the time—"

"Shh, shh, *mija*. Don't go throwing doubts on my good hopes." She chuckled warmly. "I never had a daughter of my own, but Pia wore this dress."

"Did she?" Katie's face heated at the possibilities.

"*Sí*, and now you can wear it too." She passed the dress to Katie. "Please. Try it on."

Katie clasped the bodice to her chest. "Oh no, I couldn't."

"I don't have any granddaughters," Abuela said. She giggled. "So I'll have to marry into them." She viewed Katie with keen dark eyes. "One at a time."

"I...er." Katie felt trapped, but she didn't want to disappoint the older woman. Her gaze was so excited and hopeful. "I'm not so sure that's such a great idea. Don't you think this is rushing things?"

"Not rushing. Planning." Abuela's eyebrows arched. "*Por favor?*"

At his mom's orders, Mateo went to find Katie and show her around the property. He traversed the long hall with glistening hardwood floors, peeking through open doorways. His grandparents' bedroom door was mostly shut, and he heard voices inside.

Mateo knocked and Abuela called, "Come in!"

He pushed back the door and his heart stilled.

Katie was a stunning beauty in his grandmother's wedding dress, and for a moment, he was swept away. Her ponytail had been knotted into some kind of bun at her nape, and tendrils framed her face. She pressed her palms to her bright red cheeks. "Mateo! Oh!"

"I was, uh…" He forgot what he was saying and started over. "I was looking for you to show you around. My folks want you to see El Corazón."

"She'll come in a minute," Abuela said. She gestured with her hands. "Doesn't she look lovely?"

His heart pounded in an unsteady rhythm. Then he gave himself a swift mental kick. He and women were *done*. He had no business thinking that Katie was attractive—even though she was. Or that she looked incredible in Abuela's lacy dress. It was an abstract observation anyway, and not one that meant anything.

Still. Things seemed to be moving pretty fast with Katie and his family. What was her game, really? It was hard to understand for sure without Juan to talk to. Mateo wanted to trust her, but something in his soul gave him pause. A small feeling kept niggling at him, saying she was holding something back. She didn't seem like the sort to be concealing another boyfriend. She wasn't flirty or self-focused like Gabriela. No. It was something else.

But he didn't think he could fault her for the pretty picture painted in front of him. Knowing Abuela, she'd probably insisted that Katie try on her old wedding dress. Abuela had been dropping hints about wanting great-grandchildren for a decade, even before Juan and Mateo had been old enough to consider getting married. Once Gabriela had come along, Abuela had become ecstatic about the prospects, until learning of Gabriela's betrayal. Not that Katie was anything like Gabriela. Why would she betray anyone? What would she have to gain?

His jaw tensed when he imagined Katie marrying Juan. Somehow that just felt...wrong.

"Yeah." He raked a hand through his hair. "Very."

Katie's blush deepened, and she addressed Abuela. "I should probably take this off."

"Shut the door when you go," Abuela commanded as Mateo left the room.

Katie couldn't conceal her humiliation at being caught in Abuela's wedding dress. Mateo had appeared so shocked, she couldn't pretend like it hadn't happened, so she decided to address the issue head-on. "I'm sorry about the dress," she told Mateo once they'd stepped outdoors. "I didn't really want to try it on. I mean, it's beautiful but—"

"Let me guess." He searched her eyes and her pulse fluttered. "It was Abuela's idea."

How did he always *know* things? Like about her and what she was thinking? It was a different kind of connection than she'd ever experienced before, and it made her happy but left her feeling conflicted too. Like she shouldn't be getting along so well with Juan's brother.

"Yeah."

He chuckled. "Thought so."

She didn't have to force conversation with Mateo. It simply

flowed out, maybe a bit too easily. She'd probably blabbed too much about herself at lunch and, before that, in the wine cellar. Although thinking of it only made her want to tell him more. He seemed to want to know her in a way few people did anymore. Authentically. Mateo was so open and kind. If Abuela's far-fetched dream of wedding bells became a reality, he'd make a great brother-in-law someday.

It was a gorgeous afternoon with the sun warming the air and white clouds hanging over the vineyard. Mateo led them through rows of vines and up a sloping hill. She was glad that he'd accepted her explanation about trying on Abuela's wedding dress and that he didn't blame her.

Mateo was a trusting man. Good-hearted. Even when he'd questioned her in the wine cellar, he'd done so in a careful way. Like he was trying to find answers without hurting her feelings. She'd never met anyone so considerate or careful. It made her want to be careful with his emotions too. Maybe once she was actually together with Juan, she and Mateo could become friends. Even good friends. She'd like that.

"Where are we going?"

He peered over his shoulder. "To see the heart of Los Cielos. Where it all began."

They crested the hill, and Katie spied a family cemetery on the other side, marked by a large granite cross and surrounded by a low stone wall. It contained four large engraved headstones and a smaller one that looked like it belonged to a child. A short row of grapevines stood outside the wall's boundaries.

Mateo stopped at the opening in the wall and smiled at Katie.

"When my great-great-grandparents came here from Mexico, the legend says they brought nothing with them but two horses and a mule. That mule carried saddlebags of roots and vines. The first grapevines that were planted at Los Cielos."

Katie gasped at the breathtaking sight of those original plants offsetting the small family plot and framed by the surrounding mountains. Everywhere she looked, grapevines spread out in all directions. "This all started here?"

Mateo pointed to a distant ridge. "Abuelo's grandparents—his Papi Monchi and Mamacita—crossed over Mount Hood from Santa Rosa. When they reached the top of that mountain, the Pacific Ocean lay to the west and the Sierra Nevada mountain range to the east. It was springtime, and right down below them, this valley was flooded with golden mustard flowers. They took that as a sign that this was fertile ground. Then they glanced up and saw the heavens, so close they could almost touch them."

"Los Cielos," Katie sighed.

"Yes." His eyes sparkled. "That's where the name came from."

"I love the history here," she said. "I never had anything like this growing up. I mean, it must have been so great."

"Your house is in town?"

"At the edge of town, yeah. Near the trailer park."

"It's nice out that way. Scenic."

It was also the poorest section of Castellana. He was too kind to comment on that though.

"It was my dad's house..." Her chin wobbled and her words fell off. All of a sudden, her past was so present again. "And before that, we lived there with my mom." Heat prickled her eyes, and she sucked in a breath, steeling her emotions. She hadn't fallen apart in years, and she didn't know why she was tempted to do that now. Maybe it was being around Mateo and his kindness. He made her feel accepted and not judged. But this wasn't the moment to be selfish and feel sorry for herself. Not with the Martinezes facing a crisis.

She hung her head. "I'm sorry."

"Don't ever be sorry, Katie." Mateo drew nearer and she looked up. "About how you feel." His gaze pored over her, blanketing her soul. "You've had a tough time of things. I get that. And I'm sorry. Sorry for what you've been through."

Her heart pounded and her head reeled, and oh, how she wanted to melt into him. She had an instinct that his embrace would be tender and warm, comforting. And Katie had lacked true comfort for so long, it was hard not to want it.

But wait. No.

It was *Juan* she needed to have these feelings for, not Mateo.

"There you are!"

Mateo stepped back. Katie hadn't even noticed how close he'd stood until now.

"Mom?" he asked with a worried frown. "What is it? What's wrong?"

"We got a call from the hospital," she said, breathless. It was clear that she'd run here. "It's Juan."

SIX

KATIE SQUISHED INTO THE BACK seat of Mateo's SUV, sand-
wiched between Abuelo and Abuela. Pia rode up front in the passenger seat. Raul was already on his way to the hospital with Titi
Mon. They'd gone on ahead the moment they'd gotten the call,
leaving Pia to round up the others. Katie had offered to take her
own car, but Pia had insisted she ride with the family.

If the diuretics they'd tried did their trick in reducing Juan's
brain swelling, chances were good Juan's induced coma could be
lifted today. Mateo kept a steady grip on the wheel as they wound
through the vineyard past their production facilities.

"It's all right, Mom," he said, glancing her way. "We'll be
there in an instant." He exited the grounds and peeled onto the
paved road, accelerating. The road was lightly traveled this time
of year, with them only passing an occasional other vehicle. They
seemed to be passing them quickly though.

"No speeding," Abuelo said in his gruff voice when Mateo
swerved around a slow-moving tractor. "One Martinez in the hospital is plenty."

Mateo peeked at his speedometer. "*Está bien*, Abuelo. No worries."

Abuela tightened her grip on her rosary, appearing very worried indeed. She cast a glance at Katie, and her dark brown eyes misted.

Katie wanted to issue some words of comfort, no matter how small. "I'm sure he'll be fine."

Abuela nodded. "*Gracias*, Katie."

Katie's stomach knotted. Things were going too far with Juan's family. A Christmas dinner date, okay. But the incident with Abuela and her wedding gown had been too much. She'd told Juan she'd play his girlfriend, not his fiancée. That had merely been Abuela's hopeful assumption. Or maybe her wish about what might someday come to pass. Katie fiddled with her purse strap in her lap, knowing that was what she'd secretly hoped for too. A real future with Juan someday, the now-and-forever kind.

She wound her purse strap around her fingers, recalling the unexpected urge she'd had to fall into Mateo's arms when he'd showed her El Corazón, the special place where it all began, and the legendary vines that had spawned a family legacy. When he'd stared at her with his warm brown eyes, her resolve had crumbled.

Once Juan was better and they began authentically dating, *he'd* be able to provide that sort of comfort for her. *So much better* than Mateo, like she'd always dreamed of. Juan was her natural fit. The guy she had the thing for and had wanted forever.

Pia glanced over her shoulder and spoke gently. "We know you're anxious too."

Katie's emotions were so twisted into a knot, she wasn't sure where the gnarled truth lay. She stared down at her fingers, which were turning white. They throbbed, and she unlaced them from her purse strap.

She tried to insert a positive note. "I hope the nurse's call means good news." Katie caught Mateo's gaze in his rearview mirror a second time, but he quickly looked away, focusing back on the road. Was he going over their earlier conversations like she was? Questioning the silent pull between them, which was in every case *wrong*.

Abuelo stroked his heavy moustache. "Good news is what we all need right now."

Abuela nodded. "*Un milagro, sí.*"

"Juan's very strong," Pia said. "He'll pull through this." She dabbed her cheek with a tissue, and Katie's heart clenched. Naturally, Juan's family was worried sick. But she remained hopeful Juan was improving. Pia's phone buzzed, and she read a text. "It's Raul! He's gotten to the hospital, and Juan is stable. The doctor will be in soon to chat with the family."

Mateo took a ramp onto a much larger highway. "We'll be there in a flash," he told his mom.

"Not too fast a flash," Abuelo groused.

"*Tranquilo*, Esteban," Abuela whispered. Her voice trembled, and she clutched her rosary against her chest.

Pia turned toward her, frowning. "Placida? Are you okay?"

"As well as I can be. Under these circumstances." Abuela sighed. "At least we have Katie with us." She patted Katie's hand, and Katie's heart thumped.

"Yes," Pia said. "It's a good thing that you're here. Once Juan knows you're at the hospital again, that will help too."

Abuelo harrumphed and Abuela cut him a steely glance.

The older man glanced around the SUV, then spoke blithely. "What?" he asked with upturned hands. "She came out of the blue," he said. "She's not like one of us."

Pia shot her father-in-law a look. "Of course she is, Abuelo. Juan told us all about how special she is."

Abuelo frowned. "At the very last minute."

A lump wedged in Katie's throat. Maybe she should tell them now? But what good would it do to admit that Juan and she were just pretending? They'd be at the hospital at any minute, and Juan was hopefully coming around. Then he could decide what to tell his family.

"Let's not blame Katie for landing in the middle of this mess," Mateo said reasonably. "She was as broadsided by Juan's accident as the rest of us."

"Plus, she *prevented* Juan from more serious harm," Pia added pointedly. She spun in her seat and peered at Abuelo, who crossed his arms.

Katie's pulse skittered nervously when Abuela smiled at her. "You saved him, and now he will save you, hmm? By asking you to be his bride."

Heat swamped through her at the memory of Mateo catching her in Abuela's dress.

"We don't know that," Mateo snapped. He set his jaw, like he hadn't meant to speak out loud.

"Mateo?" Pia surveyed her son. "Why so testy?"

"I'm not testy, Mom," he said. "Just worried about Juan, like the rest of you."

Katie was worried too. About Juan, definitely. And also about herself and the strange tingling sensations that took hold every single time she glanced at his brother. She had to snap out of this and focus her energy back on Juan, and she would soon. As soon as he woke up, which—with any luck—would be shortly.

———————

Mateo stayed with the others while his mom joined his dad in Juan's hospital room to consult with Juan's doctor. Titi Mon arrived in the family waiting area, wringing a tissue in her hands. Dark circles rimmed her eyes. No. Wait. Those were mascara smears. Mateo's heart lurched. Titi Mon had been crying.

"Titi Mon?" he asked, sidling up next to her. "What happened?" Abuelo was busy situating Abuela in a chair, with Katie helping him.

Titi Mon sniffed. "The ICU nurse tried to downplay Juan's progress."

"But he called us in?"

"Not *that nurse*." She shook her head. "The other nurse, who went off shift, called. The day nurse is a lot more cautious about potentially giving false hope to the family."

"So then, he's not—?"

Titi Mon's shoulders sank. "We'll know more after the neurologist talks to your parents." Her gaze fell on Katie. "I see she's still here."

"Mom insisted."

Titi Mon narrowed her eyes. "There's something about Katie," she said, leaning toward him with a whisper. "Something that doesn't feel right."

Katie caught Mateo staring and he looked away, leading Titi Mon to a small couch. "I agree their relationship is sudden."

"Too sudden, if you ask me." Her eyebrows arched. "No mention of her until yesterday, Mateo?"

Titi Mon had a point. Then again, Juan didn't generally discuss the litany of women he dated. Something about Katie had to be different. Otherwise, why would Juan have invited her home for Christmas dinner? He'd never brought any of his previous girlfriends around for a holiday before.

Mateo kept his voice down. "I'll see what I can find out." He wanted to learn more about Katie, as much for himself as for the family. As genuine as she appeared, she and Juan didn't seem to fit. Like two pieces of a puzzle that wouldn't join due to disparate edges. Juan was flamboyant, Katie reserved. Juan a big talker, Katie evidently shy. While it was true that opposites could attract, there typically had to be some common ground between a couple. Mateo was determined to learn what that was between Katie and Juan.

Titi Mon nodded before taking a seat. "*Gracias*, Mateo."

Katie strolled over in her reindeer sweater and jeans. The woman was seriously into Christmas. Her earrings looked like sparkly snowflakes too. He'd noticed them down in the wine cellar but had decided not to remark on Katie's physical appearance.

He'd been having enough trouble trying not to be captivated by her warm brown eyes and the way they sparkled when she smiled. And when she'd laughed at his dad's Mate-oreo jokes, her entire face had lit up like a sunrise. A really gorgeous sunrise, the sort that sweeps over the Andalusian hills, bathing sunflowers and olive groves in its glow. That didn't mean he had designs on his brother's new girlfriend.

She looked up at him and his heart thumped. "Did Titi Mon have news?"

Mateo raked a hand through his hair, his mind racing. Juan needed to recover for his own sake as well as Katie's so the two of them could start acting like a couple. His neck heated at an uncomfortable realization. When Katie's eyes had brimmed with tears at El Corazón, he'd had the urge to hold her—in a purely platonic embrace. *Not* in a romantic way. But still, that would have been overstepping his bounds, big time.

He'd never envied his brother's relationships before, and he wasn't starting now. Or yesterday. Or any day. He was taking an intentional break from women. A long break. He had his hands full enough with the business and his brother's medical situation. Which was why he intended to keep Katie at arm's length. Very politely, yet intentionally.

He cleared his throat. "We'll know more from the doctor soon."

Katie nodded, but her face remained awash with concern. "I was going to get coffee for your grandparents. Want some?"

"That's a lot for you to juggle," he said, trying to imagine her balancing three cups, possibly four, if she was also grabbing some for herself. He supposed she might get a carrier tray of some sort, but still.

"I don't mind. How do you take yours?" Her caring tone was convincing enough, but he had a persistent feeling she was hiding something.

Mateo's stomach churned, but then he sensed an opportunity to learn what Katie knew about Juan's business dealings. "Tell you what," he said, accompanying her as she headed for the elevators. "Why don't I come with you?"

———

Katie filled one paper cup with coffee from the coffee urn and then another. Mateo hovered nearby, opening small packages and handing them to her one at a time. "Abuelo and Abuela take theirs with cream."

She nodded and picked up a coffee stirrer, swirling in the half-and-half as the coffee turned milky white. It was easier to focus on this task than to stare into Mateo's eyes. His gaze was so penetrating, like he was trying to peer into her soul.

"I suppose you know how Juan takes his coffee?"

"What?" She'd started snapping a lid on a cup, and it tilted in her hand and hot liquid sloshed over the side. "Ow!"

Mateo yanked a napkin from a dispenser and dabbed at her wet fingers. "Are you all right?"

Katie set down the cup, drying her fingers with another napkin Mateo passed her. "Yeah, thanks." She laughed.

He selected another paper cup and filled it. "How do you take yours?"

She grabbed a cup for herself. "I'll make my own, thanks!"

He studied her as she filled her cup. "I guess you've had your fair share of practice at the diner." There was no avoiding his gaze now.

Her face warmed. "I do all right, although Daisy's coffee is way better."

"True." He cocked his chin. "Hospital coffee's different."

She took a sip, tasting hers, then scrunched up her lips. "Hospital coffee's *awful*."

He chuckled and filled his cup, staring down at its contents. He sampled some as well and his nose twitched. "You're right. This coffee leaves a lot to be desired." He watched her dump sugar in her cup. "You take yours like Juan. Extra sweet."

"He takes his with sugar *and* milk."

He considered her a moment. "You must know a lot about Juan by now."

Katie bit her bottom lip. "What do you mean?"

Mateo snapped the lid on his cup. "From dating him."

"Umm-hmm." She snapped the lid on her cup too, avoiding his gaze. If Juan would only wake up, he could explain the whole thing quickly so she wouldn't have to. She tried to console herself with the fact that Juan's condition was only temporary. Soon, everything would be right with the world again. In Juan's world and hers. She peeked at Mateo. And in Juan's really unnerving brother's world as well.

She picked up one of the cups meant for Mateo's grandparents, and he took the other.

Mateo strolled toward the register with her at his side. "Even though Juan didn't mention taking over the family business some-day," he persisted.

Gah. He was still on that?

"He's bound to have told you other things?"

Katie grinned tightly. "He *does* like to talk," she said, pur-posely failing to add, *about himself*. It was okay that she hadn't confided in Juan yet. When he woke up, he'd probably be a lot like Mateo. Kind and interested.

Insecurities clawed at her. What if Juan never came to care for her romantically? In that case, she would have gotten herself into this huge mess for absolutely nothing.

No. Not true. She was helping Juan by allowing him to assert his independence with his family. It was almost like community service! *But not.* Because when this whole thing started, she'd mostly been trying to do a service for herself. By thinking she'd actually win over Juan.

They got in the checkout line behind some hospital workers dressed in scrubs.

"So what's it's been?" Mateo asked as they ambled along. "Three months, you said?"

He was very keen on this. Too keen. Her nerves skittered anxiously. "Since I met Juan? Yeah. Three months or thereabouts."

Mateo inched along, slightly ahead of her. "So when, during those three months, did you two start dating exactly?"

He evidently wasn't going to lay off. She had to find a way to derail him—for Juan's sake. A promise was a promise, and Juan had hinted strongly that he'd been let down by others before.

Juan leaned toward her with an earnest look in his eyes, and she went all fluttery inside. "If only I could find that one person who had my back," he said in smooth tones, his words oozing out like butter. "Someone to really believe in me, you know?" His eyes glinted wistfully as he whispered, "Someone to trust in my ideas for once."

"Ideas?"

"Of course," he said. "My ideas for Los Cielos."

For a moment, she'd hoped he'd been talking about relationships—maybe even her—and not business.

Then Mark had called "Order up!" and that had been the end of that conversation. Juan had settled his bill and left while distractedly texting. The next time he came into Daisy's, he asked her to play his girlfriend for Christmas dinner.

Mateo nudged her gently, and she noticed she'd fallen behind. "I was asking about Juan and about how long the two of you have been exclusive?"

"Oh, that!" She blinked, stalling for time. "It hasn't been that long, honestly." This line was moving at a snail's pace. Katie counted the people ahead of them. There was a large family in front of the people in scrubs, and they all held trays loaded down with food and drinks. Katie spotted a cafeteria clock, seeing it was nearly five o'clock, close to dinnertime for some folks.

"No?" The dimple in Mateo's chin settled, causing heat to stir in her belly.

"No, no. It's all very new." She broke a sweat at her hairline. Hot coffee was probably a bad idea. She should have gotten a chilled drink. "*We're* brand new." She stared up at Mateo. "Isn't that what Juan told everyone?"

"Funnily, Juan didn't say anything about you until yesterday."

An idea occurred to her, and she leapt at the chance to improve her situation. *Yesterday, of course.* That would make things so easy, and then everything else would make sense. She wouldn't have to claim intimate knowledge of Juan's personal life, not with their coupledom in its infancy. "Yes! That's when it was!" Katie piped up. "Then!"

"What?" Mateo's dark eyebrows knitted together. "When you and he started dating?"

Katie's pulse raced. Maybe he would buy this. It was in many ways true. "Exactly," she said. "That's when we became official." It was definitely when Juan brought up her playing his girlfriend, so when the charade began.

Mateo shot her a strange look. "That is recent then."

"*Yes*." She shifted the hot coffee cups in her hands, centering her fingers around their protective sleeves. "But you could say our mutual"—*but not really mutual*—"attraction was building for a while." They reached the cashier next, her heart hammering. All this talk about Juan was exhausting, but at least she'd cleared the air. As much as humanly possible without blowing Juan's cover and the promise he'd asked her to keep.

Mateo set down his coffees, preparing to pay. "These four," he said, gesturing toward Katie behind him. He extracted his wallet, and Katie glanced at her purse.

"You don't have to—"

"No problem." He inserted his bank card in the machine and smiled. "It's the least I can do after all you've done for Juan."

She was doing a lot more for Juan than she'd intended. Mateo and his grandmother seemed close. Maybe Katie could enlist Mateo's help in—very gently—convincing Abuela that things between Juan and Katie didn't involve pending matrimony.

As they approached the elevators, Mateo said, "It's very good of you to be here then. Given the newness of your and Juan's situation."

"Mateo," she solemnly answered. "I do care about your brother."

"Uh, yeah, I can see that." His neck flushed red. "I also over-heard you talking to him."

Katie gasped. "What? When?"

"This morning, in the ICU, when you brought over those balloons."

Her chest tightened, and for an instant, she couldn't breathe. *What* had he overheard exactly? Her confessing her feelings for Juan? Her professing her desire to have a future with him? She mentally face-palmed, knowing she'd said as much to Pia. So then why did Mateo knowing this leave her feeling oddly strangled?

"I'm sorry." He hung his head. "I wasn't intentionally eaves-dropping, but I did get that your feelings for him are sincere." He exhaled sharply. "Even if they're relatively new ones."

Oh, how she wished that were the case. Then she wouldn't be so totally mixed up inside.

Katie pushed the elevator button to go up with her elbow. "I only want what's best for Juan," she said as they stepped aboard.

There was no one else in the elevator, only the two of them. "I know you do," Mateo said. "So do I. That's why... Katie?" he asked right before the elevator doors closed. "I need to ask you about Juan and the winery."

Katie stared down at the coffee cups in her hands. "Los Cielos Cellars?" she asked, looking up when the elevator stopped on the lobby floor. The cafeteria was in the basement.

"Yeah, Los Cielos." Mateo edged closer as more people crowded into the elevator. Why did he have to do that? Smell so fresh and bodywash-y all the time? She didn't detect cologne, more like hints of woodsy scents. "Did Juan mention any of his plans for the vineyard?"

"P-plans? I'm not sure what you're asking." His incredible eyes met hers, and she nearly dropped both cups. *That* would be a disaster and could even cause injury. She glanced around the packed elevator. It stopped on the second floor, and a few more people entered, forcing Katie and Mateo closer together. He was so close now she could almost count his heartbeats. No, those were hers, thudding in her chest and in her throat.

"For changing up the business?" he asked, scooting closer and out of somebody else's way. "Maybe rebranding?"

"Rebranding?" She had no clue what he was talking about. "No."

The elevator doors clipped shut, and Mateo surveyed her warmly. "I didn't think so."

Her pulse spiked, causing fire to burn in her cheeks. A strange, silent tug seemed to sing out between them. Boy, oh boy, like a chorus of Christmas angels. Which made her think of mistletoe. And then of Mateo and her standing under it. *No.* It was *Juan* she should be imagining herself with and thinking of kissing. Not his devastatingly adorable brother.

The elevator jolted to a stop, and people gasped.

"Oh!" Katie stumbled forward but she held out her cups so they wouldn't slosh into Mateo.

He raised his cups in his hands at the same time, and she crashed into his chest with hers.

Mateo's body warmth seeped into her, penetrating her Christmas sweater. Her pulse spiked through the roof. He stared down at her as the elevator lights pulsed off, then on.

"Are you all right?" Thankfully, neither of them had spilled their coffees. It helped that all the cups had lids.

"I hope this is only temporary," a man behind them grumbled.

"Yeah. I…" She regained her balance, righting herself on her boots. She slowly peeled herself off him, but wait. Something snagged. Katie gaped at the glittery sequin on her reindeer sweater that had latched on to a thread of Mateo's green pullover. "Oh gosh."

He saw it too and tried to squirm away. It was hard for him to do much else with both hands full. He dipped slightly on his knees, pivoting to one side and then the other.

The thread unwound further, leaving a tiny gaping hole above—she guessed—his left nipple. She blushed superhot. He wore a black T-shirt underneath.

"Yikes!" She bit her bottom lip. "Sorry about that."

"No"—the sequin popped off and flitted to the ground— "problem," he said, watching it fall in lazy circles. At least they weren't tethered together any longer. The flimsy green thread floated against his very solid and muscled chest. Perspiration swept her hairline, and her mouth went dry. She was *not* attracted to Mateo. No.

She looked up to find him gazing at her, his face beet red. "I guess that solved that problem." He laughed and she laughed too. But in an embarrassingly goofy way. Heat flooded her face and swamped to her toes, making her feel like she'd taken a big swig of habanero hot sauce. Mateo Martinez hot sauce. *Latinx spicy*. She quickly tried to conjure an image of something cool and calming. Anything. Cold, cold, cold. Yes, good. *Snow*.

The elevator jerked to a start again, causing them both to firmly clutch their coffees, and a few of their fellow elevator riders cheered.

"Sorry about your sweater," he said.

Lots of twirly snowflakes flitted around him in her mind's eye, making him appear even more enticing than ever. They started sticking to his hair and his really sexy eyelashes.

She blinked. "Sorry about *yours*."

The world finally stopped turning, and she caught her breath. *Stop it, Katie. Just stop.*

Potential brother-in-law. Hel-lo!

Boy, it was stuffy in here.

Definitely not blizzard-like.

The elevator doors swung open on the third floor, ushering in a fresh blast of—ugh—acerbic hospital air. Mateo waited for her to go first, and they exited after the others.

"That was a close one," a woman complained to her companion while the pair walked ahead of them.

Katie stole a peek at Mateo, her heart hammering.

Yeah.

SEVEN

THEY RETURNED TO THE WAITING area, handing Abuelo and Abuela their coffees. The older couple thanked them, and Pia addressed the group. "Who'd like to see Juan next?"

Raul's gaze swept over his parents. "Mamá, Papá, you two should go."

Abuela solemnly shook her head and pointed at Katie. "His *novia* first."

Katie's stomach churned. *Novia* could mean *girlfriend*, but also *fiancée*, or worse, *bride*. Despite Abuela's sentimental longings, she was *not* getting engaged to anyone anytime soon.

"Oh no, I couldn't," she demurred. "It should really be you all."

Abuelo started to stand, but Abuela grabbed his elbow with one hand while motioning with her coffee cup in the other. He frowned at his wife, his gray mustache dipping toward his chin. "Raul's right. We're family."

"And she could be family soon." Abuela darted a glance at Katie, who stammered.

"Oh no, Abuela. Seriously. Juan and I, we're not like—"

"*Ay!*" Abuela gave a dramatic cry and slumped back in her

chair, and Katie's heart lurched. She had to seriously watch her step around Abuela to avoid upsetting her.

Abuelo hovered over her, taking away her coffee cup. "*Querida?*"

She grimaced and folded her shawl against her chest.

Pia hurried toward her. "Do you need your inhaler?"

Abuela breathed in deeply, closing her eyes. When she opened them, she said quietly. "No. I think I should sit for a bit."

Raul laid a hand on her shoulder. "This is probably too much for you. We should have left you at home."

"Me?" Abuela set her lips in a thin line. "Never."

"But, Mamá." Raul scrubbed a hand across his face. "All this excitement and uncertainty—"

"Is something we Martinezes need to face together." Her eyes glimmered at Katie. "With the help of Juan's special one."

Katie stared up at Mateo, who whispered, "Don't worry. I'll talk to them later this evening when we get back to Los Cielos. Tell them what you said about you and Juan being new. In the meantime"—he nodded toward Juan's room—"maybe you should explain things to him."

———————

A few moments later, Katie sat alone with Juan in his ICU room. Pia and Raul had reported the doctor was pleased with the reduction in his brain swelling, but he wasn't out of the woods yet. Not enough to bring him out of his coma.

"So hey," she said, leaning forward in her chair. "Dr. Giblin says you're doing better, which is really great news."

Juan lay there impassive, beeping equipment and breathing apparatuses swirling around him. Despite his trauma, he didn't appear to have a hair out of place. Even in a head bandage, Juan was picture-perfect. Classically handsome.

Katie tried to insert a light note in her voice. "Everyone's hoping you'll be home for Christmas." She paused, realizing it wasn't *her* home. "Home to Los Cielos, I mean." Juan made no indication he heard her, but she decided to continue anyway. "Listen, Juan." She dropped her voice to a whisper, angling closer. "This pretend girlfriend thing is going too far. Your folks all believe...well, that we're a lot more serious than we are. Which we aren't. Not at all. I explained that to Mateo, and he's promised to tell the others."

She waited for Juan's heart monitor to increase, with its tiny blips skipping faster, but it stayed steady.

"But don't worry! I didn't blab. Didn't say a word about not being your girlfriend." She hugged her upper arms with her hands, rubbing the tops of her sweater sleeves. "I mean, I promised, and my promise is good." Her forehead burned hot, and she swept back her bangs, finding them damp beneath her fingers. "But, Juan," she whispered huskily. "You have to wake up. Your whole family needs you." She swallowed hard. "I need you too, of course." Her voice squeaked, though she didn't mean for it to. "This was only supposed to be for *one day*. A Christmas date. But now, things are getting complicated." She peeked out the glass window to the hall and leaned closer. "Abuela's getting her hopes up about the future. *Our future.*" She scrutinized his face for any signs of comprehension, but he appeared deep in slumber. Katie sighed. "She even had me try on her wedding dress."

She stared straight at Juan, but still she got nothing. No response.

"I don't want you to worry," she continued. "I'm holding my own. But please, Juan? Can you get better soon?" She stood, preparing to leave. "Your family loves you, and I—" Katie blanched when a shattering truth hit her. She'd once believed she loved him as well. But what if she'd gotten things wrong? No. She was confusing herself over this. Juan's accident. His coma. It had all thrown her for a loop. *Of course* Juan was the person who she wanted to be with. Absolutely. "I want you to get better too."

―――――――――

When Katie returned to the waiting area, a middle-aged couple followed her from the ICU wing and into the room. They glanced around, seeing that the Martinezes had mostly dominated the small space. "Maybe we should go down to the cafeteria," the man told his fair-haired companion. "Grab some supper."

The blond's face was pale and her expression drawn. "I don't think I could eat a thing."

"Come on, sweetheart." He wrapped an arm around her shoulders. "Let's try."

She headed toward the elevators.

"Your father!" Abuela said as they turned away. "He's going to be all right."

The woman spun around slowly. "What?"

Abuela gestured down the hall toward the ICU unit. "He'll be home for Christmas."

The man held his wife closer. "I'm sorry," he said to Abuela. "How do you know?"

Abuela tightened her shawl around her shoulders. "I had a vision." She sat up straighter and sent a sly glance at Katie. "And my visions are never wrong."

The woman nodded gratefully. "Well then, I hope you're extra right."

Abuela stood with some effort, and Abuelo rose to help her. She tilted her head toward the couple and approached them with gingerly steps. "Here," she told the blond. She handed her a small coil of beads. "Say a prayer."

The woman flushed. "Oh no, I'm not Catholic."

Abuela smiled. "Then let this rosary pray for you." She folded the blond's hand around it, then gave her fingers a pat. The woman realized what she was doing and stammered.

"I can't keep this."

Abuela gave her a steady look. "You won't need it for long." She turned and scuttled back to her chair and Abuelo, who helped her get seated, while the blond gawked at her hand.

"Just take it and say thank you," her husband whispered.

"Thank you," she said. Her light-colored eyes misted. "I appreciate the thought."

"Waste of a good rosary," Titi Mon grumbled once the couple had gone.

"It was not a waste," Abuela answered. "Besides that, I'll get it back before long."

Katie was speechless. Could Abuela really have the ability she claimed? That seemed so far-fetched. One thing was clear though. Her heart was in the right place.

Mateo motioned to the empty chair beside him, and Katie

joined him in the corner. "I watched over your coffee, like you asked."

"Thanks." Katie puzzled over the scene she'd witnessed as she took her seat. She sipped from her cup, but the brew had gone cold.

Mateo noticed her frown. "There's a microwave in that kitchen area over there." Brown curls spilled past his forehead, grazing an eyebrow. "I can heat it up for you?"

"That's very kind," she said, "but I'd hate to bother—"

"It's no bother."

Mateo warmed up her coffee and returned it to her, with Titi Mon's gaze trailing him. His parents sat with Abuelo and Abuela, and the four of them chatted quietly.

"How's your breathing?" Pia asked Abuela softly.

"Fine, just fine," Abuela answered. "*Muy bien.*"

Mateo waved his fingers at Titi Mon to get her to stop gawking. "We can take it from here, Titi Mon."

Her eyebrows arched sharply. "I'm sure that you can." She pointed at Katie from behind the back of her hand, not entirely discreetly. Titi Mon obviously wanted Mateo to say something to Katie. Katie's first guess was for her to go on home, and she should probably do that soon. But she couldn't go far without her car, and that was still back at Los Cielos.

Katie lowered her voice. "Your Titi Mon doesn't like me much, does she?" She sipped from her coffee, which was hotter, so about a hundred times better than before. But it was still hospital coffee, so not great.

"She doesn't dislike you," he whispered. "She's just protective."

Katie got that. She also understood that Abuelo was too. They'd appeared more receptive to her at dinner, but it had probably just been the moment. Or the wine. Possibly both. Katie's shoulders sank. She hadn't been completely forthcoming with the group.

Still. She'd done her best to walk this very tight line between playing Juan's girlfriend and not giving his secret away while trying not to become too firmly entrenched in his family. Titi Mon and Abuelo made things easier by keeping her at arm's length. Pia and Raul were so open and caring though, it made it harder to step away. Then there was Mateo...

She glanced at him, and his gaze took her breath away. "You have this one strand, right...here." He reached up and tucked a lock of her hair behind her ear, and Katie's heart hammered. Part of her ponytail had come undone, and she was sure she looked a wreck.

But when Mateo stared in her eyes, she didn't feel that way.

Heat bloomed in her cheeks.

She felt beautiful.

A nurse appeared in the waiting room. "Juan has time for one more visitor." The nurse checked her watch. "Or two."

Katie had to stop this. Feeling swoony about Mateo. When Juan woke up, she'd feel doubly this way about him. Triply, probably. They just needed more time together. Bonding time. Where Juan was present and able to actively participate in the moment.

"Juan's grandparents need a turn," Raul said, since they were the only ones in their group who hadn't seen Juan today.

Abuelo and Abuela exchanged tired glances. "Yes," Abuelo

said. He took his wife's hand. "That would be good. We should go and see Juan."

Abuela's face crinkled in a wan smile. "Of course." Today had to have been tiring for her on top of yesterday's excitement. Everyone would sleep soundly tonight, including Katie.

She fumbled for the notebook in her purse, determined to focus on something else—anything except the tantalizing guy beside her. She located her notebook and a pen, withdrawing them from her purse. The small spiral-bound notebook wasn't more than four inches tall, but it was large enough to hold her doodles. She carried it along in case she was stuck waiting for something, and Katie didn't wait well. After keeping up with the fast pace at the diner, slowing down made her uncomfortable. Creating random sketches seemed to calm her nerves.

Mateo gazed at her holding her notebook and pen. "Taking notes on the Martinez family?" he said, clearly trying to make a joke.

She laughed. "No. Just looking for a way to pass the time."

"You must be pretty bored here, huh?"

When he looked at her like that—or, well, pretty much any way at all—she was anything but *bored*. "No, it's not that." She grimaced. "I'm kind of an outsider around here, aren't I?" She glanced around the room at the others. Pia and Raul discussed something quietly, and Titi Mon was busy on her tablet. "I don't really belong."

"Not according to Abuela," he teased.

Katie blew out a breath. "She's so sweet but mistaken."

"I know, but she has hopes."

"Hopes?"

His eyebrows arched. "For great-grandchildren."

Great-grandchildren, right. That would mean a marriage first, more than likely. Somehow, Katie felt a whole lot less certain about the dreams she'd had of marrying Juan only twenty-four hours ago.

Mateo's eyes lit on a page in her notebook. "Whoa. Did you draw that?" he asked, staring at her drawing of the Christmas wreath on the diner's front door.

"Yeah. I was just playing around."

"Well, you play pretty expertly." He examined the notebook and held out his hand. "Mind if I take a look?"

It was a little awkward sharing her work, but he seemed so genuinely interested, Katie decided to risk it. Not many people knew about her hidden artsy side. Daisy and Mark did, because they'd seen her sketching things from time to time at work. They'd both said she was good, but Katie had figured they were only being kind.

Katie passed Mateo the notebook, and he started going through its pages. He pressed his lips together and then looked up. "You're really good. Did you draw these from photos?"

She shook her head. "From memory, mostly. I have this little camera in my head that takes snapshots sometimes." *When things are important to me.*

"Like a photographic memory?"

She nodded. "In a way."

He viewed her admiringly. "That's very cool."

Katie blushed. "Thanks, Mateo."

He pointed to her rendering of Daisy. "Who's this?"

"Daisy."

"She a friend?"

Katie nodded. "My boss too, and almost like a mother. A mother hen, mostly." She laughed. "Daisy always thinks she's right."

"Is she?"

Katie laughed at the truth. "Yeah, a lot of the time."

He flipped back to a drawing of the hills behind her house. "Where's this?"

"My backyard."

"Nice."

She shrugged. "It's not as nice as it seems. You ought to see the neighborhood."

He chuckled and closed the notebook, returning it to her. "Maybe I will someday." Mateo crossed his arms, his brow furrowing. "Your drawings are really great. All of them. But your landscapes—they remind me of something."

"Oh?"

Mateo snapped his fingers. "Wine labels, that's what it is."

"Labels?" Katie brightened, pleased with the comparison to something as professional as that. "Really?"

"Yeah. We're working on some new ones for the winery. Not quite as artsy as yours but in a similar vein."

Her cheeks steamed at the compliment. "That's nice of you to say."

"Mateo," Pia said, walking over. Beyond her, Raul spoke to Abuelo and Abuela as they slipped on their coats. The temperatures had crept up into the high forties, but now that the sun had set, things would be cooling off again. "Raul and I were talking about Christmas."

Mateo frowned. "I'm hoping Juan will be there." He stood, and so did Katie, and both reached for their jackets.

"Yes," Pia said. "We all are, which is why your dad and I thought it would be nice to get things ready." She turned to Katie. "Picking out our Christmas tree has been the boys' tradition for years, Juan's and Mateo's. We used to go as a family, but then when they became teenagers, they took the task upon themselves of selecting and felling the perfect tree."

Katie put on her jacket and reached for the zipper. "What a nice tradition." Funnily, Juan had never mentioned doing this with Mateo. Then again, he hadn't expressly *said* nobody else was with him.

Mateo sank his hands in his pockets. "This year, we're running a little late with our preparations. With my trip to New York, we decided to wait until I got back."

Pia nodded sadly. "Unfortunately, this year, Juan won't be participating. So!" She beamed at Mateo. "Your dad and I were thinking that maybe Katie could fill in?"

Katie's zipper got halfway up and jammed. "Oh, uh, me?" She gazed at Mateo, who appeared broadsided as well. "I'm afraid I've got to work tomorrow." She couldn't wait to go in and tell Daisy everything. Mark too. They'd definitely ask.

Pia's eyebrows knitted together. "What time do you get off?"

Katie swallowed hard, feeling railroaded into this plan. But the Martinezes had been so good to her, how could she say no? Her voice squeaked when she said, "Three."

Pia clapped her hands together. "Great! You'll still have plenty of daylight left to pick out a tree." She beamed at her son. "Mateo can pick you up at Daisy's."

Mateo's ears turned red. He shifted on his feet and glanced at Katie. "Sure."

Katie yanked at her jacket zipper, getting it the rest of the way up. Imaginary flames leapt at her face. She was not going Christmas tree shopping in her diner clothes. How embarrassing. "I'll need to go home and change first."

Raul smiled from beside Pia. "Why don't you give Mateo your address?"

Abuela scuttled over, hanging on to Abuelo's arm. "Do it now, before anyone forgets," she said cheerily.

Katie bit her lip as Mateo took out his phone. He stared at its screen, apparently trying not to look at her. Which was just as well. That way, he couldn't detect the panic behind her pasted-on grin.

"It's 224 Westside." If Mateo had his doubts about her relationship with Juan, him seeing her place in person would make matters even worse. Her modest house was definitely not in the Martinezes' league. With less than eight hundred square feet, her entire two-bedroom, one-bath house could fit into the great room at Los Cielos.

"That's past Broad Street?"

He glanced up, and she flushed even hotter. It wasn't only about him seeing where she lived. The notion of the two of them being alone together on an outing seemed dangerously like a date. But it wasn't, of course not. Although there'd probably be mistletoe for sale. Katie's jaw clenched. No. She was *not* going to think about those magical little berries and Mateo in any sort of related way. That was a nonstarter.

"You'll want to dress warmly," Titi Mon advised, joining the group. She slid her tablet in her purse. "The weather tomorrow's going to be extra chilly."

"You'll also want to come back with Mateo to Los Cielos afterward," Pia offered. "We'll have our traditional winter chili and decorate the tree."

Pain seared through her, and Katie felt torn down the middle. That sounded so tempting, like the sort of big family holiday gathering she'd always longed for. But she couldn't ingratiate herself any more with the Martinezes. Not until Juan was around to grant his approval. He'd asked her to Christmas dinner, not to move into his parents' place.

Titi Mon scrunched up her lips and stared at Abuelo as if willing him to say something. He lifted his hand, but Abuela shoved it back down by his side. "That's a good idea," Abuela said. "Juan will like knowing Katie's helped decorate the house."

Abuelo rolled his eyes and Abuela pinched his arm. "Ow," he groused quietly, rubbing his coat sleeve. Though it couldn't have actually hurt, he was good at making a show.

Pia took her hand, cementing the deal. "Please say you'll come." She smiled, and small lines formed around her mouth and eyes. "It would mean the world to me."

A tender knot formed in Katie's throat, throbbing and raw. She missed her own mom so much, and Pia was so caring and warm.

Raul placed his arm around Pia's shoulders. "It would mean the world to both of us."

Abuela batted her eyelashes. "And Juan!"

Mateo shrugged, like he figured it was settled, and Katie could see that it was. There was no battling the Martinezes who wanted her in attendance, and the others seemed resigned to the fact. "All right then," she said. "I'd love to."

———————

Mateo and the others exited his SUV when they returned to Los Cielos. Titi Mon and his dad pulled in next and parked abutting the split-rail fence. The vineyard's south-facing hills tumbled out ahead of them, cloaked in nighttime shadows. Beyond those, the Mayacamas Mountains loomed over the valley. What trailblazers Mateo's great-great-grandparents had been, crossing formidable Mount Hood from Santa Rosa before settling here. There was a certain romance in their journey. His gaze swept over Katie as she told his parents and Titi Mon good night. She turned to Abuelo and Abuela with a soft smile.

"I guess I'll see you all tomorrow."

Her eyes lit on his, and Mateo's heart jolted. He and Katie were going Christmas tree shopping, out on an adventure. Nothing as rugged as traversing the Mayacamas Mountains, and he didn't even know why he'd made the comparison. His great-great-grandparents had been bonded together, deeply in love. Heat warmed his neck. He was not going to fall for Katie. She was his brother's girl, and he'd sworn off women. But that didn't mean he couldn't like her. Be a friend. He wedged his hands in his jacket pockets, deciding that was what they would be: amigos.

"Night, Katie. Guess I'll see you tomorrow at—?" He realized they hadn't set a time for him to arrive at her house. She presumably needed some time to get home and change.

Katie opened her car door. "Three thirty works."

Mateo nodded. "Three thirty it is."

Titi Mon gave him a funny look, but he wasn't sure why. His poker face was pretty good, and he'd done nothing to let on about his inconvenient attraction to Katie. Okay. So maybe his mom had caught him and Katie standing awfully close in the vineyard. She hadn't said anything about that. Then again, with their dash off to the hospital, there hadn't been time.

"She's such a sweet girl," his mom said as Katie's taillights disappeared down the drive.

Abuela smiled over her shoulder as they entered the house. "My visions are never wrong," she told the group. "Katie looks beautiful in my wedding dress."

Titi Mon shut the door extra hard. Her eyebrows shot up. "What?"

"When did this happen?" Mateo's mom asked in surprise.

His dad removed Abuela's coat, and she straightened her shawl. "I asked her to try it on," Abuela explained. "Today, after lunch. Mateo saw her."

All eyes travelled to Mateo, and his ears burned hot.

"He can tell you how lovely she looked. No, Mateo?"

He shifted on his feet. "She, um, did look very nice in it, yeah." He raked a hand through his hair, hoping to sweep the image from his mind. He'd been attempting to do that all day long, but it plagued him anyway, like the tune of a song you couldn't get out of your head. Then there were the memories of them together in the vineyard, playing over and over again in his mind like a soft serenade, and now he had new recollections to compound those. Katie's artistic talent had surprised him. Made him want to know more about her. Not for himself. Because of Juan, of course. If Abuela had her wish, she'd be Mateo's sister-in-law someday. So getting to know her better—as a friend—only made sense.

His mom smiled. "Isn't that sweet? Abuela taking to Katie so strongly?"

"It is very strong and very soon," his dad commented from beside her. He hung their coats in the closet as well, then took Titi Mon's.

"Yes." His mom nodded. "True."

"Which is why"—his dad slowly spun toward his mom—"we should put on the brakes about discussions of weddings for a bit."

Abuela's cheeks sagged. "But, Raul—"

"Mamá," he said gently, cutting his mother off. "Juan is in the hospital. Let's wait until he gets better so we can see what he has to say about her. Hmm?"

"He's already said a lot," Titi Mon said, glancing at her phone.

"His texts were pretty glowing," Mateo's mom conceded.

Mateo held up his hands. "Dad is right. Maybe we should wait to hear what Juan has to say about Katie?" He unzipped his jacket. "From what she's told me, their relationship is pretty new. Not serious at all. They only started dating right before his accident. Like, *immediately* before. As in yesterday."

"No," his mom said. "She specifically told us they'd been seeing each other for three months."

Titi Mon removed her coat. "That's right, she did."

His dad hung Titi Mon's coat in the coat closet and reached for Abuela's coat when Abuelo handed it to him. "I recall hearing that too."

"That's when they met," Mateo insisted. "When Juan first came into Daisy's. He didn't ask her to be exclusive until yesterday."

Abuela scoffed lightly. "Young people and dating!" She turned to Mateo. "There were stars in her eyes when she put on my wedding gown," she said defiantly. "You saw that too."

"Abuela," Mateo said gently, "isn't it also possible that Katie was simply being kind? Sweetly going along with your wishes?"

Abuela crossed her arms, but when Abuelo stared at her, she relented. "Okay," she said on a sigh. "I suppose that's possible."

His mom's eyebrows arched. "Well, I, for one, agree with my husband about putting any wedding talk aside. We can reopen that topic if—and when—the time comes." She walked into the kitchen and peered into the refrigerator. "Okay," she said with a bright smile. "Who's hungry?"

They decided on *bocadillos*, and Mateo removed six dinner plates from a cabinet, preparing to set the table. "What else can I do?"

His dad glanced over his shoulder as he filled water glasses from the dispenser in the freezer door. "Why don't you go down to the wine cellar and grab us a cab franc or two?"

Mateo's mom grinned. "That sounds like the right choice."

Mateo headed for the wine cellar, thinking about when he'd been down there with Katie. Everyone seemed to like her so much. Well, mostly everyone. Titi Mon and Abuelo weren't shy about expressing their reservations. Mateo had harbored a number of those himself. But being around Katie today had changed his mind. She didn't seem the conniving sort or like the type to be after Juan's status or money. She seemed gentle and kind. Good-hearted. And yet there was something she was holding back, and that secretive edge made him uncomfortable. Maybe he'd learn more about what she was hiding tomorrow.

EIGHT

Five Days before Christmas

KATIE ARRIVED AT THE DINER bright and early. Daisy was opening the register, and Mark stood at the griddle, firing it up. Their first customers already waited in the parking lot, their headlights painting the window of the lit-up eatery from the outside. They had several regulars. Joe from the auto parts store down the street. Dougie and May, who were married and also served on a road crew together, laying down asphalt, which was much less taxing to do in cooler weather. Jules, who worked at Castellana's independent bookstore, the Blank Page.

There was also a construction crew that often stopped in before beginning their jobs, and a group of nurses from the hospital typically showed up for breakfast after completing their night shift. They had to have heard about Juan, as his tragic hit-and-run had made the local paper and was also probably big buzz at the hospital.

Then there was the banker, Mr. Elroy, who for some reason had taken a special shine to Katie. He claimed she reminded him of his granddaughter, who lived in Wyoming. He was a kind man but also a little lonely, Katie suspected. Which was why she always took extra time to listen to his stories.

"Katie," Daisy said as she breezed in the door. "How are you holding up, darling?"

Mark turned from his post behind the counter. "What's the word on Juan?"

Katie sighed. "He's still in the coma," she told Daisy. She glanced at Mark. "But he improved a little yesterday."

"That's good to hear." Mark nodded and flipped the switch on a coffee machine, helping her out as she stowed her purse and coat on a hook in the kitchen. She'd had to wear her mittens and hat this morning. Titi Mon had been right about this cold snap. It wasn't predicted to get out of the thirties all day. Which wasn't unheard of in Castellana in December, but it was unusual, since daytime temperatures generally stayed in the forties, sometimes higher.

Daisy's brow furrowed as she counted out bills. "Have the doctors given a prognosis?"

Katie scooted behind the counter, strapping on her apron. "Once they've gotten his brain swelling under better control with medication, they're confident they'll be able to restore his consciousness. He's young and healthy otherwise, so all indications are good."

Daisy frowned. "You poor dear. You must be knotted up with worry."

"Poor Juan," Mark added. He shook his head. "So that Christmas date of yours?"

Katie carted a bucket of clean coffee cups and saucers in from the kitchen, stacking them behind the counter near the coffee maker. "Don't know if it's happening." She grimaced, because with the object of her affections laid up in the ICU, it was awkward to admit it. "But I have been to Los Cielos."

"What?" Daisy shut her register drawer. "Already?"

Katie pulled the chilled pies from the refrigerator in the kitchen, arranging them in a glass case on the counter. Coconut cream and gingerbread cheesecake, which was Juan's favorite. An apple pie already sat in the case. Daisy made the desserts herself daily and took the excess home each evening to share with her family. Though there were rarely any of Daisy's goodies left.

Katie looked up from her work. "Juan's parents invited me out there for lunch yesterday." She shrugged. "Sort of as a thank-you."

"For saving Juan's life," Mark surmised. He tossed a large pat of butter on the griddle, and it sizzled. He was getting started on making stacks of pancakes that the construction crew devoured by the dozens. "That was very brave of you."

"I didn't really have time to think about it," she admitted honestly. "I just reacted."

"What about you?" Daisy glanced toward the counter stools, almost like she could see through them with X-ray vision, viewing the scrapes on Katie's bare knees. The heels of her hands had taken a mild beating too, but she'd avoided getting more banged up by landing partially on top of Juan. His overcoat had helped cushion both of them from the fall, but his head hadn't been protected from banging against the curb. "I gave you yesterday off to rest and recover." She frowned sympathetically. "You could have taken today too, you know."

"It's fine," Katie said. "I'm fine."

Another server entered the diner. Caleb was in his thirties and in between restaurant jobs as a chef. He wore his long blond hair in a man bun. "Morning, all."

They exchanged greetings.

Daisy sidled up to the counter when Caleb entered the kitchen to hang up his jacket. "So Los Cielos?" she asked quietly. "How was it?"

"Every bit as beautiful as it appears in pictures." Katie sighed. "Dreamy." Just like Juan. *And* Mateo. *No, stop that.* She couldn't—wouldn't—let herself keep thinking of Juan's brother that way. Mateo was cute, sure, and very easy to get along with. But Juan was the dreamiest one of all, hands down. He was her destiny.

"Katie?" Daisy leaned toward her. "What is it? Is something wrong?"

The scene flashed through her mind of Mateo and her standing at El Corazón beside those original vines. The story he'd shared about his great-great-grandparents had been so romantic. She couldn't imagine loving someone enough to venture with them to a new land and start a brand new life. But Mateo's Papi Monchi and Mamacita had, and their legacy still lived on.

"No, not wrong exactly." She shoved away the memory of the caring look in Mateo's eyes when she'd told him about losing her family. "I learned a lot more about Los Cielos and about how things all began with Juan's great-great-grandparents."

Daisy's dark eyes sparkled. "That background should prove useful in getting to know Juan better."

Katie nodded, deciding not to mention it had been extra helpful in getting to know his brother. Mateo was the one who seemed to care about the history of the place, not Juan. In all the times he'd come in here, Juan had never mentioned the legacy of Los Cielos. Only his notion that a lot of their practices needed updating.

"And Juan's family?" Daisy asked her. "How are they? Nice enough?"

Katie nodded. "Very sweet." She opted *not* to tell Daisy about Abuela and her vision—or the wedding dress. Now wasn't the time. And maybe the time would be never.

Caleb appeared beside her, his apron tied on. "Should I set up?" He glanced at the empty booths surrounding them.

"Yeah, thanks." Katie handed him a few fistfuls of packaged silverware rolled up in paper napkins. "If you could put these out."

"Look," Daisy said, pointing toward the door. "Here comes Mr. Elroy, first one in line."

Katie smiled at the older man scuttling up the walkway that led into the diner. "As usual," she said to Daisy, preparing Mr. Elroy's customary spot at the counter.

Caleb peered out at the packed parking lot. "Looks like a full house."

Good. That was good. That way, she'd stay busy and get to focus on her work. Rather than on her pounding heart and the fact that she'd soon be seeing Mateo. Going out alone with him to pick out a Christmas tree. And *not*—oh, how she hoped—any mistletoe. Because thinking about mistletoe and Mateo together was a dangerous mix.

———

Later that afternoon, Mateo stopped at a railroad crossing as a train rolled by, clickety-clacking across the tracks. When it cleared, the gate went up, showcasing the modest neighborhood ahead of him. Single-story houses lined either side of the street. Some were made of wood, others stucco. None appeared larger than one- or two-bedroom places, and many were in poor repair. His GPS gave a command, and he turned left onto Katie's street. Her house was on the right-hand side and had a small covered stoop. Katie's car was in the drive. He pulled into her driveway and parked behind it.

An old chain-link fence rimmed the backyard, abutting an empty field, where a passel of chickens pecked at the dirt. He supposed they belonged to the dingy farmhouse with the worn tin roof and an open-faced barn beside it. A family of goats nestled inside the barn and out of the wind, their bearded chins visible through its overhang's shadows. A towering hay field served as a backdrop, and hills rolled toward the mountains. Mateo exited his SUV and shut the door. It wasn't a bad view. Bucolic. A touch homey.

The neighborhood, though, looked pretty worse for the wear. Katie's house particularly. Did she compare it to Los Cielos, finding his home overly grand? Pretentious even? To him, it had always been home. But then, his home had never looked like Katie's. Sadness crept over him, and he found himself wishing he could do something about her troubling circumstances, but he wasn't sure what.

He approached Katie's house, noticing the peeling paint on the siding and shutters. The roof appeared ancient too. A Christmas wreath hung on the front door, though, lending the place a festive touch.

What was he doing taking Katie out to shop for a Christmas

tree? Just because his mom had suggested it, that hadn't meant he had to go along with the idea.

Oh yes, he did. It would help his family by relieving them from worrying about decorating for Christmas, and the entire Martinez clan could use a little Christmas cheer. Shopping for trees was his thing, his and Juan's. Now that Juan was unable to go himself, it made sense for Mateo to go on ahead.

It made less sense in his mind for Katie to accompany him. But with Juan in the hospital, she was essentially taking his place. Right. That was how he should think of her today: as nothing more than his brother's surrogate. That would help keep his head on straight and prevent his heart from misbehaving, as it kept trying to do every time he'd laid his eyes on Katie.

He started to knock, but the door flew open.

"I saw your SUV in the drive." She smiled, and all thoughts of her serving as his brother's surrogate flew out the window. Katie Smith was definitely *not* Juan. She was pretty and fresh-faced, with her hair worn loose to her shoulders, and dressed in a cute Christmas sweater and jeans. This sweater was red, and as far as he could tell, it had candy canes on it. She wore a white pom-pom hat to match her puffy white coat and held white mittens in one hand. Her purse strap hung over her shoulder. She quickly shut the door.

"All ready to go?" he asked her.

Her face reddened as she locked up. "Yep."

Maybe she hadn't wanted him to see the inside of her house because it was modest compared to Los Cielos. His heart clenched again. Her childhood had clearly been different from his and

Juan's. If things went well between her and his brother, her life and financial situation would improve—assuming the family was able to dig the vineyard out of the current hole it was in. He clung to the hope that they would, though he still couldn't see how.

She spun toward him and shrugged. "So," she said brightly. "I guess we're getting a Christmas tree." Her brown eyes sparkled, and his neck warmed.

Surrogate. Surrogate. He tried to superimpose an image of Juan's face over Katie's, but the effort was a major fail. He inwardly groaned. Fighting his growing attraction to Katie seemed like a losing battle. But that only meant he needed to try harder.

"Are you all right?" she asked.

Mateo cleared his throat. "Yeah, yeah. Fine." He turned on his heel as she came up beside him, walking along the short path to the drive. "How was your day at Daisy's?"

"Pretty good," she said. "How was your day at Los Cielos?"

"Same." They reached his SUV, and he opened the passenger door for her so she could climb inside.

"And Juan?" she asked, scooting into her seat. "How is he?" She peered up at Mateo, looking so unbelievably adorable in that hat of hers he had to mentally kick himself *again*.

"Not much change from yesterday, unfortunately." She nodded, and he shut the door, hoping that Juan's situation would change. Very soon. Because these feelings Katie brought out in him didn't help his determination to stop thinking about women for a bit. Juan was supposed to be the one experiencing that slow simmer in his soul every time Katie smiled. Not him. Which was why he planned to focus extra hard on picking out the biggest and best Christmas tree for his family ever. With him and Katie working on that common goal, their outing would seem more like a trip between friends rather than any sort of romantic excursion. Which it absolutely wasn't. *And...*

Mateo was going to keep telling himself that.

———————

Katie tried not to look at Mateo during the drive to the Christmas tree farm north of town, because every time he caught her peering in his direction, her heart stuttered. And she did *not* need anything stuttering around Mateo, least of all her heart. So she tried to keep a casual conversation going. They talked about this and that, including their current cold snap. The topic of the weather was harmless enough.

Mateo found a space in the busy gravel parking lot and set his SUV in Park. "At least we won't have to worry about snow this Christmas," he said, turning to her.

Katie had always dreamed about seeing snow, but she never had. She laughed at Mateo's comment. "This Christmas or *any* Christmas."

"True." He thumped his steering wheel with his gloved hands. He wore a heavy bomber jacket and a stocking cap on his head. "But you never know..." His winked and her stomach fluttered. "This year, we might get lucky."

"Sure we will." She lightly shoved his arm, then wished that she hadn't. The motion had swayed her closer to him, and in that instant, she'd caught a whiff of that heady pine scent that was unique to Mateo. "And the moon is made of blue cheese."

"Blue?" His eyebrows arched. "Not Swiss?"

Katie folded her arms, feeling sassy. "Ever heard of a blue moon? As in once in a...?"

Mateo shook his finger at her. "Very funny." He leaned back in his seat and studied her. "You're right about the snow though. In Castellana, it's unlikely."

"In Castellana," she corrected, "it's unheard of."

He turned up his hands. "So maybe this year will be different?"

"Now, that would be cool." She sighed, trying to imagine building a snowman. But that was too far of a stretch for around here. Even a few flakes would be nice. She had a vision of standing in the snow with Juan. But when he laughed and took her in his arms, his face morphed into Mateo's, while beautiful snowflakes swirled all around them. Katie blinked, batting away the illusion with her mitten.

Mateo cocked his head. "Everything okay there?"

Katie's cheeks warmed because he stared at her so intently. "Everything is extra okay!" She laid her hand on her door handle. "Should we go pick out a tree for Los Cielos?"

He nodded. "Let's do it."

There was an open-air shed up ahead of them with an overhang covering bins of greenery like garlands. Another bin held small swags of twigs holding glossy white berries, tied up in silky white ribbons. Mistletoe. She avoided Mateo's gaze, but he was looking at something else.

He gestured to a family walking by holding steaming paper cups. They left a trail of cinnamon-apple aromas behind them. "Looks like they have cider again this year. Want some?"

The wind picked up, howling up from the valley. Katie shivered and wrapped her arms around herself. "Hot cider does sound good."

A worker stood at a cash register located on a rustic wooden countertop, and loads of fresh Christmas tree wreaths hung on the back wall. Stacked shelves held other Christmas decorations and knickknacks, like stands of wooden reindeer. They spotted the hot beverage station on a table to the right. One large urn was labeled *spiced cider* and the other *coffee*. An array of candy canes was displayed in open jars. A big sign on the table had been painted with the word *Complimentary* in green and red letters.

People gathered around the table fixing their own cups, but it didn't take long for the crowd to move along. As they waited in line, Mateo explained about the Christmas trees.

"The ones closest to here are the precuts," he told Katie, pointing to the collection of trees hugging either side of the sales shed. "Some are from this farm, but certain others, like the Fraser firs, are brought in from Oregon."

"Oregon? Wow." She wouldn't have guessed that. Then again, she and her dad hadn't exactly done Christmas trees. She steeled herself against the melancholy that she often found pervasive this time of year. In her heart, she'd always loved the holidays and had longed to embrace them, but so many of the joys of Christmas had been taken away from her when she was young. She had vague memories of shopping for Christmas trees with her mom when she was little. But they'd usually gone to the grocery store parking lot, not to a farm.

Mateo nodded. "The Cortinis mostly grow Douglas firs and

white firs. You have to hike up toward the mountains a bit to get the best picks."

"Which kind are we after?" Katie asked him as they inched closer to the cider table. There was only one group ahead of them now.

"Juan and I usually go for the Douglas firs."

Katie smiled, enjoying the idea of walking around with him. "Sounds like a plan." She liked that they could get their cider and linger a bit. She did so very few Christmassy things with other people, apart from working at the soup kitchen.

Part of her felt like an imposter for participating in this ritual with Mateo. But a deeper, needier part of her so desperately wanted to experience a real family Christmas, like she hadn't had in far too many years. The sort she read about in books and saw in movies, with a happy family gathered around a tree, laughing and sharing stories.

They reached the table, and Mateo fixed them both a cup, handing one to her. "Candy cane?" he asked, his eye on a stash of them.

Of course it's okay to want this. Who wouldn't want this?

Katie grinned up at him. "Why not?" She'd always loved candy canes and peppermint anything. Which made Daisy's homemade peppermint cheesecake her absolute favorite.

Mateo picked up two candy canes and passed one to her, sliding the other in his flannel shirt pocket beneath his jacket. "What kind of Christmas tree do you usually get?" he asked as they strolled back out into the open. Daylight was fading, casting long shadows off the towering trees all around them. He motioned straight ahead with his cup, and they walked in that direction.

She shrugged. "I have a smallish fake tree that stands in the corner next to my TV." She lifted a shoulder. "It's only me."

"Right." He frowned as they continued walking. "And before? With your dad?"

She gritted her teeth, trying to act like it was silly and didn't matter. But it did matter, privately, to her. "Dad wasn't big into Christmas. At least not after."

"After?" His eyebrows rose.

She frowned. "We lost my mom."

"I'm sorry, Katie. Looks like you carried on in spite of that."

She thumbed her chest with her free hand. "Me?"

He smiled warmly. "Yeah, you." He nudged her with his elbow, and current buzzed through her. "Just look at you in those Christmas sweaters of yours."

Her face warmed because she hadn't realized he'd noticed.

He leaned closer, bringing his gorgeous mouth so extremely close to hers that she nearly died. "Plus, aren't those jingle bell earrings?"

She chuckled with embarrassment. "Okay, yes. They are."

"So see." He gave a self-satisfied grin. "You do like the holiday."

Katie blushed hotly. "Never said that I didn't." When he widened his eyes at her, she continued in sassy tones. "I'm just more used to celebrating by myself."

"Then you'd better brace yourself for plenty of company this year."

The sparkle in his eyes warmed her and confused her all at once. Though she was happy about not spending the holiday alone, she wished it wasn't under such convoluted circumstances, with her pretending to be someone she wasn't.

Mateo led them to a stand where a worker stood handing out tree-cutting equipment to people.

"What's all this?"

"We've got to get our saw and our pull cart," he told her. "Otherwise, it's going to be pretty hard to fell and bring back that tree."

"So you're Paul Bunyan now?"

"Yep." He tugged at his flannel shirt collar beneath his jacket. "At least as close as they come in Castellana."

She grinned at him. "I think there are probably one or two real lumberjacks around here."

"Okay, okay!" He held up a hand, but he was chuckling. "As close as they come in the Martinez family then."

Katie tried to imagine perfectly coiffed Juan cutting down a Christmas tree, but somehow she couldn't.

"So who usually does the chopping? You or Juan?"

"The chopping?" He rubbed his chin. "Generally me."

"And the cart pulling?"

He pointed to her, and she took a giant step back.

"Oh no! Not me!"

He shot her a smug look. "Something tells me you're plenty strong from all that heavy lifting at Daisy's."

"Mateo." She huffed and set her hands on her hips, but she was playing, because he definitely had to be.

"You're filling in for Juan," he said mildly. "So…"

"So *no*. You're going to help me!" She shoved his arm again, and he trapped her mitten against his coat sleeve. His eyes locked on hers, and time stood still.

"Am I?" he rasped, sending shivers down her spine. The way he was looking at her was *not* like she was his brother's girlfriend. Even his brother's very new girlfriend. He was staring at her like he wanted her for himself.

Heat swamped through her, and she couldn't breathe. Or think. Of *anything* other than kissing Mateo.

"One saw and one cart?" the worker asked them, breaking the spell.

Mateo blinked and wheeled around. "Uh, yeah. Thanks!"

He took out his wallet and gave the worker a few bills as Katie watched him, her heart hammering about a million miles per minute. What had just happened? And why now? Why here? And why, *oh why*, with Mateo?

NINE

KATIE LAGGED BEHIND MATEO SCALING the hill. He paused and stared over his shoulder. "I can seriously take that from you if you want." He held up the saw. "You can bring this."

She set her chin, looking determined and—God help him—so beautiful, huffing and puffing and tugging that cart along. "I'd rather bring this up the hill than drag it along once it's loaded with a jumbo Douglas fir."

"Ah, but in that case," he pointed out, "you'll be going downhill."

Her face brightened. "Maybe I can ride on the cart? Like a sleigh."

He chuckled. "There won't be room for you once the tree's on it." She stuck out her tongue at him, and he couldn't help chuckling. "Spoiled much?" he teased.

"I'm not spoiled," she countered. "You're the one who lives at the ritzy winery."

"We run a boutique business."

"*Boutique* means *expensive* where I come from."

"Come on." He latched on to the cart handle and helped her

pull it along. His glove slid into her mitten, but they both tried to pretend it hadn't happened. He couldn't let go now and act like that was a problem. That would be awkward. So he stared straight ahead and kept trudging up the hill between the neatly planted rows of Douglas firs. They got taller the farther uphill they went, and Mateo needed one at least six feet tall to fill the space in their great room. Seven feet tall would be better.

"How far are we going?" Her breath clouded the chilly air, coming out in tiny puffs. He tried not to think about her pretty pink lips as she posed the question. He didn't think she had lipstick on, more like a shimmery lip gloss. Her cheeks held the same rosy hue, likely thanks to the cold. With the sun sinking low, temps had to be approaching the low thirties.

"Up there." He nodded to a high ridge.

She gasped. "All the way to the top?"

"Over the top."

"You're kidding."

"Nope, and it will be worth it."

"What will?"

"The view."

She stared around at the thicket of pines surrounding them. "What's there that's not here?"

"A clear view of Mount Saint Helena."

Her face glowed happily. "That sounds amazing."

"It is amazing. Just wait and see." He winked, then regretted being too forward. Maybe even slightly flirty. But he couldn't help wanting to impress Katie. He wanted her to like being around him. Enjoy his company. Because... A lump lodged in his throat.

She could very well be joining their family someday. Which was why he needed to *stop* trying to banter with her and *start* learning more about her and how she fit together with Juan.

"So you and Juan," he said as they walked along. "Must have tons in common, huh?"

She bit her bottom lip. "Er, I don't know about *tons*."

"You like the same music?"

"Sure!"

"Which is?" He arched an eyebrow at her, and she blinked.

"The exact kind he's always liked."

"Opera?"

Her jaw dropped, but then she quickly closed her mouth. "Yes. Love that! All the—arias!"

"So which is your favorite?" He hadn't figured Katie for an opera buff, so this was news.

She coughed into her hand. "Which what?"

He grinned. "Opera."

Maybe she and Juan were more alike than he'd given them credit for.

"Oh! Ah." She seemed to search her brain. "*Oliver!*"

Or not.

Mateo chuckled, charmed by her. "That's more like a musical."

"Ha! Yeah. I know that." Her eyebrows knitted together, making her look adorable. She seemed to be stewing over her answer and trying to think up what to say next.

"That's okay," he said breezily. "I like that one too."

"Do you? That's cool." Her face reddened. Was that at their connection or the fact that she couldn't tell a musical from an opera?

Not that this mattered to him. He doubted it would matter much to Juan either. "It's pretty ancient though," he continued, amused.

"It *is* ancient. My mom had the record and used to play it a lot. I've still got it."

"An old vinyl?" he asked her.

She grinned. "Yeah."

"That's fun. Vinyls are becoming hot again, in a retro sort of way."

Her blush deepened. "Oh yeah? Well, I've got plenty. My mom's whole collection."

"Guess you're on the leading edge then," he teased.

"A real trendsetter!" She beamed brightly, and his heart skipped a beat. "Yep! That's me!"

Brisk winds nipped at his face, and he squinted against a chilly burst of air. When they'd begun walking, they'd had fellow tree hunters in their row, and they'd heard people chatting in the next rows over. Now, though, they'd left the others far behind.

"I played Oliver once, you know," he said conversationally. "I was just a kid. Children's theater, but I got the part."

"Was Juan in the play?"

Mateo laughed. "Yeah, as the Artful Dodger."

She batted her eyelashes against the cold. "I bet you were the cutest. Both of you!"

"Did you ever do any acting?"

She pursed her lips. "Not me."

"Not even in school?"

"Definitely not in school. The idea of getting up in front of an audience terrified me."

"Never bothered me," he said. "Juan either."

She tugged harder on the cart as they continued uphill. "I can see where you guys would be naturals, Juan especially."

Of course, Juan especially. He was always the star of every show, upstaging Mateo in the title role. Juan wasn't the best actor technically. He actually had a habit of flubbing his lines. But his smile was so bright and his presentation so captivating, he won over every audience with his charisma.

"Are you sure we're still on the property?" She glanced over her shoulder with a worried frown. "Because we seem to be the only ones up this far."

"We're almost there now," he assured her. "So if you weren't into acting in high school, what kinds of things did you do?"

"You mean like clubs and such?"

He nodded.

"I was always into art and volunteering. I started a community service group in high school."

"Did you?" His gaze swept over her. "That's pretty wonderful."

"Some of it wasn't so glamorous. We raked leaves for the elderly, picked up trash along the highway, sang Christmas carols at retirement homes."

He was intrigued. "Do you have a good voice?"

She shrank back a bit and laughed. "Not really. You?"

He cocked his chin. "I was in *Oliver!*"

"Come on." She playfully shoved his arm, and electric current rippled through him. "You were a kid."

"I'm still pretty good," he said with no false modesty.

"Well, I'm *not*."

He paused to stare in her eyes. "Wait a minute. You said you didn't like getting up in front of people? So what about the Christmas caroling?"

"I never did it on my own. Besides which." Her grin sparkled prettily. "It was for a good cause."

He admired the fact that she'd taken pains to think of others, even as a teen.

"Were you in any clubs?" she asked him.

"In high school? Sure. I was big into foreign languages. Juan was big into debate."

Katie rolled her eyes, the picture of cuteness. "I bet he was."

Mateo laughed at some memories, but then he grew sad. He'd give anything to hear Juan arguing a point with him now, even if they stood on different sides of an issue, like they did about Los Cielos.

"I know this is hard on you," she said. "Hard on your whole family, having Juan in a coma this way."

"He'll pull out of it." He forced a smile. "So you can show him your place and play those old vinyls of yours."

Pink spots formed on her cheeks. "That would be great."

They crested the ridge, and a valley opened up below them, sweeping toward Mount Saint Helena. Its snow-covered peaks kissed the dusky purple curtain blanketing the sky.

Katie gasped, covering her mouth with a mitten. "It's gorgeous."

"Yeah. And our perfect tree should be right about"—Mateo glanced down the hill at the tallest section of Douglas firs—"here." He pulled the cart along a little farther and stopped, angling it sideways so it wouldn't accidentally start rolling away. "So!" he said, wielding his saw. "Want to help me choose?" He'd rather be thinking about Christmas trees than wondering for the millionth time what Katie was doing with Juan. They seemed so different. Then again, opposites could—and did—attract.

She examined their surroundings, then stretched her mitten out toward a tree, gingerly grasping its piney branch. "This one looks nice."

Mateo eyeballed it, guessing it was about the right height. Its shape was nice and full too.

Katie bent toward the tree and inhaled deeply. "It smells like Christmas."

He beheld her standing there by the tree, thinking she smelled a lot like Christmas to him. Minty and fresh like a candy cane. He figured it was her body wash or shampoo. He'd noticed it in his SUV when she'd playfully shoved his arm, causing his heart to nearly leap out of his chest. She'd surprised him with the move, but not as much as he'd been stunned by his own reaction to her. Which was overwhelmingly inconvenient.

He walked around the tree, examining its base and deciding where to cut. "So you and Juan," he tried a second time, as casually as he could. "You've probably really been looking forward to this holiday."

"Well, like I said." She licked her lips. "We weren't even official until a few days ago."

He stopped circling the tree and came up in front of her. "Yes, but he did ask you home for Christmas dinner. You must have talked about that."

"We were going to talk more! Work out the details." She shifted on her feet. "But that was before his accident."

Mateo rubbed his cheek. "At least you had all that time talking at the diner first. Getting to know each other."

"Yes! That's right."

"You must have learned a lot about each other. Favorite foods—"

She grinned and then said coyly, "I know Juan loves gingerbread cheesecake."

He laughed but then narrowed his eyes at her. "There has to be something more."

"Of course," she said sassily, and his neck warmed. "He told me about your business and how much he loves it." She adjusted her hat, tugging it down over her ears. It was getting colder by the minute.

"I'm sure you told him tons about your life too," Mateo said. Even assuming her relationship with Juan was brand new, they had to have shared some kind of connection. Otherwise, Katie being with his brother made zero sense.

Her face reddened. "Er, somewhat."

Mateo's eyebrows rose. "Somewhat?"

Katie bit her bottom lip. "We were so busy talking about him, the truth is we didn't totally get around to me. I mean, not in extreme detail. But!" She inhaled sharply. "There will be time for that!" She held her breath, then let it go. "Eventually."

Mateo cocked his head. "You and Juan don't really know each other that well, do you?"

"That's what I've been trying to tell you, Mateo. Tell all of you. But that doesn't mean that it won't happen once Juan recovers."

"I'm sure that it will." A secretly jealous part of him hated that fact. "Because a guy would have to be crazy"—his voice went rough below the wind—"not to want to know more about you."

She blushed, and he mentally kicked himself for that sounding like a come-on. He hadn't meant to be so blatant about it. In fact, he hadn't meant to say it at all.

He studied her a long moment. "What kinds of things *do* you like anyway?"

Her eyebrows arched below her hat. "What? You mean now?"

"Yeah. What are your hobbies?"

"I do online crosswords."

She sounded very embarrassed about it, but he didn't know why. He loved doing those.

"No way! I love those too."

"Do you?" she asked.

He nodded. "And sudoku."

"Me too!" She grinned. "It's fun figuring things out."

Somehow, he hadn't figured *her* out yet, or why she was dating his brother. Storm clouds rumbled in his soul. Women tended to flock to Juan. But Katie didn't seem like the women who'd flocked to Juan before. "I guess you also have your art," he reminded her. "That's a pretty great hobby. You're so good at it."

"Thanks, Mateo."

"Ever want to go professional?"

"There was a time," she admitted sadly. "But that was before."

He stepped closer to her. "Before losing your parents?"

She nodded and then seemed to want to redirect. "What about you?"

"I spend what free time I have working on my guitars."

She searched his eyes. "The ones for your business someday?"

"I'm not sure if there will be a business. But yeah, maybe." He shrugged to brush off how badly he wanted that dream. It was impossible to see how it would happen. He couldn't abandon Los Cielos and leave it in Juan's hands, especially not now with the vineyard so badly struggling. Juan often meant well, but he wasn't the most business-minded person at heart.

"I'd like to see some of your guitars sometime." The look in her eyes said she meant it, and his heart danced. If things were different, and she weren't with Juan...

He cleared his throat. "Any time you'd like."

She gazed up at him with her big brown eyes, and Mateo was a goner. Completely swept away and wishing he was the lucky guy who was going to get to hear about Katie's hopes and dreams. A strand of her hair blew across her cheek, and he reached out to stroke it back.

She grabbed his wrist, stopping him. "Mateo," she whispered. "It's getting dark."

He dropped his arm, alarmed by how much time had gone by without them actually chopping down a Christmas tree. Instead, he'd been flirting with Katie, presumably trying to draw her out on account of his brother while secretly dying to learn more about her for himself.

A shadow draped over his soul. He was falling for his brother's girlfriend, which was about a million times wrong. "You're right," he said, hoisting the saw in both hands. He smiled to hide his inner turmoil. "Let's take this puppy dog down." He squatted near the ground, grasping the base of the trunk in one hand. "Can you hold it steady up there?"

Katie gripped a higher portion of the trunk with her mittens. "Got it!"

"Great! Hang on!"

He needed to hang on too. Hang on to some semblance of dignity in this situation, in which he was destined to be the loser. He faced the raw truth, and a pang of anguish shot through him. Though he'd dated around, he'd never cared seriously about those women. Even after dating a few of them for months, none had captured his interest or attention the way Katie had in just a few short days. Nobody had since Gabriela. Now, Gabriela was getting married. The vision of Katie in Abuela's wedding dress flashed through his mind, and his ears burned hot.

Katie would likely be the next bride down the aisle after Gabriela, but she wouldn't be marrying him. Mateo had to get his head out of the clouds, because he stood no chance of becoming Katie's groom. Which was exactly as it should be. He had other worries to contend with anyhow, like the ailing state of his family's business and his desire for a professional career apart from the vineyard altogether. And then there was his comatose older brother. Juan needed to recover ASAP. So the two of them could make amends and start fresh—and before Mateo's unwilling attraction to Katie grew even stronger.

TEN

"WE'RE HOME!" MATEO HOLLERED AS Katie held the door open. He tugged the huge tree through the entrance, carrying it in backward, bottom end first. A few pine needles shook off in the process.

"Don't worry about those," Pia said, approaching them happily. "I'll get the broom." Winds whipped in from outside, scattering the pine needles across the tile, and Pia shut the door, observing the darkened sky. "It really has grown chilly," she said. "Good thing we started a fire."

Gas logs blazed in the hearth, and Abuela and Abuelo sat beside it in two sling chairs, draped with faux animal furs and made of wood and leather. Raul bent over them, handing them each a drink. His face lit up when he saw Mateo and Katie.

"What a tree!" Then he said more quietly to his parents, "Have a *coquito*. On Titi Mon."

"We did get a good one," Katie remarked. She removed her hat and mittens, feeling more at ease around the family. Despite the grandeur of the great room and its high wood-beamed ceiling, it was cozy. "How has everyone been here?"

"Good," they all said, and Abuela added, "*Muy bien*."

Katie didn't ask about Juan, because Mateo had checked his phone before leaving the Cortinis' farm. A nurse had said the family could check in for updates anytime by accessing Juan's latest charts through an app. If there was a breakthrough of any kind, the nurse promised someone would call. In the meantime, there hadn't been much change since the family visited Juan today at noontime.

Titi Mon stood at the kitchen counter with a blender in front of her and several ingredients beside it, including what looked like cans of coconut milk and a large bottle of rum. She was clearly in the process of whipping up some kind of libation. "Will you have a *coquito*, Katie?" she asked after adjusting her festive necklace. It was made from replicas of Christmas tree lights in bright colors: red, green, yellow, and blue.

Katie glanced at Mateo, who said, "It's a Puerto Rican Christmas drink, and *very good*."

Katie laughed at the way he'd said that. "How can I refuse?" She walked toward the kitchen. "Is there something I can do to help?"

Titi Mon nodded at the counter as Katie removed her coat. "Yes, fill the glasses."

Raul took Katie's coat and hung it in the closet while speaking to Mateo. "We've got the Christmas tree stand all ready by the window. I'll help you set things up."

Pia clasped her hands together. "And I'll go bring those last boxes out of storage."

"I can grab them, Mom," Mateo said. "After we're done with this." He angled his head toward the tree.

"Why don't you let me?" Katie offered. Titi Mon filled two

short glasses with the frothy concoction as Katie held them under the blender, and then Titi Mon dropped a long cinnamon stick into each. Katie glanced at Mateo.

"You can leave mine in the kitchen," he said.

Katie set his glass and hers on the island separating the great room from the kitchen. "That looks delicious," she told Titi Mon. "I can't wait to take a sip."

Titi Mon's eyebrows arched. "What's stopping you now?"

"I was waiting on"—Katie peeked at the men setting up the tree—"Mateo."

Titi Mon tsked. "No need for formalities, *mija*. You're among family." She mumbled under her breath, "Juan's family, but still."

She gestured toward Katie's glass, and Katie picked it up. She fell under the spotlight as the rest of the family focused their attention on her. Even Mateo and Raul paused in their work to assess her reaction. Whether or not it was delicious, she needed to rave about it like it was. She'd never been one for eggnog, and it looked a lot like that. Katie took a tentative sip, and a chilled coconutty goodness filled her mouth.

"Oh wow." She grinned at Titi Mon. "This is amazing."

Titi Mon wore a proud mug. "Secret family recipe." She laughed and waved her hand. "But not really so secret. I can tell you how I made it if you'd like."

"I would." She noted Pia disappearing down the hallway. "But let me go and help Pia first."

Katie turned a corner, having lost sight of Pia. She stared up and down the corridor as Pia slipped through a door. Katie hurried that way to catch up with her.

"Oh, Katie!" Pia looked up from sorting through some stacked containers. "Hi!" She stood in the middle of a storage room that was no bigger than a large walk-in closet. It was mostly filled with boxes and sturdy containers with snap-on lids. Two collapsed card tables and a bunch of folding chairs leaned up against the back wall.

"I came to give you a hand."

"That's very nice, thanks." Pia tucked a lock of her brown hair behind one ear and studied the labeling on one container. It said *Halloween*, but that had been crossed out with heavy permanent marker and *Christmas tree stand* had been written below it.

"Are you looking for something specific?" Katie asked her.

"Yes. The crèche."

Katie smiled and pointed to the container Pia held in her hands. *Crèche* was written on the side facing Katie.

Pia stared down at it and laughed. "Sometimes things don't get put back into the boxes they came from. The labeling can get a little convoluted." Katie nodded and took the container from Pia, and Pia selected another that said *Cookie Tins*. She stared at it sadly. "I doubt I'll have energy for baking Christmas cookies this year," Pia said, depositing the container on top of a stack of others. "Christmas is almost here."

The exhaustion drained off her, landing at Katie's feet in a puddle of despair. Katie set down her container and reached for Pia's arm, laying her hand on it. She wasn't normally a touchy-feely person, but somehow the gesture felt natural.

"I'm sure this has been really hard on everyone, but you're

Juan's mom. So it's got to be extra tough on you, seeing your son so helpless."

Pia drew in a breath. "Thank you, Katie. I know you're suffering too." Katie started to speak but Pia stopped her. "Don't worry. Mateo explained about how you and Juan only started dating before his accident. But I did see you in the hospital with him, sweetheart. With my own eyes. I can tell how much you care."

Katie's heart pounded. "It's really early days, so—"

"So we'll see, hmm?" Pia's lips tugged into a smile. "Things that are meant to be have a way of working out, and I have faith they will for you and Juan."

Katie wished she shared Pia's faith, but she was now more confused than ever. While she'd dreamed of kissing Juan dozens of times, in her mind, she'd understood that had all been in a fantasyland. Conversely, everything about Mateo seemed so present. Not distant and abstract but close up and real. Juan was a black-and-white pencil sketch, while Mateo's quiet strength painted an entire palette of colors. Just being around him made Katie feel vibrant, energized. Her heart sighed. *Happy*. And she had no business being happy around Mateo, not in a super silly, besotted way. She needed to reserve those feelings for Juan.

Doubts clawed at her soul. Had she spent all these months obsessing over the wrong brother?

Pia looked up from where she stood in the corner, hemmed in by empty suitcases with wheels and slide-in handles. "How did it go at the Christmas tree farm?"

Heat swamped through her because she'd been distracted thinking about Mateo. "Pardon?"

"Was it crowded?"

Moisture swept Katie's hairline, and she swiped it with her sweater sleeve. "Oh yes. Very."

"Maybe I shouldn't have put you in that position," Pia admitted. "Sending you to get the tree with him, but I was worried…" Her forehead creased as her words trailed off.

"About Mateo?"

Pia nodded. "He's very strong but tenderhearted, my second son. So I hated the idea of him undertaking the task he and Juan normally did together alone." She studied Katie. "I don't know if Juan said anything to you about their disagreement?"

It was hard to imagine peaceable Mateo disagreeing with anyone. Juan though, yeah. She could see it. He was so sure of himself and used to getting his own way.

Pia frowned. "It was right before Mateo's business trip to New York. The boys had a bad falling-out." Her eyes glistened and she turned away. "They fought about Los Cielos Cellars."

Katie softened her tone. "The winery? I don't understand."

Pia exhaled sharply. "Juan's been wanting to modernize for a while. 'Improve things.'" She made quotation marks with her hands. "By bringing us into the current century." She frowned. "The rest of us weren't in agreement with his scheme. Least of all Raul and Abuelo. This winery is their legacy—our heritage—and Juan wanted to anglicize everything, strip away that history by rebranding Los Cielos Cellars as"—her voice warbled—"Cloudy Crest Wines."

Katie gasped. That was a major overhaul of the family business. "You're joking."

"I wish I could say yes." A deep melancholy filled the small room, like a chamber welling with tears. Pia set her chin, her disappointment in Juan clear. Maybe this was what Mateo had been hinting about in the hospital when he asked if Juan had mentioned his plans for the vineyard.

"But Cloudy Crest Wines?" Katie said. "The Los Cielos Cellars name has been around for generations. It's who you all are."

"I'm so glad that you understand. Juan means well, I'm sure, but frankly our wine business is struggling, and that's precisely why we can't take risks." Pia studied her a long moment. "Maybe once he's better, you can talk to him?"

If the rest of them couldn't get through to him, Katie doubted very seriously that she'd be able to, not as his brand-new and extremely fake girlfriend. But Pia looked so down, she couldn't bring herself to say so. So she offered up the ray of hope that Pia looked like she desperately needed. "I'll be happy to try."

"Thank you, Katie," Pia sighed. Her gaze landed on a long narrow container. She reached for it, removing the one on top of it first. She peeked in the container to be sure, then snapped its lid back on. "Here we are!" She lifted it in her hands. "The tree skirt and topper." She nodded toward the exit.

Katie picked up the box containing the crèche. "Anything else?"

"No, this should be it. Raul and Abuelo brought out most of the other decorations earlier." Pia paused a beat. "Did you and Mateo get mistletoe?" She winked at Katie, and Katie's face warmed. "We'll want to have some for you and Juan when he comes home."

Her and Juan, right. If only she could stop thinking about

Mateo and the fun time they'd had at the Christmas tree farm. *And* the heated look in his eyes when his gaze had pored over her, stirring desire in her soul.

She bit her bottom lip. "Er, sorry, no."

Pia clucked her tongue, holding her oblong box. "That's all right. I'll pick some up later."

Mateo watched Katie set the container she was carrying down by the tree and walk to the kitchen to retrieve her drink. He passed her *coquito* to her when she neared the kitchen island and raised his glass to hers in a toast. "*Salud!*" Was he imagining it, or were her cheeks even pinker than before? Her whole face had a rosy hue upon her return from the storage room. Had something happened in there? Like his mom prying into Katie's situation with Juan? It wasn't as if Mateo hadn't pried a bit himself, but he'd never arrived at any satisfactory answers about what Katie was doing with his brother in the first place.

She lightly clicked his glass. "*Salud!*" Their fingers brushed and his heart lurched. Katie's face grew even redder, matching the crimson candy-cane colors on her sweater. She ducked her chin, searching for her napkin, which had dropped to the floor. She squatted low to grab it, and Mateo bent down at exactly the same time.

Their knees knocked, and Mateo moved back, working very hard to ignore the bolt of electricity that shot through him— straight from his legs all the way up to his core and into some other inconvenient places. "Oh, uh, sorry." He scooped her cocktail napkin off the floor, handing it to her. The paper napkin was patterned with green and red holly berries.

Her smile trembled when she took it before swiping it across her glistening forehead. "Thanks."

Titi Mon tucked the empty blender in the dishwasher. "We have a toast in Puerto Rico," she informed Katie with a saucy swagger. She joined Katie and Mateo at the kitchen island, hoisting her glass in the air. Her eyebrows twitched until she had the room's attention. "*Arriba!*"

Mateo chuckled, because she was so good at this. Though she was in her seventies, Titi Mon had an impish side. Particularly when it came to sneakily fixing up her nephews. Fortunately, she'd laid off Mateo when he'd started dating Gabriela, focusing her efforts on Juan. Now that Mateo was single again and Juan evidently wasn't, he'd have to watch his back. Or the front door, as the case may be.

Abuela laughed. All of them did, except Katie.

"*Arriba!*" Abuela chortled, rolling her *r*'s.

The others lifted their glasses. "*Arriba!*"

"*Abajo,*" Titi Mon said in guttural tones. She lowered her glass to waist level, and the others followed suit.

Katie giggled, playing along.

"*Abajo!*" their chorus rang out.

Titi Mon shoved her drink glass toward the great room, then cried with great gusto, "*Al centro!*"

"*Al centro!*" Katie sang out with the rest of them.

Titi Mon winked, bringing her glass to her lips. "*Al dentro.*" She took a noisy slurp and licked her lips. "Ah yes." She preened at her accomplishment of the perfect cocktail. "Delicious."

The room roared with laughter. "*Al dentro!*" they all shouted, likewise tasting their libations.

Katie giggled at Mateo. "That was a fun toast. What did it mean?"

He rubbed his chin. "It's more or less a version of 'Over the lips and through the gums, look out, stomach, here it comes.'" He shrugged apologetically. "Not the most elegant toast."

Titi Mon tsked. "It certainly is *muy fino*."

Abuelo raised his glass and chortled. "First class!" he cried, and the rest of them laughed.

ELEVEN

IT WAS A GROUP EFFORT getting the lights on the tree, involving multiple overlapping arms and hands. They'd had a simple chili and cornbread supper while sitting around the fire before beginning the decorating.

"Here, Katie!" Titi Mon passed her the end of a strand. "Hand this to Pia."

She did, and Pia handed the other end to Raul, who shared it with Mateo. The grandparents sipped from glasses of wine, enjoying the show.

"Titi Mon," Abuelo said. "Your branch is sagging."

She tsked and made a minor adjustment. "We'll fix everything in the end."

Katie was glad she wasn't standing next to Mateo. She'd actually taken pains to arrange it. She didn't want to get any closer to him than she had to without looking awkward about it. She'd been so sure she'd experienced an attraction between them at the Christmas tree farm, but that could have been all in her head.

"That's it for the lights!" Mateo announced. He wound the final portion of the lights around the top branches, reaching up as high as he could. He was tall enough to make it with his arm extended fully.

Pia lifted another container, popping off its lid. "Now for the fun part," she told the group.

Raul chuckled. "Isn't all of it the fun part?"

"Yes, but." Her eyes misted over. "I do miss Juan."

Raul laid a hand on her shoulder. "He'll be home soon."

"Yes!" Titi Mon said brightly. "And just wait until he gets a load of this tree!"

"Katie." Pia motioned toward the container. "Pick any one you want."

Katie found a cute painted reindeer ornament and draped it from a bough. She returned to the open container at the same time as Mateo and self-consciously backed up. "You go ahead."

He opened his palm. "No, you."

Katie ducked her chin to hide her blush. She had to stop this, really she did. She couldn't let her stomach get all knotted up like a teenager's every time she stood close to Mateo. Thank goodness Juan's prognosis was good. If it were less certain, she'd have had to tell his family by now the truth about who she was. She should probably still tell them.

Katie glanced around the tree at all the happy faces. Pia's expression had brightened as she laughed with Raul over some silly ornaments the boys had made them as kids. Katie couldn't wreck the moment now. But it was hard to know when the right moment would come. *Oh, Juan, please wake up soon. For your own good and also for the good of your family.*

A deep melancholy took hold, cloaking her soul in darkness.

It was going to be so hard to leave all this behind and return to her empty house. She stole a peek at Mateo as he helped Titi Mon settle a colorful papier-mâché bird with a long ribbon tail on a high branch. "There you go," he said sweetly. Mateo was so good with other people. He reminded her of her dad. Even after her dad's world had been turned upside down, he'd taken pains to think of others first. Her mom had been the same way.

Titi Mon tugged on her Christmas tree light necklace. It dipped slightly to the left, and she slid it back into place. "Thank you, Mateo." It was easy to appreciate things about Mateo. He was always so caring around his family.

Katie became aware of her gloomy frown before anyone else spotted it, and she shifted her expression into a sunnier one, smiling as she settled a miniature toy sleigh on a broad branch. "This one is cute," she said, holding up a tiny lantern in her hand. "Where did you get it?"

"Santa Fe," Raul answered, walking around to the far side of the tree.

Pia chimed in. "It's a luminaria. They have them all over the streets during the holidays. It's very pretty."

That sounded magical to Katie. She'd never been to Santa Fe. Maybe she should start a bucket list of domestic travel. She'd only focused on international destinations so far because those seemed so exotic and—sadly—unattainable. Still, a girl could dream.

Abuelo dug into the box of ornaments, producing another treasure. "Hee-hee! Look at this one." He held the shiny white Christmas tree ball up in front of Titi Mon. "It's our Juan."

Titi Mon smiled at the ornament. "Why, yes, it is."

Abuela plucked the ornament from Abuelo's fingers, holding it by its silver hook hanger. "We should let Katie see." She motioned Katie over, and Katie drew closer to take a look.

Someone had transposed a photo of young Juan in elementary school onto the Christmas tree ball. His incredibly dark eyes were unmistakable, as was his gleaming white grin. Katie giggled, seeing he wore his hair gelled and slicked back even then. "How sweet! How old was he?"

Pia set her hand on her chin. "Seven or eight, I think."

"Oh look!" Abuelo chortled. "Here's another, of Mate-oreo!"

"Abuelo, please." Mateo practically jumped over the coffee table to snag it out of Abuelo's hand. He glanced at the ornament, which was shaped like a house made out of Popsicle sticks, and his whole face turned red. "Let's not put this one up this year."

Now Katie was extra curious. "Let me see?"

Mateo shook his head, backing away from her with the ornament. "No. It's really goofy."

Katie laughed. "I don't mind goofy. I bet it's cute."

"It is cute," Abuela answered. She sashayed behind Mateo and took the ornament from him.

"Hey!" he protested. "Abuela." He stared at her with pleading eyes, but his petition was no good. Abuela brought the ornament over to Katie.

Little Mateo's photo was in the center of the Popsicle stick house in a way that made it look like he was peering out of a window. Small cutouts of Oreo cookies were glued to the outside of the house surrounding his picture. Katie grinned at his little boy smile, which was huge. His two upper middle teeth were missing, and a mop of curly brown hair covered most of his forehead.

"This is adorable," Katie said. She stared up at Mateo. "How old were you?"

He self-consciously crossed his arms. "I don't know. Five? Six?"

Abuelo chuckled, pointing to the ornament. "That's when he developed his fixation with Oreo cookies."

"Juan told him that's why his teeth fell out," Abuela chimed in lightly. "Because he ate too many sweets."

Katie gasped. "He didn't!"

Mateo rubbed his cheek. "Yeah, and I actually believed him until I finally asked Mom about it. She told me all kids lose their teeth at my age. Juan had lost his too. I probably just didn't remember."

Katie chuckled and handed him the ornament. Then she put some distance between them. "Do you still like sweets?"

Mateo shook his head. "Not so much anymore. Though I do appreciate Titi Mon's *coquitos*."

The others laughed, and Titi Mon quipped, "Of course." She sat on the sofa to rest, propping her feet on the coffee table. "Juan's never gotten over his sweet tooth."

Katie considered all the cheesecake and pie he ate at the diner. "Yeah, that's true! Juan loves his gingerbread cheesecake."

Pia nodded at her. "You do know our Juan." She smiled at Raul and then around the room. "Isn't it so terrific having Katie here with us?"

Almost everyone said yes, except for Abuelo, who extracted

a pair of Christmas candleholders from a box, pretending not to have heard. "Maybe we should put out some other decorations?" he suggested. He held the candleholders up for display. "And take a break from the tree for a minute?"

Pia and Raul exchanged glances, then surveyed the older generation, who appeared to be growing tired.

"I think that's a great idea," Pia answered. "Why don't you and Abuela sit down and rest with Titi Mon? We'll unpack a few other boxes first and then finish up the tree."

Katie didn't judge Abuelo for having his reservations about her. She understood them. Perhaps he was the only one of the Martinezes who still saw through to the truth. While Titi Mon had offered some initial resistance, she'd seemed to open her heart to Katie, like Pia and Raul had. Mateo though. *Oh, Mateo.* Katie wasn't sure what she was going to do about him. At the same time as she was becoming enmeshed in his family, her attraction to him kept getting stronger.

And Juan was still in a coma, unconscious. Unable to explain to his family how he'd made all those "Katie is my girlfriend" texts up.

What a very messy Christmas this was turning out to be.

Pia handed Katie the pretty gold star that was to serve as their tree topper. "Here," she said sweetly. "Why don't you do the honors, Katie?"

Katie stared around the room, glancing at Mateo. "Shouldn't you?"

Mateo had helped Raul hang an enormous artificial wreath over the hearth, and a wooden crèche sat on the mantle below it. Abuela informed Katie that the hand-painted set had been made in Mexico. They'd added other holiday touches to the room, like the swag of faux greenery draping from the bar side of the kitchen island and a jolly Santa statue that stood in the foyer, welcoming visitors by the front door. It was over three feet tall and appeared hand-carved and -painted like the crèche. A pile of Christmas stockings sat on the coffee table, but they'd not yet sorted through those.

Mateo shook his head. "That's usually Juan's job, so why don't you do it for him?" He stood a respectful distance from her. Not too close but not so far away so as to call attention to it, like Katie had unwittingly done by sliding so far apart from Mateo on the sofa.

Awkward.

She and Mateo had spent the entire evening dancing around each other while trying to grant the other a wide berth. Katie was mortified to think that Mateo sensed her attraction to him and even more confused to believe she'd spied a flicker or two of interest in *his* eyes.

They gathered around the tree with Pia and Raul, putting on the finishing touches of a few colorful balls, bright tinsel, and cute candy canes. Titi Mon supervised from the sofa. She pointed to a lower branch, weighed down by decorations. "There are too many ornaments on that one," she informed Raul. "You need to space them out."

Raul chuckled and complied, moving things around. "Of course, Titi Mon." He raised his eyebrows at Pia's aunt after making the fix. "Better?"

Titi Mon nodded, pleased. "Much."

What would Juan's family think of her once they learned she'd only been pretending? They'd likely feel hurt, deceived. Perhaps want nothing to do with her. But Katie couldn't imagine the Martinezes feeling that way about Juan. Nobody would dare reprimand a man coming out of a coma. Not for fudging about having a girlfriend for Christmas anyway.

She accepted the star from Pia, and Mateo slid over the stepladder, situating it in front of her. "Careful going up," he said.

"And coming down!" Titi Mon piped in. Titi Mon waved her hand when Katie hesitated with her boot on a bottom rung. "Go on, *hija*. Don't keep us waiting."

Abuelo and Abuela slumped back in their fur-covered chairs, and Abuelo had nodded off by the fire.

Abuela covered her mouth in a yawn, then whispered her encouragement to Katie. "*Sí, sí*. Do this for Juan." Abuela's asthma seemed to be doing better. As long as she didn't have any further shocks, she should be all right. But what she needed most of all was likely the happy surprise of Juan coming home.

Katie climbed up the ladder, holding on to its upper handle while reaching for the very highest branch. But she couldn't quite get there, even when stretching up on her tiptoes.

"Mateo," Titi Mon instructed gruffly. "Go up and help her."

"All right."

Katie's pulse hummed when she sensed Mateo behind her on the ladder.

"*Cuidado!*" Pia cautioned.

"We'll be fine," Mateo said huskily.

Katie's heart fluttered. *Nooo*. It was bad enough having these involuntary reactions around him but so much worse experiencing them while she was on full display in front of his family.

Abuelo sputtered a snore, jostling himself awake. "What's going on?"

Katie peered over her shoulder to see him staring at the ladder.

Abuela gestured toward the tree. "Mateo's helping Katie with the star."

"That's Juan's job, isn't it?" Abuelo appeared momentarily confused, but then he rubbed his forehead. "Ah yes. Right."

"Here," Mateo said, settling his hands around her waist. "I'll steady you so you can reach the top of the tree."

Steady? Ha. Katie felt anything *but*. She locked her knees to keep them from shaking, then scooted up another rung. This was definitely it. She couldn't climb any higher without toppling off and onto the ground. She clung to the ladder's handle, holding the gold star in her other hand.

So much for keeping her distance from Mateo. He was so near she could feel his body heat warming her back. No. That was probably just nerves. A steaming wave swamped through her, and moisture trickled down her forehead. What was it about Mateo that always made her break a sweat? That was so not cool or attractive in his eyes, she was sure.

"You can let go of the ladder now so you can straighten up," he said. "Reach that very top branch."

Katie's heart raced at his steady grip. So strong. Reassuring. Sexy. *No. Not sexy.* But if it were just the two of them and she were to turn around somehow—without falling—so she could stare down into his dreamy eyes...

For a split second, she feared she might faint. Then she glanced down at the floor and at Pia and Raul. She might land on someone and hurt them or even wind up injuring herself.

She nodded, but her chin trembled. Then the hand holding the star did too as she reached forward. "Ahh!" She withdrew her arm, grabbing on to the ladder.

Mateo chuckled behind her. "Go on. I've got you."

His fingers thrummed against her waist, but then he held on tighter. If Juan were here, maybe she'd be doing this with him. But would he make her feel all fluttery inside like Mateo did now? Honestly, she had her doubts.

Katie's face grew hot, and she blew out a breath. "Okay." She set her jaw, determined to do this. "Here goes!" She straightened her spine, and Mateo kept her stabilized. He did have her, lending her the confidence she needed. She extended her right arm and gripped the tippy-top branch with her left-hand fingers, bending it so she could wriggle the gold star into place. She got it settled, then gently released the pliable branch, which sprang upright, holding the gold star in a perfect position.

"Yay!" Pia cried while Raul said, "Great job."

Abuela folded her hands together with a happy gasp. "*Que lindo!*" she said, and Abuelo agreed.

"The tree does look picture-perfect," Titi Mon conceded with a smile.

Katie flushed and backed down the ladder. She peered over her shoulder at Mateo, who'd reached the ground, and her foot missed a step.

"Katie!" Abuela cried.

"Ahh!" She tumbled backward, and Mateo sprang forward to catch her. She landed in his arms like a bride about to get carried over the threshold. Katie didn't know whose face was redder: hers or his.

Raul and Pia leapt to their feet, and Titi Mon and the grandparents leaned forward with anxious faces.

Mateo quickly set Katie down, feet first. Then he backed up really quickly. "Are you okay?"

"Yeah, yeah," she said, breathing heavily. "I'm good." *Now, that was a lie.* Her heart was beating so hard it was about to pound straight through her chest. Falling off the ladder was one thing. But it was nothing compared to her fear of falling for Mateo instead of Juan.

TWELVE

IT DIDN'T TAKE LONG FOR everyone to put the boxes away.
"Katie," Pia said as Mateo held up Katie's coat so she could slip
it on. "Thank you for joining us, and thanks again to you and
Mateo for picking out a great tree."

Abuela gathered her shawl around her shoulders and scooted
toward Katie. "*Buenas noches.*" She planted a soft kiss on Katie's
cheek. "I hope you have pleasant dreams." Her dark eyes danced
in her heavily wrinkled face. "And that those dreams are of Juan
and your wedding."

"Thanks, Abuela." Katie smiled at Abuela, then grinned
tightly at the others. Mateo shook his head, then picked up the
jacket he'd set on a barstool at the kitchen island. Something small
slipped from its pocket, landing on the kitchen tile. It was a dainty
sprig of mistletoe tied up with a silky white ribbon.

"What's this?" Abuelo asked, lifting it off the floor. He
pinched it between his thumb and forefinger, then cocked his head
at Mateo.

"It's mistletoe, *mi amor*," Abuela said cheerily.

Pia gave Mateo a puzzled stare. "I thought you didn't get any?"

His neck turned red as he avoided looking at Katie. "I forgot that I tucked this in my pocket."

"When did you buy it?" Katie asked. She hadn't seen him make the purchase, and they'd been together the whole time at the Cortinis' farm.

Okay, not the whole time. *That's right.* She'd slipped off to use the restroom before they left while Mateo settled the bill.

Mateo shrugged, but he still didn't make direct eye contact. It was more like he was looking at the others. "When I was paying for the tree."

"Well, I'm very glad you got some," Pia said. "You've saved me a trip to the nursery." She tried to take the sprig from Abuelo, but he held it back.

"I can put this up for you."

"Papá," Raul said. "It's late, and you're tired."

"I'm wide awake, Raul." Abuelo's eyes grew huge as he forced them wide open. "I'll tack it up before Abuela and I head to bed."

Abuela nudged him delightedly. "*Ay, ay, ay.* I like the sound of that."

Everyone laughed.

Pia observed the older couple and grinned. "You're never too old for love, they say."

Titi Mon held up her hand. "I'm too old. I find the whole idea of romance exhausting!" This brought more chuckles.

Mateo zipped up his jacket and glanced at Katie. "Got everything you need?"

She nodded and picked up her purse, hoping the ride home

with Mateo wouldn't prove too awkward. They'd done a good job of staying on neutral ground before the whole stepladder exchange. Katie was glad that had ended quickly and was now in her rearview mirror.

They all said their good nights, and Pia and Raul hugged her, both giving her the customary Hispanic kiss on the cheek. It was the first time they had hugged and kissed her, which only made Katie feel a million times worse. But also better. She had never known family like this before. There was so much warmth at Los Cielos. Acceptance too. Her gaze flitted to Abuelo and Titi Mon, who hadn't joined in on the hugging.

Okay. Well, by almost everyone.

Titi Mon sighed and threw up her hands. "Oh, whatever!" she said. Her eyes glimmered at Katie and then she said, "*Ven acá.*"

"Sorry?"

Titi Mon held out her arms, and Katie timidly stepped toward her and into a surprisingly fierce bear hug. Oof. Titi Mon was strong. "Will we see you tomorrow?" she asked, pulling back.

"I don't think so," Katie said. "I'm working the lunch and dinner shifts."

"Then maybe at the hospital?" queried Raul.

Katie was definitely interested in Juan's progress. "I'll try to stop by and see Juan in the morning."

"Fantastic," Pia said. "Maybe we'll see you there."

The entire ride home was eerily quiet. Mateo didn't have much to say, and Katie was hesitant to breach the silence. So she stared out at the moon looming over the surrounding hills instead. After a while, she said, "Nice night."

"Yeah. Was." Mateo seemed preoccupied, so she decided not to say anything more.

Maybe if Katie told anyone the truth about her relationship with Juan, it should be Mateo. She could talk to him first, and he could help her decide what to tell—or not tell—the rest of his family. Yes, good. Katie liked that idea, but she wasn't going to share the news with Mateo tonight. It was late, and his mind was elsewhere.

Mateo turned down her street and pulled into her driveway, right behind her car. He glanced at her briefly. "Thanks for hanging out with the family." He shifted his grasp on the steering wheel. "And also for coming with me to get the tree."

"I was glad to do both," she said, meaning that earnestly. What a different situation this might have been if Mateo had been the brother she was dating. Their excursion to the Christmas tree farm would have seemed very romantic then, and tonight with his family almost like a date. But it hadn't been a date. She shouldn't have to keep telling herself that.

He shut off his engine and grabbed his door handle.

She stopped him from opening his driver's side door. "It's okay. You don't need to get out."

He nodded toward her stoop. "I was planning to walk you to the door." His voice came out a little rough.

"Mateo, I'm fine, really." She rolled her eyes and tried to make a joke of it. "I can take it from here." Even in the shadowy vehicle, she could see his ears go red. "What I mean is—"

He reached out and touched her coat sleeve. "That's okay." His words were still gravelly. "I get it." He sat back in his seat, glancing at her door. "I'll wait here until you get inside."

Katie bit her lip and nodded. "Thanks, Mateo. Thanks for everything." Then she did something she'd probably live to regret the rest of her life. She leaned over and gave him a very quick peck on his cheek before scooting out the SUV's passenger-side door. She slammed it a little too hard, her heart racing, and made her way up to her front porch with brisk strides. She slid her key in her lock and peered over her shoulder. Mateo had his palm pressed to the side of his face where she had kissed it and her lips had grazed his stubbly warmth. Seeing her look, he instantly dropped his hand, cranking his ignition.

Why, Katie? Why, why, why did you do that?

She slammed her way inside and shut the door, falling back against it in a slouch.

It was nothing, she lied to herself. *Just a simple good-night kiss.*

Very Latin.

Yeah, well. So was Mateo.

Her heart hammered.

And she liked his kind of Latin—a lot.

———

Mateo had trouble getting Katie's kiss out of his head. It was a simple goodbye kiss, like he was used to exchanging all the time with members of his family. But Katie wasn't in his family—yet. As innocent as it was, the sweet pressure of her lips against his cheek had left its branding mark, leaving him unable to think of anything but her sweetly kissable lips and those big brown eyes of hers.

It still boggled his mind that Abuela had enticed Katie into trying on her wedding dress, but that was Abuela. Besides that, on that first day after Juan's accident, none of them had understood how new Katie's relationship with Juan was. Logically, Mateo understood that detail shouldn't matter. But emotionally, he was relieved that Juan and Katie weren't anywhere close to becoming engaged. Not that he didn't want the best for his brother. He did. And Katie Smith was probably one of the best women in Castellana. Wait. Scratch that. Not probably. Definitely.

His headlights painted white trails on the dark road ahead of him as he snaked through the hills, approaching the vineyard. He was letting himself get carried away by dwelling on Katie. It wasn't like she spent inordinate amounts of time thinking about him too. Or maybe she did? Was that why she'd tried so hard to stay out of his way during the tree decorating? And why she'd appeared mortified when she'd fallen from the ladder and he'd caught her in his arms?

He flipped on his blinker and turned right onto the gravel drive leading under the big wooden sign that read *Los Cielos Cellars*. The tasting building was up ahead, with his apartment located upstairs. He kept his guitar-building studio to the rear of the tasting area, and his parents didn't mind it. They viewed Mateo's guitars as his hobby, but oh, how he yearned to make them so much more than that. If things had fallen into place the way he'd wanted, Juan would be priming himself to take over the vineyard solo instead of lying in a hospital bed.

Abuelo and his dad had already privately expressed their doubts to Mateo about Juan single-handedly running the business, but he'd always defended his brother, saying he was sure Juan would rise to the occasion once given the responsibility. Abuelo and his dad weren't so sure. Fortunately, Juan didn't understand the lack of faith they placed in him. He was so sure of himself, his self-confidence was all he needed to forge ahead. It was only when everyone had learned he wanted to forge ahead in a drastically different direction for the vineyard that they'd gotten up in arms. Converting to screw caps instead of corks? Great idea. Valid and contemporary. It preserved the integrity of the wine. *Okay.* Renaming the whole family enterprise? *No way.*

Mateo parked behind the tasting building, which cast an enormous shadow under the light of the full moon. There were eight parking spaces in front of it, but the gravel lot could accommodate as many as twenty vehicles, and there was an additional area for parking in an adjoining field that came in handy when they hosted weddings or other events.

The other side of the building faced the vineyard, visible through the broad bank of windows in the tasting room with its warm oak walls and exposed ceiling beams and from the wide covered porch outside it. Picnic tables sat on the grounds below the porch along with wrought-iron tables that held oversize umbrellas providing shade during the hotter months. The view from Mateo's apartment upstairs was even more spectacular. He could see all the way to Mount Hood from there, and when he stepped onto the balcony, he could make out the central part of the vineyard where he'd taken Katie, its heart.

Mateo reached for his phone on the console charging station where he normally kept it, but it wasn't there. He hunted around the front seats and peeked in the glove box. Right. He'd been so distracted by Katie when he'd gone to drive her home, he must have left it in the main house on the kitchen island. He had a memory of setting it down when he'd put on his jacket.

Good job, Mateo.

It wasn't like him to be absent-minded. Generally, he stayed very on top of things. He had to around here, because some other people didn't. Namely Juan. Mateo set his SUV in reverse, prepared for the short errand. He'd grab his phone and say his good nights to anyone in his family who still happened to be up and about. Then he'd come back here and pour himself a glass of *tinto* while trying not to think about women dressed in white. Including Katie and his ex, Gabriela, who'd be walking down the aisle shortly.

It was fine that Gabriela had made her choices, and he was glad she'd moved on. He probably needed to move on too. Katie had taught him he could become attracted to a woman again after swearing off dating, even as wrong as it was for him to be attracted to her. Mateo sighed, considering his plans for the evening. Maybe he'd grab his favorite guitar—the first one he'd made in Seville—and come up with a song. Something to take his mind off everything.

Mateo parked at the main house, which looked dark inside. The porch light was still on. He crept in the door, assuming the household was sleeping, and quietly shut the door at his back. When he turned to face the foyer, Mateo froze in his tracks. Abuelo held Abuela in his arms. They were *dancing*.

The colorful lights of the Christmas tree bathed them in a warm shimmer as flames flickered in the hearth and Abuelo hummed a sweet, serenading tune. His eyes stayed on Abuela's as he led her in one lazy circle around the room after another with an incredible measure of grace, the wispy fringe of her shawl fluttering behind her.

Mateo recognized the melody as a Mexican love song, one of his grandparents' favorites. Abuelo pulled something from his pocket as he cradled Abuela in his arms. She giggled in surprise. "You were supposed to hang that up, Esteban," she scolded him lightly, but it was all in fun.

Mateo's neck warmed. *Fun* and *flirtation*.

Abuelo nuzzled his nose against Abuela's and said huskily, "I'll do that tomorrow." Then he held the sprig of mistletoe high above their heads.

Abuela blushed like a bride. "Esteban, what are you doing?"

"Kiss me, Placida," he commanded in gravelly tones.

She placed her palms on his cheeks and did.

Mateo skittered toward the kitchen island and his phone, feeling hugely intrusive. He wasn't about to announce his presence now. He nabbed his phone and slipped stealthily back out the door, leaving Abuelo and Abuela with their arms wrapped around each other, the mistletoe now on the floor.

Mateo welcomed the cold rush of air that slapped him across the face as he hurried toward his SUV. It had been getting a little toasty back in the main house between his grandparents. He shook his head, but then his heart warmed. The exchange had been *very* unexpected but about a billion times sweet. Rascally old Abuelo and deeply romantic Abuela still kindled flames of desire for each other, even after so many years.

Mateo sat behind the steering wheel and gazed at the main house and its darkened windows. Then he looked out over the vineyard and up at Mount Hood. His great-great-grandparents had also shared a romantic passion, and the warmth and mutual admiration between his parents was clear. That was the kind of love worth waiting for. The sort you'd build a future on, a legacy.

He scanned the vineyard and rows upon rows of vines stretching out below the moon and beneath the backdrop of the mountains. Maybe if he had the right kind of woman as a partner, he'd feel differently about leaving Los Cielos behind. Maybe he'd want to stay here and build his life with the woman he loved.

THIRTEEN

Four Days before Christmas

KATIE WALKED INTO THE HOSPITAL holding a plate of Christmas cookies. She'd tacked a bright red bow on top of the tinfoil she'd used to cover the plate. She'd had so much nervous energy last night after her day with Mateo, she'd been able to do everything but sleep. So she'd padded to the kitchen in her slippers and pj's, deciding to bake for the Martinezes.

Pia had said she'd be too tired to make Christmas cookies this year, and Katie had everything on hand she needed to make sugar cookies and snickerdoodles. She still had the candied sprinkles she'd used to decorate the cupcakes she'd made for Daisy's birthday at the diner too. So she'd been able to make her Christmas tree, wreath, and angel-shaped cookies bedazzled. She'd set aside additional cookies, packed in small tins, to take to her friends at the diner and stashed those in her freezer to keep them fresh.

She checked the time on the hospital wall at the same time as the guy manning the front desk did. He handed her a visitor pass when she said she was going to the third floor. "Family?"

Katie pursed her lips. "They know me. I've been up there before."

The man shook his head at her plate. "You won't be able to take baked goods in there."

Katie smiled at him politely. "These are for the patient's mom and dad, not him."

The man nodded and waved toward the elevators. "Have a good visit."

As if Juan could visit with her. But Katie was going to try getting through to him. Even if he couldn't respond now, maybe some of what she said would seep into his consciousness and make an impact when he awoke. She passed through the family waiting room outside the ICU, but it was empty.

A couple emerged from the elevator behind her. She recognized the woman as the one Abuela had given her rosary to. Her blue eyes lit up when she spotted Katie. "You're part of Juan Martinez's family, aren't you?"

Katie shifted the cookie plate in her hands. "I've been here with them, yeah."

The lady continued speaking. "Juan's room is right next to my dad's. My dad's former room, I mean. He's been moved downstairs. We just came from there after seeing him all settled in."

Katie's eyebrows arched in surprise. "Downstairs?"

"To the second floor, yes. In a regular room." Joy and relief flooded the woman's face. "They've hinted that he'll be home by Christmas."

That was huge. That was only four days away.

The woman glanced around. "Is the older lady here? Your grandmother, I think? The one who wears the shawl?"

Katie craned her neck to peer toward the nurses' desk in the

ICU ward. No one was there except for a person in scrubs typing on a laptop. "I don't believe the others have gotten here yet," she said to the woman. "Is there a reason you needed her?"

The woman opened her purse and took out Abuela's rosary, which she'd slipped into a simple mesh bag, the sort with a drawstring that holds precious jewelry. Her face brightened. "I wanted to return this with my thanks. My dad came through his operation with flying colors."

Her husband further explained to Katie, "It was triple bypass surgery. Very touch and go there for a while, but we kept the faith." He glanced at the rosary. "And apparently so did Edgar." He titled his head toward his wife. "That's Roonie's dad's name. Edgar Thomas." He held out his hand. "I'm Heath Robinson."

Katie freed one of her hands to shake hands with the couple. She was still wearing her mittens and hat, because it was another brisk morning outside. The cold snap that had started yesterday was predicted to hang on, possibly all the way through Christmas. Maybe they would get some snow, which would be magical and fun. But almost too much to hope for, just like hoping for her relationship with the Martinez family to work out, given the way it had started.

The best she could do was thank them for the kindness they'd extended to her, and these cookies would be a start. She wanted to do more but didn't know what at this moment.

Roonie handed her the mesh bag containing the rosary. "Can you please give this to your grandmother?"

"Of course," Katie told the couple, accepting the rosary. Her backup plan was to drive out to Los Cielos to deliver her cookies if she didn't run into the family here.

"Don't forget to relay our thanks," Heath said as they peeled away.

Roonie latched on to his arm. "We hope you get good news about Juan soon too."

"Thanks." Katie inhaled deeply, wishing that with all her might. "So do I."

She set her plate of cookies on a side table in the waiting room, removing her hat and mittens. Then she set those gingerly on top of the cookie plate before covering everything up with her coat. At least her trip out to Los Cielos would be a quick one. Since she was working at eleven, she wouldn't be tempted to linger and stay for lunch. Or spend any more time than she should around Mateo. She was in a quandary about speaking with him, because she wanted to tell him the truth about Juan not being her boyfriend, but she also didn't want to find herself in any more compromising situations where she was alone with him either. She'd gotten herself into enough trouble last night with that goodbye kiss.

Part of her wanted to believe that he'd blown it off, thinking of it as nothing. But the way he'd kept his hand pressed to his cheek had left her with a different impression. If he brought it up later, she could always act like she was trying to fit in by following the customary greeting—and parting—gesture for Latinos.

It was a thin excuse, and Mateo might see through it, but it was better than admitting what had really happened. That she'd been so inexplicably drawn to him, she hadn't been able to stop herself from scooting close to kiss his handsome face. And then, when she had, her heart had sprouted wings, making her all giddy inside. Just like a silly teenager with a major crush.

Katie fanned her too-hot face with her purse and approached the ICU desk. The nurse looked up. He recognized her from before. "Juan's had a good morning. If the brain swelling continues to go down as predicted, he could be out of here in another couple of days."

Katie grinned. "That's really great. Have you communicated that to his family?"

"His mom and dad came in very early to see the doctor when she made her rounds. So yes, they've heard the news."

Katie nodded, deciding to text Pia about stopping by after her visit with Juan. Knowing Pia, she would say that was all right and maybe even invite her to lunch. But Katie wouldn't stay. She was grateful to have the excuse of working the lunch and dinner shifts today, because being around the Martinezes was becoming increasingly unbearable, with her on the cusp of losing them.

Katie entered Juan's room, where seemingly endless monitors beeped. In reality, there were probably only two or three.

"Well, hey there," she said brightly. "I hear things are looking up."

Juan didn't move, so it was hard to see his improvement. He looked peaceful though. Well rested. Very well rested, in fact.

Katie pulled a chair over and sat beside his bed. "I'm so glad you're getting better because, Juan, this whole thing with your family has become really involved. I've tried to downplay our relationship. I never said we're not dating, but I keep feeling like I need to tell someone the truth. Maybe Mateo."

She waited for his reaction but got none.

Katie sighed. "He's a good brother and a good person. I

know he'll understand and help me figure out what to do." She pursed her lips and continued. "In the meantime, keep improving, because everybody wants you to come home. Your mom. Your dad. Abuelo and Abuela. Mateo, of course, and Titi Mon."

She wished for the tiniest movement, a sign that he could hear her, but nothing in his expression changed.

"I want you back at Los Cielos too, because there's *so much* we need to talk about." She held her breath, then decided to brave it. "Including your plans for the winery. You never told me much about those, and I'd love to hear more. Maybe I can even help you somehow?"

When Juan woke up, he might actually be impressed with the way she'd finessed things. Grateful to her for not blowing his cover. She'd exhibited courage under fire. Remained loyal to her word—and to him—under extraordinary circumstances. That would make her a hero in his eyes. Then his family would tell him about her additional heroism in saving him from greater physical harm.

Given both things, Juan might start to see her with newly appreciative eyes. Which was one hundred percent what she wanted one week ago. Now though, she felt totally disconnected from the fantasy of Juan Martinez being the guy for her. And then there was Mateo. Would Juan ever look at her the way Mateo did, like she lit up the night sky like a million stars? It was hard to believe that he would.

"All right," she said, getting to her feet. "I suppose I'd better go now. I've got to drive out to Los Cielos and take your family some cookies and a rosary." She chuckled softly to herself. "Long story."

The heavier swath of wraparound bandages had been removed, and he now only wore a wide stick-on bandage on his forehead. A lock of Juan's hair had fallen forward, and she reached out to gently stroke it back. She hesitated with her hand in midair. Maybe it wasn't okay to touch him? But no. This was Juan. The guy who prided himself on his physical appearance.

She leaned closer and whispered softly, "Get better soon," shoving the errant strand of his hair back in place. She wasn't sure what she expected. Maybe a silent buzz. Some sense of connection or a hint at her destiny. But she experienced nothing like the reactions she'd had while being physically close to Mateo. No flutters, not a one.

Katie pulled back her fingers, and guilt enveloped her. This was *not* a contest between the two brothers. That was not what she'd meant to happen and absolutely not how it should be. She wrung her hands together. Of course she'd felt nothing while interacting with Juan. The poor man was in a coma. Unconscious and not really here. But secretly, she suspected she'd never experience the kinds of feelings for Juan as she had for Mateo.

Not when Mateo kept awakening her heart.

FOURTEEN

PIA OPENED THE DOOR WHEN Katie reached Los Cielos. She stared down at the covered plate with the big red bow on top. "What's this?" she asked with pleased surprise.

Katie smiled at the attractive brunette in a fitted black turtleneck, boots, and jeans. "Christmas cookies. I hope that's all right?"

"All right?" Pia's grin grew huge. "That's wonderful." She took the plate, lifting the foil to examine the cookies. They had come out picture-perfect, and Katie was glad. "Oh my, these look delicious, and so pretty too!" She let Katie indoors. "Thank you."

"I know you said you might not have time to bake any yourself this year."

"I probably won't." Emotion clouded Pia's eyes. "How kind of you to remember."

Titi Mon held up her hand from where she worked by the sink. "I never bake. Only cook." She swiveled her hips. "And blend cocktails."

Katie laughed at her shenanigans. "Hi, Titi Mon."

Titi Mon nodded in greeting. "Such great news about Juan,

no? We're all in lighter spirits today." Titi Mon seemed to have come around to accepting that Katie was on the same side as the rest of them. Which she was, just not girlfriend-wise like his family assumed.

"Yeah, for sure," Katie agreed. "It's the best news ever." She addressed Pia next. "I was at the hospital when I got your text."

"It's no wonder he's improving, with so much support," Pia answered, like it was partially on account of Katie. Pia placed the cookie plate on the counter beside Titi Mon, who worked rolling out dough on a large cutting board. She had bowls of ground meat and cheese beside her.

Titi Mon looked up. "Will you stay for empanadas, Katie?"

They looked tempting, but then the food around here was always fantastic.

Katie's shoulders sank. "I'm afraid I can't stay. I've got to work."

Katie stood in the foyer beside the Santa statue, and Abuela scurried toward her down the hall. "I thought I heard voices out here." She held open her arms, and Katie went to hug her. Abuela's hug was warm and tender, and she smelled of heavy perfume. Her dangling jade earrings matched the stones in her silver necklace.

"Hi, Abuela." Katie broke their embrace and dug into her purse. "This is for you." She extracted the rosary in its mesh bag. "The lady you gave it to at the hospital asked me to return it when I saw you."

Abuela shared a worried frown.

Katie rushed to correct her mistaken perception. "With her thanks. The lady's dad is doing super well. His family thinks he'll be home for Christmas."

"Oh *sí?*" Abuela beamed brightly. "Just like our Juan." She clapped her hands together. "You see, Monsita and Pia, my visions are never wrong." Her eyes twinkled at Katie, and Katie held her breath, because she doubted very seriously that Abuela's particular vision of her marrying Juan would become a reality.

While she'd fantasized about that prospect in the past, the idea of her marrying Juan anytime soon—or even in the future—was holding less and less appeal.

It wasn't like she could imagine herself marrying Mateo either. She recalled the vision she'd had of him in Paris, then she quickly shook it off. They would *not* be travelling to France together, because they were *not* becoming involved. Things were messy enough at the Martinez household this holiday, and Katie didn't even know for certain how Mateo felt about *her*.

Raul ambled in the front door, wearing his zipped-up jacket and muddy work boots. Pia pointed down at the floor, and Raul unlaced his boots, removing them one at a time like a scolded kid. "Oh, hi, Katie," he said, noticing her. He scanned the room. "Has anyone seen Mateo?"

"He's down at the barn," Pia said. Katie had learned that was how they referred to the tasting building, which looked like it might have been a barn at some point. They had an actual set of stables for horses farther down the hill, but she'd yet to see it.

Raul reached into his shirt pocket under his jacket and pulled out his cell phone. "I tried calling him, but he didn't answer."

Abuela laughed and pointed to the counter where Mateo's phone lay. "That's because it rang through here."

Pia strapped on an elf apron, getting ready to help Titi Mon make the lunch. "Mateo's been leaving his phone around a lot lately," she informed Raul.

Raul placed his hands on his hips. "That doesn't sound like Mateo."

"He put it down this morning," Abuela said. "When he helped me tack up the mistletoe." She pointed over Katie's head into the foyer, and Katie instinctively stepped back. It was a silly reaction to have, given that no one she might have kissed romantically was here. If Mateo had been in the room, she might have blushed.

Raul wore a confused frown. "Didn't Papá put that up last night?" he said, referring to the mistletoe.

Abuela flipped back her shawl. "He got distracted," she said coquettishly.

Katie noticed this shawl was turquoise and green, sporting tropical flowers and ferns. Abuela had to have an entire collection of shawls, and she always accessorized with her jewelry to match them.

Pia and Raul raised their eyebrows at each other, and Titi Mon glanced over her shoulder at Katie. "Latin lovers," she teased. "They're all the same." She lowered her voice huskily. "Insatiable."

"Titi Mon!" Pia elbowed her, but she was laughing.

Raul winked at his wife. "Titi Mon could have a point."

Pia shrugged and blew her husband a kiss. "Maybe."

Katie giggled with embarrassment. This family talked about *everything*. Her parents never mentioned sex at all. Of course, her mom had died when she was young, but if she'd had to go by what her dad had told her, she'd been an immaculate conception. She supposed the topic had been too sensitive for him to discuss with his teenage daughter. Katie'd had to learn the basics from her friends at school and later more accurate information in health class.

She didn't see Abuelo anywhere around and assumed he might be back in his and Abuela's bedroom. Maybe recovering from whatever Abuela had hinted at happening last night. Could she have been serious? They had to be in their eighties. She glanced around the prettily decorated great room, needing to think about something other than members of the Martinez family becoming amorous with each other. Mateo and Juan were probably used to this kind of talk by now, but she wasn't.

"Everything looks so pretty," Katie said, "very festive." She noticed they'd hung their Christmas stockings from the mantel. There appeared to be too many of them though. She started counting mentally. Two for Juan and Mateo, two for their parents, another set for the grandparents. That made six, but there were eight stockings.

Pia noticed her staring at the hearth and waved a hand. Her fingers were covered up to her knuckles in flour because she'd been assembling empanadas. When she pushed back her hair, some flour stuck to her cheek, making her look so motherly. Katie experienced a pang in her chest, and sadness seeped through her. She still missed her mom.

"The extra two are for you and Titi Mon," Pia said, and the tender spot in Katie's throat throbbed, making it sore. She was humbled to be included, already taken under their wing. But this wasn't her nest. It was theirs. And she definitely couldn't be here for Christmas. If Juan got better before that, like the doctors thought, he'd be here then, and the two of them could explain about Katie never really being his girlfriend. That would be the end of their pretending then, and none of the Martinezes would want her around any longer.

Katie's voice warbled when her eyes grew hot. "You all didn't need to—"

"Of course we did." Abuela slid up onto a barstool, draping her long gray skirt across her knees. She wore cute fashion boots beneath it and settled those on the lower barstool railing. "You're practically family."

Katie pursed her lips, unsure of what to say. So she forced a grateful smile and said, "Thank you."

"How are you feeling, Placida?" Titi Mon asked. Then she turned and explained to Katie, "She woke up this morning breathing heavily." She playfully rolled her eyes at the older woman. "Perhaps now we know why."

Abuela adjusted her position on the stool while hanging on to the bar. "That had nothing to do with anything, Monsita. I just had a moment this morning after breakfast."

Pia scolded Raul. "I told you we shouldn't have brought up Juan's rebranding efforts over *café con leche*."

Raul placed a hand on his chest. "That wasn't me. That was Papá."

Abuela replied to Pia in soothing tones. "I feel much better after lying down."

Raul shook his finger at her. "*And* taking your inhaler?"

Abuela lifted her chin. "Of course, Raul. I'm your mother. You don't have to baby me."

Great. This definitely wasn't the time to cause more excitement around here by sharing the truth about her and Juan with anyone but Mateo.

Abuela patted the counter beside her. "Why don't you take your coat off, Katie? Come and sit down."

Katie checked the time on her watch, not wanting to interfere with their lunch preparations. "I really should run. I don't want to leave Daisy shorthanded." Although she *could* afford to stay a moment more before her shift started, Katie's guilt wouldn't allow it. They'd gotten her a Christmas stocking now. Every time she turned around, it seemed that instead of disentangling herself from the Martinezes, they kept winding her in tighter.

The pathetic thing was that she enjoyed their company so much, she didn't mind being held close. In fact, she kind of craved it. This group made her feel welcomed and accepted. Like she was already one of their fold. Though she had friends at the diner, being around the Martinezes gave her a true sense of family, which was something amazing to have at Christmas. Despite her awkward interactions with Mateo, being here to help them decorate their tree had been like a dream come true. She'd always wanted a big Christmas tree. Her heart pinged painfully. And a big family like this one. But she'd never had either, which was why she worked at the soup kitchen every year on Christmas Day.

Principally, she wanted to give back to those less fortunate. While she wasn't rich by any stretch, at least she had a roof over her head and didn't have to worry about putting food on the table. Plus, it was easier not to feel sorry for herself, being totally alone during the holidays, when she was out there doing something for others. She'd established a routine that worked for her, and she was okay on her own. Most days. At Christmas, though, the solitude was a little sadder somehow.

Raul had his grip on the Christmas tree, adjusting it so its fuller side could be better viewed from the kitchen, while Abuela gave him directions, pointing to the left and then to the right as he shifted it around. But no adjustments needed to be made in Katie's mind. Everything was perfect. Even Titi Mon's colorful necklace made of oblong Christmas tree lights had its charms. It draped down the snowman apron that covered her glittery green sweater.

Katie's heart seized up. She needed to go. Now she was growing misty-eyed over Titi Mon.

Pia placed her finished empanadas on a cookie sheet lined with parchment paper. "Are you sure can't stay?" she asked as Katie walked toward the door.

Katie turned away when her eyes burned hot, but no. She wouldn't cry. She'd forgotten how. "I'm sure, but thanks for the invitation." She laid her hand on the doorknob, and Raul called out.

"Oh, Katie!"

She spun around.

"Would you mind doing me a favor? When you drive by the barn, can you stop in and tell Mateo I need him in the office up here? There are some inventory reports I want to ask him about before lunch. I'm afraid I can't make heads or tails of the notes Juan left behind."

Katie forced a cheery smile, though her heart was aching. Because this family never could be hers. "Of course," she told Raul. "I'll let him know."

"Oh, and, Katie!" She turned back around, and Raul smiled.

"Please ask Mateo to round up Abuelo. He went to check something in the cask room ages ago, and I need his opinion on something too."

Katie stopped in front of the heavy double doors to the tasting room. They were made of thick pine and had big brass door handles. She could see the expanse of the tasting room through the latticed window inserts in the doors. The darkened space seemed to go on forever and contained several round tables with chairs. A long bar lay straight ahead of her, and behind it, a bank of windows framed the beautiful vineyard and mountains. She knocked lightly, not sure exactly where Mateo was or if he could hear her.

She stepped back off the stoop to examine the top story of the building, which had five windows across it. The one in the center was smaller than the others. Probably a bathroom. Window wells down below gave evidence of a basement. That was shadowy too, but she made out copious bottles of wine arranged neatly in racks that went from the floor nearly to the ceiling. The far end of the building housed what appeared to be its original barn door. A tractor and other farming equipment were parked in front of it. There was also a flatbed truck that looked like it was used for hauling things, like cases of wine.

No one answered the door, so she latched on to one of the handles and pushed. The door latch clicked, then disengaged, and the door swung slightly open. She pressed it farther ajar. "Hello? Mateo?"

Her voice echoed in the cavernous space, but there was no sign of anybody here. She walked inside and shut the door, observing the vineyard through the windows. The landscape was gorgeous, with the sun shining brightly, and the azure sky dotted with puffy white clouds. She tiptoed to the polished oak bar and ran her hand along it, imagining enjoying a tasting in this room. Did Mateo sometimes play the bartender, sharing stories about Los Cielos Cellars wines while pouring out samples? He'd make an awfully handsome one. Then again, so would Juan. Both were great-looking men, but Mateo's appearance was less polished. More natural. *More Mateo.*

She glanced around and called out once more. "Hello? Anybody here?" Raul hadn't told her where to look for his son. She hadn't expected the inside of this barn to be so big. A hallway at one end of the room had signs beside it indicating the restrooms were that way. She peeked down the hall and spied a swinging door labeled *Staff.* She checked it out, learning it led to a kitchen, but it was empty. Another sign in the hall said *Tickets, Tours* with an arrow pointing to a closed door. She pulled it open, finding a metal staircase that led to the basement.

She headed for the other hallway off the tasting room. A sign on a plaque on the wall said *Private.* Katie noted an extendable belt mounted on poles, which had been moved aside. A sign dangling from the belt read *Not Open to the Public.* She had to be getting warmer.

She peeked inside a door on the same side of the hallway as the elevator. It was a closet containing cleaning supplies: a mop in a bucket, a dustpan and push broom, and an industrial-style sink. The door across from it, facing the parking area, led to some sort of woodworking studio. Wait. Her eyes adjusted to the dim light coming in through the partially shaded windows. Those were guitars.

A workbench with a stool stood in the center of the room, and an unfinished guitar lay across it, while a wide hanging lamp fanned out overhead. If she switched on the light, she'd be able to see better, but she didn't want to invade this sacred space any more than she had. It seemed so special and solitary, like a private sanctuary.

The guitar on the workbench looked expertly made, but it had not yet had its strings attached. Other specimens, in various stages of completion, sat on tables and leaned against the walls, and assorted equipment lay about. Hand tools hung on mounted pegboards. This had to be where Mateo worked on his hobby, the one he hoped to turn into a business someday. She guessed it would be hard for him to leave Los Cielos after having grown up here, but if he did finally strike out on his own, at least he'd have the comfort of knowing the vineyard was in his brother's hands.

Katie trusted that people rose—or fell—to their expectations. Everyone was so worried that Juan's unannounced plans would destroy the family business, but Juan was smart and capable and had a certain visionary aspect about him. Maybe he'd seen a unique way forward for the vineyard that nobody else had?

Maybe she wasn't giving Juan enough credit. Maybe none of them were.

She quietly backed out of the guitar-building room, searching the hallway and finding one last door. It revealed another metal staircase that ran up to the second floor. *Aha.*

The door to Mateo's apartment must have been open, because bands of light spilled through it, crowning the landing in a golden hue.

FIFTEEN

KATIE COCKED HER HEAD, THINKING she heard music. "Hello? Mateo, are you up there?"

She didn't want to startle him, but she'd told his dad she'd do him this favor, which was taking longer than she'd anticipated. It was good she wasn't in as much of a hurry to get to the diner as she'd acted like in front of the others. She still couldn't linger, since she needed to be in by eleven. It was half past ten, but the drive was only twenty minutes, so she had time for a quick chat with Mateo. She aimed to relay Raul's message and then tell him the truth about her and Juan before she could turn tail and run. It was nerve-racking to think about facing Mateo and revealing the truth, but she needed to fix this holiday mix-up.

She slowly climbed the staircase, calling out again. "Mateo?"

The music grew louder with sharp staccato beats. That had to be Mateo playing his guitar. The tune listed, growing fluid and tumbling down the staircase as she ascended. His fingers thrummed against the guitar, mimicking the sound of clacking castanets—or the heel taps of sprightly dancers—before he began strumming faster and faster, the music rising and falling in frenzied crescendos.

She imagined the ocean with its tumbling waves. Wild, reckless, untamed. Cresting and then falling in a deep well, creating eddies of heat in her belly that went around and around until she felt dizzy from their sway.

The sound was passionate, sexy, dousing her in wave after wave. She grabbed the railing on the landing, her heart pounding and her skin sizzling hot. She was a pool of liquid heat. Then she saw Mateo, and she totally melted. He stayed intent on his music, eyes closed, his expression serene, almost euphoric, as he carried forward the tune, releasing it into room...up to the ceiling...and beyond that, to the heavens.

Katie stood there, mesmerized, and scanned his apartment. He sat on a brown leather sofa surrounded by rustic furnishings. There was not one frilly thing in the place. No curtains or throw pillows. Not even any artwork, except for one framed poster of a flamenco guitarist with swirly letters written in Spanish above him. Simple, southwestern-patterned rugs covered the wide-planked wood floor. An assortment of a dozen or so guitar cases shared the corner by the open doorway to the bedroom.

Katie bit her bottom lip, imagining Mateo lying in that inviting king-size bed.

His chin jerked up and he stopped playing. "Katie." He set down his guitar, holding it by its neck and resting it against his leg. He wore jeans and a navy blue sweater, and the instrument glistened like polished cypress wood. He cocked his head to study her, and it was like her whole body went up in flames. Had she really been thinking about Mateo being in bed? Oh yeah, she had. She'd also imagined being in there with him.

The french doors to the balcony behind him were cracked open, letting in a bracing chill, which Katie desperately appreciated. Her cheeks couldn't have burned any hotter. She held on to the doorframe, not trusting her own legs to support her. "That was beautiful."

"Thanks." His face relaxed in a smile. "What are you doing here?"

"Your dad asked me to come and get you. He needs you for some accounting stuff back at the house." Good. This was good. She should quickly deliver Raul's message and then leave.

Seeing Mateo in his lair made her heavy crush on him a thousand times worse. And there was no denying it any longer. She was developing a major thing for him. Juan wasn't who she wanted. Maybe she never would have wanted Juan to begin with if she'd known Mateo first. *The way he played the guitar.* So in command of everything. He'd make an incredible lover. The sort poetry gets written about. *Ballads.* She swallowed hard. *Love songs.*

"Yeah? Okay, thanks." His eyebrows rose. "So what are you doing at Los Cielos?"

He beckoned her inside, but she was reluctant to release the doorframe. Her head still swam from his unintentional serenade, and her heated blush hadn't subsided. She wiped her sweaty palms on her pant legs, daring to let go for a few bold seconds. "I, uh…" Argh. She went light-headed again, so she gripped the doorframe with her right hand. "Brought some cookies for your family."

"Christmas cookies?" His eyes twinkled, and tiny tingles shimmied through her, like dancing snowflakes, all dazzling and glittery.

"Yeah." *Please don't let me sound breathy.* But she probably did.

"I love Christmas cookies." His voice was so husky, it caressed her from across the room.

She loved Christmas cookies too. She really did. And big Christmas trees and holidays. She was loving this holiday especially.

His gaze pored over her in the same way it had at the Christmas tree farm, then later at the main house, and she couldn't even count how many other times. Her breath came in little fits and starts, like she'd just run a marathon. A Mateo marathon. Oh, she could totally envision going the distance with him under the mistletoe.

No. Stop. This wasn't helping one bit. She needed to get out of here. *Go.* But first, she should tell him about Juan. Yes. This was the time and the place, when it was just the two of them.

First, she remembered about Abuelo. "Your dad also asked you to get Abuelo before you go back to the house and bring him with you. Do you know where he is?"

Mateo laid his guitar on the coffee table. "He was down in the cask room last time I saw him." He chuckled warmly. "Even though everything is automated now, he still insists on double-checking our inventory in person."

"Inventory, yes!" Katie said. "That's what your dad had questions about. Something about Juan's notes not being clear?"

Mateo shook his head and laughed. "Juan's notes are never clear." He winced as if remembering her relationship with Juan. Her *supposed* relationship with Juan. "But he definitely has his strengths!"

"Mateo. About Juan?"

He motioned to a chair, and this time she entered the apartment and took a seat. She needed to get this done before she lost her nerve.

"It's great, isn't it?" He grinned. "He could actually be home for Christmas."

"It is great. So great." Katie rubbed her hands together as the brisk wind was at her back. "That's what I wanted to talk to you about."

"Oh, sorry." Mateo got up and shut the French doors. "I like playing in the open air, and when I'm not outdoors..." He laughed. "I like to let the air inside."

"Even in December?"

"Even in December." He got a dreamy look on his face. "Reminds me of Seville. It gets cold there in winter too, you know, and a lot of the places don't have heating since it stays toasty so much of the year."

"Where did you live there?" She didn't know tons about Spain, but she'd perused photos while putting together her travel collage. She recalled one of the cathedrals that had been built on the spot of a former Muslim mosque. The architects had preserved its minaret during the conversion, reclaiming it as a bell tower.

"In a rooming house in el Barrio de Santa Cruz, Seville's former Jewish quarter." Mateo leaned forward on his elbows, bracing them on his knees. "You know about Seville?" He appeared pleased, and she hated to disappoint him.

"Not too much, honestly." She unzipped her coat. Now that the doors were shut, his apartment was getting warmer. "I've seen some pictures of its main cathedral tower, that's all."

"Ah yes, La Giralda."

"Giralda?"

"The former minaret. The site was taken over by the Catholics."

"I read something about that," she said, trying to remember the details. Spain had never been on her bucket list of travel locales. Listening to Mateo play the Spanish guitar made her feel differently. It would be an interesting place to visit with someone like him, who was familiar with the culture and the language.

"There's a lot of Moorish influence in Seville. It's said that the flamenco dance and music emerged from the early intermingling of three cultures: that of the Roma people—Roma people—who migrated to southern Spain from northwest India, with those of the Sephardic Jews and Moors, who already lived there."

"Is that what you play?" she asked him. "Flamenco guitar?"

He grinned. "Among other things."

"Well, you're very skilled at it." *Juan*. She needed to talk about Juan, not Mateo and Spain. Although she was intrigued to learn more about the time he spent there, now was *not* the time to get into that.

He settled back on the sofa and crossed his arms. "Just takes practice."

It had to take a *lot* of practice to play the way he did, in a way that could totally sweep a woman off her feet. But not her. No. And not today.

He still believes you're Juan's girlfriend.

You've got to speak up. Now.

Raul was waiting on Mateo and Abuelo. The funny thing was, Mateo didn't make Katie feel rushed. When she was around him, he made her believe he had all the time in the world to listen to whatever she wanted to say. He would have made a great doctor or a counselor. Or a priest. *There! That's the right image.* It was also a lot more helpful than remembering being with Mateo at the Christmas tree farm. She needed to stop thinking about Mateo and mistletoe and start spilling the beans.

"I'm sorry," he said. "I sidetracked you earlier. You were about to say something about Juan?"

"Yes." She squirmed in her chair, which would have seemed roomy and comfortable under any other circumstance. "It's about Christmas dinner. Our *original plans* for Christmas dinner."

Confusion flickered in his eyes. "Original? What?"

Katie licked her parched lips. Her mouth felt like great big cotton balls had been wedged into it, making it hard for her to speak. Okay, fine. She was nervous, but she was *not* chickening out. She owed it to Mateo and all the Martinezes to tell them the truth. First though, she had to get her swollen tongue unstuck from the roof of her mouth. Yuck. "Er. Do you think I could have a glass of water?" she asked, speaking from behind the back of her hand.

Mateo leapt to his feet. "Of course." He pulled a glass from a cabinet in the kitchen and filled it from a dispenser in the freezer door.

Katie drew in a deep breath to quell her anxiety. She fiddled with her coat collar, which was suddenly too tight. Like it was choking her on her soon-to-be-delivered truth.

Katie unzipped the top part of her coat, noting the fancy brass light fixture hung over the dining room table. The oak dining table had its legs painted ivory, and the dining chairs' oak spindles and legs were ivory as well, tying the lighter-colored kitchen cabinets in with the dining room. Interesting accent pieces lent bright pops of color to the otherwise natural-toned apartment, like the mustard-colored retro clock in the kitchen. A sleek ceiling fan with only three wooden paddles turned overhead, providing a lofty breeze that probably wasn't normally needed in December. But boy, did she appreciate it now. Maybe Mateo had needed it to keep cool during his very hot guitar playing.

He handed her the water, and her face warmed. "Your place is really great." Her voice squeaked, and she took a look sip of water. "Did you decorate it yourself?"

He glanced around his apartment. "Yeah. It took a while to get everything right, but now it feels like home."

"It looks great."

"Thanks." He smiled. "I like it." He sat back down on the sofa and met her gaze. "So what's this about Juan?"

She took another sip of water and set her glass on a coaster. Enough stalling. "Yeah, so. Here's the thing..." *Think, think, think.* How was she going to put this? "You. Your whole family have such a mistaken impression."

His eyebrows arched. "Mistaken how? You've already cleared things up about your relationship being new."

"It's newer than you think."

He cocked his head.

"Mateo, me and Juan?" She winced, narrowing her eyes. "We never really got started."

"Started what...?" He frowned, perplexed. "Dating?" Mateo

laughed like she'd told a joke. When she didn't respond, he stared out the French doors, considering the vineyard and the mountains. "Well, of course you have," he said, turning back to her. "A new relationship is still a relationship after all. Baby steps."

She gaped at him, petrified, unsure of how to proceed.

"Katie?" he said gently. "What's this all about?" His face fell, and then he stared at her wild-eyed. "Oh no. Oh, man. Oh, oh, oh *no*. I get what this is." He raked a hand through his hair. "You've changed your mind, haven't you? About Juan. Now that he's incapacitated, you're going to bail on him."

"Bail?" Her voice cracked. "What?"

Mateo squatted right in front of her and took her hand. "Katie, please. Listen to me."

Her heart practically leapt out of her chest.

"You *can't* do that to my family. You can't dump Juan at the height of his illness. That would be uncharitable. Unkind. Now's not the time."

Katie gasped. "No. It's not like that."

"Look," he said with a serious stare. He squeezed her fingers more tightly, so tightly they pinched. "Maybe this relationship is brand new to you and not a super big deal, inconsequential, but I don't think my brother feels the same. Because, Katie, Juan has never brought a girl home. I mean, *never*. Not even in high school."

Her head spun. This was getting worse by the minute.

"He sent us all text messages," Mateo continued. "Bunches of them! Singing your praises. You couldn't possibly do anything to hurt him now." He dissected her with his gaze, and her lungs seized up. "Not when the man's in a *coma*."

Katie went hot, then cold, then hot all over. *What's happening?* "But...he's coming out of it, right?" The words were all garbled like she had marbles crammed in her cheeks.

"Of course he'll come out of it. We need to think positive. All of us do." He tugged her toward him and leaned closer, bringing his face near hers. "Which is why I'm asking you not to do this. Don't dump Juan. Not now. Later, when he's better, sure. Okay. Whatever you want—then. When he and you can discuss it, I'm sure he'll understand. Just please don't do it now. Not right before Christmas. You have to think of Juan and his recovery. Think of the family. Think of Abuela. I don't believe Abuela can handle one more upset right now."

But she *was* thinking of his family. So, so hard. How was this backfiring on her? Her eyes burned hot, and wet spots marred her cheeks. Wait. Was she crying? At last?

No. She was perspiring again. Great.

Mateo reached toward an end table with his free hand and passed her a tissue. She used it to dab at her damp face, her forehead, her throat, the back of her neck...

"Look, I know this is tough on you," he said, watching her worriedly. "I can see that. But, Katie, can't you please give Juan a little more time—at least until he's out of the hospital—before lowering the boom? The doctors say it will be any day now. Is that really asking too much? You've already made it this far." His grin trembled. "View this as the homestretch!"

Time? He wanted her to give Juan time? Okay, she'd read Mateo's signals all wrong. He wasn't even remotely interested in her. He was trying to get her to *not* ditch his brother. The brother she couldn't possibly ditch, because she'd never been going out with him in the first place. She blinked, fearing her head would explode. From the way it was pounding, that seemed a very real possibility.

"I'm begging you." His hand gripped hers like a vise. "It's Christmas." Emotion filled his eyes. "And you've already given my family so much hope. They haven't known you long, but they already love you."

Katie's pulse spiked through the roof. She had to stop this runaway train.

"Mateo, wait!" She jerked away her hand, and he stumbled, catching himself on the arm of her chair.

He stared up at her with earnest eyes. "What is it?"

She wrung her hands together, massaging her aching fingers. "You've got this all wrong, you and your family. Juan and I aren't really dating. We never were." She grimaced and shrank back in her seat. "It was all a big ruse."

"A ruse?" His eyebrows knitted together. "Are you saying that your relationship with Juan is all made up?"

She nodded adamantly. "*Yes*, that's what I've been trying to tell you. Juan asked me to *pretend* to be his girlfriend to ward off Titi Mon and her fix-ups."

He frowned. "That's a terrible thing to say when Juan isn't here to defend himself."

"Defend? What?" The room started spinning around her.

"He's not even conscious, Katie. Wow." He stood and began pacing back and forth. He blew out a breath, evidently trying to piece together the whole supposedly sordid picture. "Are you telling me that when you showed up at the hospital the day of Juan's accident, when you first met my family, you lied to them about being Juan's girlfriend?"

"Well, um, it wasn't *exactly* a lie."

He stared into her soul. Deep, deep down into the darkness.

"Okay, maybe yes. Just a little white one." She slunk down in her chair. "I mean, when they assumed that I was with Juan, I didn't disagree."

"And then later, when I met you, and afterward, when you came out to Los Cielos—"

"Mateo," she pleaded. "You've got to believe me. I didn't mean for any of this to happen."

He rubbed his chin. "I bet that you didn't." He stopped walking and hung his head. After a while, he set his hands on his hips and looked up. "Sorry. I don't buy it."

Katie's heart caught in her throat. "Which part?"

"The part about the girlfriend ruse. But it's all right. I get it." His shoulders dropped. He sank down on the sofa with a haggard look. "I don't blame you. This has all been too much." He gestured toward the French doors framing the vineyard. "My family, our business problems, Juan's accident..." He pursed his lips in shame. "I'm sorry for judging you. Honestly I am. Of course you're freaked out. What woman wouldn't be?" He stared blankly up at the ceiling. "You think you find a great guy, and then you become exclusive." He met her gaze, his eyes wide. "The very next day, you're confronted with a crisis, and a very big—and involved— family. Then, before you can get your head around that, Abuela pulls her stunt with her wedding dress." He turned up his hands. "Hey, if I were you, I'd probably be running for the hills too."

She had no idea what to say to that. Mateo had everything so twisted around. She grabbed on to her purse, holding it in a death grip. At least Mateo was no longer squeezing the life out of her hand. Her knuckles still smarted.

He frowned. "But you really didn't need to go that far, acting like you and Juan had never happened."

Her temples throbbed. She was starting to feel sick and trapped. More trapped than she'd ever been in this endless predicament. The more she protested she wasn't Juan's girlfriend, the more Mateo appeared to disbelieve her. Oh, *why* had she made that deal with Juan? It had seemed so harmless at the time. One date! One dinner! Not her whole life.

Mateo looked her up and down. "You're only what? Twenty-five?"

"Twenty-eight," she said, although she could hardly see how that mattered. "How old are you?"

"Thirty-one, and Juan's thirty-two. Old enough to know his own mind. So if he asked you to be exclusive, I'm certain he had his reasons." Mateo's neck reddened. "I mean, I *know* he had his reasons."

He laughed sadly, but Katie couldn't tell who he was sad for: Juan, her, his family, or himself. Maybe all of them. Katie wanted to weep, but she couldn't.

"Come on. Look at you," he said. "It's easy to see what Juan saw. You're...perfect."

Katie bit her lip. *Oh, Mateo.* So far from it. Her heart fluttered, but then she became incredibly nauseated. She wasn't sure whether she wanted to hug Mateo, throw up, or bolt for the door. What was she supposed to do? Insist on her truth *now*, making Juan out to be a liar and ignoring the fact that she lied to the family before? Her stomach ached and her throat went raw. At least she wasn't sweating any longer. Oh wait.

More perspiration formed on her forehead, then ran down her temples.

Please don't let him notice. *Please, please, please.*

He noticed. "Do you want to take off your coat?"

"No, I really can't stay." She stood unsteadily. "I'm probably already going to be late for work, and you need to find Abuelo."

"Do me one favor," he said before she reached the door. She turned on her heel. "Let's keep this discussion between us for now. I don't want to go upsetting Abuela or my parents any further. Not until Juan is safely home."

"And then?"

Mateo shoved his hands in his pockets. "Then, it seems that you and my brother will need to talk."

Oh my gosh, she was in it. *Deep breaths—in and out.* But okay, she could do this. She'd done it so far, and it was only for a few more days. *Homestretch!*

A loud siren blared, and Katie nearly jumped out of her skin. "What's that?"

Mateo raced to the French doors, jerking them open. He jogged to the balcony railing, peering over it.

"Fire alarm?" she asked as he darted back inside.

His jaw tensed. "No, we've sprung a leak."

SIXTEEN

KATIE CALLED AFTER MATEO AS he dashed toward the door. "A leak? What? Where?"

He glanced over his shoulder. "That's what I'm going to find out."

"Mateo, wait!" She followed him out of his apartment, determined to help with whatever it was. She'd made such a big mess of everything, maybe she could do some good. "I'm coming with you!" She was definitely going to be late for work, but Daisy would understand once she'd told her everything.

She pulled her cell from her purse, close on Mateo's heels as he bolted down the stairs. He reached the ground floor and raced through the tasting room as Katie sent a frantic text to Daisy.
Be in late! ER at LC!

Hopefully, Daisy could decipher that. Katie would text to explain further when she got a chance.

Mateo yanked open the door that led to the basement and darted down the metal staircase. Katie was right behind him. The alarm was still blaring. Then a loud whooshing noise met her ears. It sounded like rushing rapids. No, not water. *Wine.*

"Help!" Abuelo called. "I'm down here!"

"This way!" Mateo called. They cut through a large room containing a checkout counter with a register below a partial window. It appeared to be the vineyard's gift shop, with built-in shelving holding knickknacks, like customized wine goblets, fancy corks, and grape-themed kitchen towels. This was the room she'd seen from outside with all the racks of wine on display.

Additional bottles lay in open wooden crates on tables. Those seemed to have special seals on them and blue ribbons, but it all went by in a blur.

The interior wall on the vineyard side was one huge glass window overlooking a series of stainless steel fermentation tanks a few feet below them. The tanks all had hoses connecting to them and running somewhere out of view. The floor was a sea of red.

Mateo stared at the scene in horror. "Oh no."

Katie gasped. Abuelo had his hands around a dislodged hose that had somehow broken free from the tank. His arms strained to hang on to it as he tried to force it back onto the valve of the tank. Wine spewed everywhere. Up the side of the fermentation tank, across the room. All over Abuelo and his clothes. The hose seemed to have a mind of its own, refusing to stay still and let him attach it. It was an impossible task with the wine gushing out of the tank so fast.

Mateo held his head with both hands and ran even faster. "Why hasn't he shut it off?" he yelled, more to himself than to Katie. He burst through another door and down a short set of steps. Red wine seeped toward the bottom step, emerging from a tunnellike room lined with oak casks. "Crap!" Mateo cried, racing through it, kicking up wine spray as he ran.

The liquid covered the floor and was at least an inch deep, maybe more. Katie's canvas shoes became instantly soaked, squishing and squirting wine up onto her pant legs and puffy white coat.

They reached a closed-off area, and Mateo barreled through the entrance. The production room was flooded. Mateo grumbled in frustration. "The drains? Why aren't they working?" The production room held conveyor belts, bottling machines, stacks of boxes and such. The bottom portions of some of the boxes were soaked with wine. "Great."

Katie's heart pounded. "What's in those boxes?" she asked, chasing after him.

"Our new labels."

He finally reached the door to the area where Abuelo was. He located a handle on the alarm system on the wall and yanked it down. The blaring alarm fell silent.

"Will someone come?" Katie asked. "911?"

Mateo frowned. "Not for this."

"The drains aren't working!" Abuelo screeched.

"Shut the valve!"

"I can't!" Abuelo held up a broken piece in his hand.

Mateo set his jaw. "Double crap." They trudged toward Abuelo through the sludge. Mateo reached his grandfather and braced his shoulders. "Abuelo? Are you all right?"

Abuelo dropped the hose with a stunned look. "Yes." He nodded. "I'm all right." He viewed Mateo with sad eyes. "This is no good."

More wine spewed out of the tank in a steady stream. It was now up to their ankles.

Katie tugged on Mateo's arm. "What can I do?"

Mateo briefly patted her back. "Stay with Abuelo. Try to stem the flow."

Stem the flow? Katie's nerves skittered. She stared around the room, seeing nothing that could be of help.

Abuelo stared at her clothing, getting an idea. "Your coat!"

It was already ruined anyway. Katie shed it quickly and squished it, rolling it up. It was plush and puffy but could be compressed into almost nothing for packing.

"Is that made of down?" Abuelo asked her.

"Synthetic, I think." She handed him one end of the wadded-up coat and then shoved it up against the tank. The force of the cascading wine jolted them backward like a bucking bronco. Katie gritted her teeth. "Whoa!"

Despite the terrible circumstances, Abuelo had the good humor to laugh. "Very glamorous, this wine business."

"Ha! Yeah!"

They tried again, pushing against the coat harder. This time, it absorbed the wine, growing heavy. Wine seeped through it like a sieve, but the flow was slower. Katie's arms ached with the strain of holding her coat in place. This was like trying to contain a breaking dam. She put her back into it and pushed hard, and Abuelo did the same. Wine ran over her knuckles, saturating her sleeves. Poor Abuelo had wine in his hair, and his mustache dripped red.

"Your sweater!" Abuelo said above the noise. "It's ruined."

Katie stared down at her wine-splattered clothing. Of course she'd worn white.

"Your snowman," Abuelo said. "He looks like he's been through the war."

"It's okay! He'll survive it!" She wasn't sure that was true, but if the stains wouldn't wash, she could keep it to wear around the house. Her wardrobe was the least of her worries.

She surveyed the tall tank in front of her. There was a second spigot a short way up from the larger one they blocked. "How much wine does this hold?"

"Over two thousand gallons."

Katie winced, shifting her hold on her sopping wet coat as she pushed against it. "How much do you think is left?"

Abuelo scowled at the floor and the wine that lapped up around his ankles. "Maybe not much."

Mateo returned in a jog, holding tubing in his hands and a big clamp. "I might be able to get this one to work." He heaved a breath, winded. "It's all set up on the other end."

Mateo scooted between Katie and Abuelo, and Katie noticed a change. The wine wasn't running at full force. Her coat seemed to have plugged its escape like a cork. "Hey!" she exclaimed. "We stopped it!"

Abuelo raised his eyebrows at Mateo, and he and Katie slowly released their hold on the coat. It dropped like a soggy rag into a wine puddle below with a *plop*. More wine splashed up and splattered against Katie's jeans.

They all stared at the spigot as a small dribble of wine escaped. The dribble eased to some drips and then irregular, isolated drops.

"No." Abuelo frowned. "It's empty."

They sloshed back to the production room where Mateo flipped a series of levers.

"What are you doing?" Katie asked him.

"Trying to clear out the drains. Sometimes if we open and close them—"

A huge sucking sound emerged from the tank room. Katie looked down to see the wine below their feet running in that direction. She hadn't noticed the slight tilt to this floor until now.

Abuelo's furrowed brow eased. "*Gracias a Dios.*"

Mateo ran his hands through his hair, surveying the damage. Boxes all around him had their bottoms soaked through, and wine still reached into the cask room, although at least now it was flowing toward the drains. "It's going to take a while to clean this up."

"I'll help," Katie said.

Mateo smiled softly. "Thanks, Katie, but you've already done a lot."

"She did do a lot." Abuelo puffed up his chest. "Pitched in—like family." He leaned in to hug her. "I hope you don't mind my clothes," he said gruffly.

Katie fell into his sturdy embrace, feeling sheltered and warm. She'd never known her grandparents but had always wished she had. "Mine are a mess too."

Abuelo pulled back and chortled. "We're all a mess, aren't we?"

Mateo chuckled too, and then so did Katie. Soon, they all belly laughed in the hilarity that comes from shock and relief. Mateo called himself up short and stared at Katie. "Don't you have to go in to work?"

Katie held her middle, gasping. "Yeah. I should probably check in with Daisy at least."

Abuelo observed her outfit. "You'll need to go home and change first."

"That's all right," Katie told him. "I keep a spare uniform at the diner."

Mateo stared down at her feet. "And shoes?"

Katie nodded. "Those too." She sometimes got held up on her way in to work and liked being prepared just in case. She suspected she looked a wreck, but she could clean up well enough in the diner's employee washroom. This was their busiest time of day, so Mateo was right; she should get going and not delay any longer.

"Wait," Mateo said. He hoisted a box from the floor and set it on a counter, then did the same with another box and another. The bottoms of the boxes dripped with red wine. "I need to get a few of these off the floor and check our new labels. We've just ordered an update with a redesign of our family logo. We hired a local artist, and the work reminds me of those sketches you like to do. Maybe you'd like to have one?"

Katie guessed it would only take him a second to open the box and grab a label. "Sure!"

Abuelo viewed her admiringly. "You're an artist now too?"

Katie blushed. "Not in a serious way. I just doodle."

Mateo grinned. "But her doodling's very good." He took a folding knife from his jeans pocket and broke the seal on the box. "These are only advance samples," he said to Katie. "The supplier said if we like them, we can keep these as a bonus to the larger order once we place it. Let's hope most of them can be salvaged. If they look anything like the mock-ups, I know they'll be great." He removed some packing paper from on top and then pulled out a stack of labels wrapped in what looked like cellophane. He broke the package open and separated the label on top from the others. "Here you are."

Then he blanched and pulled the label out of Katie's view, gawking down at it. He looked like he'd been slapped in the face.

"I can't believe this."

"Mateo?" Abuelo asked. "What's wrong?"

Mateo turned his doleful gaze on them, and Katie's stomach clenched.

"This isn't the label I approved, and it doesn't say *Los Cielos Cellars*." The words scraped from his mouth like he could scarcely bear to say them. "It says *Cloudy Crest Wines*." He held the label up, and his fingers shook.

Abuelo covered his mouth with his hand and stumbled. Katie caught his elbow, and he latched on to her arm. He turned to her in dismay. "Did Juan tell you about this?"

A lump wedged in her throat. "No, Abuelo. I swear."

He sadly met her gaze. "Don't worry," he said. "I believe you."

The color returned to Mateo's face, which now went beet red. "How could he?" he wailed. "Without telling any of us?"

Abuelo shook his head. "Maybe he planned to?"

"Oh yeah? When?"

Abuelo still held on to Katie's arm. "At Christmas?"

Katie's stomach roiled. Was that really Juan's plan? To let

his family know he'd gone ahead with his gentrification project anyway? Had he intended to use her as a buffer? Thinking they wouldn't explode if he'd brought his "girlfriend" along?

"I'm so sorry about this," she said, because she was. Sorry about the labels, sorry about the wine disaster, sorry Juan was such a jerk. And super sorry about the misunderstanding she'd had with Mateo earlier and about the way he'd misjudged her.

Abuelo patted her hand. "None of this is your fault." His tone was so gentle, so understanding, she would have cried if she could have.

Mateo sighed. "This makes me wonder what else he's done."

Katie had questions about that too.

Katie arrived at the diner covered in wine. She'd left her coat at Los Cielos, telling Mateo he could pitch it. She didn't think there was any coming back from where it had been. There was only one place for it to go: in the trash. What a mess this whole thing was. She wanted to stay and help clean up, but Mateo'd said not to worry. They had staff they could call in to assist.

Most folks ignored her entry, but a few people turned to gawk. Daisy's eyes grew huge when she spotted her. She served two customers in a booth their lunches, then whispered as Katie went by, "What happened to you?"

Katie walked around the counter. "They had a flood at Los Cielos."

Daisy frowned. "Looks like you were in the center of it." She set down her empty tray. She'd been filling in for Katie waiting

tables, while doing double duty working the register. "ER at LC...
emergency at Los Cielos. So that's what you meant!" She shook
her head and laughed. "I honestly had no idea, child."

Mark turned from flipping burgers on the griddle. He tugged
down his cook's cap. "That *is* wine, right?" Rows of bacon strips
and sausage patties sizzled to the right of the burgers while he
cracked eggs onto the glistening surface.

"Yeah," Katie said. "They had a big wine emergency at the
vineyard. I tried to help out."

He nodded. "That was nice of you." He surveyed her soiled
clothing. "Everyone okay?"

"Yes, thankfully."

"Oh, say!" Daisy stopped her before she could slip away.
"Guess what I saw in the paper today? They caught the kid driving the white van."

Katie turned to her. "Kid?"

"He was only seventeen." Daisy fixed the tie on her apron,
which had come undone. "His first day on the job with a house
painting company, and he was running late." She pursed her lips.
"Poor boy was beside himself. When Juan fell, he was sure he'd
hit him. Maybe even killed him. It took him days to turn himself
in, but when he finally admitted to his parents what he'd done,
they insisted."

Katie gasped. "Did he get arrested?"

"No." Daisy's eyebrows rose. "Juan's family evidently didn't
press charges."

That sounded so much like them. Charitable and forgiving.

"He did lose his license though," Mark said. "For at least a year."

Daisy nodded. "And will have to take a remedial driving class too." Well, that was something. Katie guessed the teenager's own fear and guilt had punished him enough.

Mark gingerly turned each bacon slice and sausage patty over with his spatula, then quickly flipped some eggs, scrambling a second batch of them. He peered at Katie. "So what were you doing at Los Cielos again anyway?" A stack of steaming pancakes sat on a platter by his elbow.

Katie bit her lip, because she hadn't told either of them about shopping for Christmas trees, and somehow that didn't seem to matter in the scheme of things. What mattered was the discovery Mateo had made today. "I took the family some Christmas cookies this morning. They've been through so much with Juan." She didn't want to speak ill about Juan while he was in the hospital. Mateo was right about Juan being unable to defend himself for his actions at the moment. But *how* had he not believed her about the pretend girlfriend pact?

What a mangled confession that had turned out to be. She couldn't wait for Juan to wake up and completely clear the air. She also couldn't wait to hear what he had to say about the new wine labels. Would he invent excuses? Say he'd only done what was best for his family and the vineyard? Probably so.

Mark began serving up plates of bacon and eggs. Although it was lunchtime, they served breakfast all day long. "Well, I'm glad they got everything under control out there."

"Yeah," she said. At least about the leak. About other things, not so much. "Me too."

Daisy went to give Katie a one-armed hug, then she thought

better of it. She glanced at the register where a line had formed. "You'd better go wash up."

Katie scooted through the swinging doors to the kitchen. "Back in a flash!"

SEVENTEEN

Three Days before Christmas

AFTER GETTING THINGS UNDER CONTROL at Los Cielos, Mateo headed to Juan's condo the following day. He and Abuelo had agreed not to share anything about finding the Cloudy Crest Wines labels with the rest of the family until they learned more. Mateo couldn't wait for Juan to come out of his coma so he could find out what he'd been plotting. Evidently, some of those plans were already underway. Juan had been taking meetings with suppliers, supposedly gathering competitive quotes to secure them the best deals. It was true their business was hurting. But rejecting the vineyard's history wasn't the way to fix things.

Mateo fumed as his key slid into the lock on Juan's condo's front door. He had a top-floor unit with stunning views of the Mayacamas Mountains. Mateo entered the unit, where everything was made of chrome and glass. The furniture had hard edges and stark geometric forms. Mateo would have been uncomfortable living here. Each item in the room was either black or white, including the black-and-white photos on the wall, picturing their vineyard. At least Juan appreciated Los Cielos enough to showcase it in his large photo display.

One photo showed the barn in summertime, its outdoor tables holding open umbrellas under the gleaming sun. Another portrayed the main house in autumn, with turning leaves on the trees. A third winter scene captured the stables on a chilly day while horses grazed in the frosty meadow nearby. The final shot was of the tombstones at El Corazón, the special heart of the vineyard. That photo had been taken in the springtime. The part of the valley that hadn't been planted with vines was flooded with mustard flowers.

Mateo's gut twisted. While he'd been in Juan's condo before, he'd forgotten about his brother's sentimental side. There was a time when Juan had appreciated his heritage. Mateo wasn't sure when he'd lost his way.

The photo of the large valley oak tree in autumn recalled him to an episode in their past. He and Juan had been little kids, probably just a year or two younger than those images of them on the Christmas tree ornaments, and Juan had become fixated on another fanciful notion. For a while, he'd professed to be a fire-breathing dragon. Then he swore he had gills like a fish. After that, he'd claimed he could fly.

Their parents had indulged Juan's fantasies, while Abuelo and Abuela had found them endearing. Although he was a year younger than Juan, Mateo had a clearer sense of reality than his older brother by then. After learning that his teeth hadn't really fallen out due to eating so many Oreo cookies, he'd grown unilaterally suspicious of his brother's stories. He'd seen a circus performer swallow flames on television but knew for a fact that real people didn't breathe fire. He also got pretty clearly that humans couldn't fly, not unaided by an airplane or something like a parachute anyway.

Juan insisted it was true though, and that he had these magical abilities. He'd dreamed he'd been soaring over Los Cielos miles up in the sky and was determined to prove it.

Mateo could still remember that day in perfect detail.

———————

Juan climbed the big oak tree and was five or six feet off the ground, crouched on a sturdy limb. He wore a striped shirt under a light jacket and high-top tennis shoes, his shiny hair glinting in the sun.

Mateo didn't like Juan's hair. It was as if he was trying to look older, like their dad, but on Juan, the hairstyle looked dumb. Juan didn't care what Mateo thought. At six, he already had a girlfriend. Her name was Guinevere, and she had red hair.

Mateo squinted up at Juan, shielding his eyes with his hands. His curls flopped down to his knuckles. "Juan!" Mateo called up at him. "What are you doing?"

"I'm going to fly like a bird!"

Juan grinned, and Mateo self-consciously stuck his tongue into the spot where he was missing his two front teeth. He'd never have Juan's perfect teeth. Or a girlfriend, probably.

"Just watch me!"

Mateo's face heated. Juan couldn't jump out of that tree. Had he lost it? "Stop being so stupid! You know you can't fly!"

Juan lifted his chin like he was so superior, in on the universe's secrets. "My teacher says if you can dream it, you can be it!"

Mateo huffed. "That was when you said you wanted to be an astronaut!"

Juan glared down at him. "Who told you that?"

Mateo shook his head and sighed. "You did."

Juan inched toward the edge of the branch, ready to spring out of his crouch. "You're such a doubter, Mateo," he said meanly. "Maybe we should call you Doubting Mate-oreo."

"Oh yeah? And maybe we should call you Juan Bobo," Mateo punched back, referring to the fictional Puerto Rican character who made lots of dumb mistakes.

Juan's face turned red. "Why don't you get a haircut, Mateo? You look like a girl!"

Mateo's jaw flinched. "Why don't you come out of that tree, Juan! You look like a squirrel!"

"Okay," Juan said defiantly. "You think I can't fly?" He inched farther down the branch, releasing his hold on the branch above him. "Just watch me!"

"Juan! Noooo!"

But it was too late. He'd jumped!

Mateo raced toward his brother, crumpled on the ground. "Juan!"

"Ow, ow, ow, owwww!" Juan whined and clutched his shoulder, rolling onto his side, his knees drawn up to his chest.

"Are you crazy? Why did you—"

Juan's voice shook, and tears streaked down his cheeks. "Why didn't it work, Mateo? Why?"

Mateo frowned, hovering over him. "Don't move. I'll get help."

He broke into a sprint, but then Juan called out, "Mateo!"

Mateo stopped, glancing over his shoulder.

"Don't tell Mom and Dad I jumped. I might get in trouble."

Mateo hung his head. "Okay."

Juan's smile trembled, and for once, it didn't look so perfect. He winced and grabbed his injured arm, then quickly released it, sucking in a breath. "Hurry!"

Mateo ran and ran, as fast as he could toward the main house. "Help! Help!"

Abuelo appeared at the door, his forehead furrowed.

Mateo raced toward him, panting. "Juan fell out of a tree!"

Juan had broken his arm, but in retrospect, his ego had been damaged more. He never pretended to be able to do anything magical after that. But as he got older, he still remained convinced he could accomplish anything he set his mind to, no matter how long the odds. Which was Juan's greatest strength as well as his biggest weakness. Juan was always in such a hurry to find the next great thing and jump on the latest bandwagon. Generally, the others had been able to help Juan see reason. What was different about this time was that even though his family had had their say, Juan had apparently tuned them out, going ahead with his plans for Los Cielos Cellars anyway.

Mateo walked to the Lucite desk by the sliding doors to the balcony. Juan's laptop was on it, but it was password protected, so he was out of luck. Juan's phone had been smashed to smithereens during his fall, so there was no gaining information from that either. It was probably password protected anyway.

He sank down in Juan's desk chair and slid open the narrow top desk drawer. He found pens and paper clips, a pair of scissors, and tape inside it. A phone charger, blank sticky notes, and such. He shut the desk drawer and pulled open a deeper one below it on the right-hand side, holding file folders for personal finances: utility bills, credit card payments, and the like.

The lower left desk drawer was for business. Several said *Los Cielos Cellars*, others *Marketing* or *Promotions*. A few carried the names of get-rich-quick schemes Juan had pursued then abandoned. The files were arranged in alphabetical order. Mateo's fingers lingered on the file labeled *Inspections*. They had routine equipment and safety inspections at the vineyard, and one of Juan's duties was staying on top of them. Contracting with the inspectors, recording their reports and recommendations, following through with any fixes. Mateo's mouth went dry when he opened the folder. He hadn't seen this report. Nor had his parents or grandparents.

The last inspector in June had noted that the drain system needed repair and the valve on Tank 17 looked iffy. The December inspection had lapsed, never having been scheduled or completed. Mateo released a hard breath, thinking of the disaster yesterday morning. The one that could have—should have—been prevented, had Juan not been so enamored by other ideas he'd failed to take care of the basics.

That was why his parents had left the general running of the operation to Mateo. He oversaw their daily wine-making ventures; he employed and supervised field workers to plant and harvest the grapes and others to maintain their facility and work in production. He trained additional staff to host wine tastings, give tours, and run the gift shop while ensuring things went smoothly with deliveries to wholesale and retail vendors.

By contrast, Juan was given very few—but important—jobs and was trusted to do them well. Mateo hadn't realized Juan was being two-faced in his efforts, pretending to support the family business while secretly sabotaging its legacy. Juan's other duties were basically administrative. He balanced the books, ran automated inventory reports, placed orders, and set up facilities inspections.

Or, in this case, not.

Their parents and grandparents filled gaps where they could: Abuela in the gift shop, Abuelo in hosting tastings, because they enjoyed doing these things and not because they had to. Their parents led tours and assisted with managerial matters. But Abuelo and Abuela were essentially retired, and their mom and dad hoping to be on their way out. The transition had already begun.

Mateo reached the Rs in the business file drawer, and his pulse raced. Two file folders were labeled *Rebranding*. He pulled the files from the drawer, opening the first one on the desk and flipping through its pages. There was lots of correspondence between Juan and various suppliers, laying out specifics in each proposal submitted with a competitive bid. Mateo flipped the file shut, unable to read any more. But he still had the second file to look through. He braced himself and opened it, extracting some printed pages.

His heart lodged in his throat. These weren't merely estimates in this file. *They were receipts.* Juan hadn't only purchased enormous numbers of new labels and twist-cap bottles without consulting the family, he'd submitted down payments for a substantial advertising campaign with a big public relations firm as well. Not only that, he'd signed a major distribution deal with an international distributor. Mateo slumped back in Juan's desk chair, unable to believe his eyes. The words *Cloudy Crest Wines* jumped out at him again and again.

His family vineyard's products weren't getting shipped around the globe under the Los Cielos Cellars name. They were being sent everywhere, from Alaska to Australia, as Cloudy Crest Wines. The logo was the same as the one he'd seen on the wine labels in the production room: two illustrated wineglasses—one containing white wine, the other red—toasting over a cloudy mountain ridge.

If these numbers were right, they were out *tens of thousands* of dollars already, with another hefty sum due after the start of the year. The agreements were notarized too. All official. Undertaken recently while Mateo was away in New York.

Mateo's stomach soured.

He hadn't done it on purpose, but he'd done it nonetheless.

Juan had bankrupted Los Cielos.

EIGHTEEN

Two Days before Christmas

THE NEXT MORNING, MATEO DIDN'T feel any better. In fact, he felt worse after sharing the news about Juan with his family. Cleanup from the fermentation tank leak was going to cost them additional money, as they'd had to pay their workers overtime for coming in during their vacations. Since the winery was typically closed for these two weeks, a lot of their staff had made holiday plans. Mopping up a flooded basement was definitely an imposition. Then again, the disaster had also provided an opportunity for his employees to earn some extra cash. Opportunities like that would be in short supply in the foreseeable future, if not nonexistent.

Titi Mon sat on a barstool at the kitchen island while his mom refilled her coffee. Abuelo sat on the patio outdoors, despite the frosty weather. He wore a heavy coat and held a coffee mug, his gaze on the Mayacamas Mountains. Mateo couldn't imagine what he must be thinking. His heart had to be breaking over the entire Martinez legacy going down the drain.

"Good morning." Mateo pursed his lips, knowing it was anything but a good morning. December 23, and they all should be looking forward to Christmas and Juan's recovery. Yesterday afternoon, his parents had received more encouraging news about Juan when they went to see him at the hospital. His brain swelling had almost resolved completely, and his vitals were good. The doctors expected to bring him out of his coma very soon. Maybe as early as tomorrow. Mateo was supposed to have joined his parents during that trip, but after making his discovery at Juan's condo, he hadn't been able to stomach the visit.

"Coffee, Mateo?" His mom covered her mouth in a yawn. The dark circles under her eyes indicated she hadn't slept much last night. He suspected none of them had.

"Thanks, yeah. But I'll get it."

Titi Mon sagged against the kitchen island, hunched over on her elbows. He didn't see his grandmother anywhere.

"Is Abuela still sleeping?" he asked, pouring himself some coffee from the pot. His normally fresh-as-a-daisy Abuela had looked like a wilted flower last night over dinner, with all the sparkle gone out of her dark brown eyes. Perhaps Mateo should have waited until after the evening meal to tell everyone about Juan, but he'd wanted to get the bad news out in the open so they could all start dealing with it.

His mom frowned. "Abuela had a rough night and had to take her medication."

Mateo's heart thumped. "Oh no. Is she okay?"

"She insisted nobody call the doctor," Titi Mon added.

His mom sighed. "She seemed better this morning, but I don't know. This whole situation with Juan has been a big blow."

Mateo understood. The truth had crashed down on the family like a ton of bricks.

His mom walked absently to the Christmas tree, gazing up at the star on top. "I was hopeful for so many things this year. When Juan told us about Katie, it was like a dream come true. Our Juan had finally found somebody. Someone he was proud of and wanted to introduce to the family. Then we met her." She smiled at Mateo. "We could see why Juan loves her so much." She held up her hand. "You can say they're brand new all you want, Mateo, but I saw Katie's face at the hospital that first day after Juan's accident." She sighed and laid a hand on her heart. "She was obviously so adoring, very much in love with your brother. No doubt just as he is with her."

Mateo's gut tensed, because he'd witnessed the same thing himself. He considered Katie's story about Juan asking her to pose as his girlfriend, claiming their relationship was a ruse. Putting those two things together didn't make sense. How could Katie have authentically acted so smitten if she and Juan were just pretending? She hadn't known Mateo was listening to her private conversation with Juan when she'd begun confessing her love for him.

His mom sat on the sofa. "After having gotten to know her a little," she continued in low tones, "it's impossible to believe that Katie's affection was all one-sided. Just look at her, Mateo."

Yeah, he'd been looking a lot more than he should have.

"She's so sweet. She brought us Christmas cookies when she knew I'd be too tired to bake them."

Titi Mon raised her coffee mug. "*And* she helped out with the flood."

"That's true," his mom said. She glanced out a window at the patio. "Your abuelo hasn't stopped talking about her." His mom slumped back against the sofa, wrapping her hands around her coffee mug. "I hope this new discovery about what Juan's done won't affect how Katie feels about him, but I fear that it might." She spoke with a defeated edge, like Juan's huge deception had been too much for her to bear.

His mom was normally so upbeat, so positive. It broke his heart seeing her so down. He didn't know what had gotten into Juan, because he honestly wasn't the sort of man to devastate his family on purpose. In his heart of hearts, Juan must have believed he was helping them as well as helping the business. Which had been as delusional as Juan thinking he could fly. How was gutting Los Cielos going to save it? Juan might as well have ripped his family members' hearts out one by one. Didn't he have any sense of that? Mateo scoffed to himself, because he doubted it. Juan could never see the downside to any proposition. He was a glass-half-full guy to a fault.

Mateo went and sat beside his mom, sensing she needed reassurance. But his insides had gone all topsy-turvy too. It was like their entire world stood on end, and it was impossible to know how to right it. He didn't know who was taking it harder, Abuelo and Abuela or his parents.

Sunlight poured through the windows, threading through the bare-limbed trees. "Where's Dad?" Mateo asked.

His mom set her mug on the coffee table. "Down at the stables."

Mateo and his dad had that in common. When they needed to think, it helped to go for a ride. They kept four horses on the property, one for each of his parents and the other two for him and Juan. Abuelo no longer rode, and Abuela had never been much of a horsewoman. She did enjoy seeing the animals, though, and feeding them carrots and apples. Their eagerness always made her laugh and smile, and they'd learned to be careful with elderly Abuela.

Who knew what would become of their horses now, or the winery and their land. Would they have to sell everything off to provide for their basic needs? Mateo and Juan were young, and the two of them would land on their feet. But what about his parents and grandparents? Apart from the modest Social Security payments they'd receive, they didn't have major retirement funds set aside. They'd invested in Los Cielos.

"Mom," Mateo said gently. "This can't be the end of Los Cielos. There has to be a way to fix this." He raked a hand through his hair, wishing with all his might he could think of what to do. But the shock of yesterday's discovery still clanked around in his brain like a prison cell door slamming shut, sealing this dismal fate.

"I'd give anything in the world to believe that." Her shoulders sank. "But this hole that Juan has dug for us is so deep. He made *deposits*, Mateo." She wrung her hands together, massaging her wedding band and the diamond engagement ring beside it. "With our money."

Now wasn't the time to mention his repeated warnings to his parents about the dangers of leaving Juan on their business checking account. He held it jointly with Mateo, and Mateo had already had to help Juan cover his tracks over more than one financial misadventure. Mateo had argued against letting Juan have control of any purse strings, suggesting he oversee arranging their promotional opportunities and facilities maintenance appointments without actually paying the invoices. Mateo wanted to be in control of those so he could oversee their expenses.

But removing Juan from the account would have involved closing down the existing account to open a new one, and his parents had only recently transitioned their financial holdings into the names of their two sons in preparation for their approaching retirement. They already had a number of autopay commitments tied to the new account, including payroll, so making a change would have created a substantial disruption for the business and very likely would have upset Juan.

It also could have saved Los Cielos.

Mateo patted his mom's shoulder and stood. "I'm sorry."

Her eyebrows rose when he opened the coat closet by the Santa statue in the foyer. "Where are you going?"

"Probably out for a ride in a bit. But first." He glanced through the glass panels in the door. "I think I'll have a chat with Abuelo."

Before he left, his mom called out, "Mateo!"

He turned with his hand on the doorknob.

Her eyes held a sad glimmer. "I think Katie needs to know."

"Yeah," he answered. "She probably does."

His mom pursed her lips. "I'll tell her."

"Thanks, Mom." He was glad for the offer, because for an instant, Mateo worried his mom was going to ask him to do the honors.

Katie had already been itching to leave Juan. Now that he'd torpedoed the family business, she could point to his thoughtlessness and poor judgment as another excuse. Shame washed through

Mateo as he questioned whether he'd really been looking out for Juan or secretly for himself by selfishly wanting to have Katie around a little longer. For what? So he could moon over a woman he could never have? *Get your head out of the clouds, Mateo.*

He sighed and shut the front door, knowing his mom was right. Since Katie was involved with Juan, she had a right to better understand who she was involved with and why his family was suddenly at odds with him. Katie had to have an inkling about what was going on after witnessing Mateo finding those Cloudy Crest Wines labels, but she clearly couldn't know the full extent of it. Couldn't know that Juan had contracted with advertisers and had gone so far as to sign an international distribution agreement under the Cloudy Crest Wines name.

But no matter what he'd done, Juan wasn't a malicious guy. And Katie needed to understand that about him too. He simply had trouble seeing the world from anyone else's point of view. Still, his actions meant he'd soon be out of a job and maybe his home. Maybe all of them would.

Abuelo turned when he heard Mateo cross the patio.

"How are you holding up?" Mateo asked the older man.

Abuelo stared deeply into Mateo's soul. "How do you think?"

"Yeah." Mateo heaved a breath, sitting beside him. "I guess we're all still in shock." The chair's frame was chilly, its cold seeping into Mateo through his jeans. But that did nothing to match the giant icicle that Juan had wedged through his heart like a sharp, jagged knife. He felt so betrayed by his brother, but this wasn't just about him; it was about something so much bigger. Their legacy, their vineyard. Their *family*. How could Juan have done this?

Abuelo took a sip of coffee, then spoke above the rim of his mug. "My father left this land to me," he said, his eyes on the mountains. "And his father before him to him. They made enormous sacrifices, your Papi Monchi and Mamacita. Both of their families were against it, begged them not to come to California.

"Santa Rosa had been destroyed just a few years before by the same earthquake that leveled San Francisco. Mamacita's family took that as a bad omen. Papi Monchi's parents told him if he left to never come back. Once he'd deserted the family in Oaxaca, he'd no longer be welcome. And *still*." Abuelo's breath clouded the frosty air below his heavy mustache. "They did it. They came here to start fresh, to build their legacy. Do you know why, Mateo?" He locked on his grandson's gaze. "Because they had two things!"

Abuelo set his jaw. "They had *faith* and *love*. And *love*"—he raised a hand and swept it over the vineyard—"created this." His eyes twinkled sadly, but then he smiled. "Faith helped a lot. My grandparents' faith in each other, faith in the land, in God." He made a fist, thumping it against his chair arm. "They held on to the things that were good and worked day and night until they had their first harvest." He sat back in his chair. "And the rest, as they say, is history. *Our history*. It guts me to see it destroyed."

Mateo squeezed his hand over Abuelo's coat sleeve. "I know, Abuelo."

Abuelo stared at him with pleading eyes. "Mateo, you're so clever. Isn't there something you can do? Juan has always had the looks. But you"—he leaned over and slapped Mateo's chest—"have been the brains of this operation."

If that wasn't a double-sided compliment, Mateo didn't know

what was. But he didn't fault his grandfather for speaking his mind. Abuelo always did. Mateo wasn't *that* terrible looking, just maybe not as picture-perfect as Juan. Still, he had his own strengths. His commitment to his family, an analytical mind, a certain kind of tenacity and... He swallowed hard, feeling it rise up inside him. *His faith.* His eyes panned over the vineyard, and then his heart warmed, growing fuller and fuller, so huge it almost ached. Mateo raked a hand through his hair as his heart beat faster and stronger.

He was falling in love with Los Cielos. Maybe he'd loved her all along.

He had to do something to keep her from going under.

He just didn't know what.

"You know the one I feel really sorry for?" Abuelo shook his head, then stared at Mateo. "It's Katie. She has no idea about any of this, does she?"

Mateo shook his head. "I don't expect she does, but Mom's going to fill her in."

"Well." Abuelo sighed heavily. "I guess that's the end of her and Juan."

Mateo shrugged off his discontent. "Maybe so."

Abuelo frowned. "That's such a shame too. She's such a nice woman. Fits in so well with the family." Abuelo shot him a look. "You don't suppose *you*—?" His eyes sparkled like he'd arrived at an idea. A very far-fetched and impossible one in Mateo's estimation.

Mateo rubbed his knees and stood. "No, Abuelo. I don't suppose that would work out at all." If they lost Los Cielos, what would he have to offer Katie anyway? Other than his broken heart? He needed to go for a ride and clear his head.

THE HOLIDAY MIX-UP 215

His focus right now should be on saving Los Cielos Cellars and *not* on someone who'd briefly been—or had only posed as—his brother's girlfriend. Whatever reasons she'd had for her actions, those had all been related to Juan and not on account of him.

He'd do really well to remember that.

———————

Katie arrived at Los Cielos at a little after 1:30 p.m. She'd worked the opening shift at the diner and hadn't seen Pia's text message until she got home. Her stomach knotted with nerves when she rang the doorbell. Pia hadn't said what she wanted to talk about, but it seemed a little unusual being summoned here by Juan's mom. Though Mateo hadn't wanted to hear her confession, maybe he'd reconsidered later, deciding to believe her.

She hadn't expected to be confronted by Juan's mom about it though. She felt like a kid getting sent into the principal's office. She drew in a deep breath and released it, trying to calm her anxiety. Pia wasn't vindictive. She was gentle and kind.

Titi Mon answered the door. "*Hola, hija,*" she said with a mournful gaze. She drew Katie into a hug and kissed her cheek. "We've been waiting for you." At least she didn't seem angry. Her vibe was more like disappointed. No doubt in Katie, for perpetuating an untruth. She got it.

Katie spied Pia sitting on the sofa by the Christmas tree. "Katie, take off your coat." Pia patted a cushion. "Come on over here and sit with me." Her wan smile caused a mellow sadness to wash over the room. Raul wasn't around. Neither were Abuelo and Abuela. Mateo's absence was the most notable of all, maybe because Katie was looking for him the hardest.

Katie hung her coat in the coat closet. It was an older one that had belonged to her mom and not very modern or fashionable. She wore her mom's old leather gloves and black stocking cap too. Her white mittens and hat had been in her white coat's pockets, so they'd also been ruined. But fashion was the last thing on her mind at the moment. She reached for a hanger and her hand trembled. Whatever Pia and Titi Mon had to say to her, she prayed they'd do it quickly and be merciful so she could—once and for all—get out of the Martinezes' hair.

Her heart wrenched. Soon, she'd be leaving this place and never coming back. The great room was inviting, with a fire blazing in the hearth. Eight stockings still hung from the mantel, but she suspected that one would come down pretty soon. The panorama of the vineyard through the windows took her breath away.

Every which way, vines, planted neatly in rows, crested the rolling hills, reaching up toward the mountains. Pinkish clouds hugged the peaks and ridges of the Mayacamas range like big swirls of cotton candy. She could see why Abuelo's grandparents had fallen in love with the place. It was beautiful. Serene.

Titi Mon stood at the kitchen counter, stuffing wrapped packages and bottled water into saddlebags. It was a little late for a picnic, and Titi Mon didn't seem like the horse-riding sort, but Katie realized there were probably lots of things she didn't know about Titi Mon. Just like she hadn't known certain things about Juan. Her head still reeled over the fact that he'd commissioned sample labels without consulting his family about the change. At least they were only samples, according to Mateo.

"Titi Mon," Pia said, capturing her attention. "Would you mind?" She swept her hand toward a hallway, and the other woman immediately read her signal.

"Of course." Titi Mon nodded and closed the latches on the saddlebags. "I've got a bit of Christmas wrapping to do anyway." She winked slyly at Katie, and confusion swirled through her head. Not presents for her, surely. Though she definitely had some for the Martinezes. She'd started working on them last night and intended to finish this evening if she could.

She wanted to apologize to everyone, and maybe she should start now before putting Pia through the trouble of confronting her. Katie sat with Pia on the sofa. "If this is about Juan," she said, once Titi Mon had slipped down the hall, "I think I know what you're going to say."

Pia's eyebrows arched. "Do you? But how?"

"Mateo probably told you about the other day." Katie hung her head.

Pia gently raised Katie's chin in her hand. Her eyes probed Katie's. "Is this about Mateo finding those Cloudy Crest Wines labels?" Pia asked.

Katie shook her head, and Pia dropped her hand.

"Then what?"

"It's, uh…" Katie shifted in her seat. "About what happened in the hospital. The day of Juan's accident." She gripped the sofa arm tightly, gathering her courage. "The day we first met."

"Oh, Katie. Sweetheart." Pia surprised her with a hug. "I

know how much hope you held in your heart for you and Juan. Your future."

Katie gasped, her heart pounding. "What?" She pulled out of Pia's embrace.

"You were very much in love with my son."

Katie blushed hotly. "I did think that once, but—" *Now, I'm so much more in love with Mateo.* Katie swallowed that hard truth, nearly choking on it. *In love? No.* But then she considered the million ways Mateo made her heart sigh and her soul sing. *So maybe?*

"But?" Pia said, latching on to her hesitation. "Not so much anymore?" Her eyes shone warmly.

Katie's forehead furrowed. "You mean because of Cloudy Crest Wines?"

Pia grabbed on to Katie's hands. "I'm sorry, honey. It's so much worse than we knew. Probably worse than you knew." She licked her lips, then added, "I'm sure of that. You never would have been complicit."

"Complicit?" Katie's pulse raced. "In what?"

Pia frowned. "Juan has already started his rebranding of Los Cielos."

"You're talking about those labels Mateo found? Weren't those only samples?"

Pia's frown deepened, causing lines to form around her mouth. "Juan evidently approved those samples and put in orders for hundreds more. He also set up a major advertising campaign for Cloudy Crest Wines *after* securing an international distribution deal."

Katie's head spun. "But how?"

Pia squeezed her hands. "Juan has access to our corporate checking account. He made his move when Mateo was out of town in New York." She sighed. "And unfortunately, this is the last straw breaking our backs here. The vineyard's been under quite a financial strain, and now..." Her chin trembled and she stopped talking, releasing Katie's hands.

"Did Juan know this?" Katie asked her. "What a precarious state the business was in?"

Pia's face said of course he knew. "He's always gone his own way. Only this time—" she blinked—"It's all of us who will suffer." Her eyes went moist. "Katie," she said solemnly. "We could lose everything."

Katie's heart lodged in her throat. How could Juan have done this? Taken such a huge risk for his family? One that might now land them all in the cold? "Isn't there someone you can call to stop this? I mean, given Juan's accident and medical condition, maybe there's a way to put on the brakes? At least until you can figure out a solution?"

Pia slumped back in her seat. "Raul and I were on the phone first thing this morning. Every place we called had already closed for the holidays. Some won't reopen until after Christmas. Others after New Year's."

"In that case," Katie said, "no action will be taken either, right?"

Pia pursed her lips. "Hope not."

Katie stared at the blazing hearth and then the pretty Christmas decorations adorning the room. This was supposed to be such an awesome Christmas with Juan coming home. Now, it seemed that it was Juan who was ruining it. "I'm sorry, Pia. This sounds like an awfully big mess. I hope you all can find your way out of it."

Pia sighed. "Yes. Me too."

Katie looked at her, a question forming in her mind. "This is all very personal family information." She studied Pia's distressed gaze. "So why are you telling me?"

"I thought you should know about Juan. In case..." Pia exhaled sharply. "In case this changes your mind about how you feel about him."

Katie had already changed her mind, but only partially on account of Juan's duplicitous behavior. Still. She was shocked Juan hadn't considered this outcome. That he'd endanger the well-being and livelihood of everyone he loved. Would he operate in the same manner as a boyfriend or a husband? By refusing to entertain other opinions? Taking life-altering risks? Katie couldn't see herself with that sort of person. No. No matter what Juan's reasons or motives were. He'd been pigheaded, prideful, and wrong, and the fallout was catastrophic.

A pang of shame shot through her.

She hadn't exactly been a paradigm of virtue this holiday season either.

"Please don't judge my son too harshly." Pia's smile trembled. "As a mother, I'm upset with his choices, but I also know in here"—she placed a hand on her chest—"he has a good heart. Juan's always been so..." She sounded wistful. "Cheerful. Optimistic." She frowned. "Unfortunately, sometimes that gets him into trouble too. Dreaming those impossible dreams."

Katie remembered a song by that name, "The Impossible Dream," from the musical *Man of La Mancha*. Her mom had owned the soundtrack from the movie, but Katie hadn't played that old vinyl in years. In its lyrics, Don Quixote sings about his valiant quest. Following his far-flung dreams, bearing sorrows, reaching for the unreachable star... Maybe with her unrequited attraction to Mateo, she'd also been tilting at windmills. The truth welled up inside her, making her throat tender and raw. "Pia, Juan wasn't the only one who was misguided. I've also made mistakes. Some huge—"

Pia touched her arm. "Don't blame yourself for anything, Katie." Her eyebrows arched. "Please. We all understand. You and Juan were just getting started, yes. But news like this could make you want to end things. I just have one favor to ask you. Don't do it now."

Katie felt faint. Mateo had asked the same thing. "But, Pia. You don't under—"

Pia locked on her gaze. "I do understand, sweetheart. But I also have the rest of our family to think of." She glanced at the long hallway by the kitchen. "Abuela's been in her bed all day, heartbroken. She's taken this move by Juan very hard. So has Abuelo." She tilted her head toward the patio. "He's been out there for hours, just staring at the mountains."

"And Mateo?"

Pia shook her head. "None of us have seen him since this morning. He went out for a ride, and Raul passed him in the stables, just coming back from one himself. Those two are so alike in that way. When they're troubled, they go to the horses."

Katie suspected Mateo must be very troubled by what Juan had done. He'd already been upset before by Juan's refusal to accept his family's input on the rebranding. Now that he'd gone on ahead with it secretly behind their backs, that was bound to sting even more.

"So, Katie. Please, *mija*. Whatever you feel about Juan, whatever your plans for the future." Pia lightly patted her cheek. "Please let some people here hang on to the illusion that you're still a part of this family."

"But I'm not," Katie said on a breath. Her voice trembled when she added, "A part."

Pia leaned toward her. "You have to know that Abuela wanted you to become one of us, and to break the news to her would be too much for her fragile health. I know I have no right to ask this, so if you want to refuse, I of course understand. But if you could find it in your heart to at least not say anything to Abuela and Abuelo about your decision to leave Juan for a few more days. Let this family get through Christmas as best as we can first."

Katie's heart thudded dully. "Of course. I won't say a thing to Abuela or Abuelo, I promise." Maybe telling Pia and Raul the whole truth now wasn't the right thing either. It would be selfish to unburden her soul just to make herself feel better when she could easily wait a few more days and until Juan hopefully got better.

"Thank you, Katie." Pia hugged her so tightly Katie wanted to cry. For the Martinezes, for herself. For everybody. Even for Juan. He had such a wonderful family. A family that had always supported him, despite him sometimes going astray. It was clear that they'd still support him while trying find a way forward out of this disaster.

Oh, Juan. What a very big mess you've made.

———————

Titi Mon peeked her head around the corner. "Is it safe to reenter?"

Pia laughed sadly and waved her in. "Yes, yes."

Raul appeared behind Titi Mon, his shoulders hunched forward and his hands wedged in his jeans pockets. "I've been in the office," he told Pia. "Trying those phone numbers."

"No luck?" Pia asked him.

His face hung in a frown. "No luck." He appeared to suddenly notice Katie. "Oh, hi, Katie. Nice to see you." He frowned again. "Sorry about the circumstances."

Pia held up her hand and said sunnily. "Katie's agreed not to make any decisions—about anything," she added pointedly, "until *after* Christmas."

Gratitude glimmered in Raul's eyes. "Thank you, Katie." His expression telegraphed, *You have to know we're already dealing with a lot around here.* And she did. She wasn't going to pour fuel on the flames by highlighting still another way in which Juan had deceived his family. The fake girlfriend ruse was a tiny white lie when compared to the whopper of a transgression about rebranding Los Cielos Cellars.

Katie swallowed past the lump in her throat. "Um-hm. Sure."

Titi Mon hefted the heavy saddlebags in her hands. "I've prepared lunch for Mateo like you asked, Raul, so you can take it to him."

"Great. Thanks, Titi Mon." He strode into the kitchen.

"Mateo has to eat," Pia confided to Katie. "He completely missed lunch, and we're worried about him."

Just as Titi Mon said that, Pia's cell phone rang. She reached for it on the coffee table. "Oh! It's the hospital!" She answered and had a quick conversation, her tone growing more and more animated. "Of course," she said in closing. "My husband and I will be right there." She ended the call and stared at her husband. "We're wanted at the hospital. There's some paperwork we need to sign."

Raul opened the coat closet, removing two heavy jackets. "I hope there'll be good news."

Pia got to her feet and stuck her phone in her jeans pocket. "Yeah, me too."

Titi Mon let the weight of the saddlebags settle in her hands. "And Mateo's lunch?"

All eyes turned to Katie.

"Do you know how to ride?" Pia asked her.

Katie flushed when she got what Pia was asking. Would she be willing to take the lunch to Mateo? She couldn't say no. Titi Mon probably didn't ride, and she was skeptical about the grandparents.

Katie nodded, feeling like she should step in. The Martinezes needed her, and how long could it take to find Mateo and deliver his lunch after all? Katie's stomach rumbled, and she realized she hadn't eaten either. She'd been in such a hurry to get here after receiving Pia's text, she'd skipped lunch. "I had a friend in high school with horses," Katie told them. "She used to take me riding with her a lot."

Titi Mon grinned. "Excellent." She stared at Katie's stomach as if she'd heard it growl. "I'll toss some extra food in for you," she said, opening a saddlebag and then reaching in the refrigerator for another wrapped sandwich.

"I'm not sure about doing the tack part though," Katie said. "Saddling up and all that. Jane always did that for me." The nuances to getting a horse ready to ride could be tricky, and she didn't want to risk making a mistake. Mistakes like that could be dangerous, for the rider and the horse.

"Don't worry." Raul glanced out the door and at Abuelo. "We'll get my father to help you." He stared out at the sky. "Very pink. The weather's turning. Mateo shouldn't stay out there much longer anyway." He observed Katie's clothing, jeans and another Christmas sweater. "Are you okay to ride in that?"

"I should be all right."

"Bundle up," Pia said. "It's really chilly outside."

Titi Mon beckoned her over, and Katie walked into the kitchen as Pia and Raul prepared to go. They stepped onto the patio, and Raul sent Abuelo inside.

"I hear someone's going for a ride?" He grinned.

"Yes," Titi Mon said. She opened one of the saddlebags and tucked in a wine bottle. "She's taking the new cabernet franc."

Katie blinked. "What?"

Titi Mon shrugged. "Mateo will probably need it." Her eyebrows rose. "And maybe you'd like a little *tinto* too?"

She was suddenly being sent on a picnic in the countryside with a man she majorly crushed on who evidently didn't like her back. At least not in *that* way, since he'd basically urged her to keep on seeing his brother.

So okay. Maybe she *would* take a sip of wine. *Or two.*

Just not so much that she couldn't get back to the stables on her horse.

NINETEEN

ABUELO TIGHTENED THE STRAP ON the saddle and patted the horse's haunches. "Okay, Toro. Be good to Katie." He'd already attached the saddlebags, checking that they fit snugly.

Katie stepped forward to stroke the horse's nose. "His name is Toro?" He rubbed his muzzle against her hand, and she laughed. "He seems gentle enough."

"He's very tame," Abuelo assured her. "And very old."

"How old?"

"Twenty-three years old. Juan got him when he was twelve."

"Wow." Katie examined the horse's shiny black coat and chestnut-colored mane and tail. He was impeccably groomed. "He looks great."

Abuelo nodded. "Juan takes good care of him. We also have Alonzo, who oversees the stables. He often grooms the horses, and not because we request it. Mostly because he says they're like his family. Alonzo and his wife, Bettina, never had children of their own. Bettina cooks for us in the main house normally."

"Are they on vacation?"

"Yes, visiting her sister in San Francisco. We have two younger helpers, Cheme and Gildita, who come in early each morning to feed the horses and clean their stalls. They're here and gone by seven; that's why you've never seen them."

Katie stroked Toro's silky mane. "I always wanted a horse when I was little."

Abuelo turned up his hands. "I always wanted an airplane."

She laughed. "Did you ever get one?"

"No, but I had a good friend who took me flying. He was a pilot in the air force for a while."

Katie considered Abuelo's stocky build. He was compact but muscled. As a young man, he must have been fairly strong. "Did you serve in the military?"

"My number never came up," he said, referring to the draft, she guessed. "Which was for the best. I was my parents' only child, so I was needed here."

Katie hadn't considered Abuelo's birth family before.

"I did have a little sister." Abuelo frowned. "But she died when she was a baby."

Katie's heart broke for him. Then she remembered the smaller grave marker at El Corazón. "How awful. I'm sorry. How old were you at the time?"

"Only four, but I still recall it vividly. My mother's wail shook the house when she found Isabella not moving in her crib. They call it SIDS now. Back then, they didn't understand it so well. Though it wasn't my parents' fault, they never got over it. They didn't want any more children after that. Couldn't bear to try again. So they poured all their love into Los Cielos." He gave a wan smile. "And me."

"They were very lucky to have you," Katie said, certain he must have been a wonderful son. "How long ago did you lose them?"

"Many years ago. Before Juan was born." He seemed to shake off the melancholy. "But enough of the Martinez family history!"

She hadn't minded hearing about Abuelo's parents or his childhood. In fact, she was honored that he'd shared those private memories with her.

Abuelo motioned toward the horse. "Now, young lady, it's time for your ride." He led Toro out of the stables by the reins. "Do you need a boost up?"

It was kind of him to offer, but she didn't need to impose on Abuelo. "I think I've got it." She grasped the saddle horn with one hand and slid her boot into a stirrup, holding the back of the saddle with her other hand. In one quick move, she'd swung her leg over the horse and mounted the saddle. It was a long way up since the horse was large, leaving Abuelo dwarfed by comparison on the ground. He was much shorter than his grandsons and Raul but still slightly taller than Abuela.

She settled in on the saddle, and Abuelo passed her the reins.

His eyes twinkled approvingly. "Looks like you're a natural."

Katie had longed for horseback riding lessons as a kid, but her dad had never been able to afford them. Riding with her friend Jane had always been a special treat. She'd been secretly envious of Jane having a horse, and then later, a husband and a family. As she got older though, she found herself feeling happy for Jane. She'd always been a good friend, and Katie didn't really blame her that they'd lost touch. It had just happened.

She leaned forward, pressing her face to Toro's neck. "I think Toro and I are going to be good friends."

The horse whinnied and flicked his tail, eliciting chuckles from Abuelo.

"I think he likes you already." He studied her a beat. "That's impossible not to do."

Her face warmed. "You and your family are pretty great too."

"I'm glad you still think that." He set his hands on his hips and frowned. "I know Pia told you about Juan."

Katie's heart thumped. "She did."

"And?" His eyebrows rose.

Katie blew out a breath. "I'm hoping everything can still be fixed."

"Cloudy Crest Wines!" Abuelo grumbled. "What was he thinking?"

"I don't know." She shrugged. "Maybe, in his own way, he was trying to help?"

"That's what we all want to believe." Abuelo's shoulders sank. "But that doesn't make it better."

"No," Katie said. "Not yet. But, Abuelo?"

His forehead creased.

"Maybe things will look brighter tomorrow?"

He pursed his lips, then said gruffly, "You're a good person, Katie Smith." He shook his finger at her in a teasing fashion. "Maybe too good for Juan." He paused to stroke his chin. "I do have another grandson though." His eyes held a devilish gleam. "He's no chopped liver."

Katie gasped. "Abuelo!" She laughed with embarrassment, unsure if he was joking.

"Humor an old man." His mustache twitched. "Can I help it that I like having you in the family?"

Katie's heart wrenched, because she loved being a part of this family too, but that wasn't going to last. She stared at him fondly. "Thanks, Abuelo." Katie hadn't known her grandparents, but if she'd ever had a grandfather, she would have wanted him to be just like him.

"So you'll be here for Christmas?" Hope glimmered in his eyes, and she hated to let him down. But she also didn't think she could handle opening presents around the tree as the fraudulent girlfriend, knowing she'd soon have to reveal the truth.

"I'm not sure," she hedged. She lifted a shoulder. "But we'll see?"

"That's good enough." Abuelo nodded toward the hills, getting back to the business of her intended picnic. "Do you know El Corazón? The heart of the vineyard?"

"Yes." She flushed at the memory. "Mateo took me there."

"Good." Abuelo's gaze scanned the rows of vines and distant mountains. "Ride in that direction, to the east, with the sun at your back. When you reach it, you'll be at the highest point in the vineyard."

She recalled the sweeping view and nodded.

"Mateo will probably be on the other side near the stream."

"Thanks, Abuelo." She straightened her back and sat up taller in the saddle, preparing to ride.

Abuelo winked at her. "Enjoy the wine."

"What?"

Abuelo shouted, "Yah!" and swatted Toro's rump, sending him into a trot. Katie glanced over her shoulder and Abuelo grinned. "I peeked in the saddlebags!" He chortled and waved. "Have a good time!"

Mateo sat with his back against a tree, strumming his guitar. It was a quiet tune, the soft serenade of his strings resonating like tears. His music floated up to the heavens, sifting over the vineyard in sonorous waves. It filled the air and flitted on the breeze but did very little to soothe the storm clouds rumbling in his soul. He'd always loved this place, but his bond with the land was stronger than he'd understood. Nearly as strong as his ties to family. Cemented deep inside him. *A part of him.*

Maybe it was true what they said about not appreciating something until it was gone. It had taken being on the cusp of losing Los Cielos for Mateo to fully grasp how much he loved it. How much he needed to protect it at all costs. He had his music and his guitars, and those were important to him, yes. But not more important than his heritage. *His legacy.*

Mateo's horse grazed nearby, wandering into the pebbled part of the stream to take a drink. Blaze always stayed close. He was faithful that way and getting up in years. Mateo had gotten him when he was eleven, the same year Juan got Toro. Where other boys got bikes for Christmas, he and Juan had received stallions. They'd had tons of fun together, riding through the vineyard when they were young. For a moment, he allowed himself to get lost in a memory.

Mateo raced Juan to the crest of the hill at El Corazón, but Juan's horse was faster. Toro stopped beside the low stone wall surrounding the family graves. Papi Monchi and Mamacita were there. Abuelo's parents, Safiro and Luciana too, as well as Abuelo's infant sister, Isabella.

Mateo supposed Abuelo and Abuela might be buried here someday, but he didn't like thinking about it.

"Beat you again, baby brother." Juan shared a triumphant grin. A lock of his nearly black hair spilled across his forehead, giving him an atypically unkempt demeanor.

Juan looked like a man at sixteen. Mateo was still gangly in his growing fifteen-year-old body. Unsteady in his gait, like a foal, while Juan had already settled into his swagger.

Juan hopped off his horse to examine the view of the Mayacamas Mountains. "We came from over there." He set his jaw proudly pointing at Mount Hood. "All the way from Mexico."

Mateo jumped off his horse as well. He grabbed Juan's elbow, steering his arm south rather than east. "We came from Oaxaca," he corrected. "And Puerto Rico." He motioned with his chin to where Juan had initially pointed. "Over that way's Santa Rosa, California."

Juan balled his hand into a fist, using it to playfully pound Mateo's skull while wrapping an arm around him. "You are always so knuckleheaded smart."

"Stop!" Mateo pushed him away and shook out his curly hair. "Am not." He widened his eyes at Juan. "I just know my geography."

"You with the books, and me with the women." Juan fixed his fallen lock of hair, smoothing it back into place. *"I think we've divided things nicely."*

"Women, sure." Mateo smirked. *"They're teenagers, Juan."*

"Some of them," he teased. *"Others might be older."*

From the twinkle in his eyes, Mateo couldn't tell if he was joking. *"Mom would have your head. Titi Mon too."*

Juan dragged a hand down his cheek. *"Don't get me started on Titi Mon."*

"She's coming to stay with us again this Christmas."

Juan arched an eyebrow. *"She's always here at Christmas."*

Mateo nudged him. *"That's because you're her favorite godson."*

"I'm her only godson, Mateo."

"Which is why she needs to watch out for your 'morality.'" He held up his hands, forming quotation marks with his fingers, and Juan rolled his eyes.

"My morality's in great shape," he quipped. *"Thank you very much."*

"If you say so, man."

"I say so." Juan put on a wistful air. *"I'm saving myself for the right woman."*

"Right." Mateo coughed into his hand, wondering if he'd ever have any experience with women at all. Probably someday. But he'd never have half as many experiences as Juan.

Juan surveyed the rows upon rows of planted vines. Mateo stared at the view as well, caught up in it for a long moment.

Juan sighed. *"It's hard to imagine this will all be ours someday."*

"*Yours,*" *Mateo corrected.*

Juan's forehead creased. "What? No. Yours and mine, Mateo."

Mateo sank his hands in his jeans pockets. "You're the oldest."

"So? You're the smartest."

"Don't sell yourself short."

"All right. I won't." Juan crossed his arms. "Which is why I'm smart enough to know I'd need you by my side running the winery." He swept his hand over the hills. "I could never do this alone. And anyway." He cocked his chin at Mateo. "What would you do instead?"

"I don't know. Something." Mateo shrugged. "One thing's for sure." A smile tugged at his lips. "I won't be trying to fly out of trees."

"I was only six." Juan roughly pushed his chest, and Mateo fell back a step, laughing.

"Don't worry," he told Juan. "I'll take your secret to my grave."

Their gazes locked on Papi Monchi's and Mamacita's tombstones, and they both grew silent. Reverence penetrated the breeze as light gusts of wind riffled through the historic vines.

"They were very brave," Juan said after a beat.

Mateo met his eyes. "I know."

"Mateo," Juan said. For some reason, his voice went shaky. "I don't want to… What I mean is, I can't—" He huffed and grabbed Mateo by his shoulders. "I don't want this all for myself. It's too much." His grasp was so firm it pinched. "I'll never handle it. But with you? With you, I could do anything." He shot Mateo a tilted grin. "Even fly to the moon."

Mateo bursting out laughing, because him helping Juan run Los Cielos? No. That wasn't what he wanted. Not the practicality of running a business day to day. He wanted to spread his wings! Do something creative! Write or maybe make music. Fortunately, as the younger brother, he'd never have to worry about Los Cielos being left in his hands. He pulled Juan into a bear hug, pounding his skull with his knuckles. "Now, who's being the knucklehead? Huh?"

"Me." The word was muffled, with Juan speaking into Mateo's coat collar.

Mateo tightened his squeeze on his brother. "What's that? Say it louder!"

"Me!" Juan burst out of his hold, his whole face red. "I'm going to kill you, Mateo."

Mateo leapt onto his horse, jamming his boots into the stirrups. "You're going to have to catch me first. Come on, Blaze! Yah!" He dug in his heels. "Let's go!"

"Argh!" Juan jumped up on Toro and cantered after him, faster and faster, closing in on Blaze at a brisk clip as they tore across the vineyard, weaving through rows of vines, their horses' hooves thundering against the earth and spewing up dust behind them.

But this time, Mateo's horse was faster.

TWENTY

MATEO HEARD A SOUND. HE'D been so lost in his reverie, he'd stopped playing his guitar. It rested idly on his knee, so he set it aside, leaning it against the tree. He raised his hand to his forehead, squinting into the daylight beaming down on him. There, at the top of the hill, just on this side of the small cemetery and historic vines…

Wait. Is that Toro?

Yes. His heart pounded. *And Katie,* her lovely silhouette framed by the distant mountains. She scanned the area, then her eyes lit on his. A smile graced her lips, and it dazzled like sunshine. All at once, he could see his Papi Monchi and imagine how he must have felt arriving on that summit with Mamacita. The image of Katie wearing Abuela's wedding gown wedged into Mateo's brain, and his palms went damp. It was almost like he'd seen a glimpse into his future. A future that involved Katie—with him and not Juan.

He shook off the vision and waved her over, and she guided Toro down the hill, poised in the saddle like an expert horsewoman, her brown ponytail bobbing behind her. It held a reddish cast in the sun, almost auburn, though he'd never noticed that indoors. Mateo stood as she approached, trying to ignore the intense humming in his veins. The attraction. The rising heat as his heart galloped in tune to Toro's thundering hoofbeats, carrying Katie closer.

"Abuelo...said...you might be here!" Her words came out in gasps of air as she caught her breath. She was dressed in jeans and a heavy jacket. She wore a hat and mittens, and her cheeks were bright pink.

"Katie." He walked toward her as she stilled her horse.

"Whoa, Toro." She gently pulled back on the reins. "Whoa."

He stared at her, perplexed. "What are you doing here?"

"Your family was worried about you."

"Yeah, I"—he raked a hand through his hair—"lost track of time." He met her eyes, and they shimmered like gemstones, richly beautiful and warm. She and Toro made a stunning pair. So stunning, he couldn't stop goggling at them in wonder. Of all the things he'd expected out here, it wasn't Katie and Toro surprising him.

"That your horse?" she asked, observing Blaze lift his head from the stream where he'd been drinking.

Mateo nodded.

"He's beautiful. What an incredible dark brown coat. What's his name?"

"Blaze."

She smiled. "I might have guessed that from the jagged white stripe on his nose."

Blaze moseyed on over to greet Toro and Katie. He snorted and scraped his hoof against the ground.

Mateo laughed. "Blaze wants to know what happened to Juan. He looks so different!"

Katie placed a hand on her chest, getting his joke. "Yeah. I guess I *am* a little shorter." She rolled her eyes.

"You're a lot more than that." He hated that his voice went scratchy.

She peered down at him. "What do you mean?"

"You're a lot more girly."

"Guilty." Her tone was a touch saucy, causing more heat to rise in his neck, and he was already burning hot. She dismounted Toro while Mateo watched her, mesmerized.

"Where did you learn to ride?"

She rested her hand on a saddlebag. "My friend Jane taught me."

"That's cool."

"Yeah, we were friends for a lot of years."

"You still in touch?"

Katie frowned. "Not really."

"I'm sorry."

"It's okay," she said. "Time moves on." She reached into a saddlebag and removed a package, holding it out toward him.

"What's that?"

"Your Titi Mon called it a *bocadillo*. She was concerned about you skipping lunch."

"I'm sorry if anybody worried." Mateo stepped toward her, accepting the package. "Thanks."

She stuck her hand back into the saddlebag, fishing for something else. She located a second package that looked like the first one. "Can you hold this?" He took that from her as well.

"Two sandwiches?" he asked. Mateo chuckled. "I'm not sure I'm that hungry."

"Well, I am." She shot him a playful pout. "I'm starved."

"Oh no. You haven't eaten either?"

"Not yet." She opened the other saddlebag.

"How did you get roped into being the delivery person?"

Katie shrugged. "Your dad was going to come looking for you, but he and your mom got called in to the hospital."

Mateo's panic spiked, but then he read Katie's calm expression. If Juan were in trouble, she wouldn't look so relaxed. "Is Juan okay?" he asked, just to be sure.

"Yes. The doctors want to do more scans, and your parents had to give permission."

"I...see."

She stood up on her tiptoes, attempting to reach something in the saddlebag that was eluding her.

"Can I help?"

"Nope. I've got it." She yanked harder, twisting her arm around.

Mateo stroked his chin, amused by her acrobatics. "What's in there anyway?"

She produced a bottle, and her grin swept the gloomy storm clouds from his soul. "Wine!"

Mateo studied the label of the bottle as Katie handed it to him. It was their newest vintage of cab franc, freshly out this year. "Whose idea was this?"

"Titi Mon's."

He laughed. "Titi Mon's full of good ideas."

"Abuelo thought the wine was a good idea too."

"Did he? Huh." Mateo's face warmed when he recalled Abuelo's insinuation about him getting together with Katie, assuming she was ready to break up with Juan. But Mateo would never in a million years steal his brother's girlfriend, fake or not. Visions and images were one thing, because those had been involuntary. Actions were different, and Mateo was very good at controlling his actions. He'd always been. Until Katie came around, making it harder for him to maintain his resolve—and keep his distance. But he'd done both those things so far and could easily keep himself on the same course. If he worked at it.

She glanced at Toro as he followed Blaze to the stream. "They won't run away?"

"Those guys? Never." He cocked his head at the horses. "They have it too good here to want to leave."

Katie smiled at their surroundings. "Los Cielos is pretty ideal. I don't blame them."

Yeah, Mateo was starting to get that now.

He stashed the wine bottle under one arm, holding the sandwich packages in his hands. "Did Titi Mon send a blanket?" There was nothing inherently wrong about the two of them sharing an innocent meal together in the countryside. Even though they were alone and very, very far from other people, that didn't mean there was anything untoward about this. He intended to play the perfect gentleman. His shoulders sank. Per usual.

"Toro!" she commanded. "Wait!"

The animal stopped in his tracks, eyeing her carefully. She tucked a lock of hair behind her ear and plodded toward him. Toro waited patiently like she was his owner.

"I just need to check one more thing." Katie peeked into a saddle-bag. "We have...napkins!" she announced, extracting a small pile of paper napkins. "And water..." She removed one bottle and then another.

Good. He could take a long cool swig from one of those and clear his jumbled head. He'd had no business thinking those things about Katie before. She wasn't supposed to be *his* vision. She was Juan's, assuming she even wanted to be with Juan anymore. And if she didn't, it would be a stretch to imagine her wanting Mateo. That would prove doubly awkward anyway, seeing as how she'd started out with his brother.

She scooted around to the other side of the horse, passing by Toro's head. "You're a good boy," she said, rubbing his nose. He nuzzled against her palm like they were best friends.

How had she and Juan's horse bonded already? It was incredible. Then again, animals could sense the goodness in people. Katie was sweet and kind.

She stretched way up on her tiptoes, rummaging around in the bag. "Hang on," she said, hopping up and down a little.

Mateo couldn't help but grin. She was one hundred percent adorable but two hundred percent hands-off. *No touching, no holding, and definitely no kissing.*

He blocked out the mental image of him devouring her sensuous mouth with his. It was bad enough he'd thought of it at the Christmas tree farm and then agonized over the fantasy, again and again.

But okay. He had to get her attention somehow. Very properly. He cleared his throat, but she was too preoccupied with her saddlebag hunt to hear him.

He lightly tapped her on her shoulder with just his pointer finger. Really fast.

She wheeled around, her eyebrows arched.

"Why don't you hold all this?" he said, handing his bundle of stuff to her. "I'll grab it."

"The blanket got kind of scrunched up in the bottom." She grimaced cutely, and his heart took another dive.

Come on, man. Snap yourself out of it. Now's definitely not the time.

And the time would be *never*.

He peeked in the saddlebag, then plucked the plaid picnic blanket out with his fingers. A corkscrew lay beneath it. "Good old Titi Mon." He held up the corkscrew for Katie to see. "She thought of everything." He strode over to the tree and shook out the blanket. "How about this spot?"

"Looks perfect." She grinned at his guitar. "Guess you were out here playing?"

He settled the blanket on the ground, stretching out all four corners. "Playing sometimes helps me think." Which was great when the thoughts were welcome ones. Unlike the night he'd written that tune while thinking about Katie, the one she'd embarrassingly caught him playing in his apartment. He could never tell her he'd composed it, pouring his unrequited passion for her into the piece. He motioned for her to sit, and she did while he did the same. They both positioned themselves on the picnic blanket, getting comfortable.

"Did it help this time?" She darted a gaze at his guitar, and he sighed.

"A little." While reminiscing about the past hadn't solved anything, it had made him feel better about Juan by reminding him of the brotherly relationship they shared. "So," he said, wanting to address this. Otherwise, it would be hanging over them the whole time they had lunch. "I'm guessing Mom told you about Juan?"

She sighed. "Yeah, I'm afraid she did."

"I'm sorry, Katie. I'm sure that was another blow to you."

"Another?"

"On top of his accident."

"Right," she said dourly. "Nobody expected that."

He decided not to bring up the fake girlfriend issue. He still had his doubts as to why his brother would engage in such a scheme, but then again, Juan was full of surprises these days. Maybe that part didn't matter so much at the moment anyway. Katie either *was* or *wasn't* Juan's pretend or very new girlfriend. This had to be an incredibly confusing situation for her either way.

"Katie, about what I said the other day about you not dumping Juan. It was wrong of me to interfere." Remorse filled his soul, because the last thing he wanted to do was make things harder for her. "Forgive me?"

"It's fine, Mateo. I don't blame you for what you said. You were only looking out for your brother and your family." Understanding filled her eyes, and then she made an admission. "Your mom asked me to stick around through Christmas too. With Abuela not doing well, she didn't want one more change."

Mateo's jaw tensed. This was all too much. Too big an ask. "I'm really sorry about my family putting pressure on you." He swallowed hard. "Myself included. None of this is right." The waning sun cast a circle of light around her, like an angel's halo. "No one should be in your position, Katie. If you want to go—"

"I don't!" She cupped her hand to her mouth like she hadn't meant to say that. "I mean." She shyly ducked her chin, then peered up at him through long lashes. He nearly lost his mind. She was *so* incredibly beautiful. "I like being around Los Cielos." She paused and licked her lips, those make-a-man-crazy kissable lips. Then, she added softly, "And you."

His heart pounded. "I like being around you too."

She stared into his eyes so long it was almost like they were on a journey together. The two of them on horseback, riding into Los Cielos, arriving from Mount Hood. No. Wait. That was Papi Monchi and Mamacita. But the feeling deep in his heart said, *Yes, this is the same. This is how it was for my great-great-grandparents when they accepted the challenge to move here together from Mexico.* How it was when Abuelo met Abuela and when his dad first fell for his mom.

Mateo's breath hitched. He was *not* falling for Katie. Was he?

Katie's cheeks burned bright red, and wait. Was that a shimmer of interest in her pretty brown eyes?

Maybe he'd been kidding himself by thinking that he and Katie could never be together. Suppose she'd never been meant to be with Juan but had been meant to be with him all along? His heart would burst with happiness if she'd be willing to give him a chance. But that wouldn't solve the here and now and their problems with Juan and the business.

He reached for the wine, and she gave it to him, then watched as he uncorked it. "Will you have some?" he asked hoarsely. He needed a sip, a big one. He needed to stop getting so easily reeled in by her heartwarming smile and gorgeous brown eyes, and tantalizing himself with the excruciating possibilities. No. *Impossibilities* that could never come true.

"I guess I'd better." She frowned playfully. "After Titi Mon went to all that trouble." She tossed her ponytail behind her in a sassy move, and his heart slammed against his chest.

Okay. He couldn't help it. She was freaking adorable. Her tenderhearted kindness beamed brightly like a brilliant burst of sunshine streaming through the clouds.

Mateo's eyebrows arched. "I didn't see any cups. Did you?"

She shook her head.

"I guess we'll have to wing it." He winked, and her face reddened. He enjoyed the sweep of color on her cheeks and the way her eyes sparkled like starlight under the dark canopy of the tree. He tipped the bottle up, taking a drink. A hint of sweet cherry hit his tongue, then a burst of birch and pine, followed by a black pepper finish, tangy and delicious, lighting up his taste buds. Mateo smacked his lips. "It's a party in a bottle," he told her. "Taste it."

"A party, hmm?" She took a drink, swishing the liquid around in her mouth like he had done, her eyebrows knitted together in concentration. After a moment, she swallowed and wiped her mouth with the back of her hand. Her eyes flew wide. "Wow. Delicious!"

He laughed with delight. "Look at you, becoming a wine connoisseur."

"Hardly. Most wines that I drink cost under ten dollars. Some of them under five."

"No reason you can't develop expensive tastes."

She examined his smirk. "Oh yes, there is. It's called a budget."

"All right." He settled back on his elbows, ready to talk about anything for a while other than his failing family business and Juan. Mostly, he wanted to talk about her and probe into that intriguing mind of hers. Make her laugh a few more times. Elicit that heart-melting smile. "If cost were no object, what would you do?"

"Like travel, you mean?"

"Sure. Why not? You can start with that."

"Well." She shrugged shyly. "I think I mentioned I've always wanted to go to France."

"Paris, yeah?"

Her face lit up in a grin. "That's right. I'd love to see the Louvre."

"It's very nice."

Her expression grew animated. "You've been there?"

"I wouldn't mind going again." *And I'd take you in a minute.* "Where else?"

She started to tick off her list of dream vacation spots, and many matched places on Mateo's own list. He gauged she'd make a great travel partner. As a girlfriend—flames leapt through him—or a wife.

"Where would you like to go?" She passed him a sandwich package, and they both unwrapped their *bocadillos*, which were made of cheese and Spanish ham on French bread. Mateo hadn't realized how hungry he was until now. He dug eagerly into his food, enjoying the scenery and his picnic companion. As much as he loved his brother, it was nice not to think about Juan for once and all the trouble that he'd caused.

It felt good to relax. Take a breather.

"I made a collage, you know." She wiped her mouth with her napkin. She reached for the wine bottle, and he passed it to her with a grin.

"What kind of collage?"

"Of all the places I'd like to travel."

"That's cool. Where is it?"

She took a sip of wine and closed her eyes, savoring the taste. "Mmm. This is very tasty." She handed him back the bottle. "The collage is over my couch."

"I'd like to see it."

"I'll show it to you sometime." She dropped her head and giggled. "Want to know something else?" She pursed her lips, looking impish about it. "I added Seville."

He was so incredibly pleased. "Did you?" He splayed a hand on his chest. "On account of me?"

"Yeah, on account of you." She nudged his arm, and her eyes danced.

Tingles coursed through him like an electric rain. A rain that he ached to become drenched in. "Then I'm very honored."

She absorbed the landscape around them. The sun was already sinking low. It had to be past four, approaching five. But Mateo was having a good time and didn't want to go.

"I've learned a lot about your world by being at Los Cielos."

"I'm really happy about that." He was eager to delve into hers. "I'd love to hear more about your art."

She blushed deeply. "What? Why?"

"Because," he said, "it's important to you. I could tell that at the hospital."

She quirked a grin. "You learned all that based on me sketching a coffee cup?"

Warmth spread through his chest. "I'm a very intuitive guy."

She bit her lip and studied him. "Yeah, you are." She gazed out over the vineyard, leaning back on her hands while bracing herself on her arms. "You're right though. My art is important to me, just not in the way I thought it was at first."

His eyebrows rose. "What do you mean?"

"I mean." She pursed her lips and mulled it over. "I wanted to work commercially before. Way back when I was a teenager and thinking of going to college, that was my dream."

He leaned toward her. "But not anymore?"

She shrugged. "I think my dreams are changing."

When she didn't add anything more, he decided not to push her on it, figuring she'd share when she was ready. He was appreciating the gentle camaraderie between them and didn't want to endanger the easygoing vibe.

"Well, whatever they are," he said, meaning to encourage her, "it's not too late to make them happen."

"No." She appeared distant a moment. "I suppose not." She cocked her chin to study him. "What about you and your dreams?"

He exhaled heavily. "Ah. Those are a bit complicated right now." All this while, he'd believed his dreams were about his music: making and playing guitars. He understood now those would never be enough. He wanted—needed—more.

"Because of"—she seemed like she was about to say *Juan and the winery* but changed her mind—"everything?"

Mateo leaned back, propping himself on his elbows. "Yeah. That's an understatement."

"You want to know what I think?" she asked in perky tones.

"I do. I really do."

She wore a pert smile on her lips. "I think you shouldn't give up on your dreams either. I mean, you're only thirty-one. So you never know."

He valued the sentiment and her kind words. He hadn't really talked to anybody about his desire to build and sell guitars, except his ex.

Gabriela had basically dismissed the idea, asking why he'd want to do that when he could have a vineyard. She'd never really understood a lot of things about him, just like he'd never totally gotten her. It was honestly for the best that she'd gotten back with Tomas. The best for both Gabriela and Tomas. And also for him.

"Thanks, Katie," he told her. "I'll definitely keep them in mind." She was so great at making him see situations clearly; he wanted to know even more about her. "Will you tell me about your mom?"

Her eyes grew misty, and he worried he'd made a misstep. "Why do you want to know?"

"She must have been a very special person."

"She was." Katie stared at the picnic blanket, then met his eyes. "So was my dad."

"Will you tell me about him too?"

She turned away, and Mateo sat up on the blanket.

"Katie. Hey. Whoa. I'm sorry. What's wrong?"

"Nothing, really." She crumpled her paper napkin in her hand, gazing back at him. Her lips trembled. "You're just being so sweet."

He steadied her wobbly chin with his hand. "If any woman deserves sweet, Katie…" His voice combed through the wind. "It's you."

She smiled softly. "Thanks, Mateo."

"Besides which." He leaned back on his elbows, crossing one ankle over the other as he stretched out his legs. "I really do want to know."

"All right." She shifted her position and leaned back on her elbows too. "I'll tell you."

He held up the bottle. "Want one more swig?"

"Yeah." She chuckled. "I do."

Mateo got lost in her stories about the volunteer work she did and how she'd used helping others to cope with the loss of her mom as a kid. Her folks had been good parents, and she'd been loved, but tragedies had ripped them from her life too soon. Mateo's life was so filled to the brim with family, it was hard—and heartbreaking—for him to imagine a life without it. But Katie had soldiered on, doing the best with what she had. What impressed him most about her was that she didn't seem bitter about her past and somehow remained grateful for the memories.

"So wait," he said in surprise. "You mean to say that after your mom died, you and your dad never celebrated Christmas?"

She sadly shook her head.

"But you're all about Christmas in those Christmas sweaters and earrings of yours."

"I've never given up on the true spirit of the season, that's true. I've still got my fake tree, even if it's a small one."

He laughed good-naturedly. "The one we bought at Cortinis' must have looked like a monster to you!"

She nudged him with her elbow, and he appreciated her body warmth, scooting a bit closer to her on the blanket. If she noticed, she didn't let on. "It *is* a monster," she agreed, "compared to my tree." She peered up at him, and his heart stilled. She was not only beautiful but also had such an amazing outlook on life.

He didn't know how her most special Christmas memory had involved receiving a large crafting board, glue, and scissors—those seemed like such meager gifts—but it had. Mateo almost felt ashamed by the embarrassment of riches he'd been treated to over the years. While his parents weren't billionaires by any stretch, they and his grandparents were all very well set. He frowned to himself. *Had been well set until Juan had driven their finances into the ground.*

"What about your past Christmases?" she asked him. "Any favorites stand out?"

He ran a hand through his hair, glad to focus on a lighthearted memory. "There was the year Juan and I got Toro and Blaze. That was epic." His gaze fell on the horses in the afternoon shadows growing long. He and Juan adored those *beasts*, as they jokingly called them. He and his family were *not* going to sell them or the land that they grazed on. He didn't want to let any staff go either and had been working on a modified schedule. Reduced hours were better than no hours at all. He only wished he could do better, but this latest maneuver by Juan had been so unsettling, it was hard to understand how they'd come back from it. Maybe he'd been kidding himself about finding a solution. He might have found a tentative one before Juan's wild outlay of the vineyard's cash. Now, though, he just didn't know.

The sun had started going down, so he and Katie couldn't stay here forever, but he hated the thought of leaving this beautiful spot and her company. He was also glad to have something to focus on other than the failing state of his family business.

"Did Santa bring them, or were you boys too old to believe in the jolly old elf?"

He laughed, his tension easing. Katie was always so great to be around. "We probably were too old for Santa. I was eleven and Juan was twelve, but my parents went along with the whole Santa thing all the way up until we went to college." His neck warmed. "They still fill our stockings, as you saw."

She grinned sweetly. "I think that really nice. Having traditions." She cast her eyes over the horses. "So about getting Blaze and Toro?"

"Oh yeah." He chuckled at the funny memory. "Mom and Dad both knew we wanted horses of our own but said we'd have to wait another year until I was twelve and Juan thirteen, which really got Juan worked up, because I'd be getting my horse a year sooner than he would."

"A little brotherly competition?" she teased.

"Yeah, somewhat." He shook his head. "In any case, Santa came and left us video games, which were great and all, but just not—"

"Let me guess," Katie said. "Horses."

Mateo clucked his tongue. "Right. Horses. Then Three Kings' Day comes along—"

"That's the holiday you told me about in the hospital?"

"Yeah, it's the twelfth day of Christmas, January sixth. But normally the Three Kings just brought me and Juan small trinkets. The bigger things came from Santa."

"But not that year?" she guessed.

"Nope. After breakfast, Abuelo said in his gruff voice, 'Juan, Mateo, last night, your Abuela and I heard a big commotion down at the stables.'

"'Yes,' Abuela said, 'so we went to investigate, and we saw— camels! Three men in royal garments rode them into the sky!'"

Katie laughed at his imitation of Abuela's Spanish accent. "That's so cute."

"It was cute," Mateo assured her. "Juan and I took one look at each other and ran all the way down to the stables in our sweat-pants and T-shirts without even putting on any shoes."

Katie giggled, evidently trying to imagine the two boys racing down the dirt road to the stables, barefoot in the December chill. "No coats?"

"No coats." He grinned, reliving the moment that he and Juan had burst through the stable doors. "Alonzo was waiting. He told Juan three mysterious strangers had left a shiny black colt for him, and then he smiled at me, nodding toward Blaze." Mateo sighed. "It was love at first—" He turned back to Katie and caught his breath.

Her eyes sparkled in the waning light. "Sight?"

"Yes." His pulse pounded in his ears. The breeze caught

loose tendrils of her hair, sending them spiraling around her pink cheeks, and in that moment, he wished he had Katie's artistic talent. Because if he were a painter, he'd create a portrait of her beauty in the twilight, immortalizing this moment forever. "Do you believe in that?"

"What? Love at first sight?"

Was she wanting, hoping what he was? That she was never meant to be with Juan?

He placed a hand on her cheek. "Yes," he said, diving into her eyes.

She licked her lips and they glistened, moist and inviting. "I'm not sure."

Man, how he wanted to kiss her and erase all doubt.

TWENTY-ONE

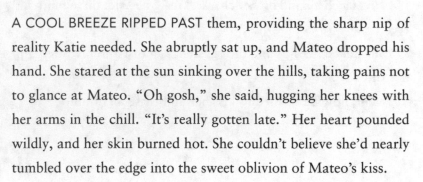

A COOL BREEZE RIPPED PAST them, providing the sharp nip of reality Katie needed. She abruptly sat up, and Mateo dropped his hand. She stared at the sun sinking over the hills, taking pains not to glance at Mateo. "Oh gosh," she said, hugging her knees with her arms in the chill. "It's really gotten late." Her heart pounded wildly, and her skin burned hot. She couldn't believe she'd nearly tumbled over the edge into the sweet oblivion of Mateo's kiss.

His mouth had been so near, with just the width of a butterfly's wings between them, his dimpled chin closing in. Had he really been about to kiss her, or had that been all in her head? Maybe it had just been in the moment? A fleeting instant of weakness inspired by their intimate conversation and the wine.

He seemed to shake the spell off, sitting up as well. "You're right." Toro and Blaze appeared to be growing restless, pacing by the edge of the stream. "We need to head back. The others are probably wondering about us."

She and Mateo had to have been out here close to two hours. Not that she regretted a minute of it. She'd never had a picnic like this. She'd also never known anyone like Mateo either.

He scooted into a crouch and stood, holding out his hand. Katie set her palm in his, her heart racing. Then he tugged her to her feet and her heart beat harder. They stood close enough for him to hold her. But then it would be all over, because once they started kissing, she'd never want to stop. And they had real-world worries to contend with at the main house. They couldn't avoid facing those any longer.

She backed up a step and so did he, both equally raising their defenses. Even if he was becoming interested in her, Katie could *not* become involved with Mateo. Not now. Not until Juan had recovered and the problems concerning the vineyard had been solved. If he'd even want her then.

Mateo hung his head. "Guess we didn't really solve anything, did we?"

"Not exactly." They'd actually made things more compli-cated. Their conversation had flowed so naturally that Katie had almost forgotten the troubles looming over Los Cielos until now. Maybe so had Mateo for a bit. They seemed to be full-tilt crashing down on him at present. "But, Mateo?"

He looked up.

"I don't think you should give up either. I mean, there has to be a way to undo what Juan has done or at least amend it."

He sighed. "Yeah. I was awake half the night thinking about that, but the pit that Juan has dug for us is so deep, it's hard to see a way out." His laughter was tinged with melancholy. "I mean, we don't even have a ladder."

Katie's gaze travelled up the hill to the heart of the vineyard and the historic vines, held by a trellis and climbing toward purple twilight. "No," she said. "But you do have your history."

He followed her line of vision, then looked back at her. "What are you saying?"

"Mateo," Katie said, a solution occurring. Her heart skipped a beat. "What if Juan's ideas weren't all bad? Maybe wider distribution is *good* for the business. Can help make it more money."

"But, Katie?" He raked a hand through his hair. "Cloudy Crest Wines? Are you kid—"

"No. Not Cloudy Crest Wines." She held up both hands. "Los Cielos Cellars wines, gone global."

His face was awash with confusion. "How?"

She snapped her fingers, thinking of Papi Monchi and Mamacita. "Your great-great-grandparents," she said. She stared up at him, her pulse humming. "That's it! They're the key!"

He rubbed the side of his neck. "Key?"

"To this!" She thumped him lightly on his chest with the back of her hand. She gestured around the vineyard. "All of it. Your Martinez family history. Your legacy. That amazing story about your Papi Monchi and Mamacita."

"What about it?"

"You should *market* it." She grinned broadly. "Think about it, Mateo. You could print a short version of their story on the back of every bottle of Los Cielos Cellars wine. Maybe you do need a new logo. Maybe your old one of an oak cask is outdated, but you don't have to replace it with clinking wineglasses."

Understanding broke over his face. "Like a map of my great-great-grandparents' journey, for example?" He ran both hands through his hair. "Or—" He stared at Toro and Blaze. "A sketch of the two of them on horseback?" His eyes glinted with inspiration. "Or maybe even of their mule carrying the vines?"

"Yes!" Katie bounced up and down on her heels and clapped her hands together. "The vineyard could expand *and* rebrand—just not as Cloudy Crest Wines. You could keep your family name and just update things. Modernize."

Mateo grinned in amazement, his eyes growing huge. "New logo. New labels. Twist caps!" Then his face fell in a frown, disappointment crashing down on him. "All those things cost money, Katie. And Juan has already sunk us deep in the hole."

She set her chin, deciding to share her connection. It couldn't hurt. "Listen, I know almost everyone in town because of the diner. Mr. Elroy comes in nearly every day."

"Elroy who runs the savings and loan?"

"Yes, him." She nodded. "He's big on supporting local businesses. Maybe it's not too late to put the brakes on some of what Juan's set in motion. What if there's a way to keep the advertising contract by changing up your product? Same with the distribution agreement?"

Mateo sighed. "I don't know if those businesses will go for it."

"You don't know that they won't," Katie stubbornly replied. "And maybe Mr. Elroy can help you all with a small business loan to get you over the hump?"

The twinkle in his eyes said he was already strategizing a way to make this work.

"So?" she asked, walking toward him. "What do you think?"

He placed his hands on her shoulders. "Katie," he said. "You're a genius!" Without warning, he pulled her forward and into a kiss—right on the lips. His clumsy kiss landed hard with a smack, and Mateo jerked back, releasing her like a live wire. "Oh wow, Katie." His neck went red. His face too, and the tops of his ears turned crimson. "I'm so, so sorry about that."

Her lips burned hot from his chaste kiss, and her cheeks steamed too. "It's, ah, okay." She stepped back and so did he as they both caught their breath. "It was in the moment." If it had lasted another second, she would have latched on to Mateo and never let him go, giving back as good as she got.

"Yeah, but still." He appeared mortified. "I didn't mean to—never would have—" He scrubbed a hand across his face. "What I mean is, it *wasn't* like that."

Katie's heart wrenched. He might as well have stuck a great big pin in her fantasy bubble about actually getting together with him. His exuberance over saving the vineyard had caused that kiss, and the joy on Mateo's face was worth any small ounce of heartache it caused her. If the plan actually worked, that would be a hundred times better for the entire Martinez family and their winery.

She exhaled shakily. "Same. Me either." She'd been just as guilty of laying a kiss on his cheek the night they'd decorated the Martinezes' Christmas tree. "I guess now we're even." She laughed, trying to make light of it, because if she didn't, she might cry from sheer disappointment.

Where had her head been anyway? Thinking that she and Mateo could make it as a couple? Even for an instant? No. What she'd taken for romantic desire had merely been polite interest on his part. That was so Mateo. Gracious to a fault.

He stared at her, puzzled, so she explained. "My good-night kiss a couple of nights ago?"

He pensively rubbed his cheek, then shook off his stupor. "Oh, that!" He pursed his lips. "That was nothing. I mean, I didn't read anything into it." But still, his eyebrows twitched.

Gah. He'd probably thought she'd been making a play for him while the man she supposedly loved was in a coma. Awesome. Doubly awesome, because maybe she *had been* doing that without even knowing it.

"That's great," she said, playing it off. She swallowed her lie. "I didn't read anything into *that* either." She rolled her eyes like it would be silly to think otherwise while mentally kicking herself. The tragic thing was, she hadn't meant to fall for Mateo. Somewhere between their Christmas tree shopping and listening to him playing his guitar, major feelings for him had snuck up on her—and then landed like an avalanche. Despite trying to convince herself she was destined to be with Juan, her attraction to Mateo had persisted, growing stronger and stronger, until it had become inescapable.

Mateo sure looked like he wanted to escape somewhere, putting greater distance between him and her, and she got it. He didn't need one more complication in his already complicated life. His focus was on his brother getting better and on saving his family business, just as it should be.

She helped him pick up their trash and wrap what was left of their sandwiches to stuff back in the saddlebags. When they began folding the picnic blanket, they nearly bumbled into each other, then quickly jumped apart.

"Oh, uh, sorry!" He released his portion of the picnic blanket, letting her fold it the rest of the way up. Great. He didn't even want to come within arm's length of her.

"No problem," she said, although her face felt just as hot as his looked. What did he think? That she would pounce on him and tug him into her arms? No. She wouldn't chase after a man who clearly had no interest in her—for all the right reasons. She'd been deluding herself with her vivid dreams about dating Mateo.

Mateo cleared his throat and moved even farther away. Yep. He was steering clear. "So we're, um, good?"

She inched back too, not eager to give him the impression she'd pursue him anyway. She wasn't that dense.

"All's forgiven?" He stumbled over a tree root, and something clanged. The strings of his guitar left a haunting echo filling the valley. He'd knocked it over with his foot. He gaped down at it, mortified, and Katie shot him a glance.

"Absolutely."

"Great." He hastily scooped up his guitar and slid it into his case.

The poor guy was beside himself over that innocent kiss. Hurt welled in her throat. Well, what did she expect? That one accidental kiss would change everything? The only thing it had done was cement Mateo's inclination to keep his guard up around her. How humiliating for him to intuit she'd harbored this secret crush. He'd never believe her if she tried to explain how her feelings for him were different from how she used to feel about Juan. She was still unpacking that herself.

"I can't wait to tell Mom and Dad about your idea," Mateo

said. "Abuelo and Abuela too." He walked toward Blaze, strapping his guitar case in behind his saddle. "Want to be there with me?"

"I don't think so," she said. She clicked her tongue at Toro, nabbing his attention and getting her grasp on his reins. "This should be between you and your family."

He nodded and didn't insist, assuring her she'd made the right choice. "How soon do you think you can talk to Mr. Elroy?" He'd finished with Blaze and had begun reattaching the saddlebags on Toro.

"The man is as punctual as clockwork," Katie said while Mateo yanked on the saddlebag straps. "Predictable too. He'll be in at seven for two eggs over easy with a side of bacon and rye toast."

Mateo laughed. "That sounds delicious." He patted Toro on the neck and returned to Blaze, getting ready to mount his horse. She was glad to have moved on to another subject and away from that kiss. Mateo seemed ecstatic to be talking about anything other than that too.

"It is pretty delicious," she said. "Mark's a great cook."

He watched her place one hand on the saddle horn. "Need help over there?"

"No thanks," she told him, climbing up on Toro. She hadn't realized how easily the horseback riding would come back to her.

Mateo brought Blaze around, facing the steep hill with his back to the stream, and Katie did the same with Toro. "I'll talk to my folks tonight," he said. "I'll want to go and see Juan in the morning. I'm betting the rest of my family will too. Tomorrow's Christmas Eve." He tilted his head at her as they began moving along at a steady trot, their horses plodding toward the family graveyard. "You'll be there, right?" When she hesitated, he added, "You did say you'd stick around until after Christmas?"

Katie swallowed past the raw burn in her throat. "I did," she said weakly, but inside her heart was breaking, because every time she saw the Martinezes, it was like another silent goodbye. And now she had that impulsive kiss from Mateo to additionally mess with her head.

"I, uh, have to work early." She hung her head, trying to block the memory of that kiss and all the other special moments they'd spent together. "But I'll try to stop by...sometime." She avoided his gaze, intentionally remaining vague.

As she rode alongside him, their horses' companionable strides oddly broke her heart. It wasn't so much that Toro and Blaze's easy camaraderie made her sad; it was more that the way they got along accentuated the fragility of her connection with Mateo. During their picnic and their talk, their conversation had flowed so easily, and the mood had been lighthearted and warm. Like they were old friends who'd chatted all their lives. The way they rode in tandem now seemed familiar as well. Like it was natural for the two of them to be traversing the gorgeous grounds of Los Cielos on horseback together. And yet this couldn't last.

The sun dipped below the mountains, sending long shadows over the hills and weaving dark trails through the vineyard. She let the clip-clopping of the horses' hooves carry her years back in time to Mateo's great-great-grandparents and their romantic journey. Could she ever love someone enough to make that kind of sacrifice? She stole a peek at Mateo's handsome profile on Blaze, and her present zoomed into focus, causing a dull ache in her heart. Maybe, yes. If that someone was half as stellar as Mateo. But Christmas Day was the day after tomorrow, and her role here as Juan's fake girlfriend would soon be over.

Then she'd be back to her lonely little bungalow while the Martinezes gathered together to celebrate their holiday. She couldn't fathom how she could participate with them, given the secrets she held in her heart. About how she felt about Mateo and all the lies she'd allowed them to believe concerning her relationship with Juan. There wasn't any doubt that Juan would recover. The question was *when*. And when Juan got better, the existence she now clung to by a tentative thread would go up in a poof, like a helium balloon disappearing into the clouds.

TWENTY-TWO

MATEO BURST INTO THE MAIN house alive with excitement. "*Familia*," he said. "I've got great news!"

His grandparents sat by the fire in their favorite chairs, and his parents read on the sofa. His mom lowered her book, and his dad placed his e-reader on the coffee table.

"Mateo?" his dad asked. "What's going on?"

Titi Mon rested in the recliner with her swollen ankles elevated. She set her tablet in her lap. "Did something happen?"

Abuelo's ears perked up. "On your picnic?"

"*Bueno, hijo?*" Abuela asked expectantly. She yanked on her shawl, leaning forward.

The whole room keened toward Mateo like he was some sort of amazing bright light. And he did feel brimming with sunshine. If he was able to reorganize things as planned, there'd be real hope for saving the vineyard.

His mom's eyebrows rose. "Well, come on. Don't keep us in suspense."

Mateo deposited the saddlebags on the kitchen counter, planning to stow away the leftovers from his picnic with Katie. "I believe we've found a way to keep Los Cielos afloat." He'd been mulling it over ever since Katie revealed her inspired proposal. Of course they could expand and rebrand. By revamping the Los Cielos Cellars label while maintaining the vineyard's name *and* capitalizing on its compelling history.

"We?" Abuelo's eyes twinkled. "You and Katie?" He peered at Titi Mon. "Didn't I tell you that I sensed something?"

"You did," Titi Mon said. "It's true." She stared at Mateo. "I'm not sure I approve of you stealing your brother's girlfriend, but given what he's—"

"Stealing? Whoa!" Mateo flagged a hand in her direction. "Titi Mon, nobody's stealing anything. Or, uh."—he cleared his throat—"Anyone."

Abuela peered at Titi Mon, then scrutinized her husband. "What do you know about this, Esteban?"

Abuelo tugged on a corner of his mustache. "Nothing."

Mateo turned up his hands. "Because there's nothing going on!" All eyes locked on him, and he lowered his voice. "Between me and Katie." He shifted on his feet. "We've just become... friends."

"Oh *sí*?" Abuela studied him, then Abuelo shot her a wink.

"If she no longer wants Juan..." he whispered gruffly, motioning with his hands.

Abuela clearly got the implication. "*Oh sí.*" She clasped her hands together, wearing a happy grin.

Wow. It wasn't like he and his brother were interchangeable parts in Katie's mind. Guilt trickled through him when he recalled his kiss and the somewhat romantic picnic they'd shared. Maybe he had been trying to usurp his brother subconsciously. Which was one hundred percent *wrong*. Also why he'd stopped himself from kissing Katie a second time and like there was no tomorrow. And man, how he'd burned to do that.

He pulled over an ottoman, taking a seat near the hearth, where the heat from the fire masked the warmth on his face. If he'd been thinking more clearly, he would have stopped himself from kissing her to begin with. But his joy over possibly saving Los Cielos had been overwhelming.

"Okay, here's the deal." Mateo rubbed his palms together, holding the group's rapt attention. Then he filled them in on Katie's brilliant suggestions.

His dad sat back on the sofa and crossed his arms. "I like it," he said. "I like it a lot."

His mom nodded. "This just might work."

His parents turned to Abuelo and Abuela.

Abuelo concentrated on the flames in the hearth before addressing the others. "I think my grandparents would be very honored to have their story included on each bottle of our wine."

Abuela tittered. "Their *love story*." There were stars in her eyes when she glanced at Mateo. "Your Katie really came up with this?"

"Oh no." Mateo laid a hand on his chest. "She's not—"

"I think the idea's stellar too," Titi Mon chimed in. "If you want an outside opinion. And if you don't?" She squared her shoulders. "You're getting it anyway."

Everyone laughed and Mateo was glad to feel the tension easing in the room. "We can start making calls tomorrow," he told his mom and dad.

His mom shook her head. "Everything's already shut down for the holidays, and tomorrow is Christmas Eve."

"Yes," his dad said. "And besides, maybe some of these calls should be made in person?"

"I agree," his mom answered, typically in accord with his dad. "The personal touch could be important when requesting these modifications."

"I'll go too!" Abuelo stood.

Abuela latched on to his arm and struggled to her feet. "Me as well!"

Titi Mon collapsed the recliner, preparing to stand. "I'm not staying here while—"

"Wait!" His dad leapt off the couch. He tugged on Mateo's mom's hand, and she stood beside him, reading his eyes. "Too many of us will prove overwhelming," he said in placating tones.

"That's right," his mom added calmly. "It would best to send an emissary." She cast her gaze on Mateo, and he was definitely up to the challenge.

"I'll go." He braced his hands on his knees and stood. "It would be my honor."

"Thank you, Mateo." His mom hugged him; then his dad added a bear-hug embrace. He caught a glimpse of Abuela's shawl and Abuelo's mustache, Titi Mon's red hair, as they all piled on with their hugs.

They broke apart and Abuelo raised his fist. "We can do this— together! We will save Los Cielos!"

Mateo wanted that more than anything. He also needed to square things with his brother, because until he did that, he had no clue how to resolve his very messy feelings for Katie. He and Katie had grown close over this past week, almost like friends, and she seemed like such a special person. A person who fit in so easily with his family.

His heart stuttered as a doubt crept in. Had it been too easily? In the beginning, he'd been wary of her motives in getting close to Juan and the family. But Katie wasn't the scheming sort. Even if her own background had been lonely and sad, she'd never try to fill that void by immersing herself at Los Cielos. She didn't even want to be here at Christmas among them and had expressed so many reservations about continuing to date his brother.

Still. That didn't mean that she'd want to be with *him*.

But did he want *her*?

Mateo sighed. His emotions concerning Katie were all so twisted around, he wasn't sure there was a way to untangle them.

"So," he asked his folks as they all sat back down. "What did the doctors have to say about Juan?"

"The new scans were very promising." His mom lifted her book off the sofa and shut it after sliding a bookmark into place. She set it on the coffee table beside his dad's e-reader. "They're hopeful that tomorrow will be the day."

"To bring him out of the coma?" Titi Mon crossed her puffy ankles. Then she winced and uncrossed them on the footrest of the recliner. When his mom nodded, she declared, "*Fabuloso!*"

Abuela pulled her rosary out of her skirt pocket. "How soon can we go and see him?"

His dad answered. "First thing tomorrow if you'd like."

Abuela nodded, lightly fingering her rosary beads. "I'd like."

Titi Mon held up her hand. "I'd like too!"

Abuelo surveyed the room. "Naturally, I'm coming."

Mateo was too. He needed to speak with Juan himself.

"We'll all go," his dad assured them.

"We'll leave right after breakfast," his mom offered.

"Good idea," his dad said. "In the meantime, we should all sleep on Katie's plan and put our heads together over coffee."

"Already on it, Dad," Mateo said, because his mind was suddenly racing miles ahead, pondering different scenarios, mulling over label designs, considering a short yet succinct way to frame Papi Monchi and Mamacita's touching story. He'd probably get very little sleep tonight, keeping track of his thoughts and writing them down. But he didn't care. He was on a mission to save this vineyard and preserve his family's legacy. For his grandparents and his folks, for Juan and himself, and maybe—just maybe—for a family of his own one day.

His mind mentally shared a snapshot of Katie in Abuela's wedding dress, but he quickly shut that image down, burying it deep in his heart. *One issue at a time, Mateo.* Maybe if he solved their problems at the winery first, the rest of it would fall into place. He sighed. Sure, as if it was all so simple. *Not.* If it were, the moon would be made of Swiss cheese. His mouth twitched. Or *blue cheese*, according to Katie.

He envisioned her lips giving that cute little pout, and every fiber of his being didn't want to give up on her. What if she had been telling the truth about her and Juan? If they'd never actually dated, would that make a difference?

Then he recalled her tender words to Juan at the hospital when she'd sat by his bedside, and Mateo's heart sank like a stone. He was kidding himself. Katie had always been *all about Juan*—and not him.

Any other illusions he'd had were as fanciful as Juan once believing he could fly.

TWENTY-THREE

Christmas Eve

WHEN KATIE REACHED THE DINER, it was still dark outside and only Daisy's car was in the parking lot. Katie juggled the cookie tins in her hands as she unlocked the front door with her key. The baseboard heat inside instantly warmed her cheeks while leaving a musty hot coil smell in the air. The weather seemed to be growing chillier each day. It was particularly brisk this morning with winds howling along the two-lane highway after roaring down from the hills.

Daisy had most of the interior lights turned off, with tables and booths illuminated by the colorful Christmas lights she'd draped around the walls. Katie smelled baking apples and cinnamon, telltale scents of Daisy's delicious homemade apple pie.

Daisy walked out of the kitchen wearing an apron and holding a large cheesecake sprinkled with crushed candy canes. She shared a broad smile, then checked the clock on the wall over the register. "You're in awfully early."

Katie set her cookie tins on a booth table to remove her gloves and coat. She yanked off her hat next, stuffing it in her coat pocket. "I wanted to go by the hospital before their morning shift change."

Daisy set the cheesecake in the refrigerated section of the display case on the counter. "How's Juan doing? Any better?"

"Actually." Katie heaved a breath. "Much. They're bringing him out of his coma today. At least that's what the nurses said when I asked them."

Daisy slid the display case door shut. "Why, Katie!" Her face held a happy glow. "That's wonderful!"

Katie's heart melted at Daisy's tender expression. She'd consistently been there for Katie, reaching out and being supportive, but it was always Katie who had pulled back. Maybe pulling back wasn't always a good thing. She'd adored being embraced by the Martinezes. Pia reminded Katie so much of her mom, and in a way so did Daisy.

"It is wonderful," Katie agreed, unwrapping her scarf. It also meant that her world would soon be changing. But who was she kidding? It had started changing already.

Daisy walked around the counter and approached her with a worried frown. "If Juan's doing better," she asked softly, "then why the long face?"

"Oh, Daisy, I—" Katie drew in a shaky breath, needing to confess to someone, craving the motherly warmth and understanding she no longer had. After having caught a glimpse of it in Pia, it was going to be twice as hard to live without it now. "I've made such a mess of everything."

"A mess?" Daisy's eyebrows lifted. "I don't see how." She braced Katie's arms in her thick hands. "You saved the man's life. That's huge." She leveled Katie a look. "*And* he asked you out to Los Cielos for Christmas," she said in lighter tones. Her dark eyes sparkled. "That's huge too."

She was so sweet, so tender. Katie couldn't help but let her in. She hated disappointing Daisy, but the truth telling had to begin sometime. She pursed her lips before saying, "I'm afraid it's not what you think." Her heart ached at the admission. "It never was."

Daisy searched Katie's eyes. "What's not what I think?"

"It was never for real." Katie blubbered out the words. "It was all a ruse." Now that she'd started, she let it fly. "Juan never really liked me at all! He asked me to *pretend* to be his girlfriend at Christmas."

"Pretend?" Daisy blinked and held her closer. "Why?"

Katie sighed. "Because he didn't want the holiday fix-up his Titi Mon had planned. So he asked me to"—she inhaled deeply, collecting herself and holding back the burn in her eyes—"play his girlfriend at dinner to get his family off his back."

"Oh boy."

"Only Juan avoiding that fix-up has led to this gigantic holiday mix-up." Katie winced as the weight of the week settled on her shoulders. "That's huge."

"Oh, honey." Daisy pulled her into a firm embrace, pressing Katie to her cushiony frame. She smelled of apple pie and candy canes, enveloping Katie in her warmth.

Why had she resisted this? Because she was afraid of deepening their bond and then having another fragile bond break? Like it had with the deaths of her parents? But no, Daisy wouldn't let her down, not if she could help it, and Katie desperately needed to trust someone.

Daisy's hushed words washed over her. "I'm so sorry. So you and Juan—?"

Katie pulled back to stare at her. "No," she said sadly. "Not ever. And truthfully? Maybe it was never meant to be."

Daisy held her gaze. "But you've adored that man forever."

"I didn't know him like I thought I did, Daisy. And then, I met"—Her chin trembled—"Mateo."

"Uh-oh." Daisy still had her arms around Katie. She tried to read her eyes. "Oh no?"

Katie pouted and gave a sharp whimper.

"Oh *yeah*." Daisy observed her sagely. "The brother." Daisy stared at her a moment longer and gasped. "You've got a thing for *him*? Mateo?"

Katie folded her face in her hands.

"Katie?"

She peeked between her fingers. "Maybe."

"Okay," Daisy said, taking charge of the situation. "Don't go anywhere!"

"What? Why?" Katie asked as Daisy strode away. Maybe her admission had been too much, and Daisy was going to scold her. But when Daisy turned around, she wore a soft smile.

"This deserves coffee." She motioned toward the booth where Katie had set her cookie tins. "You sit. I'll pour."

Katie's cheeks steamed as she tried to protest. "But—"

"No buts about it!" Daisy raised a hand. "The pie is on a timer, and we don't open for another thirty minutes." The finality in her tone said the decision was as good as done. She was opening her heart to Katie, and this time, she wasn't letting Katie push her away.

Katie took a seat in the booth, knowing it was impossible to argue with Daisy. Besides that, she didn't want to argue. She badly needed Daisy's listening ear and always great advice. And yes, also a bit of the motherly comfort that radiated out from her smile like sunshine after a storm. "Still," Katie said, teetering on the cliff of their deeper connection, "Mark and Caleb will be in soon."

Daisy filled two coffee mugs and carried them to the booth, setting them on the table. "In that case," Daisy said sweetly. She slid into the booth opposite Katie, passing her a coffee. "You'd better talk fast."

Mateo and his family filed into the family waiting room of the hospital's ICU wing. This morning around seven, they'd received the phone call they'd been waiting for. Juan's brain swelling had completely receded, and the anesthesiologist was bringing him out of his induced coma later this morning. They'd driven here as quickly as they could while mostly obeying the speed limits. Nobody wanted to miss Juan's big reentry into the waking world, least of all Mateo, after the terrible way things had ended.

Mateo stared into Juan's ICU room from the hall, seeing his brother was no longer on a ventilator. He had small oxygen tubes below his nostrils instead, which meant he'd soon be awake and breathing on his own. It would be the first time that they'd seen each other since their big altercation. Juan had barely contained his temper then, and Mateo was ashamed to think he'd had trouble reining his in as well. He regretted that now as the painful memories of their blowup flooded him.

Juan stormed angrily through his condo, cutting from the kitchen into the living room. He held a glass of Los Cielos Cellars wine in his hand. "Why won't you ever listen to me?"

Mateo followed him, holding his own wineglass. "I would listen! If you made sense!" He'd come here with a pinot noir at his parents' urging. Juan's ideas were getting out of hand and starting to worry Abuelo.

Juan wheeled on him before he reached his desk, and wine sloshed in his glass. "Everything I do is for the winery."

"That's just it. It's not your winery to run." Mateo sighed. "Yet." He hated the idea that his parents were right in opposing his plans to break away and start a guitar business. Even though Juan was the oldest, his folks maintained that Juan couldn't handle the responsibility on his own. He needed Mateo's guidance. Overseeing daily operations at Los Cielos Cellars was one thing. Babysitting his older brother for the rest of his life seemed untenable.

Juan's dark eyes glinted. "I don't want it all for myself. I've already told you that a dozen times. Maybe hundreds since we were kids."

"There won't be anything left of the winery, period, if you run it into the ground."

Juan set his wineglass on his desk and leaned back against it, folding his arms across his chest. "What's wrong with Cloudy Crest Wines? It's elegant, contemporary."

Mateo grated out the words. "It's not who we are."

"Not yet." Juan set his chin. "But it is who we can be. You have to think big, Mateo. Reach for the stars! Los Cielos Cellars

sounds provincial. Outdated. But Cloudy Crest Wines?" He waved his arm toward the wall with his framed photos. "Now, that holds possibilities."

Mateo stared at the photo of El Corazón portraying the family cemetery and grumbled, "A chance to send Abuelo and Abuela to their early graves." He blew out a breath. "Maybe Dad and Mom too."

Juan pouted. "Stop being so melodramatic."

If that wasn't the pot calling the kettle black.

Mateo lunged for him; then he stopped himself short.

"Mateo!" Juan bumbled backward into his desk, knocking over his wine, which dribbled onto the floor. His eyes flew wide. "Stop!"

"If you destroy Los Cielos," Mateo said, bearing down on him, "it will destroy the family." A muscle in his jaw tensed. "I won't let you do that."

Juan righted the wineglass, which thankfully hadn't broken. Red streaks ran down its sides and splattered its base. His eyebrows arched. "Nothing's going to be destroyed." He picked up the wineglass, wiping its outside clean with a napkin. "Only improved." He held the glass up in the light before setting it back down. "Made better."

Mateo rolled back his shoulders, fuming. "We don't need this now. It's practically Christmas." He picked up his keys and strode toward the door.

"Which is why we need to make this change ASAP." Juan squared his bullish frame. "A new plan for the new year."

The steam practically blew out of Mateo's ears, because Juan

didn't seem to understand even the most basic things about the
business. "You don't know what you're saying—or doing." He
turned and opened the door. "Sorry about the wine."

"Oh right. I forgot." Juan's sarcasm dripped off his lips.
"You're the smart one."

Mateo's body tensed.

"Yeah?" He glared at his brother. "And you're nothing but a
bigheaded fool with some slicked-back hair!"

Then Mateo stormed out the door—and slammed it.

Mateo rubbed the tender spot in his chest, staring into Juan's ICU
room through its glass window in the hall. He'd been over that
conversation with Juan so many times in his mind, not regret-
ting his position but extremely sorry about the way he'd voiced
it. By mutual agreement, they'd all decided to hold off on dis-
cussing Juan's underhanded dealings at the winery with him for
the time being. They needed to ensure he was completely healthy
first. Once Juan was back at Los Cielos and recuperating nicely,
but before businesses opened at the new year, they'd broach the
subject of his rebranding endeavors with him.

Medical personnel buzzed in and out of Juan's ICU room,
whisking IV bags and other paraphernalia with them. Mateo's
mom removed her jacket, handing it and her purse to Mateo. "I'm
going to see what's going on." She glanced at her husband, who
quickly shucked his coat. Mateo took that too as they hurried
toward the nurses' station.

"What is it?" he heard his mom ask the head nurse as she

walked from behind the desk. "What's happened? He's not awake already?" His mom had wanted to be there. All of them had. Still, if Juan was awake now, that was fantastic.

"Not yet," the nurse answered.

His mom's forehead creased. "How much longer?"

"Soon, very soon." The nurse smiled. "I'm sorry, ma'am." She tried to step around his mom, who was blocking her path. "We're undergoing a shift change. You'll need to stay in the family waiting room for another few minutes while we transition reports."

His dad pulled his mom aside to prevent her from colliding with Juan's doctor when she pivoted out of the nurse's way. The doctor, Elena Giblin, nodded at them. "I'm very happy to say all systems are go for bringing Juan out of his coma."

His mom heaved a breath. "Oh, thank goodness."

Mateo and his grandparents and Titi Mon shared grateful sighs too. Though they'd been told this on the phone, it was an enormous relief for everyone to hear it in person. Directly from Juan's neurologist too.

His dad addressed the doctor. "Can we see him?"

"As soon as we clear the room." Dr. Giblin glanced over her shoulder as others checked monitors and adjusted tubing around Juan. "The anesthesiologist and I will remain, along with one of the nurses, but having family at his bedside could help. Sometimes it's less of a shock, and less scary, for the patient to be surrounded by loved ones when they awaken. It helps to reassure them that they're all right."

Mateo's dad wrapped his arm around his mom. "This is the moment we've been waiting for."

His mom spoke to the doctor. "How many of us can be in the room when you wake him?"

Dr. Giblin peered down the hall, then looked at them. "As long as none of you have been ill and there's no risk of infection, I don't see why you all can't be there."

His mom gave a happy gasp. "The whole family?"

"You'll need stay out of our way," the doctor cautioned. "And leave the minute I give the signal if anything goes wrong." When his mom wrung her hands, Dr. Giblin said kindly, "I have every confidence though, that things will go right. Still. We have to be prepared for any situation."

His dad nodded solemnly. "Of course."

His mom embraced Dr. Giblin, stunning the younger woman with a tight hug. "Thank you." She grew weepy-eyed. "Thanks so much for everything you've done for Juan."

Dr. Giblin stiffly patted her back. "I'm always happy to give good news." She smiled. "I only wish I could give it more often." The doctor stuffed her stethoscope into her shirt pocket and stared down the hallway again. "How many of you *are* there?"

"Six," Mateo's dad answered, but his mom corrected him.

"Seven." She nudged his arm. "You're forgetting Katie."

The doctor tapped her temple. "Of course, the fiancée's welcome too."

"Fiancée?" asked his mom.

Dr. Giblin smiled at Abuela. "A little bird told me a wedding was in the offing." Her tone held a singsong lilt, and Mateo's neck warmed. Rumors of Juan and Katie's upcoming nuptials were highly exaggerated indeed.

Sweet Abuela really did want her grandsons to marry. So did Titi Mon. After a while, his grandfather had piled aboard that matrimony train. Mateo would never tell Juan that Abuelo had started hinting about Katie dating *him* instead of his wayward big brother. Juan didn't need to know that, now or ever, probably.

But he did need to understand the sacrifices Katie had made on his behalf, first by saving him during the accident and then by blending in so well with the family. Her upbeat attitude and quiet smile had lent them all an added dose of holiday cheer when one was so badly needed. She'd provided a happy distraction for everyone, including Titi Mon and Abuelo, and had been exceptionally stellar at putting that star on their Christmas tree.

It was hard to imagine that Katie might no longer be around once Juan recovered. But that was up to Katie and—Mateo supposed—Juan. Depending on the defense Juan concocted for himself about sabotaging the family business, Katie might be swayed by Juan's explanation. So many other women had been taken in by Juan's glib excuses. But Katie wasn't like those other women. She was unique. More into substance than flash. Someone who was no stranger to tragedy but who'd kept her chin up—as well as her good heart. A woman Mateo found impossible to get out of his head.

Another group entered the waiting room, so his dad spoke in a low whisper. "I saw Juan through his doorway," he said. "His color is much better today."

"*Gracias a Dios.*" Abuela tightened her fingers around her rosary beads. "I've said so many prayers."

They'd all said many prayers, and they were finally being answered.

His dad pursed his lips, steeling his composure. "Dr. Giblin said, if all goes well…" His voice trembled, and Mateo's mom laid a hand on his shoulder. He set his chin, and Mateo went shaky inside as well. His dad never got emotional. He was a rock, but even rocks could be tested under fire, and this had been such a difficult situation. Even though Juan's prognosis had been good from the start, it was hard not to have doubts. Not to fear for the worst when those doubts got the better of you. Mateo had been in that dark space himself.

"If all goes well," his mom finished for her husband, "Juan could get moved to a regular hospital room later today. Once he's awake and fully lucid, they'll keep him there for another twenty-four hours for observation."

Mateo's spirits lifted at the outstanding news. That would mean Juan being home for Christmas, the miracle they'd all hoped for. Katie should know about this too. He pulled out his cell to text her. "When should I tell Katie to come?" he asked his mom.

She glanced at Juan's ICU room, and Dr. Giblin waved her inside.

Mateo's mom met his gaze, her expression urgent. "Right away."

Mateo lagged behind his folks and grandparents, who approached Juan's room with Titi Mon, to dash off his text, but before he could send it, the group got stopped by the nurse attending to Juan. She glanced at his mom's shoulder bag and Titi Mon's enormous purse and then at his dad's cell phone sticking out of his coat pocket as they all stood in line to sanitize their hands from the dispenser mounted on the wall. "I'm sorry," she whispered.

"You'll need to leave any electronics in the waiting room." Since they'd only been visiting Juan a few at a time, they'd normally had other parties with whom to leave their belongings in the past.

"Can we leave them at the nurses' station?" his mom asked.

The nurse grimaced in apology. "I'm afraid if everyone did that—"

His mom nodded. "Yes, yes. Of course." She stared helplessly at Mateo, who held out his arms.

"Here," he said, accepting the pocketbooks and his dad's cell. "I can run everything down to my SUV." He glanced past the nurse into Juan's room. "But I definitely want to be here."

The nurse checked with the doctors and came back to the doorway. "You have time."

"Great," Mateo said. He addressed the others. "Be right back."

Before he could leave, his mom said, "Don't forget to text Katie."

"Right," he said, intending to pause in the waiting room to do that.

Before he could leave, a nurse behind the desk caught his attention. "Since you're going to your car, you might want to take your packages." Her pink lipstick matched her pale pink scrubs. "There's bound to be a lot of happy commotion when Juan wakes up, and I don't want to forget to give them to you."

His eyebrows knitted together. "Packages?"

The nurse smiled and nodded over her shoulder. "Juan's fiancée left something for your family when she came in this morning." He didn't see the point in correcting her about the "fiancée" part.

"Wait. When was she here?"

"She came in to see Juan very early," the nurse explained. "It was probably around six or six thirty. She left the packages then, saying the family would be in later, but she wasn't sure if she'd be able to get back, depending."

"Depending on what?"

"I'm afraid she didn't say." The nurse shrugged. "I assumed depending on her workday? Something like that?" The nurse pushed out her chair, and it rolled back on casters. "Hang on. Let me go grab them for you." She disappeared behind a glass wall shielding an internal office and returned with her arms full of packages. They looked like Christmas gifts. "Do you think you could, um—" She held out her packages, and he shifted the other items in his grasp to accept them. "Can you get all that?"

"Yeah, no problem." He settled the gifts in his arms, a deep melancholy taking hold. Katie had been acting uncertain about coming out to Los Cielos for Christmas. These gifts said she'd made her decision. The packages had gift tags on them, addressed to different members of his family. There was even one for him.

He carried his stash into the family waiting room and paused in a corner, setting it all down by a glittery snowman decoration to send his text. Would Katie even come back to the hospital now? He surveyed the packages, knowing he had to give her the chance. His mom and the others wanted her here.

His throat burned raw.

So did he.

TWENTY-FOUR

LUCKILY, THE DINER WAS SWAMPED, and that helped keep Katie's mind off the hospital situation. Still, she couldn't help but worry. Had Juan been lifted out of his coma by now? Had he gone ahead and told his family about who she really was—and *wasn't*? Maybe the entire Martinez clan had written her off already.

She reached for the coffeepot and came over to refill Mr. Elroy's cup.

The gray-haired man held up his hand. "I'm fine, thank you." He wiped his mouth with a napkin, then balled it up in his fist. "Breakfast was delicious, as usual."

She'd been trying to work up her nerve to ask him about Los Cielos. Now that he was leaving, she had to act fast. "Mr. Elroy?"

His kind brown eyes settled on hers. "Yes, Katie?"

She licked her lips, unsure of how to proceed. "Your bank is a savings and loan, right? I mean, you support local businesses?"

He chuckled warmly at her awkward approach. "Are you thinking of opening one of your own?"

Katie flushed. "Oh no, not me. I'm, um..." She swallowed past the lump in her throat. "Asking for some friends."

He set his elbows on the counter. "Which friends are those?"

"The Martinezes," she confided softly.

"Ah yes." He stroked his chin. "They run that winery, Los Cielos Cellars."

She nodded. "That's right."

He cocked his head. "Is their business in trouble?"

She winced, shrinking back a little. "Hard times, you know?"

Mr. Elroy set his jaw, appearing distant a moment. "I do indeed." He withdrew his wallet from his vest pocket, laying an extra big tip on the counter. "Tell you what," he said, standing. "Why don't you ask the Martinezes to come talk to me, and I'll see what I can do? Their winery is legendary in town. No doubt it's very deserving of some extra support."

Katie wanted to leap across the counter and hug him, but of course she didn't. "That would be fantastic. Thank you so much."

He studied her as he slipped on his coat. "I didn't realize you were close with the family."

Katie held her breath as her heart pounded. "Only recently." And up until now. After today, she had no idea what would happen next.

Finally, after what seemed like eons, her cell phone buzzed in her apron pocket.

Katie's pulse raced when she paused by the coffeepot to read Mateo's text.

Juan's waking up.

Family wants you here.

Daisy peered over her shoulder. "Is that the Martinezes?"

Katie's chin jerked up, and she lowered her phone. "Mateo," she said, her heart still pounding. She showed the text to Daisy, and Daisy answered without hesitation.

"You have to go." She gave Katie's shoulder an affirming squeeze. Daisy hadn't told her what to do earlier. She'd merely absorbed Katie's story with her calm understanding. Now though, she was steering Katie toward the hook in the kitchen where she'd hung her coat.

"Daisy, no." Katie's knees wobbled, and her mouth went sandpaper dry. "I can't."

"Listen to me, girl. You *can* and you will." Daisy leaned toward her and whispered, "Otherwise, this will haunt you. Unfinished business always does."

Katie glanced around the busy diner. "But—"

"We'll cover for you here."

Daisy was right. She had to make things right with Juan and his whole family. After they'd all been so good to her, she owed them that much.

Katie licked her lips and whimpered. "Oh, Daisy. What am I going say?"

Daisy's eyes shone warmly. "Why don't you start with the truth?"

———————

Katie hurried into the hospital lobby, beelining for the registration desk. Juan was waking up! *Yes!* She was so happy for him and his family, but her pretense for hanging out with them was about to go up in smoke. Raw nerves clawed at her gut as she unzipped her coat. She checked in and got her visitor pass, taking the escalator and then the elevator to the third floor. As strange as it seemed, this was all familiar territory by now. After today, it would probably be a while before she set foot in a hospital again. *Which is a good thing*, she tried to tell herself.

Her heart landed with a dull thud at her feet as she stood outside Juan's ICU room. Through the big glass window, she could see bustling activity inside. His entire family was present, and official-looking medical people kept a watchful eye on Juan's IV and his machine stats. She recognized the middle-aged redhead as Dr. Giblin, Juan's neurologist. The other doctor appeared to be an anesthesiologist, and a nurse in scrubs stood by, double-checking the sensor pads attached to Juan's chest beneath his hospital gown.

This was really happening. They were bringing Juan around.

Katie removed her gloves to tuck them in her coat pockets so she could sanitize her hands, and her fingers shook. In a matter of minutes, Juan's life would take a turn for the better, and hers would take a total nosedive.

Abuela looked up and spotted Katie first. "*La novia*," she proclaimed softly. "She's here!"

Pia hurried over with a hug when Katie entered the room. "Thank you for coming," she said in hushed tones.

Mateo's heartfelt plea had been short and to the point. The last thing in the world Katie could have said was no.

Abuelo's eyes sparkled when he saw her. Titi Mon's did too. Raul shot her a thumbs-up, like all was about to be right with the world, and his confidence in Juan's full recovery was contagious.

The others in the room seemed to sense it, observing the doctors work with bated breath. Mateo stood apart from the group, a little behind Titi Mon. He'd crossed his arms, his forehead furrowed in concentration. He caught a glimpse of Katie and sent her a sad yet hopeful smile as Abuela clutched her rosary.

"Can I say a prayer?" Abuela asked the nurse quietly.

The nurse glanced at Dr. Giblin, who nodded. "Go right ahead."

Abuela began reciting something in Spanish. From its cadence and a few of the words, it sounded like the Lord's Prayer.

Titi Mon said, "Amen."

The others stared at the doctors for permission to speak.

The anesthesiologist surveyed the machines. "Juan's regaining consciousness, so anything you can say to help bring him around..."

The beeping sounds from the monitors grew louder as the family gathered near the bed. Pia held out her arm, encouraging Katie to join them, and she tentatively stepped closer.

"You know, Juan," Abuelo said gruffly. "You need to wake up, because I have a bone or two to pick with—"

Abuela shushed him. "Esteban, not now."

His bushy eyebrows arched. "What? I do."

Abuela elbowed him and whispered, "After."

Raul widened his eyes at Abuelo as if to say, *Cool it.*

"We're all here with you, *mijo*," Pia said sweetly. "Your dad, me, Mateo, Titi Mon, and even Katie." She smiled across the room, and Katie's cheeks grew hot.

What if Juan didn't remember the deal that they'd made?

She'd read up on people coming out of comas. They sometimes experienced agitation, anxiety, confusion...even amnesia. Sweat beaded her hairline.

None of his family would believe her about the agreed-to ruse if Juan couldn't remember agreeing to it. They might even think what Mateo had when she'd tried to tell him the truth, that she was only inventing that story as an excuse to break up with Juan. Katie's stomach fluttered with nerves. Then she told herself to calm down.

Juan had done other things that could provide her with *ample* reasons for wanting to end their supposed relationship. Her gaze swept over his grandparents, and her heart ached.

Abuela sent Katie a tender smile. "Your *novio* will be back with you soon."

Katie's jaw clenched in the same painful fashion that it had on the very first day, when this entire holiday mix-up began.

"And if you don't want him—" Abuelo whispered, jerking his chin toward Mateo.

Katie's stomach flip-flopped, and her heart beat faster.

"Esteban!" Abuela swatted his hand, and Mateo dragged a hand down his face.

Of course, he was humiliated. Katie was too. There was no hope for her and Mateo. He'd made that pretty clear. The fact that his family hadn't gotten the memo though, was incredibly awkward.

"Maybe he *should* know," Titi Mon said boldly.

Mateo spoke between gritted teeth. "*Titi Mon*, please."

She tsked at him and stood up straighter on her heels, leaning toward Juan. "If you don't wake up," she called loudly, "you're going to lose your girl to your brother!"

Both doctors blinked, and the nurse pursed her lips.

Pia gasped. "*Tía!*"

"Well." Titi Mon set hand on her hip. "It's true."

Katie's pulse fluttered. Maybe Juan already had lost his girl to his brother. Because it was no longer Juan that she pined for with a heartsick longing. She'd known since catching Mateo playing his guitar in his upstairs apartment that he was the Martinez brother she wanted. He was also the brother who didn't want her. Probably neither of them would after today. Her face burned hotter, but this torment would end soon.

Juan's eyes popped open, and he stared around the room. "Where am I?"

Joyful gasps erupted from his family, and Katie brought her hands to her chest. It was Juan! He was here, fully conscious. And looking so totally adorable. Picture-perfect handsome, even dressed in his hospital gown. Her heart should have fluttered, but oddly, it didn't. So okay. That infatuation was over. Was that all on account of Mateo and the way he'd made her feel? *Cared for. Comforted. Heard.* She caught a glimpse of his face, so awash with relief, as he carefully watched his brother.

Juan's face screwed up in terror as he gaped at Dr. Giblin and the nurse. He angled forward to peek at the anesthesiologist before collapsing back on his bed. "Is this a hospital?"

"It's okay," Dr. Giblin said. "You had a bad fall and hit your head. You've been in a medically induced coma."

"A coma?"

"But you're better now," Dr. Giblin reassured him.

The nurse smiled and took his blood pressure. "Everything's going to be okay."

His grandparents scuttled over to hug him. "*Ay*, Juan!" Abuela's shawl fluttered across Juan's hospital gown. "We were so worried."

Abuelo wiped away a tear. "Welcome back."

Raul gripped his shoulder and grinned. "We really missed you around here."

Pia kissed Juan's forehead. "So, so much."

Juan startled, seeing Katie. "Who's she?"

Titi Mon gasped. "Oh my god, he doesn't recognize her?"

Please don't let it be true.

Please, please, please. Please.

That would make the nightmare of their fake relationship continue, and she couldn't bear deceiving the lovely Martinezes for one more day. Not one more hour even. She cut a quick glance at Mateo, who observed her interactions with Juan. And she definitely was done pretending in front of Mateo. Her heart sank. About so many things. If only she could tell him that he was the brother she'd come to care for. But given the present situation, that would be an impossible admission to make. She also doubted it would be well received, since it had been Mateo who'd insisted she keep dating Juan.

Juan's gaze locked on hers, and his eyes widened. "Katie?"

Titi Mon threw up her arms. "*Gracias a Dios!* He remembers!"

Heat flooded Katie's face. At least he recalled that much. She would soon see about the rest of it. She swallowed hard. Very, very soon. She hoped.

Maybe the whole story would spill out gradually.

She smiled and said shyly, "Yeah, that's me."

Dr. Giblin grinned at Juan. "She's your fiancée."

Or not.

"My *what*?" Juan looked like he'd been hit by a truck, or maybe the white van this time. Full throttle.

Katie felt like she'd been flattened by its tires rolling over her chest. She could barely breathe.

"No, I'm sorry," Pia said to the doctor. "That was a misunderstanding."

Dr. Giblin's forehead rose. "Oh?"

Katie winced in agreement. "Kind of a big one, but no."

"She's only his girlfriend," Titi Mon added authoritatively.

Juan visibly blew out a breath and reclined back against his pillow. "You think I would have recalled something like that, having a fiancée. Or a"—he shut his eyes and rubbed his closed eyelids—"girlfriend?" His eyes popped back open, and he stared at Katie. "Wait."

Katie's tongue was stuck to the roof of her mouth. She needed to say something, but the words caught in her throat.

Juan's perplexed gaze travelled to Mateo, who stepped forward and took his hand.

"It's really good to see you, Juan."

This diverted everyone's attention away from Katie, giving her time to think. How could she put this? What would she say? What's more, when would she say it? Katie bit her lip. Maybe Juan would say it first by telling them all about the girlfriend ruse. Assuming he remembered them arriving at that arrangement. And

by the way he kept snatching cagey glances at her, it looked like it
was coming back to him.

Juan tugged Mateo down toward his bed and whispered, "Did
we have a...fight?"

Mateo patted the back of Juan's hand. "We'll talk about that
later."

"Later," Juan said, like he was still making sense of the situation. "Okay."

At the moment though, Juan didn't look like he was capable of saying much more of anything. He gawked at them all like
they'd descended from the mother ship.

"Don't worry," Dr. Giblin informed everyone. "He's still getting oriented." She signaled to her colleagues before addressing
Pia and Raul. "If you all could step outside briefly," she said,
"we'll give Juan a quick exam, then give you and your family some
time alone with him."

———

Pia approached Katie in the hall as she nervously twisted her purse
strap in her hands. She'd left her phone down in her car, knowing
she wouldn't be able to carry it in here. "Don't worry about Juan
and the engagement misunderstanding," Pia whispered. She cast
a quick glance at Abuela, who chatted with Mateo, Abuelo, and
Raul. Titi Mon had made a quick trip to the restroom. "We'll
explain to Juan that Abuela was mistaken." Raul sent her a nod,
and she turned to Katie. "My husband's talking to his mom about
that now."

Katie overheard Abuela's partial protest. "*Pero*, Raul—"

"Mamá," Raul returned in low tones. "Now is not the time to confuse Juan further."

Abuelo placed his arm around Abuela's shoulders, leaning toward her. "He's right, *querida*."

Abuela smiled at Katie, then leaned toward Abuelo and whispered, "Well, if Juan is out of the picture—"

Mateo cleared his throat. "Abuela. No."

"No?"

Mateo shook his head and said in hushed tones, "Definitely not."

A red-hot arrow pierced right through Katie's chest.

Of course not.

No way was that happening, and Katie hadn't even made her confession yet.

Abuela frowned and tucked her rosary beads in her skirt pocket. She centered her gaze on Abuelo, and then on Raul and finally Mateo. "Well, it has to be one of you." She held up her chin. "My visions are never wrong."

Mateo gently rubbed her arm. "Maybe this time? Hmm?"

Pia pretended like she and Katie had been unaware of the entire exchange. "In any case, sweetheart."—she wore a pained expression—"The family is holding off on confronting Juan about the winery's rebranding until he comes home. But whatever you have to do concerning your relationship with him is up to you, of course. I don't want to get in the middle of that. Again, I'm very sorry I tried to insert myself before."

"Pia—"

Her eyebrows arched. "Yes?"

"I have something to say." Katie swallowed hard. "But I'd rather say it back in there." She nodded to Juan's room. "When everyone's present."

"Would you like to have a word alone with Juan first?"

That was so like Pia. Thoughtful and understanding. "You know what?" Katie stared through the window as the nurse pulled back the curtain she'd drawn during Juan's exam. "That would be good."

A few moments later, Katie approached Juan's bed, and he gave her a tentative smile. "Katie, right?" He shook his finger at her like he was putting it together. "From Daisy's Diner."

"Yep." She sat down beside him. "That's me!"

Juan peered out the window at his family. They all spun back around like they hadn't been trying to watch. Well, everyone but Titi Mon until Pia tugged on her arm. He scratched his head. "So what was that Titi Mon said about you and my brother?"

Katie's whole body flushed hot. "Oh, that? That was nothing." She shifted on her feet. "Your Titi Mon was mistaken."

He squinted at her. "So why did that doctor think that you and I were engaged?"

"It's such a long story." Katie blew out a breath. "Short version. When you had your accident—"

"The van!" He sat up in his hospital bed, and the IV line tugged against his arm. "That was you, right?" His eyes scanned hers. "I heard your voice. Then someone pushed... Wait. That was you who saved me?" He leaned back and rubbed the side of his head. Then winced.

Katie grimaced. "Still hurts?"

"Some." He fiddled with his IV, slackening its tug on his arm. "This thing bothers me more."

"From what I hear, you shouldn't need it for much longer. They'll be moving you to a regular room pretty soon."

He glanced around. "So this is...?"

"You're in intensive care. You've been here all week."

"That's what the doctors told me." He shook his head. "It's super freaky to lose seven days like that. So what did I miss?" He gave her the charming smile that used to make her knees weak.

Somehow though, its effect fell flat. No butterflies stirred in her belly, and her heart didn't pound, the way it still did every time she looked at Mateo. But Mateo didn't want her any more than Juan did. Not romantically.

"Uh." Katie lifted a shoulder. "Kind of a lot."

Deep lines furrowed Juan's brow, giving him the serious look that used to make her heart sing. Now, the only tune that played in her soul was a sweet serenade from one of Mateo's guitars. But she was foolish to hope Mateo would ever serenade her. Once she and Juan revealed their truth, it would be game over with the youngest Martinez brother—and probably his entire family. Her heart clenched. And yet somehow she'd known this moment was coming all along.

"So," Juan said, "since you're *not* my fiancée, obviously, and *not* with Mateo, then what—?" He sighed and massaged his temples, seemingly trying to conjure a memory. "Wait," he said, looking up. "The girlfriend thing?"

Katie sucked air through her teeth. "The girlfriend thing. You pretty much told your whole family we were involved before your accident, and then when they saw me at the hospital—when you were unconscious, they immediately assumed... And I didn't know what to say without breaking my promise to you."

"Oh wow, Katie. I'm sorry. I really am. So when did you tell them the truth?"

She felt the blood drain from her face.

"Wait." He blinked. "Never?"

"It's been a really long week."

He stared back out the window, and his family members quickly turned away again.

Juan set his chin. "I'll bet."

"We're going to need to tell your family what happened," Katie said. "Let them know you concocted the whole girlfriend story." She paused, thinking. "Maybe you should do it? If you're ready?"

"Me?" He gawked at her. "What about you? You had a part in this too." He peered past her shoulder and out at the hall. His family spun away again. "A very big role, it sounds like."

Nerves skittered through her, and her face burned hot. "You're right, I did, and I plan to apologize too."

Juan peeked out the window to the hall. "I'm not sure I can do this alone."

Katie took his hand, but there was no romantic tension in their touch, only a unified solidarity. "Then maybe we should tell them together."

His dark brown gaze pored over her, and he squeezed her hand. "Thanks, Katie."

"Okay then." She blew out a breath, gathering her courage. "Shall we do it now or later?" She glanced over her shoulder. "Abuela's been having some health issues."

Juan frowned. "Her asthma?"

Katie nodded.

Juan sighed. "Then maybe it's better to get this over with. Honestly, sometimes prolonging things can only make them worse."

Katie's stomach churned. Didn't she know it.

"Hey," he said gently. "I'm not mad at you, you know. I mean, how could I be?" His eyebrows rose. "You're the woman who saved me." He smiled, and she waited for the tingling sensation that didn't come. "Also the one who kept my secret. That was a very tall order, I'm sure, and I thank you. That's some display of loyalty from a guy's waitress at a diner."

Oof. There, he'd said it, as plain as day. *A guy's waitress at a diner.* She couldn't believe she'd spent so much time thinking—hoping—he viewed her as something more. What a terrible fool she'd been. Needy. Ridiculous.

His face screwed up in embarrassment. "I'm sorry, Katie. I didn't mean that *at all* how it sounded." He pushed back a lock of his hair that had fallen across his forehead. "It must be the drugs. They're still wearing off. Of course you and I"—he seemed to be fumbling with his words while also searching his memory—"are friends, right?"

"It's okay," she said gently. "I get it. You were never that into me." Maybe a part of her had always known Juan would never have amorous feelings for her. As much as she'd wanted to believe they could make the perfect pair, they didn't completely fit.

"Wait." He wore a look of utter shock. "You mean you...?" Juan placed a hand on his heart, then groaned. "I'm so sorry, Katie. What a colossal jerk I am. I totally don't—and never did—deserve you." His eyebrows knitted together in a very sincere fashion. "But thanks for standing by me anyway."

She released a slow breath. "It was no problem," she said, even though it had been an enormous one. But even so, there'd been so many benefits to playing his girlfriend, it was hard to believe she'd take anything back, even if she could. Because the hard truth was, she wouldn't. Not the sweet times she'd had with the family or the happy memories she'd made with Mateo. No, she'd hold on to recollections of those forever in her heart. But first, she needed to make amends for the part she'd played in this fiasco. "All right," she said on a shaky breath. "Let's do this then. Should we ask everyone back in?"

Juan nodded. "Yeah." His eyebrows arched. "And thanks, Katie. Thanks for everything you've done. You're a champ."

She didn't feel like one though. She felt like the world's biggest loser, and she was about to lose even more. The respect and admiration—and most likely the affection—of the Martinezes.

Juan waved toward the window, motioning his family into the room. This time, they didn't act like they hadn't seen, because they arrived at his bedside within seconds.

"Family," Juan said once they'd all gathered around him. "Katie and I have something to tell you." He pursed his lips and then spoke firmly. "Katie's not my girlfriend."

Katie tried to read their long faces, but she didn't detect surprise as much as sorrow. Mateo appeared the most sorrowful of all.

"Any longer." Titi Mon shared a sympathetic frown. "We know."

"No," Juan said. "Not *any longer*." He scanned the group. "Never."

Pia gasped. "What?"

Abuela's dark eyes glistened with tears. "Katie? What's this about?"

She hung her head, the truth searing through her like a white-hot flame. "I'm sorry, Abuela," she said, looking up. She glanced around the room, and when she stared at Mateo, her heart ached the hardest. "But I never really was Juan's girlfriend. He only asked me to pretend to be that for Christmas."

Abuelo's mustache dipped with his frown. "But why?" He spoke directly to Katie, but the gruffness in his tone seemed to come from hurt and not anger.

Raul wheeled on Juan. "*Another* betrayal?"

Pia steadied his arm. "Raul, please."

Juan goggled at his parents. "Another?"

Mateo folded his arms across his chest, and his gaze went misty. "You know." He swallowed hard when his voice cracked. "She tried to tell me." He spoke to the others, avoiding Katie's gaze. "She said it was all a ruse."

"What?" Pia's jaw dropped. "And you didn't tell us, Mateo?"

"I didn't believe her, Mom." He exhaled heavily and stared at Juan. "I thought she was hunting for excuses to leave you because of your suddenly serious condition. That it was all too much for her to deal with, given that your supposed relationship was so new."

Juan sadly shook his head. "Man, oh man."

Pia turned to Katie with anguish in her eyes. "Is this true, Katie? You and Juan?" She glanced at her oldest son, then back at Katie. She sounded heartbroken. "Never?"

Katie's chin trembled. "I'm so sorry, but no." A heavy pall fell over the room, and Katie hated that it was partially on account of her. She stepped back from Juan's bedside, sensing distance from the group. She was once again the outsider she'd always known herself to be.

Abuela stumbled, and Abuelo caught her.

Abuela grabbed on to his arm. "I think I need to sit down." Mateo scrambled for a chair and pushed it over, and Abuelo and Raul helped Abuela sit. She gathered her shawl around her, slowly perusing the room. "What do we do now?" Her sad gaze lingered on Katie.

Raul smoothed back his hair. "Tomorrow's still Christmas, and—God willing—Juan will be coming home."

Pia walked over and took Katie's hand. "I think Katie should come too."

Her kindness was so overwhelming that Katie wanted to weep, especially when she looked at Mateo, who paled, appearing physically ill. The idea of being around her evidently turned his stomach, and she didn't blame him. Some of the others didn't seem thrilled about her being at Los Cielos for Christmas either. Namely Abuelo and Titi Mon. Raul and even Abuela seemed to be undecided. The invitation was far from unanimous, that was clear.

Katie released Pia's hand. "Thank you, but I've already made some plans."

Titi Mon's gaze flitted between Katie and Mateo; then she

addressed Juan. "And why did you do this thing? Ask Katie to pose as your girlfriend?"

Juan sighed heavily. "Because, Titi Mon. Every year, it's the same. Another holiday fix-up. And this year, *for once*, I wanted to make my own choices." He studied the ceiling a moment, then screwed up his face, like a new memory had hit him. "About, uh, a lot of things." He glanced around the room. "I'm the oldest, okay? But all of you have always made me feel like I'm not fully capable of anything. But I am capable—of lots."

"We *know*." Abuelo shot him a steely look, and Abuela nudged him with her elbow.

Pia raised her eyebrows at the group and said coolly, "Which is a topic for *later*."

Titi Mon wrung her hands. "You should have told us sooner," she said to Katie. "We all took you in. It wasn't right."

Katie's heart twisted. "I know, and I want to apologize. To all of you, sincerely. But once everything got started..." Heat pooled in her eyes. "I'm sorry."

Mateo hung his head, and that simple gesture broke her heart.

Her words came out all shaky, but she was trying so hard. "Once everything got started." She stared at Pia and Raul. "You made me feel so welcomed." She turned to Abuela and Abuelo. "Even loved."

Abuela and Abuelo frowned sadly.

She spoke to Titi Mon. "Accepted. Like the family I never—"

Mateo's face contorted in anguish. "So you used us?"

"What?" Katie's pulse spiked. Of all the things she'd meant to do, it had never been that. Her gut wrenched. Not intentionally. "No, of course not."

"And on the picnic, Katie?" Mateo gaped at her. "When you shared about your life, was that only to rope me in? Get me to pave your way into the family?" His tone emanated hurt, and it crushed her.

"Rope you—?" Her heart stuttered. "No."

"What picnic?" Juan asked.

Abuelo grumbled in his direction. "They rode out into the countryside with wine."

"Oh!" Juan said. Then the idea settled. "*Ooh*."

"It wasn't like that at all," Katie said, responding to Mateo. "I didn't do or say anything to hurt anybody. My intentions were always good. I wanted to help Juan and help the family. I still hope to help concerning the winery. I spoke to Mr. Elroy." She gasped, catching her breath.

"The man at the bank?" Raul asked.

Katie nodded. "He says he's going to help you."

Mateo's Adam's apple rose and fell, but it looked like his whole world was caving in.

So was hers.

"Well, that's great," Mateo said hoarsely. He pursed his lips. "Thank you."

A painful knot welled in Katie's throat, but then Titi Mon stepped in. "Maybe Katie was wrong for concealing the truth about her and Juan, but none of us should blame this poor girl for wanting a family. Not after everything's she's been through."

"It wasn't *just* about family," she said weakly to Titi Mon. She stared around the room. "As wonderful as all of you are."

"No?" Mateo challenged, stepping toward her. "Then what?"

The words froze in her heart and on her lips.

It was about you.

"Everyone!" Juan held up his hands. "This is enough. No one should be piling on Katie. If there's anyone to blame, you should blame me. I put her up to it. It was my secret she was keeping."

"She kept it very well too," Abuelo said sadly.

Titi Mon shook her head at Juan. "I'm sorry you felt pressured to do something so extreme."

"It wasn't *that* extreme at the time," Juan protested. He observed the trappings of the medical equipment around him. "It only became worse because of my accident."

"During which Katie saved you," Pia pointedly reminded everyone. "And we're all very grateful."

The rest of them mumbled their agreement and thanks, but Katie sensed she'd overstayed her welcome. Now that she'd said her piece, it was time for her to leave. The nurse would give the Martinezes their presents, if they even wanted those.

"Well," she said, withdrawing further from the group, "I'd better go. Things are really busy at the diner."

Pia held open her arms. "One last hug."

The word *last* hit Katie like a sucker punch as she hugged Pia tightly. The others all hugged her in turn, and the air hung heavy with their bittersweet goodbyes. The moment Katie had dreaded was finally here. "Don't forget about Mr. Elroy," Katie said to the family in general. "He'll be waiting to hear from you all."

Pia nodded, and there was gratitude in her eyes. "Thank you, Katie."

Instead of coming forward to embrace her, Mateo stepped

back. The hurt in his eyes shot straight to her core. Maybe she should have expected this outcome. She had no future with the Martinezes any longer. Least of all with the one of them she wanted the most.

"Mateo," his mom reprimanded, but Katie hustled toward the door, unable to endure the sting of his dismissal. Her stomach tensed and her insides ached. But she wouldn't fall apart here. Not in front of Mateo, the guy who'd unintentionally broken her heart.

"It's all right," she said as she scurried into the hall. She tried to keep her voice steady, but it shook anyway. "I'm already running late." Then she hurried down the hospital corridor, onto the elevator, down the escalator steps, and went racing through the lobby and out the hospital's front door as fast as she could go.

This year, she'd had a glimpse of what lay on the other side of her loneliness. Family. Acceptance. Love. A set of parents, two grandparents, a lovable, meddling great-aunt, Juan, and Mateo all tied up in a shiny red bow. But that package wasn't hers to open, and it never had been. She'd just gotten to peek inside it.

A burst of cold air slapped her in the face, delivering a rude shock to her senses.

Then an icy ping hit her cheek. Then another and another.

Katie looked up at the cloudy gray sky and burst into tears.

It was snowing.

TWENTY-FIVE

Christmas Day

MATEO PUSHED JUAN'S WHEELCHAIR OVER the threshold and into the foyer, stopping in front of the Santa sculpture. He shook the light smattering of snowflakes from his hair. The sky had been sprinkling small powdery flakes since yesterday, and a fine coating of white blanketed the vineyard. He and Katie had joked about it never snowing in Castellana, and now it was doing exactly that. Guilt washed over him. He hadn't seen the look of surprise on her face when she'd seen her first snow and would never get that chance again.

Juan stared down at the collapsible wheelchair. "I don't really need to be in this thing," he told his mom. "I can walk fine."

"But we want you to take it easy," his mom said. "At least for the next few days. Also," she whispered, leaning toward him, "Titi Mon ordered this for you online the day after your accident. She's been counting the days until we could use it to bring you home."

Titi Mon worked busily at the kitchen counter by the sink. She called over her shoulder, "Welcome home!"

"Hi, Titi Mon!" Juan chuckled and quietly answered his mom. "In that case, I'll use it in good health." He glanced around the great room, taking in the decorations and stunning Christmas tree. "Wow. Everything looks great!"

"Katie helped us." His dad frowned the instant he'd said it.

Mateo's gut twisted. She'd attempted to confide in him, and what had he done? Shut her out. Refused to listen.

Abuelo and Abuela traipsed down the hall. Abuelo had Mateo's potted plant, and Abuela held Katie's collection of partially deflated balloons. The big Mylar smiley face balloon still bounced along, bobbing up toward the ceiling.

Mateo saw Katie in his mind's eye, striding up ahead of him while one of those balloons escaped, and his heart clenched. He'd spent a restless night trying to make sense of her duplicity. She honestly seemed to think she'd been helping Juan. He'd been way too hard on her at the hospital by accusing her of attempting to worm her way into his family. That had been an incredibly harsh thing to say, above all to a woman who had nothing left of her own family.

Mateo was keenly embarrassed by his rudeness, but he'd been so thrown, he hadn't exactly been thinking straight. He'd fought tooth and nail against developing feelings for her, all the while believing she was Juan's girlfriend. Even if she *wasn't*, that didn't change the fact that she had to have been very interested in Juan at the outset. That was the only way she would have gone along with Juan's ruse.

Maybe part of her *had* wanted that to come true. Mateo had called Juan the fool, but perhaps he'd been the idiot. Getting ideas in his head about Katie liking him for who he was. More than liking him. *Falling for him*. Like he'd found himself falling for her. Clearly, he'd imagined the whole thing.

That was all in the past anyway, and there didn't seem to be a whole lot he could do about his bad behavior now. His family and Katie had already said their goodbyes. Him reaching out to her at this point would prove uncomfortable, even if it was to apologize. No. Contacting Katie would only be like reopening a big can of worms or ripping off a bandage on a wound that hadn't anywhere near begun to heal—for any of them.

Titi Mon emerged from the kitchen carrying a big birthday cake with glowing candles. They all started singing "Las Mañanitas," a typical Mexican birthday song that Abuela loved, and Juan laughed out loud.

"Hang on!" he said when Titi Mon approached him. "It's not my birthday."

"It is to us," Titi Mon replied. "I made your favorite: a rum cake with coconut icing."

"Well then," Juan said graciously. "How can I refuse?"

Their dad stepped up behind him. "Here, son, let me take your coat."

"Make a wish!" their mom commanded when Titi Mon lowered the cake in front of Juan.

Juan briefly closed his eyes and then blew out the candles. Everyone clapped and cheered.

Juan noticed the cake's seven candles. There was an indented spot in the icing like an eighth candle had been stuck in and then removed. "Why seven?" Juan asked Titi Mon.

She proudly squared her shoulders. "One for each of us here to welcome you: your father, mother, Abuelo, Abuela, Mateo, and me. The seventh one—the blue candle—is yours."

"How sweet." He stared down at the indented spot. Titi Mon had originally included a candle for Katie. In just a few days, she'd become almost a dedicated part of their group.

Juan rubbed his hands together and smiled at Titi Mon. "Well, I think that looks delicious. How soon can I have a piece?"

"As soon as we all get settled in the living room," their mom answered.

Their dad approached the bar area of the kitchen. "Wine anyone? Something stronger?"

"I think this occasion definitely calls for a toast," Titi Mon quipped, and they all laughed.

"I'll pour," Mateo offered. He glanced at his dad. "Want me to grab something from the wine cellar?"

"That would be great, Mateo." His dad grinned. "Your choice."

Mateo got halfway down the spiral staircase, and a lump wedged in this throat. His chest tightened and his stomach flip-flopped. He braced himself against the railing with one hand, thinking of Katie and the conversation they'd had right here the first day she'd come out to Los Cielos. The same day he'd showed her El Corazón and Abuela had insisted Katie try on her wedding dress. That was sadly one of Abuela's visions that was never coming true.

Katie's time with the Martinezes was over, and any chance that Mateo could have had with her was in the past. He raked a hand through his hair, thinking that things might have been different if Katie had met him first instead of Juan. It was the two of them—Mateo and Katie—who seemed more like kindred spirits,

as if they were destined to get along. Ride together into many sunsets, just as they'd done while returning from their picnic.

But things *weren't* different, and Mateo and his family had
other things to deal with, including saving the winery. There was
no use in Mateo lamenting the sorry state of his heart. He rubbed
his fist across his chest, massaging the dull ache inside it. This was
supposed to be such a happy Christmas with Juan back at Los
Cielos.

But with Katie out of the picture, it fell flat.

Katie scooped mashed potatoes, turkey, and gravy onto another
paper plate and passed it to the older volunteer standing next
to her. His name was Brad, and they'd both worked at the soup
kitchen together before. Brad added green beans and cranberry
sauce to the plate, then gave the meal to a gray-haired guy in a
tattered overcoat.

"Thank you, my son." The guy receiving the food couldn't
have been many years older than Brad, who had salt-and-pepper
hair and was probably in his sixties.

Brad smiled, loading up another plate. "Merry Christmas."

Katie glanced out the window on the other end of the cafeteria. Snow was still coming down in dainty white flakes. It wasn't
sticking to much of anything, but it sure was pretty, dusting the
hedges surrounding the shelter building and gracing the moun-
taintops, which appeared buried in white. They'd gotten more
accumulation in the higher regions, and the uncharacteristic but
Christmassy weather was predicted to hold all day. Cortinis'

Christmas tree farm probably looked magical about now, and the great room in Los Cielos must feel so cozy with the hearth brightly glowing along with the shimmering lights on the Christmas tree.

Katie's heart ached at her foolish hope that she might have been there for Christmas, experiencing a real family holiday for the first time in forever. But she was far better off staying out of the Martinezes' way. Not all of them wanted her there after the truth had come out, least of all Mateo. She pushed her tangled emotions back down below the surface, refusing to let them interfere with her service to the community today. But they worked their way back up in insidious waves of regret and sorrow, casting a shadow of loneliness across her soul.

She forced a smile at the next lady in line, who reminded her in some ways of Abuela. In spite of her threadbare clothing, she had colorful jewelry on and a cheerful sparkle in her eyes. "Merry Christmas," Katie told her, heaping food onto her plate.

The older lady grinned, her sweet, wrinkled face a palette of cheer. "*Feliz Navidad.*"

Katie spied some red beads spilling out of the woman's coat pocket, and her heart pinged. "Is that a rosary?" she asked kindly.

The woman removed it from her coat pocket with gnarled fingers. "Yes. Isn't it beautiful?" She displayed it in her palm as she scooted along with the line.

Katie swallowed hard, desperately missing Abuela. Abuelo. Pia. Raul. *Mateo*. Even Juan. All of them. "It's lovely."

The woman reached under the protective glass shielding the food, passing the rosary to Katie, who followed along, keeping up with her. "Here, you have it."

Heat flooded Katie's face as others turned to stare. "Oh no, I couldn't."

The woman extended her reach so that her coat bumped into her tray. "Please," she pleaded with a smile. "A gift."

Katie didn't feel like she deserved this kind of gift, such a selfless action of the heart. But she understood that disappointing this generous stranger would be worse than accepting her gesture. She took the beads from the woman with a quiet "Thank you." The older lady's touch was smooth and warm, silky almost, like she'd had a different kind of life than Katie's, one in which she hadn't worked with her hands. Maybe she'd had a good life, one with financial stability, but somehow, life had changed for her, and she'd wound up here. Every person at this shelter had a story, including the volunteers, but most were stories that Katie would never know.

The lady took her plate from Brad and set it on her tray. "Are you Catholic?" she asked Katie.

Katie shook her head because she wasn't anything really and hadn't been in a while.

The woman smiled. "Well, maybe you know somebody who is?" Her eyes danced. "It's Castellana," she said, meaning a largely Hispanic population with lots of Catholic families, including the Martinezes.

"Yeah, I do." Katie tucked the rosary beads in her apron pocket, and her fingers shook. She recalled returning Abuela's beads to her after she'd loaned them to the couple at the hospital. In Castellana, it seemed, certain people were eager to share their faith. But it was hard to have faith in much of anything this Christmas. She'd ruined it so completely.

"You should never give up," the old woman said, snapping Katie back to attention. She'd reached the end of the line and was selecting a dessert. She placed a piece of pumpkin pie on her tray and shook her finger at Katie as if admonishing her to pay attention. "It's Christmas." Her eyebrows rose. "Remember."

How could Katie possibly forget? Forget about the week she'd spent getting to know Juan's family? The moments she'd shared with Mateo: learning about his talents and what he valued…developing feelings for him because of the solid, caring, principled man he was. Falling in love with the whole darn bunch of them. Katie looked up to thank the woman again, but she'd already gone, taking a seat with some friends at a table.

Brad stepped closer and whispered, "Are you all right?"

No. She wasn't all right. She would never be all right. Until she'd finished the business she'd started. Though she'd apologized to Juan's family, she hadn't fully told them the truth.

She peered at the start of the line, seeing it was thinning. Her shift here was nearly done. There was something she still needed to say to Juan's family though. To Mateo as well.

Daisy was right about unfinished business. Though Katie had thought she'd wrapped things up yesterday as neatly as a Christmas present, she'd been wrong.

TWENTY-SIX

ABUELO REMOVED THE BLUE BOW from his package with a grumpy frown. "Katie wasn't supposed to give us gifts." His gaze scanned the room. "Especially after"—he shrugged—"you know."

They all sat around the fire, slowly enjoying their wine. Titi Mon's delicious rum cake had served as their afternoon snack, since they'd planned a later Christmas dinner. Mateo's mom had put the turkey in the oven shortly after they returned from the hospital, and the aroma of it roasting filled the air.

Titi Mon perused her framed picture of *coquito* fixings. "At least mine looks festive." She pointed to Katie's drawing of her Christmas light bulb necklace on the counter beside the blender in the picture. "The jewelry adds color."

Mateo's dad's eyebrows rose. "The jewelry wasn't there, was it?"

Titi Mon shook her head. "Creative license."

Mateo's mom turned her artwork around so the others could see. "This drawing of the main house set against the vineyard is so pretty. Katie somehow captured its essence. Do you think she did all this from memory or took photos on her phone?"

Mateo downed his last sip of wine. "From memory's my

guess." A gloomy darkness overtook him. In spite of all the Christmas cheer, he couldn't fight the feeling that something was really wrong. *Of course it is. Katie's not here.*

"Katie's gifted, no doubt." His dad lifted his wineglass in the air. "Can I get anybody another?"

"With dinner," Abuela said, and the rest of them concurred. Abuela ran her fingers across the glass frame on the drawing Katie had made of her rosary. "It seems Katie had a way of knowing what was special to all of us."

Titi Mon got her dander up. "Are you saying rum?"

His mom chuckled. "No, Tía. Fun."

Titi Mon stiffened. "Okay," she said finally. "I'll accept that."

"Wonder what's in mine?" Juan said, holding up his gift. "I'm not sure Katie knew me that well."

"She had to have known you some," Titi Mon scolded. "For you to ask her to fake being your girlfriend."

"Yeah. Sorry about that." Juan's shoulders sagged. "Again."

Abuelo ripped the paper off his package. "Well, what do have we here?" He discarded his wrapping paper on the floor by his chair. "Oh ho! It's our best vintage." He displayed the drawing for the others, then examined it more closely. "It's amazing she got so many details on the label correct."

Mateo shifted the package on his lap. "Katie mentioned she had a really great memory, almost photographic for certain visual details."

Abuelo chortled. "She could have been a spy."

"Maybe." Mateo sighed, thinking Katie could have been anything she wanted. His dad was right. She definitely had artistic talent.

Abuelo stared at his drawing again. "Los Cielos Cellars," he said slowly. "That has such a nice ring to it." He shot Juan a look. "It always has."

"And will!" their dad added, also staring at Juan.

Juan pushed back in his wheelchair, staring at the others. "Fine." He pursed his lips. "Should we address the one-hundred-pound elephant in the room?"

Abuela leaned forward, gripping the edges of her shawl. "One *thousand* pounds, at least."

Their dad glanced at their mom, and she sighed. "I hadn't wanted to ruin the holiday."

"It will probably be ruined anyway," Mateo said, "if we don't get this out in the open."

"You all have been keeping something from me about the business," Juan said in accusatory tones. "And—"—he cleared his throat—"I'd like to know what that is."

"We? Keeping things from you?" Titi Mon laid a hand on her chest. "Unbelievable."

Mateo sat on the end of the sofa closest to Juan in his wheelchair. His parents were on the other side of him. He turned to his brother with a heavy breath. "We found the Cloudy Crest Wines labels."

"What? Where?"

Mateo set his jaw. "In the production room, after the flood."

Juan's eyes grew wide. "Flood?"

"One of the fermentation tanks sprang a leak," Abuelo informed him with a steely gaze. "Number seventeen."

Juan sank back in the wheelchair. "Oh." His gaze darted around the room, landing on his mother, who frowned.

"That's not all, Juan," she said sadly. "We know about the distribution agreement you signed and your plans for total rebranding."

His dad rubbed the side of his neck. "Son," he said to Juan. "How could you?"

Juan blanched and looked around the room. "Wait. You went through my papers? At my condo?"

"Our papers," Mateo corrected. His anger still simmered beneath the surface, but he was mature enough to repurpose that into action. His mission was saving Los Cielos now. "The winery's papers, before you commandeered them for your own."

Juan's face turned red. "Everyone, listen." He held up both hands. "You don't understand."

"I think we understand plenty." Abuelo crossed his arms. "When you couldn't get us to agree to your scheme, you decided to play tricky dicky with the family finances and forge ahead with it on your own."

"Abuelo," Juan rasped hoarsely. "It's not like that. Not like that at all."

"No?" his mom asked. The hurt in her voice was clear when she asked, "Then how is it?"

Juan stared into the fireplace, studying the gas flames as they leapt against each other, curling around the artificial logs. His gaze trailed to the Christmas stockings hanging from the mantel and then traveled to the Christmas tree. "Maybe the rest of you don't understand how it is. How it's been," he said, speaking more to the tree than the rest of them. "Never being seen as the smart one in this family." He blinked and turned his eyes on Mateo's. "It's not your fault that you're brainy. You were born that way, when I"—he cocked an eyebrow at his parents—"was born *handsome*."

"Juan," his mom said softly.

"No, Mom." Juan smoothed back his hair. "All of you. Please, hear me out." He observed his grandfather with a hangdog expression. "I know you never believed I could handle running the winery on my own." He glanced at his dad. "Like father, like son. You didn't either."

His dad scrubbed a hand down his face. "Juan—"

"Dad, no. Really. I need to say this." He sat up straighter in his wheelchair. "Say this to all of you. You were so dead set against rebranding Los Cielos Cellars. So sure that move would sink our ship, when I was even more certain that was the only way to save it. Maybe other ideas I had in the past didn't work out, but that didn't mean that this one wouldn't. It was like none of you, not a single one"—his voice cracked—"could show me an ounce of faith."

Mateo covered his mouth with his fist, his soul aching for his brother. He'd never looked at things that way. From Juan's perspective, he could understand how that had been hard.

"Not in my business dealings," Juan continued. He glanced at Titi Mon. "Or in matters of the heart."

Titi Mon hung her head, and Abuelo and Abuela looked like they both wanted to cry.

"We're sorry, Juan," Abuela said. "That's not how we meant it."

"No," Abuelo agreed. There was moisture in his eyes.

Juan balled his hands into fists. "I thought if—just this once—I could get it right..." He turned to Mateo. "You know? Be the genius with the solution, then you all would forgive me for Cloudy

Crest Wines. Actually even *thank me* when those profits started rolling in and the fate of the vineyard changed for the better." He viewed the grounds outside the windows as snow pelted the vines and hills. "You think that I don't love this place?" His jaw wobbled, and he rubbed at the corner of his eye. "That I don't love the family? Love all of you?" He gaped at them, incredulous. "I do. But." His Adam's apple rose and fell, and then he pounded his heart. "I needed to be my own man."

Your own man?

Mateo had never known Juan to be anything other than that. Juan's signature style was going his own way—always, and for better or for worse.

The room fell silent with only the sounds of the gently hissing gas flames. Mateo surveyed his parents, who seemed too stunned to speak. His grandparents looked crushed too, and Titi Mon stared at the floor with a devastated frown.

"I'm sorry, Juan," Mateo said, his heart wrenching for his brother. "Sorry if I ever made you feel that way. Like you weren't good enough. Are you kidding me? You?"

Juan looked up and met his eyes.

"You were my big brother. The one who was so cheerful. So clever. Ambitious. Fun. The guy who got all the girls—"

Juan laughed at this. "Yeah," he said softly. "I suppose that's true."

"You are smart, Juan," their dad said. "You and Mateo just have different gifts."

"And *hey*." Mateo playfully shoved Juan's arm. "I'm good looking too."

This evoked chuckles, easing the tension in the room.

"I'm very sorry," their mom said, addressing her oldest son, "if we made you feel you weren't good enough. Because you *are*. And we love you. All of us do. But, Juan," she said weakly. "Rebranding without telling us?"

Juan sighed heavily. "You're right." He shook his head. "And I was wrong. No matter what my motives were, I never should have rationalized going behind your backs."

"It might not be too late to stop it," Mateo said.

Juan's forehead rose.

"It's Katie," Abuelo explained, "who had the idea that we try to expand without rebranding."

"At least not totally," their dad chimed in. "We can still update our labels and distribute our Los Cielos Cellars brand more widely."

Juan rubbed his chin. "Katie suggested this?"

"She said we should capitalize on our family's history." Abuela's eyes glistened. "Market Papi Monchi and Mamacita's love story on every bottle."

Juan absorbed this a long moment, and then he grinned. "On each bottle of Los Cielos Cellars wines?"

Abuelo held up his drawing of the wine bottle. "Yes."

Juan suddenly appeared as deflated as one of his balloons. He frowned. "I'm afraid I've already set some things in motion."

Their mom set her wineglass on the coffee table. "Can't some of them be unset?"

Mateo met Juan's gaze. "I'll help you," he said firmly. "Do whatever it takes."

Juan smirked, but it was all in fun. "I thought you wanted to build guitars."

Mateo shifted on the sofa. "First things first."

"I think this is wonderful," Titi Mon said. "Two brothers helping each other."

Juan nodded at her. "Two brothers helping the family. I owe it to all of you to make this right, and I promise, I will."

"You two still haven't opened your packages from Katie," his mom said.

The mood in the room was lighter now that the family business discussion was over. Mateo was relieved that they'd cleared the air with Juan and still saddened about the family making Juan feel lesser. He'd played his own part in that too, but he no longer would going forward. His dad was right; he and Juan each had their own gifts. When they put their positive attributes together by combining forces, they'd make an unstoppable team and fix this mess.

Juan held up his gift with the bright green bow. "It was really nice of her to do this."

Titi Mon rested her feet on the ottoman. "She's a really nice girl."

"She is very sweet, yes," his mom said, glancing at his dad.

He placed his arm around her shoulders. "We all liked her."

Juan unwrapped his drawing and broke into a grin. "It's El Corazón."

The others sighed when he showed them the picture.

"That way, you can always remember," Abuela said to Juan. "The things that are important."

Juan sent his grandmother a fond look and said firmly, "Yes."

Everyone turned to Mateo, but he was already mulling over what was important in his own mind. And it was about more than saving the vineyard or even eventually building guitars. It was about the woman who'd helped out his family by offering them an incredible solution to their troubles when they were at their lowest point.

The person who'd gotten soaked with wine while pitching in during a family emergency. The one he'd burned to take into his arms at El Corazón and had been desperate to kiss at the Christmas tree farm and, later, during their picnic. A woman he could see himself sharing many sunsets with in the future and whom he longed to embrace during a slow dance when their hair was as snowy white as the flakes coating the vineyard outside.

A woman he'd been incredibly rude to at the hospital by refusing to share a civil goodbye, because he hadn't understood the pain in his heart for what it was. Not anger at her betrayal of his family but agony over the fact that she was leaving and never coming back.

"Mateo?" his mom said, jogging him out of his reverie.

"Oh right." He peeled back the wrapping paper, exposing Katie's gift. Mateo's heart pounded. It was a colored-pencil sketch of his workshop and the unfinished guitar, his favorite project so far. He'd had so many distractions lately, he'd nearly forgotten about it.

Titi Mon angled forward in her chair. "Can we see?"

Mateo spun the drawing around, and everyone smiled.

Juan tilted his chin at Mateo. "Katie did get to know everybody, didn't she?"

"Yes," Abuelo said. "And she got to know Mateo *very well*."

Juan blinked. "What? Really?"

"It's odd that she picked that guitar," Titi Mon said. "It's not finished."

Abuela gasped and covered her mouth with her hands. "Mateo," she said, her cheeks all rosy. "I've had a vision." She locked on his gaze. "You're going to finish that guitar."

Mateo raked a hand through his hair. "Yeah, I hope so." That was absolutely what he intended. To help get the winery on the right track and then someday run a side business of his own. He didn't need a big studio or standalone shop or any venues in which to perform. He could sell his wares easily enough online, and he enjoyed playing his music for himself. Though he could envision playing a few serenades for one special lady.

"And"—Abuela's dark eyes twinkled—"Katie's going to wear my dress."

"That's an old vision," Abuelo quipped.

"No, it's not." Abuela squared her small shoulders. "It's an updated one."

Juan chuckled at his brother. "I guess I did miss a lot."

"Mateo," his mom said. "There are still eight stockings hanging from the mantel, and we don't eat for another hour."

Mateo shot to his feet, setting Katie's drawing aside. "Right." He strode to the hall closet and took out his coat. Of course he had to fix this.

He had to tell Katie the truth about what was in his head and in his heart. He also owed her some apologies: for not listening to her about Juan, for judging her too harshly for keeping Juan's secret, and for treating her poorly when they parted.

He hoped she had it in her heart to forgive him.

TWENTY-SEVEN

KATIE STOOD ON THE STOOP at Los Cielos, preparing to ring the doorbell, and then the door flew open. Mateo was wearing his jacket.

"Katie!" He took a step backward like he'd been hit by a big gust of wind. Swirling snowflakes blew through the door, landing on the welcome mat.

"I'm sorry to surprise you." Her heart pounded in her throat. Maybe this was a bad idea. A really bad idea. "I probably should have texted first."

His neck went crimson first, and then his face, and next his ears. "No." He sounded strangled on the word. "I was just coming to"—he stopped and raked a hand through his hair—"see you."

Titi Mon and his parents huddled behind him. Abuelo and Abuela weren't far behind, toddling into the foyer alongside Juan's wheelchair as Juan steered himself along.

"It's true!" Juan stared at her in surprise. "It is you."

She waved to him and then to the others. "Merry Christmas."

"*Feliz Navidad!*" Titi Mon called.

"Mateo, don't leave her standing there in the cold," his mom reprimanded. She smiled warmly at Katie. "Let her in."

They all backed up accordingly with Mateo still in front. He shut the door behind Katie, and what he'd said finally registered with her. "Wait." She blinked up at him. "You were coming to see me?"

"We love our drawings!" Abuelo announced from behind Mateo.

"Yes," Raul agreed. "You certainly have talent!"

"Oh good." Katie flushed. "Thank you."

Mateo spun on his family. "Do you all think that Katie and I—"

"Yes, yes, of course." Pia nodded and corralled the others into the great room while Mateo and Katie stepped into the kitchen, but the others kept sneaking peeks their way.

"As long as we have our coats on," Mateo said, nodding toward the door, "do you mind?"

Katie's pulse skittered, and her soul welled with hope. "Sure."

The group turned to watch them slip outside, with Katie going first. She peered back through the door to spy Mateo glancing at the others. He held up his hand with fingers crossed, and Abuelo mimicked the gesture. Then Abuela did too. Titi Mon and his parents joined in. So did Juan, who was grinning bigger than the rest of them and pointing over Mateo's shoulder.

Mateo gasped and wheeled around, his face beet red. She giggled at his caught look. He probably looked more adorable than Katie had ever seen him. He appeared really happy too, and she could see why. Whatever he had to tell her, he clearly had his family's blessing—including Juan's—and she was glad.

He tugged shut the door as brisk winds blew, tearing down from the hills and the distant mountains. Everywhere Katie looked, the vineyard was blanketed in white.

"It's always beautiful here, but seeing it like this is special."

He smiled softly and gazed into her eyes. "A white Christmas."

Her eyebrows rose. "In Castellana! Who knew?" She studied him a moment. "So things with Juan are...?"

He grinned. "Good."

"You all talked it out?"

"We did, and I also learned something about Juan. He honestly did have the best intentions." He shook his head. "In a very misguided way."

Warmth spread through her chest. "So it's okay then? You'll be able to save Los Cielos?"

"I think so." He pursed his lips and gazed at her. "No. I know so. I sent a quick email to Mr. Elroy this morning, and he answered, even though it's Christmas Day. We're meeting to discuss the loan after the holidays." He stepped toward her. "Thanks to you."

She blushed. "I'm so glad."

"Yeah," he said. "Me too."

He clearly wasn't mad at her any longer or judging her for trying to insert herself into his family. In fact, he seemed ecstatic about having her here. Still. She needed to have her say.

She stared up at him, wanting to get this right. "Mateo, I have something to tell you."

He shoved his hands in his jacket pockets. "Me first?"

"All right." The wind picked up, but she was anything but chilled, buffeted by the warmth in Mateo's eyes.

"I need to apologize," he said. "That's why I was coming to find you." He sighed and hung his head. "I've gotten so many things wrong."

She laughed, commiserating. "You're not the only one."

He looked up at her. "No, but you had your reasons. You tried to explain them to me earlier—the day of our disaster with the fermentation tank—but I wouldn't hear you, and I'm sorry for that. Because that's one thing a guy should never do: refuse to listen to the woman he loves."

Loves? Heat flooded her face, making it burn hotter.

He tilted his head and stared at her. "Yeah, it's true. Katie Smith, I've fallen in love with you." A song was written in his eyes, as beautiful and passionate as a serenade on his Spanish guitar. "I know it's only been a week—"

"And what a crazy week it's been." Her heart hammered as he got nearer.

"Yeah, it has been wild, hasn't it? And yet." He cupped a hand to her cheek. "Here we are. And I need to tell you that I'm sorry. Again, for not listening about Juan and especially for treating you badly in the hospital. I never should have said that thing about family."

"But wait. Mateo." She licked her lips because the truth hurt. "You weren't wrong."

"It doesn't matter." His voice grew rough. "What counts is the way I said it, with intent to hurt you, but I swear I'll never do that again. I was mixed up and confused. Confronting emotions I didn't understand. And instead of sorting through them, I took them out on you." He lowered his head and peered up at her with his amazing honey-brown eyes. "Can you forgive me?"

She was still stuck on that first part. *He loves me? Mateo really loves me?* Her heart grew full to bursting as acknowledgment settled in. All that time she'd spent hoping that he cared for her just as much as she was falling for him...it hadn't been in vain, and her instincts hadn't failed her after all. He'd felt exactly the same about her as she had about him, and now the two of them were coming together like two pieces of a puzzle: his heart and hers. The emotion was beautifully overwhelming, so lovely.

"You mean it?" she asked, basking in his gaze.

He lightly stroked her cheek with his thumb. "I do."

"Mateo," she whispered. "I want you to forgive me too, for all the lies I told—or untruths I let you and your family believe about me and Juan. It was never meant to hurt anyone, only help them."

He settled his arms around her and pulled her close. "I know that now." He lowered his forehead toward hers and nuzzled her nose with his. "I also know that I'm mad about you, Katie. Crazy for the sweet way you are with my family, the gentleness you show to Abuela, and the way you charmed Abuelo and Titi Mon. My whole family's wild about you, Mom and Dad too."

A smile trembled across her lips. "I'm pretty wild about them too."

"Really?" His lips brushed over hers, and electricity crackled through her. She grabbed on to his shoulders to steady herself when her head felt light.

"Really," she said, falling into his kiss.

Mateo brought his mouth to hers for the sweetest lingering moment.

"And, Mateo?"

He gazed at her adoringly.

"I love you too."

He held her closer and whispered, "You know what I want? I want you to spend Christmas with us."

She giggled, her heart so light. "I'd like that."

He grinned playfully. "I'd also like you to *not* date Juan."

"I don't want Juan," she said, her breath on his lips. "I only want you."

"That's the best Christmas gift of all." He kissed her again, and her heart danced on the wind, darting through the snowflakes and twirling up past El Corazón, then way beyond that and over the Mayacamas Mountains.

A car door popped open, startling them both to attention. Mateo and Katie turned toward the drive and the new fancy sports car that had arrived. A woman stepped out of it, long legs first in short ankle boots. Katie glanced at Mateo, but he had no idea who she was. He was still floating on the clouds from his kiss with Katie and the fact that they had a future. Abuela's visions were never wrong.

The gorgeous Latina walked up to them. She wore a retro-patterned minidress beneath her open fake fur coat, and snowflakes stuck to her wavy dark hair. Her carefully manicured eyebrows arched at Mateo and Katie. "Excuse me? Is this the Martinezes' house?"

Mateo was too stunned to answer. It couldn't be. Was this Titi Mon's date for Juan?

"I'm Adelita Busó." She grinned with a gleaming white smile that rivaled Juan's. "I'm looking for Monsita Rebelles, and, uh…" She hesitated and checked something on her phone. "Juan?" she asked, searching Mateo's and Katie's faces.

Katie bit back a smile, and Mateo's mouth twitched. What a very interesting Christmas this was turning out to be. He laid his hand on the doorknob, opening the door for Adelita. "After you," he said gallantly, secretly winking at Katie. "Adelita's here!" he called into the house, letting her enter first.

"Adelita?" Abuelo inquired.

"*Ay.*" Abuela gave a breathy sigh, her gaze landing on the woman. "*Adelita.*"

Mateo chuckled at Titi Mon's surprised look. "Adelita!" She sat bolt upright in her chair and sprang to her feet, striding briskly to the door. "Oh yes, *hija*," she replied, remaining coolly composed. "Please. Come on in."

Juan goggled at the scene in amazement. Then he took one long look at Adelita and grinned.

"Wait a minute," he said. "I *know* you. Weren't we in school together?"

She grinned at him. "Kindergarten, before my family moved away. You're the boy who thought he could fly." Her smile turned into a frown when she noticed his wheelchair. "You're not still trying?"

Juan laughed. "No, nothing like that."

"It's a very long story," his dad said.

His mom glanced at him and then happily at the group. "We can share it over dinner."

His dad strolled over and shook Adelita's hand. "I'm Juan's dad, Raul, and this is his mom, Pia."

His mom took Adelita's hands in hers. "Adelita." She shot a quizzical look at Titi Mon, who shrugged. Clearly, in all the excitement, she'd forgotten to call off the fix-up. "Welcome." She smiled at their new guest. "I hope you like turkey with chorizo stuffing."

"That sounds delicious." Adelita surveyed the room. "Your house is gorgeous. So is your tree." She giggled, spotting the ornament with Juan's face on it. "There you are!" she told him. "Just like I remember."

Juan's face reddened. "That was a long time ago."

"Sure was." Adelita thanked Abuelo, who took her coat.

"I'm Juan's grandfather," he said, hanging Adelita's coat in the closet.

Abuela waved. "I'm the grandmother."

Mateo raised his hand in the foyer. "Mateo here, and this is Katie." His family noticed his hand linked with Katie's and gave approving smiles.

Adelita nodded. "So nice to meet everyone."

"Adelita, have a seat," Titi Mon commanded. She pointed to the sofa and Mateo's old spot, since it was right next to Juan. "I was about to whip up some *coquitos*."

"Oh!" Adelita's face lit up. "I love those."

Mateo glanced over at Katie with her pink cheeks aglow. She looked as pretty as their all-lit-up Christmas tree, and he couldn't wait to steal another kiss. Family was great. Fantastic. So was a little alone time with the woman he'd very recently realized he loved.

Mateo latched on to Katie's hand and tugged her back out the front door.

"Wait," she whispered, giggling. "Where are we going?" She glanced at the living area, smiling at his family. Her family in many ways now. She'd already become a part of them, and Mateo was so glad. From the happy sparkle in her eyes, so was she.

"Outside to enjoy our first white Christmas together," he whispered huskily, "along with one more kiss."

She seemed to like the idea, since she followed him and definitely didn't protest. Mateo shut the front door and took her in his arms, his heart feeling happy and full. There was no woman he wanted in his life more than Katie. He wanted to learn more about her and love her. Support any dreams for the future she had. In so many ways, she'd already supported his.

Before his mouth met hers, she stopped him. "Our *first* white Christmas?" A smile warmed her beautiful lips. "You mean there'll be more?"

"That's what I'm hoping." He slid his hand into her hair, bringing her closer. His lips brushed over hers, and a heated buzz hummed through him. "But as long as we're together, I'll take them any old which way. Snowy white or tropically hot, like on a beach in Puerto Rico."

"Ooh." She grinned. "We're going to Puerto Rico?"

He nodded. "And Paris. Seville. Any place you'd like."

She sighed. "I'd like any of them better with you."

"Then let's make it happen."

He kissed her again, and his heart soared.

Maybe Juan's childhood self had been right. Maybe a man *could* learn to fly. With Katie by his side, Mateo had confidence that they could go anywhere. Undertake any journey, no matter how impossible it seemed.

Just like his Papi Monchi and Mamacita had done many years before.

EPILOGUE

One Year Later

"*SALUD!*" RAUL AND PIA HELD up their wineglasses, toasting the others.

"*Salud!*" Wineglasses clinked as Katie watched the pretty Christmas tree shimmer in the background, and a fire glowed in the hearth.

The whole family gathered around the dining table at Los Cielos, and Abuela sat beside Abuelo. Raul and Pia were at the other end of the long table. Katie sat across from Juan, in between Titi Mon and Mateo. Adelita was next to Juan. Adelita had become a fixture in this family since last Christmas, and Titi Mon never missed an opportunity to tell Juan, *I told you so*. Adelita and Juan complemented each other so well. Just like Abuela and Abuelo, Pia and Raul, and—Katie's heart sighed—her and Mateo.

"This has been an awesome Christmas," Adelita said. "Thanks for including me."

Titi Mon smiled. "We couldn't possibly omit Juan's *novia*."

Juan toasted Mateo. "Or Mateo's." His gaze travelled to the ornate diamond engagement ring on Katie's hand, made from Mexican silver and gold.

Mateo had proposed at the Christmas tree farm, and Juan and Adelita had been in on it, leaving them ample privacy on that mountaintop so Mateo could surprise Katie with Abuelo's mother's ring. Adelita and Juan had surfaced just in time to take snapshots of the happy couple huddled together.

Mateo had told Katie that had been when he'd first fallen in love with her, the day they'd shopped for his family's Christmas tree. She couldn't say when she first fell for Mateo. Maybe when he'd played his Spanish guitar in his apartment, or maybe it was before that, when he'd caught her silly balloons. In some ways, it seemed as if she'd always loved him and like they were always meant to be together.

Adelita had confided secretly to Katie that she had the same instinct about Juan. The two younger women had bonded instantly over their affection for the Martinez men and the entire Martinez family, making Adelita almost like the sister Katie had never had. It was so great to have a family now and to really belong here with all of them. She always felt included and loved, and her love for the Martinezes was boundless in return. She'd remained close to Daisy too, ever since their heart-to-heart last Christmas. Letting down her guard wasn't so bad when she was blessed with the right people. In fact, being open and warm felt pretty terrific.

Abuelo lifted a bottle on the table, turning it around in his hands. "I love our new label. So elegant." He grinned at Juan. "And modern."

Juan raised his glass toward Katie. "Here's to the artist!"

They all said, "Hear, hear," and drank from their wine. With their updated labels and expanded distribution plans, the winery had turned a corner and was now more profitable than ever, cementing Los Cielos Cellars's position as an esteemed boutique business in the marketplace.

Katie smiled around the table, then nodded out the window and up toward El Corazón. "I had great inspiration." Her design featured the historic vines, seemingly climbing up toward the heavens as clouds laced through the mountains behind them. Every bottle of Los Cielos Cellars wine now included a brief version of Papi Monchi and Mamacita's story.

Mateo lovingly took her hand. "It's a good thing we're getting married, seeing how important you are to the family business as our marketing manager." That was true, and Katie was so happy about her new job. Even though she missed her friends at the diner, she still visited them often enough and kept up with her volunteer duties. For his part, Mateo had also realized his dreams. He'd begun a guitar shop online and now shipped his lovely handmade guitars all over the world. He sometimes played for the greater family, but most of his private serenades were reserved for Katie, and each time he played for her, her heart fluttered the same way it had on that first day.

"Marriage is always good," Abuela assured them. Her eyes sparkled at Katie. "And now you'll finally get to wear my dress."

"Yes." Katie's cheeks warmed. "Can't wait."

Abuela shut her eyes and clutched her chest. "*Ay!*"

Abuelo's face hung in a frown. "*Querida?* What is it? What's wrong?"

Abuela peeked one eye open and then the other. Once she had everyone's full attention, she impishly declared, "I've had another vision." She centered her gaze on Adelita, and Mateo chuckled.

"Oh boy, Juan," he teased his brother. "You know what they say about Abuela's visions."

Juan kissed the back of Adelita's hand. "I *have* heard," he said, not seeming to mind it.

Adelita's cheeks colored. "I think I might be a little tall for that dress." Adelita was very statuesque and far taller than any of the other women in the room.

"Don't worry!" Titi Mon quipped. "Abuela's dress has an underskirt."

Adelita's eyebrows arched. "What?"

"It's true." Abuela lifted a finger. "It can be adjusted for almost any bride."

"Besides that," Abuelo added, "we know an excellent seamstress."

Juan chuckled and wrapped his arm around Adelita's shoulders. "Don't let my family pressure you."

Adelita straightened her spine in her chair and took a small sip of wine. "I don't feel pressured," she said sassily, and the rest of them roared.

Pia stood to gather the plates. "Any more food anyone?"

"Not for me," Raul said. "Everything was delicious."

"I hope you all saved room for dessert," Titi Mon prodded, making an effort to stand. "I made a Christmas flan."

Katie touched her arm. "Why don't you sit?" She walked over to Pia, relieving her of her plates. "Here, let me take those," she said, and Pia sat back down too.

Adelita stood as well, addressing Titi Mon. "We'll bring the flan out here."

Titi Mon settled back in her seat. "Oh well. Okay. Thank you."

Mateo and Juan got up next, removing their grandparents' empty dinner dishes and returning with dessert plates and forks. Titi Mon didn't seem to notice they'd brought in an extra of each. Katie set the flan on the table in front of Titi Mon. Adelita held a spare wineglass in her hands, sitting back at her place.

The doorbell rang, capturing everyone's attention.

Raul checked his watch. "Who would be visiting now on Christmas Day?"

Juan pushed back his chair. "I'll go and see," he said, acting oblivious. He wasn't a very good actor though.

Pia stared at Mateo. "Is something going on?" she asked.

"Don't know, Mom." Mateo raked a hand through his hair, and Katie held in her giggles. Juan was such a secret romantic. Mateo claimed they both got it from Abuelo, but Katie had always pegged Abuela for the romantic one. Perhaps both the grandparents were old softies underneath.

"Don Luis!" Juan exclaimed at the door. "What a happy surprise!"

"Surprise?" The older man's voice carried a heavy Spanish accent. He sounded befuddled. "Didn't you invite me for Christmas dessert?"

"Yes." Juan patted his shoulder. "And you're right on time."

Titi Mon blanched. "What's happening?"

Raul shrugged, turning up his palms. Oh, he was good at this. Much better than Juan.

"I have no idea," Pia said, but her eyes told another story.

Mateo leaned toward Titi Mon. "Juan found you the perfect match," he said in hushed tones. "With a little help from Daisy Santos."

"What?" Titi Mon blinked. "Me?" Her voice squeaked.

"Yes," Mateo whispered. "He's Daisy's first cousin who's recently moved here from Panama. He's a retired university professor and an eligible widower."

"*Ay, Dios mío.*" Titi Mon grabbed for the bottle of wine, filling up her glass.

An older gentleman appeared at the table. He was very handsome, with silvery white hair and a beard and a deep brown complexion. "I hope I'm not intruding?"

"Not intruding at all." Raul stood and extended his hand, and Pia smiled in greeting as they introduced themselves. The man already seemed to know Adelita and clearly was acquainted with Juan.

"Titi Mon," Juan said. "I'd like you to meet Luis Salazar." He turned to Luis. "And this is my great-aunt, Monsita Rebelles."

Titi's Mon's face lit up like a sunrise. "Hello."

"*Encantado,*" Luis said, bowing his head.

"Let me find another chair," offered Juan, retrieving one from the great room.

Luis sat down, and Adelita passed him the clean wineglass. "Here, I have an extra."

Titi Mon filled up his wineglass too. Very full, almost to the rim.

Raul reached for a fresh bottle on the table with a screw cap. "Here, let me open this."

Mateo nodded at the newcomer. "Hi, I'm Mateo, and this is my fiancée, Katie."

Katie's heart fluttered at the sound of that. Her marrying Mateo was like a dream come true. The impossible dream she'd hoped for when she'd believed she was only tilting at windmills. But now, she'd be forever riding into the sunset with her own perfect hero and husband-to-be.

Abuela's dark eyes sparkled. "His *real* fiancée," she told Luis, like that made sense.

And it did, pretty perfectly, to Katie. By accidentally bumbling into the Martinez family last Christmas, she'd found her forever man, restoring her faith in a lot of things, including love and the importance of family. Now, Juan and Adelita looked really happy together, and Titi Mon and Luis appeared delightfully awkward with their chairs scooted so closely together. Pia's and Raul's faces reflected their absolute joy in each other and with the company gathered here.

"Shall I serve the flan?" Titi Mon asked, shyly avoiding Luis's gaze.

"My," he said appreciatively. "That looks delicious."

Katie could hardly believe it, but Titi Mon actually blushed. "Thank you, Luis."

Once they all had their dessert plates, Abuelo held up his wineglass, smiling at the group. "Here's to new friends." He nodded at Luis. "New engagements." He grinned at Katie and Mateo and then winked very obviously at Juan and Adelita. "And perhaps to new announcements to come! *Feliz Navidad!*"

Mateo took Katie's hand as they joined in the toast. "*Feliz Navidad!*"

She smiled up at him, her heart so light. "Merry Christmas, Mateo."

His gaze washed over her. "Merry Christmas, Katie."

He leaned toward her and kissed her, and everything was merry and bright.

ACKNOWLEDGMENTS

I have many people to thank for *The Holiday Mix-Up*'s publication, starting with talented senior editor Christa Desir for graciously acquiring this book and then bringing out the very best in the story. Teamwork does indeed make the dream work, Christa, and I'm indebted to you and the entire Sourcebooks Casablanca team for your outstanding efforts.

Kudos to editorial assistant Letty Mundt for her keen first-pass input, and art director Stephanie Gaffron for the adorable, eye-catching cover, with thanks as well to copy editor Sabrina Baskey, editorial assistant Jocelyn Travis, content editor Susie Benton, production editor Shannon Barr, marketing director Pamela Jaffee, author liaison Madeleine Brown, royalty associate Jessica Castle, and associate marketing manager Alyssa Garcia for their essential contributions. No acknowledgments would be complete without thanking my awesome agent, Jill Marsal, for championing my work, including this book's proposal.

Major hugs to my family for so kindly supporting this newest novel, with special thanks to my husband, John, for urging me to quit my day job to give this author gig a try. It's been an exhilarating, daunting, and rewarding journey! I wouldn't change a leg of it for the knowledge I've gained, the friends I've made, and the much-valued gift of being able to share my stories.

Finally, thanks to every cherished reader, reviewer, librarian, bookseller, book blogger, social media influencer, and audiobook listener who generously chose *The Holiday Mix-Up* this season, thereby allowing these characters into your hearts. I hope you enjoyed your time at Los Cielos with Katie and Mateo, and that their world helped yours shine a little brighter.

ABOUT THE AUTHOR

New York Times and *USA Today* bestselling author Ginny Baird writes wholesome contemporary stories with a dash of humor and a lot of heart. She's fond of including family dynamics in her work and creating lovable and memorable characters in worlds where romance is a given and happily-ever-afters are guaranteed. She lives in North Carolina with her family.

Find Ginny online at ginnybairdromance.com, on Facebook as GinnyBairdRomance, on Twitter @GinnyBaird, and on Instagram @ginnybairdromance.